THE TAKING OF SHALE CITY

DAVID J WINTERS

CONTENTS

ALSO BY DAVID J. WINTERS

BEDSIDE MANNER

Nurse-and-union-leader *turned* homicide-detective, Eminence Gray, uses her gifts of empathy and emotional labor to catch the most vicious of West Brandon's killers. Em's ability to maintain this skillset will be put to the ultimate test when the highest-profile murder case her department's ever faced falls right into her lap. Add to Em's troubles a corrupt executive from her union days, back and up to old tricks, and it might just be Eminence Gray requiring a little *bedside manner*... or a lot.

INTERVENTIONISM

Roger Jech doesn't have any superpowers but he has a super ability: harm him, harm yourself in equal measure. Hit him with a right hook, your jaw breaks. Shoot him in the head, your brains blow out the back of you. Drop him in a war zone, your enemies kill themselves killing him. Jech's a weapon to the wrong people and a savior to the right, but before he can become the former, he must learn to harness his gift before it becomes his curse.

SCARCITY

Twenty-one to forty-five-year-old armed forces members, police officers, and intelligence agents (our intended protectors) are going missing everywhere. Seemingly 'taken' out of strange agrarian communes popping up all over the planet. Now Agent Bart, fresh out of retirement, is determined to solve the mystery of these disappearances and get his people back.

ISBN 9780991680382 (paperback) | ISBN 9781068863608 (hardcover) | ISBN 9780991680399 (electronic book)

{SubGenre : Publishers}
www.subgenrepublishers.com

For our Fathers

SANTA ROSA

It wasn't my city but it wasn't his neither. Not no more. The man who'd taken the city had taken the name *Haidt*. Everyone said it like it looked. *Hate*. Some said it one time too near him and now they don't say nothing no more. The rest of us left lickin' learned that day the man's name's said like *height*. We still say *hate*. Couldn't not considering the self-refutative nature of encouraging folk to not get *hate* from *Haidt* by severing their tongues. We still say *hate*. Outta a little spite ourselves. Only now we know to say it behind all the right backs.

Ah shit! Story's getting away with itself 'fore lack of introducing itself. I wanted to tell you about my city and I will in due course. I'm going to tell you about my city by way of Haidt's penultimate.

SANTA ROSA HAS SURE LOOKED better. By the fires we know something cruel and violent occurred in the night. By the dilapidation we know some other form of cruelty set in some time ago. The bucket brigade will handle the immediate though it'll take pertineer a leap annum to handle the rot that set in over that time.

You can tell where the fires had been put out not just by the char but by the blood-red stain the well water left.

What's left of the dilapidation is only a little more subtle than the burn. Brick buildings for commerce have lost most of their corner masonry as well as chimneys all crumbled to hell. Slatted facades like of the homes are missing every third board of siding or so. Where'd they go? Not lost to fires but stole to build the odd monument. See, when one of those brick facades collapsed completely, over the rubble was built a boarded frame of a wooden man rising out-and-up-like. Looming. Like he'd done the deed and was admiring his handiwork. Crude as could be. A blasphemy.

The most striking aspect of Rosa's rot after all above is the copious amounts of what the archeologists call *graffiti*. Not that archeologists ever came to study Santa Rosa. Naw. It was the art of Haidt's people so-possessed. They put a graffito on anything with a surface not moving. Even on a few surfaces that were. At first we thought Haidt's men had been mutilating the cattle. Then we realized the blood-red defacement dripping from the cows' backs was some sort of beet-boil. Looked like wings. It was the same substance Haidt's men had slathered under their eyes so as to come across like tears.

That's how you knew his men. Their red weeping tears. That and their weakness of ethic and latter-entailed-by-former openness to mobbery.

They spiked every well in Rosa with that beet-boil poison too. It was a town of Haidt's men faux-bleeding from their eyes and innocent townfolk faux-bleeding from desperate thirsty maws.

·   ·   ·

ROSA'S A HELL OF A sight after all of Haidt. I'd sum up the town's disrepair like this: if we could all float a minute to gander at her from on high, I suspect it would be like coming across a leper whose leper hands tried to fix a leper face with a whore's pallete.

UNLIKE THE LEPER, ROSA'LL HEAL.

IF WE COULD ALL FLOAT upon Rosa a minute that would be a hell of a trick. But a trick reserved for the angels. Winged beasties too. Always will be I assume. Maybe I ought grant the man on the moon the privilege too? My kids would sure like that. We sure ain't such though. We aren't any winged angels or beasties. We aren't even those blood-winged cattle never more confused than they currently are and that's saying something for such an easily perplexed beast.

Best we can do if we want a bigger picture of Rosa is pull back from the outskirts of her a sufficient pull and get as holistic a take as we can from ground up.

Pull back far enough and our view's obscured by a lone set of train tracks running parallel to her. The tracks are as good a place as any to stop.

What we see?

Not much just yet.

There's a small station-house to the left of us. Station has an arrival and departure platform extending from either side of it. Between the rail infrastructure and the city limits sits a swath of dirt and gravel for a few hundred yards.

The sheer width of this gap might have sparked in you the idea some dummy built those train tracks in the wrong place. Or maybe Rosa herself? Naw, that was intentional.

Rosa's a mining town mining iron ore. One of fifteen towns just like it running along an iron belt that's the southern-most in all Amerika. By way of ordinality, Santa Rosa was the first along *The Belt*. My municipality was eighth. By way of the arbitrariness of geography you could just as accurately have said Rosa was the last of The Belt. Santa Rosans never did though the point still stands. We could just as easily start counting our towns facing south as we do facing north. I'm proud to say however, north or south, my town will always be the eighth mathematically. Sitting smack in the center.

Whether Santa Rosa was the first or the last it was the only iron town that had the shit-dumb luck to strike gold in addition to iron. And it *was* shit-dumb luck. It was shit-dumb luck because shit-dumb out-of-county bandits couldn't tell the difference between a boxcar full of Rosa's taconite and a snuff box full of a prospector's placer gold. So Rosa folk decided it best to move their train tracks a near-quarter of a mile out the city limits then salt the earth between. They did so on the opposite side of the tracks too. Then up and down them tracks for three miles for good measure.

It wasn't really salt. It was some kind of copper residue. Turned a few Santa Rosans the color of saffron. The presence of them yellow martyrs meant there wasn't a bush or a lean-to for a thief to jump out of for hundreds of acres all around. Irony was, it took all the town's gold fortune to buttress those tracks. Copper and gold to save iron. Better than nothing. A net benefits in perpetuity kind of thing.

If someone was going to get the better of Santa Rosa he'd have to get the better of it from the inside-out. By lulling as many of the townsfolk as he could.

You don't fell the tree by chipping away at it. You feed the termites.

Like what Hate did.

HEAT WAVES DISTORT THE SANTA Rosa city-line. Across the salt expanse to the other side of the station, air sashays in an upward-curving gesture. Light bends up and to the left first. It zigs back to the right real quick then up left again just before dissipating. Left right left. Left right left.

Now a disruption.

The wavering bending light parts slowly for *The Rider* like bulrushes as he makes his debut. He doesn't *emerge* through them heat waves so much as they *form* him. Molding him out of the distorting vapor as he rides toward.

Curiously, The Rider's mount looks dressed out with some extra meaty saddle bags. I guess we'll find out though...

Rider dismounts. Boots land in perfect simultaneity with toes out in symmetry parallel the mount. Boot bottoms stand steady a tad longer then whip perpendicular the mount. Toes kick up a little copper dust flicking grit at the horse's ankles. Well-behaved animal. Doesn't flinch. *SWIP SWIPPING* of something untied is heard atop the horse. Then...

WHOMP!

A *Body* thumps down next to those boots, hard. Thumping body's in fetal position facing away from us. Hands shackled behind back. The Rider crouches down with his back to us too. Rider grabs the shackles and births that fetus. Gets The Body half up.

Body's of a man now kneeling in the gravel. Seemingly no

pain in knees gnawed at by the worst combination of grit, chipped clay, and gravity. The man raises his head. It's *Haidt*. We know it because he's crying those same beet-blood tears his men do, a north-facing poplar bark pallor all over his face in addition. Add to him some wispy silver locks turned such— so the story goes—from some kind of poisoning in his youth, and you have near-all of what differentiates him from his Red-Eye'd disciples. Poison turned his hair silver. It also turned his teeth blue. He puts plaster of Paris in that part of his face to hide the blue. How's that better? Looks like piano keys without the sharps. Looks like the demon your gramma said would enter your nose if no one blessed ya when ya sneezed.

"Where we goin' Marshal?"

Marshal Shawk's standing to the right of Haidt. Marshal has his left hand on Haidt's right shoulder. It's like a priest comforting a man to the gallows but what Marsh's really doing is feeling for the slightest of tensions in that shoulder. If Haidt were going to try anything worth worrying about, the contracting muscles would give a good 10 milliseconds' notice to the Marshal. Marshal's other hand rests on his gun. Could be the most comfortable place to rest it. Could be another precaution.

Marshal don't look down, looks straight ahead. Obliges Haidt in half-measure nonetheless. "Up the road. To Carson."

Haidt leans forward. Marshal's hand moves with the shoulder. No resistance. Haidt looks on down the tracks.

"The steel road." He leans back. Tilts up to Marshal. "Ya ran me out."

"Wasn't hard."

Haidt Chuckles. Steam whistle blows in the distance.

. . .

SAPITZ! TRAIN LURCHES TO A stop. Marshal and his quarry stand man-and-a-half about the middle of the length of cars. Haidt turns his head to see up the tracks toward the station then turns the opposite to see toward the rear of the train. His focus sets on the unorthodox caboose. Car's unique to any train heading to a law town like Carson.

Deputy Marshal Swade exits the caged caboose a little hasty, stepping on and kicking at least less than half the men in shackles he passes. Men are on their way to the prison courts or gallows of Carson.

Swade stomps over to Shawk and Half-Haidt with a look of some sort of perturbation. Very well tended-to look otherwise. Peculiar for a place like this. Face is a window to the man's ego.

I know him. He got a gander at a painting of Narcissus one time. Painting where Narcissus is gazing at his reflection in that lake. Swade got one half-n-eyeful and said *Where can I get me one of those?* I said *The painting?* He said *Naw the mirror.*

Now that's one of those *didn't* happen, *did* happen kinda scenarios. Everything up to the mirror line happened. The fact that Swade was pretending to be a connoisseur like that in front of a bunch of dignitaries, one of them dignitary's wives in particular, meant he might as well have inquired about that mirror. The sense of self-importance in that man. Pardon my digressin'.

As I said, Swade's got some sand in his farts about something.

"We about done breaking with protocol?" he chides. "You charging into that den of *initiquey* alone..."

Marshal removes his hand from Haidt's shoulder. Doesn't break eye contact with Swade. Swade fixates on Haidt.

"I'm going to settle this man into that cage car," Marshal assures. "Then I'd about say I'm retired. You can have all the credit Swade. Say it went by the book. Even say you led the charge."

"N—now..." Swade fumfers. "It's about goddamn protocol here Mart—"

"Yeah!" Haidt bursts out. "About protocol! Protocol says better you ride with me Marshal. Allay that deputy a yours' fears."

Marshal's hand goes back on Haidt's shoulder.

Swade don't miss a self-concerned little beat. Sneers at the still kneeling captive. "You calling me *yella,* miscreant?"

"I'm calling ya *afraid.*" Haidt corrects. "Your eyeballs are too big for your head. Weren't a minute ago. I call that 'fraid. Man as officious as you clearly angling to divest yourself of the *Deputy* in *Deputy Marshal* don't want to see the only man in the way get out the way? Naw!" Haidt shakes his head.

Swade's grip tightens on the handle of his coach gun. Marshal remains unmoved. Haidt goes on.

"I saw a picture once of Mike Angelo's David. Of the statue but it was a picture of it. Tiny little pecker on that boy. Fella with the picture book, real learned fella, said that was intentional-like. *The receding of the penis and testicles* he said, was meant to illustrate the fear deep down in David. Fear of Goliath." Haidt chuckles again. Those plaster of Paris teeth are real prominent in the chuckle too. "I don't gotta get your pants down to know your pecker ain't even in your back pocket no more!" He mocks in wide-mouth grimace. "Fucken fraidy cyat."

WHOOSH!

His hands whip out from behind his back. Broke out of the shackles somehow. He makes a grabbing gesture for Swade's crotch stopping just inches before it. Causes Swade to shriek and fall backward. Haidt looks on at Swade with a shit-eating grin comprised of those fucked-up teeth. A look like it's almost saying *coulda ripped your balls off*. The prisoners in the caboose howl with laughter.

Swade lunges back up and smashes Haidt in the face with the butt of his coach gun.

SMASH!

Captive goes backward from the force as Marshal lunges forward booting Swade back onto his ass. Marshal spins to make sure Haidt, despite the daze of the walnut kiss, ain't up to anything behind him. He rolls the supine Haidt prone and pats him down. He finds nothing on him except a dislocated thumb. He pops it back into place and reapplies the shackles extra tight.

MARSHAL SHAWK LOWERS HAIDT BETWEEN two drunks in the prison car. Marsh ain't ginger about it but there ain't no animus neither. I've seen this in him time again. Not any ceremony in what he does. Real cold and clinical. In the next century when there're undoubtedly the pneumatic men made available thanks to the lightweight alloys of Amerika 'Luminum doing our jobs, folk like Shawk'll never be short a day's worth of that work.

Now don't mistake my jesting to mean Marsh ain't humane. Shawk ain't an unfeeling man though he is a man of the task-at-hand. Truth be told I've only ever seen him at work and work is work for him. There's something different about this hunt though. This hunt's lowered his jowls a little. Greyed his temples. Whitened his whiskers. Could say it's the length of the chase but naw. Shawk's been on longer hunts for more vicious men. There's just something different about this one.

My metric for Shawk's humanity and his health if you're wondering, is a single measure. The gravestone. *Martha Shawk nee Spruce b. 2032 d. 2090.* He stops by that stone exactly once a hunt. 'Bout the time he thinks we're halfway done. He's seen that stone three times on the hunt for Hate.

Marshal lowers Haidt into the space between the drunks and waves a hoopty motion to a jailer outside the car. Jailer undoes the shackles, wrenches Haidt's hands out through the bars then re-applies them. Marshal hoopties again and the jailer clenches those shackles tightest.

Marshal's gone by the *RATCH!* of the shackles' last clamping. Not just out the caboose. He and his mount have already left the scene to be reintegrated with and disembodied by the heat of them copper flats.

That's how those of us who knew Marsh knew he'd retire. No ceremony. Gone. Must say I'm happy for him though a might bereft too. As bereft as all us who worked with Marsh must be.

HAIDT ASSESSES THE TWO DRUNKS flanking him. One's got the shakes real bad. Likely not going to make it to wherever they're taking him. The other's passed out hungover. Haidt looks a little more disgusted by the suffering shaking drunk. He shifts away from the shaker moving a little closer toward the sleeper. Lesser of two lost souls? Jostling of *Sleepy* reveals the top of a mickey of whiskey in vest. Label appears to say *Dauphin Brand Rye Whiskey.* Haidt smirks, barely. Does it through them piano keys of his.

Then...

SMASH! SMASH!

Swade's driven the butt of his coach gun two more times into Haidt. Smears that demonic poplar in so doing. Smears it more with a spit of spite to follow. Wiped the smirk right off Haidt's face and wiped the jaw right off its hinges. Blooded drool and bits of plaster of Paris seep out the man's busted drooping slack jaw.

It's all darkness for him now as…

"Make sure to get that shit off his face before Carson," Swade orders. "I don't want him disturbing the locals."

THE TRAIN LURCHES INTO MOTION and all our players leave Santa Rosa. Leave her to heal.

2

—————

GOING T' CARSON FOR T' HANGING

Carson's next to Rosa but that don't mean it ain't a trek. Train left by noon and it won't arrive until after nightfall. It chunks along fearless nevertheless, guts crammed to the walls with a host of pinworms not so fearless.

Why talk of fears? The dark the bluffs and the curves of the last leg of the trip are a perfect recipe for ambush ya see. And the dark'll get to that train before that train'll get to those curves.

Why talk of worms? Train's full of a decent proportion of vermin. Though *Miscreant* is likely the better way of putting it. Despite the bulk of these passengers being perfectly wormlike and parasitic in the sense of the poets, there's also a depravity to these men that doesn't just beggar belief it obliterates the very thoughts the beggaring deprives of truth-value. Discard even the thought lest you want to lose the best of your hopes. They're no good is the point. Out-of-county scoundrels brought to settle in the reforming and redemptifying amorality of The Belt. Imported by train. So although I say these men have the worst qualities of a worm, out of respect for worms it need be said, worms ain't got a fraction of the worst qualities of these men.

Most of them miscreants are shackled. The rest done the shackling. Anyone else is just a poor old drunk who was too much a liability to whatever town gave him the boot.

THE FINAL HOUR TO CARSON is enough to make the bravest of men wary. So, by the stronger argument to weaker men, the final hour's got Swade spooked to shit. He ain't so dumb he don't know caught outlaws got representatives. Representatives with a vested interest in the freedom of those they represent. Bluffs alone would hide them agents just fine and the dark alone would do the same. Course, last hour to Carson means both the bluffs and the dark to contend with at once, all while the curves of the track slow the engine.

"Point them lanterns as far out them bars as your arms'll let you!" Swade barks at the jailers. He catches a glimpse of Haidt's demonic visage as one of the jailers' lanterns moves past it. Haidt's unconscious with a jaw just barely hanging on and yet he's still got a power over Swade in a way strange. "Jailer!" Swade's voice breaks saying this. His darting eyes go back on them bluffs. "Told you to get that shit off his face!"

"Carson," says the jailer.

"I know where we're going," Swade says indignant. Swade knows everything.

"Nah, Carson's my name," *Jailer Carson* corrects.

"Kinda dumb coincidence is that?"

"No coincidence at all. Carson City's namesake is me."

"Hangin' hub of the county's named after you?"

"My family anyhow. Great great grandaddy was the first ever Judge."

"Must have been one fecund of a judge to make so many

of Carson a Carson that that's the name and I gotta be riding with one," Swade scoffs.

"Hanged all the competin' peckers!" chuckles another jailer.

Swade smirks at that. "Get that lantern up!"

Arm raises the lantern perpendicular to torso.

"Fuck you—" says Jailer Carson at all involved in his mockery.

"Get that shit off his face!" Swade reminds.

Carson hesitates. "Make him more sympathetic to a jury like that."

"He ain't seeing any jury," Swade says matter of fact. "He had his day. Sentenced to hang a long time ago."

Logic's sound enough for Jailer Carson. Not logic he likes mind you, just logic that's sound. No one likes sound logic. Sound logic moves the hesitant man to act. It's like the old doggerel says,

> *You'd sooner shoot dead and if ya missed*
> >   *you'd run*
> *From the huckster who said 'hey listen son,*
> *What I got here, just for you'll*
> *Turn your convictions false*
> *And your worst fears true*
>
> *Make any justice sought and the good you've*
> >   *chased*
> *Oppression defined and an awful waste*
> *Any hatred banished any evil defied*
> *Lovey-dovey and the true and the tried*
>
> *I can see in your eyes, tool's new for you*
> *Wish your story'd been different*

A trick your whole life through
Then your false would be false
And your true would be true

But that's the nature of the beast
That's the essence of the tool
It's the sole of the sage
But the hat of the fool'

That's logic.

Carson moves in to do what was asked. He hunkers down, reaching for his handkerchief. Ain't shook his hesitancy yet.

As he squats in front of Haidt mustering whatever it is he needs to muster, his attention drifts to the man to Haidt's right. Man's still. Carson moves the lantern to him. Man's face is all pallor even under the yellow glow.

"Drunk's dead," says Carson.

"Which?" Swade asks.

"One with the shakes."

"He stink?"

"Yes."

"Of death?"

"Can't tell."

"Well we ain't stopping and he'll need be accounted for when we arrive. Just gonna live with the smell to town."

Jailer Carson can't get any kind of reprieve it seems. Decides to just dive in and do the job. Starts scrubbing. The vigor of his cleaning wakes the convict. Jailer jostles the broke jaw and Haidt barks out in a necessarily muffled bark of pain. Carson startles! Makes a sound like *GEEYUH!*

"Shut up I'm almost done," the jailer whispers, maybe just for himself. Muffled cries of pain continue. Carson spits a healthy dose of tobacco juice onto that hanky-on-its-last-legs and uses it to dilute the beet-boil and the poplar paint. Doesn't look much better when he's done but doesn't look demonic no more either.

More cries.

IT'S SLOW GOING THROUGH THEM curves and train's only about a halfway in. Seems slower than usual to the lawmen. Always does. Put them in the brothel car and the trip'd have been done hours ago. No such thing as a brothel car of course but them horny jailers can dream. And that is exactly what better than half of them are doing better than half the time as they try taking their minds off their fears.

Their arms are still outstretched holding those lanterns exactly perpendicular to their torsos. How'd they manage that for forty-five minutes straight? One of the jailers got the bright idea to tie his lariat to his wrist after looping it over the top bar of the cage car. Everyone else just followed suit.

What we got's a zoo exhibit chugging along a steel road. Six hanging hands a' glowing, three per side halfway up-and-out while eight pairs of shackled hands sit along the bottom of either side. A real sight.

The men are tired though fear keeps most awake. Those too dumb to be fearful can't sleep for the chafe of their lariats. Haidt's back unconscious. Doesn't mean he won't be howling again should he wake up. That's why he's got a gag in his face tight. I say *face* because there's no discernible mouth left to put it in. All the miscreants in that car just sit or stand in silence. A groggy menagerie. Appendages just dangling when...

SCHWNAPP! BANG!

One of the Jailers' lariats is shot out! The snapping of

the line catches him and his weak arm unaware sending the lantern swinging down like a pendulum. Lantern hits the iron bars with a *SMASH!* sending flaming kerosene into the jailer's thighs and crotch. He screams as the fire spreads. Screams catch the attention of the few not already attending to the sight. All have turned to see the flaming bellowing jailer stumbling toward them from the rear of the car. Length left of his shot-out lariat hangs from his wrist afire: limp spent and flaming like a dong familiar the brothel car.

All are mesmerized when...

BANG! BANG!

More gunshots! Shakes them out of that daze. All hop to it.

Jailer Carson immediately drops his lantern reaching back into the cage for his pistol. His clumsiness has left his section of the car in a darkness that won't last long as *Flaming Jailer,* now fully engulfed, is stumbling closer and closer like a screaming wailing torch.

The sleeping prisoners are all awake and screaming and shouting near as bad as Flamer. Their legs alternate between pulling inward and kicking outward as they try to avoid the flames and boost themselves into a standing posi-tion at the same time.

While all this transpires, the other two jailers on Carson's side have snagged themselves up on their lariats and are flailing helplessly. Forgot they had for all intents and purposes bound themselves to the cage wall. Jailer between Swade and Flamer moves to assist them.

BANG!

Another shot. Helpful jailer takes that bullet to the temple. He goes down dead as Flaming Jailer stumbles over him moving toward Carson. Carson's frozen in fear at the glut of horrors occurring. Flamer's about to get within arm's length of him when...

WHOOOF!

Swade wraps a lambskin coat around Flamer and wrestles him to the ground. Flamer's set still. Dead too. His last remaining flames lick at the lambskin.

BANG! BANG! BANG!

"Get them lanterns in the goddamn car!" shouts Swade. "Put 'em at the center and get the hell away!" He looks to the two hung-up jailers. "Fer fuck!" He moves to them in a hunkered shuffle pulling out his hunting knife as he goes. He's dodging bullets that haven't even been fired. He gets to *Jailer One* and starts brainlessly cutting sections of the rope away. He culls a few half-feet sections at the slack-end nowhere near the only length that matters: the rope after the snag-knot. Guess there're no instincts or intuitions gonna help Swade here. And yet there's always blind luck where due to the blind luck of it all, the right part of the rope gets cut. It snaps away freeing the Jailer. Slack causes Jailer One's lantern to drop too. Of course it did. Though better it break outside the car than in.

"Do the same for him." Swade puts his knife in Jailer One's hand and shoves him toward *Jailer Two*. He moves back to the front of the car. He crouches at the north corner while Jailer Carson crouches at the corner across. They peer around as though there's anything to be done about their invisible attackers. "Get the prisoners settled!"

Now freed, Jailer One and Two start waving their pistols at the bound men. Shackled men go back to still but they ain't silent about it.

"Shut up!" says Jailer One smashing his pistol handle into the face of a prisoner arbitrarily chosen.

Shackled men go silent but they ain't happy about it.

PWING!

Lead ricochets off the bars a few inches above Swade's head. He hunkers lower weaving according to no discernible pattern.

The shots are getting closer and so must be the ambushers. Fact appears to have exercised one prisoner in particular. He's four men down from Haidt and he's gotten decidedly animated despite the threat of a pistol handle to the chops. He's doing that dance the shackled were doing a few minutes ago. He's trying to lift himself to his feet.

Swade catches the attempted erection and realizes... "They're here for him!" He's pointing at the animated prisoner. "Shoot him dead if it looks like his friends got the upper hand!"

"No! Not me!" shouts the prisoner settling back down.

"Nice try rascal shit!" Swade says in hush. He goes back to trying to identify the source of the attack.

"Not me!"

Swade turns to face the ornery prisoner once more. "I. Said. Shut. Up."

"*Now!*" shouts the prisoner staring right through the lawman.

Swade spins to bars to see what the prisoner was shouting at. Spins just in time to face the barrel of a Colt pistol. Muzzle's pointing into his left eye. One of the ambushers had ridden up alongside while Swade's back was turned. 'Busher cocks the pistol in-eye then...

BANG!

Clenched-shut eyes burst open. Swade rolls them around. He's still got both of them. How the hell? He gets his focus and looks forward. The 'busher's horse is still keeping pace but the 'busher's keeled over and slipping away. Off the horse he goes and under the car.

"The hell?" Swade mutters.

THUH-CRATCH!

No more time for ponderin'. Swade's attention snaps around to the 'busher that's jumped onto the bars behind. This one's got Jailer Carson around the neck with both arms and's got him around the belly with both legs. A little monkey on them monkey bars piggyback riding the wrought iron overcoat of the jailer.

Swade's eyes widen as he fumbles for his pistol. About time he drew down! Jailer Carson's face is turning blue. His tongue's sagging out the side of it. Swade tries aiming at *Monkey* behind Carson and it's futile. Can't get a bead on the attacker as Carson's his shield. Real cooperative shield too since the jailer's completely motionless, near purple. Swade's taking the first steps to rush Monkey man when...

BOOOSH!

Top of Monkey's head rips off. Buckshot took it. Took it from outside. Grip loosens from Carson's neck and the ambusher falls backward still hanging by the legs.

Swade's back moving toward. He gets to Carson and pulls those legs free. Monkey slips away into the darkness.

Swade smacks the unconscious Carson back conscious and the jailer gasps awake.

CLINK! CLINK!

Sounds are coming from the other side of the car opposite the two. The men attend to it. They see the butt of a pistol grip banging against the iron above two prisoners frozen and scared to death. Who's holding that pistol? None can tell.

CLINK! CLINK!

Last two *CLINKS!* and the hand recedes into dark. Gone.

"I don't fucking believe this." Jailer One's face is pressed against the northside bars.

Swade Carson and Jailer Two do that hunker-shuffle toward Jailer One's side of the car. All of them peer on into the bluffs. What they see is a rider. Moonlight's hitting his beaming ivory face. Turns now. Takes both reins in right hand. Holds out the index and middle fingers of his left hand. Points them at Swade. Now he brings those fingers back to just under his eyes, streaks beet-boil blood down to his cheekbones. Without breaking concentration he leans back in his saddle like he needs the clearance. He whips his pistol to a draw at the jail car and...

BANG!

The four men jolt out of the collective trance. They reach for holstered pistols just as a last 'busher collapses dead above them. They look up to see him laid out lengthwise the bars of the jail car. One arm hangs through. Blood drips from a bullet hole in the 'busher's chest. The pose is almost imploring with gravity helping extend the hand while bulging the eyes.

The lawmen turn back to the bluffs. Red-eyed rider's gone.

TRAIN STOPS. SWADE GRABS A STRUGGLING STILL-GAGGED STILL-GRUMBLING Haidt upward and drags him out the jail car.

Carson's sheriff and two deputies are there to receive the prisoners. The three can't exactly see into the jail car from where they stand yet none miss the stench of the Amazonian cook-out. The sheriff ever-so-daintily puts a finger across his nostrils. Finger presses tighter into those nostrils as Swade nears.

"Get this shitbag strung up before he makes me puke!" He tosses Haidt at the sheriff's men.

"That's not protocol and you know it deputy," sheriff rebukes.

Swade bursts out at the lawman and grabs him by the collar. Deputies make a move to aid their boss as the jailers draw on them. *Don't do it boys...* Swade pulls the sheriff up close to his lapel pointing at the badge on it. Badge says *Marshal.* Just *Marshal.* Sheriff grimaces a little. We see his tongue moving behind his lips like he's fishing a whole world of food bits out of his teeth when... Resolve.

"Fine," he relents. "Go wake the warden."

"No warden. Rope."

"You really anglin' to lose that badge you just got?"

"Rope."

Sheriff shakes his head in all due defeat. "Fine."

GALLOWS ARE PREPPED. HAIDT'S MUMBLING last words through gag as a noose lowers over his head. Noose knot's cinched tight to the nape. Make-shift executioner kicks the rain barrel out from under the station mail hook and...

CRUNT!

No ceremony.

Man's hanged. Man's dead.

3

SHALE CITY: THE MAYOR

What's most striking about *Hannah Price* are the rigid features of her otherwise delicate countenance. The elements of it. All the various pairs of bells and baubs. The inputs through which the objects of her acquaintance trigger the senses. All sharp and rigid. They lay in perfect symmetry too. Eyes, ears, nostrils, lips. Two of everything lying left-to-right top-to-bottom like a mirror.

The sharpness made her appear to be in a state of steely discernment all the time. Don't get me wrong, it wasn't unpleasant and it wasn't unwelcoming, just discerning. She isn't always in a state of discernment of course though frequently. Steel came long before the perpetual philosophy. It's who she's always been. *Temperament* grew into *look* when her husband died you see, when she received her inheritance. Only bit of positive luck in all that. Not the inheritance mind you, but the temperament becoming commensurate the discernment.

Eighteen more months she thinks as she looks out to the stone. She's looking as she leans on the veranda rail of her

Queen Anne. He built the veranda all the way around it. Built it that way for her. *Eighteen months for your bold experiment my love.* She squints at the etching. Puts a hand to her brow. The sun's risen high enough behind the stone its glare makes the etching near-unreadable. *Why didn't you talk me out of putting our plot at the east again? I know I know. So you can tell me to get to work in the mornin'.* Glare always seems to blot out her husband's year of passing first. She smiles at what the occlusion suggests. *I wish you were right Tom. I wish it wasn't done.*

If she were a more spiritual woman she'd fully commit to her husband's messages as more than metaphor. More than just his impeccable foresight and planning. Nature as his agent. Executor of his wisdom in perpetuity. If she were a more spiritual woman she'd see his soul in it.

Make no mistake, Hannie *is* that more spiritual woman on the gloomier days of Shale City. The days born of going to bed feeling a tired in her guts instead of her heart n' soul. Where tired should be. Where it can be vanquished. On nights like that she sleeps a chilled restless sleep she drags along with her into the better part of her day. Dragging a tired that's moved from guts to mind. That's filled her head with a lament and sadness at all that's good in the world and a pity for all who *are* good in the world... And a hatred of herself for the unasked-for sanctimoniousness.

They're good folk. But the good will be taken from them at some point in some measure and those good people know it. They know it in some mathematical sense. They don't know it in any gut sense. Not in a way that gets them to move on it which is the same as not knowing it at all. And you want them to be happy forever because anything other than that happiness is something they'll never see coming and will be unbearable for them. Your heart aches for them because on some awful awful day… They. Will. Be. You.

On days like that Hannie'd find herself draped over that stone crying into her husband's arms honest to goodness.

NOT TODAY.

TODAY SHE FEELS a tranquility. The crisp September air was always invigorating for her. There was a clarity to it. A fresh start. A vestige of her days as a teacher maybe? She stares wistfully a last second then decides to heed her husband's advice and get to the day's work.

She walks around to the north side of the veranda, the side facing the outskirts of the south of Shale. *And you…* She's leaning, looking again—the morning sunshine at her back as dawn wraps Shale up in amber. Thought she had to get to work? This is her work. …*Time to shine them shoes.*

City does have the mud and the grit all over it you'd expect. A red slop. You know in some parts of the world they don't have the color brown? They have something they call *deep red*? They swear they even see it as redder by virtue of calling it *red* alone! Well I don't mean to say the ground of Shale is a deep red in place of brown like them folk abroad say. Nor am I saying it's a reddish-brown or even a brownish-red. It's red simpliciter. And in the morning sun it's blood.

"Mrs. Mayor!" half-shouts a Shale resident pausing on her way into the furniture store. "Morning to ya."

"Morning Rosey," Hannah half-shouts back. She leans further forward over the rail fooling herself that closing six inches of a twenty yard gap negates any need to yell. "Looks like my down came in?"

Rosey scowls slightly. "Picking out the hen feathers."

Scowl turns to contrition. "I'm sorry Hannah. You know how those intermediaries adulterate anything they can."

"I accounted for that. Will."

"Mayor." Rosey's brother Will has caught up to his sister. He's carrying a large toolbox full of woodworking implements. "She tell you about them feathers? Damn adulterators! Everywhere!"

"Still trying to shake the sawdust out the pepper myself. No hurry."

"This Saturday?" Rosey asks.

"Sure."

"Ain't never had a request such as yours ma'am." Will hoists up the box of tools. "Had to root around in my daddy's old things for these. Shouldn't be long now."

Well keep them tools at hand Will. Keep that list of importers/exporters at hand too Rosey. Shale needs more than iron. "I had a yearning for an authentic Recamier in the den. I knew you two'd be up to the task."

"Don't know how authentic a French couch made in Shale is, but it felt good honoring the old ways like that. Immen the debt Ma'am."

Hannah bows. Rosey and Will head into their store.

Just as the shop door closes a wind kicks up. A cold wind. September's crisp in Shale City only not this crisp and the wind's coming from the south. Wind seems a product of nothing. A howling gust without cause ripping toward Shale. Gust stops Hannah though not by its strength. She's curious. She doesn't realize it at first—too busy with that discerning of hers—but she's exhaling a steady plume of a steaming vapor. She bunches her shawl up into her arms wrapping it around herself tighter.

September's crisp though not this crisp.

Then...

The wind dies at once. Vapor vanishes. Where's the settling dust? There ought to be dust. It's spooky so Hannie's spooked. She's trying to reckon with the irregularity but...

A rumble from the southwest. A tremor.

THE PIERCE OF THE WHISTLE follows the rumble.

She flies around to the other side of the house. South side. Side facing the pit. Can't see a thing. She moves into the house in a flurry and not more than a quarter minute later she's crawling out her second-story window onto the peak of the house's rotunda. She sidles along its overhang. Now she can get a look into the mining pit.

She holds her field glasses up to her eyes. The men are bursting out the *main bag*. Term comes from the Latins. *Saccus* I think. It just means the corridor out the main mining shaft. They jog a few paces and slow immediately after. They're hustling to clear the exit for the others though once out the bag it appears they're out the trouble.

Whistle whines unrelenting.

She's counting. Three dozen men started their night down there. She's thinking she's subitized about the same sum from her rotunda. Needs to confirm this.

Needs to prepare for the denials deflation and hand-waving of the worst of her council too—their silver tongues about as lulling as The Mining Council silver in-pocket. She needs to get to work. She climbs back into the house.

Out the door, she heads southeast. That's away from Shale proper toward Shale station.

"ERD IT WAS ONLY A TRICKLE MA'AM," says *Jon* the office and Town Hall allman. He holds the door open for Hannah.

"Lower level'll be filled in a day," she says brushing past him.

"Trickle let the men out."

Hannah's is a tone of concession. "You're right. Could have been much worse."

"Uncanny ma'am."

She looks bemused.

Jon intuits the confusion. Smirks a little too like he's been banking on the reaction when...

"Jon!" *Maria* admonishes. "Now is not the time to be having *yewr* fun with Mrs. Price!" she softens a little at her husband. "Just show her."

Hannah's real curious now. Jon's satisfied with the level of intrigue he's elicited. He moves swiftly to what looks like a pillowcase hanging on the wall to the left of the office door. "Real uncanny!" He whips the pillowcase away revealing a framed charcoal sketch of the office front. Hannah Jon and Maria are sketched into the scene for good measure. Jon made the frame.

"Where'd you find that?" Hannah asks a little flustered.

"It's perfect!" Jon beams. "Almost on par *whit der* frame."

Maria nudges him in the ribs with her elbow. *Stop foolin'!* "It really is ma'am," she concurs.

"Where?"

"Oh just the trash where you thought you could hide it."

"I don't know what to say. I really—"

"Here he comes ma'am!" Maria's pointing across Hannah to the window.

Hannah spins to see *Waylan Burke Jr*, councilman-at-large, exiting Shale City Hall. He's prancing a little as he crosses the street toward The Mayor's office. Really, he's just trying to keep his cuffs out of the mud but what's more showy than clean clothes in Shale? As good as prancing if you ask me. He's a muckety-muck on the council too, Chairman of Labor Relations. What's more inappropriate than clean clothes on a broker for the workin' man while we're judging? The trio watch him through the office window in no sort of anticipation.

"Carpetbagger," Maria scoffs.

"He had to get elected like the rest," Hannah reminds.

"By men desperate for his papa's jobs," Maria whispers.

Burke's hand's already on the knob.

"Alright," Hannah hushes. "There'll be plenty of time for dissenting—"

"Madam Mayor!" Burke shouts as he lets himself in.

"*Erd* it was only a trickle..." Jon says demanding the councilman's attention.

Burke eyes Jon quizzically. "Y—yes," he stutters. "And barely even that... *J-on?*"

"*Y-on,*" Jon annunciates.

"Town of just 150 people..." Maria whispers at Hannah. Hannah nudges Maria in the ribs in a way all too familiar. Jon sees this and rubs his side as though in phantom pain.

Burke doesn't pay any mind to the exchange. Didn't even notice. "Well Madam Mayor! Got a lot of worried townsfolk already piling into City Hall."

"Best we head over then," Hannah says.

She Jon and Maria begin shuffling for the door. Burke puts out a prudish little arm, wedging it between Maria and Hannah, stopping the latter. Doesn't stop her by force mind you but by the awkwardness of a floaty appendage that dare not touch a woman widowed less than three years. Arm floats at barely her midriff too as Hannah's taller than Burke by several inches barefoot. She's tallish for a woman though he's mighty short for a man. Immaculate pant cuffs though.

"Um, you two head over." Burke is gesturing for Jon and

Maria to keep moving. "Tell the rest of the council we'll be there post-haste."

Hannah nods to her office managers. *It's alright you two.*

They exit though not before Maria shakes her head in mock exasperation at Hannah, for Hannah, behind Burke's back.

CALL ME 'MADAM' ONE MORE *time ya runty little bunko steer...* She's sat herself in her desk chair for comfort for Burke's sugar-coating. He stands solemn as though giving Hannah time to prepare herself for the profundity to ensue.

"It's probably the best news we could have hoped for ma'am."

There's a flush in Hannah at the first syllable of a *ma'am* so close to a *madam.*

Set it aside Hannie girl. Set it aside for the stoics.

"The earth is shifting, settling," he continues. "Happens all the time. *Transient phenomenon.*"

You're overselling it Burke. "Is that your expert opinion?"

He chuckles. "Why 'course not Miss Mayor. Got the geologist down there as soon as I could. Personal friend. Did me a favor."

"And the leak?"

"Wellspring is working some silt out. Transient."

"Wellspring runs east of the mine."

"Not since the shift."

"I just don't see it Burke. Groundwater's followed the same path for near forty years. Now a change?"

"W—well." Burke feigns indignation. "Shall I summon the geologist?"

"Where is he?"

"Well truth be told he's on his way to Washington."

"What's he gonna do there?"

"*Lie.*"

"Could get his fill of that working for you."

"Naw ma'am. *Lye.* Something about adding it to rivers to take out the acid. Or adding acid to rivers to take out the lye. Suffice to say he's probably halfway to the capital by now."

"Then it's a good thing I caught him before you put him on that train."

"Why madam—"

"That tremor was no earth settling. A dam gate collapsed. That's why the water. Thanks to the diggout last year, mine pit's left no shelter belt. Come the north winds of fall the whole rig'll collapse and we'll get more than a trickle."

"You're funnin' Madam Mayor!" Burke chuckles on.

"Enough with this *Madam Mayor* horseshit!" She stands as she says this, towering over the man. "You think I'm ignorant of the language games you and the council play? That *madam*'s the vehicle of your resentment?"

Burke affects a look as though meant to say *this is beneath me.* "Trust me missus." He pulls his lapels like an orator. "It's a might more respectful than *the widow mayor...*"

"I'd prefer that." She chooses her next words carefully. "*Next of kin governs in the interim.* It's law. Only law ever needing invocation around here it seems."

Burke starts mumbling something. Hannah can only make out the word *blood.*

"What's that?"

"I said *wrong* ma'am. *Kin* on another of our laws means *by blood or by god.* The latter includes marriage." Burke starts mumbling again. "If yours-stated were truly our only law we wouldn't have our *madam* mayor."

Hannah can just barely hear this but she *can* hear this which is likely the intent.

"Not a man for laws Burke?"

"Ma'am I simply believe in meritocracy not defaults."

"Who's the head of The Mining Council again?"

"*Hmmm.* One could argue my daddy immersing me in the business of iron from the cradle makes me the ideal candidate for Labor Chair in a town whose labor consists entirely of working that iron."

"One could say the same about Tom immersing me in the business of mayoring in a town whose labor affairs consist almost entirely of politicking. Hence the law."

"*Touché*," Burke says. Then... "You tell them folk the mine's as good as gone and they won't just be dispirited they'll die inside. Shale'll be a ghost town inside of four months."

Speaking of *shifts*... He's being honest-to-goodness earnest about things as he will from time to time. These sudden turns of decorum always provoke in Hannah an instant reckoning for what of all conditions immediate the man are its cause. As though she'll find some switch she can flip to turn off the bureaucrat in him.

"Now," he continues. "If you tell them it's temporary you'll buy all of us the time needed to make the appropriate economic shifts—"

"Specifics!" Hannah says, as though this isn't the first time she's had to remind Burke to speak directly. He does.

"Buying time to establish another form of commerce. To get these people work. It's our only hope Hannah."

She nods in a clipped almost vibratory manner. *Goddamnit he's right. I can't believe I'm in complete and utter agreement with a Burke!*

"And who knows," he adds. "Maybe the dam'll hold after all!"

And that ends that accord...

TOWN HALL IS PACKED. Fear's palpable. People are trying to mask their fear with anger which ain't so difficult.

"...Only be a temporary shutdown," Hannah says to the crowd—seated council at her back. "The earth is settling." She hates herself for this. "No more than a month. The tremors stop and we'll know the mine is safe."

The crowd jeers.

Bullshit Hannah!

You sound like Waylan Burke!

What would Tom think?

That last one stung. They're right. Hannah turns from the crowd. She wipes away tears like she's ripping her tear ducts away with them. She realizes she's doing this in front of her council. Why turn away if the aim is to not betray vulnerability to the wrong people? She stifles, inhales deep. Turns back to the townsfolk.

"Well you can't very well go down there," she almost pleads. "I admire all of your work ethics. Lord knows it's more than admiration, it's a dependence. However, we need to put your wellbeing before the iron—"

No mine, no town!

"It's just temporary."

HANNAH'S GONE OUT THE FRONT door with the townsfolk. *If you can't walk out the door of that hall,* Tom used to tell her, *with all them people, facing them come what may, you ain't mayorin' right.* Citizens just stare daggers at her. Anything they had to say they said inside. Anything they had to jeer they jeered inside really.

She stands on those steps enduring their silent disgust and judgment in a silent acceptance all her own. Antagonism's coming at her in silence, bearing it might as well travel the same.

There's contradicting opposing righteousness coming from all factions all over this landing. A righteousness in all the relevant senses despite the incoherence. Yet it was only Hannah who had to lie to attain hers. *Forgive her this trespass?*

"You want the coffee on?" Jon asks her.

"No, I'm heading home."

He watches as she sets out down the Town Hall steps. "Don't walk lonely ma'am."

HANNAH DOES WALK ALONE. SHE walks alienated. She even walks a little aimlessly having decided to take a detour around south Shale. However, she walks with resolve not loneliness. The crisp air reminds. *Early Tom. Too soon though it was bound to happen. We'll manage.* Then... Something cheerful...

"It tickles moma! Don't you want to see?"

"It's not for me pet. My toes are made for chornyy."

Hannah edges closer to the picket fence she walks along. She watches the mother watching her little girls play in the grass. The children are barefoot. Moma's in some homemade gumboots. Looks like the leather's been dipped in pine tar.

Sod's a novelty in most places around here yet a fixture in The Belt. Nobody knows why, but hybridization really took to our soils. Hence the county carpet. Our red mud can't hold a crop of anything other than dust yet it holds this.

What may not be a novelty to many Belters anymore is certainly a novelty to these kids. Near everything is to an eighteen-month-old and a four-year-old. However, there's something *extra new* about this to them. The children stomp amidst the blades.

"Mrs. Molyboha," Hannah greets.

"Mrs. Mayor," Kateryna greets in return. Greeting's guarded but comes with all due warmth. Still facing her girls, Kateryna sums the day's events with Hannah's tone. Throws in all pattern she's observed her first week in Shale for good measure. She makes a derivation. "They were more uncompromising than usual?"

"You should have attended," Hannah jests.

She turns to The Mayor. "I've never understood the iron. My husband will inform me."

4

SHALE CITY: THE SHERIFF

"**D**on't walk lonely ma'am."

Hannah bows solemn at this as she moves toward Main.

The Sheriff starts moving up the town hall steps simultaneous to Hannah passing from our view. He moves through the milling townsfolk. He plods upward, jovial-looking enough. Kind of his default. Maybe it's the upturned ends of his English-style mustache that make him come across more grinnish than he is? His wife told him to trim it that way. A matter of acculturation he assumed. Or pullin' the wool? He's a slender reed of taupe otherwise. Your standard sheriff down to the tin star. He differentiates his dress with a little leather pouch hanging off his hip but other than that, his is a swath that typifies your average iron belt lawbringer.

What about that pouch? Sheriff told everyone it's called a *moshonka*. His wife seems to have some special *even* sentimental attachment to it cuz she flushes every time folk around here ask her about it. They ask frequently too as that pouch is one of the few mysteries of our Sheriff. *What's he got in that moshonka?*

As The Sheriff continues his ascension, a few of the townsfolk behind him start grumbling. More and more join in the chorus with every step. It's a collective grumble by the last. Bit of a din even.

All they'll do is grumble? Sheriff wonders. Three towns, four years. They only grumble. They grumble all over. We only grumbled back home. Everybody grumbles. Mining Council grumbles at town councils. Town councils grumble at Mining Council. Miners grumble at both. And yet the iron either comes or it doesn't.

He meets Jon at the landing locking the hall doors. He pats him on the shoulder, "Finishing up?" Says it loud enough to be heard over the crowd starting to move away. They rove off as a mass, grumbling as they go.

"Tidy tidy first," Jon answers making a sweeping motion. He points across the street at The Mayor's office. Sheriff nods. Pointing's started Jon moving. Sheriff joins him back down to Main.

The two split away from each other at the gutter, Sheriff moving in the direction of the jail, Jon continuing on to Hannah's office.

Sheriff gets a look of recall, spins back to face the allman. "Staying in tonight?" he half-shouts.

"Should I?"

Walking backward, Sheriff points to the saloon behind Jon gesturing at near all the miners pouring in. At near a quarter the town besides.

"Lick and a promise and I lock the doors," Jon assures.

"Good," Sheriff says as his backward amble turns frontward.

· · ·

HE KNOCKS A SPECIAL KNOCK on the jail door—*cummin' the jail!*—and starts turning his key. He leans half through the doorway glancing around the place. None are in the cells. None are lodging any complaints. None are exemplifying any qualities whatsoever as none are present. None but sheriff's deputy *Bill 'Dep' McNult*. Dep's leaning on the side of the little oak desk meant for clerical concerns. More ornamental at present. He looks to be anticipating the point of the visit.

"Want me to stay later?" Sheriff asks.

Deputy chuckles a slight scoffing chuckle. "For what Sheriff? Full moon was last week!" He twists off the side of the desk and into the office chair. Real loungy about things.

Sheriff's demeanor remains fixed. "People are unsettled. They drink more tonight. Drink brings trouble."

"Shale folk drink *t'* get *t'* bed not to carouse. It'll be fine."

Sheriff gives an *I hope you're right* look. Deputy tilts his head and makes a clicking sound with his tongue, points at Sheriff and winks. Then he takes to busying himself in the left-hand drawer of the desk.

As Dep does, The Sheriff reaches for a wall-mounted lockbox within arm's reach of the door. Box is full of local storefront keys for use in emergencies. He quietly slips one of the key rings down his sleeve and looks back to The Deputy rifling through a second drawer. He *reminds* by giving the steel box a couple of wraps with his ring finger. Wedding band amplifies the *CLANG!* He drives the padlock shut with a *CLACK!* Sounds couldn't be any more significant of The Sheriff's point.

Dep notices. He waves an ameliorating hand without looking away from the drawer he's rooting in.

"Goodnight," The Sheriff relents, pulling the door closed.

"Oh sheriff!" Dep calls through it. "This came for you."

Sheriff pops back in just in time to catch a bursting bundle of envelopes. One of the corners of one of the envelopes is poking out a rip. It reads *U.S. Marshal's Service.* Sheriff grins a little happier than his mustache and puts the bundle under arm.

"SHERIFF METRO?" ASKS A SHALE resident trying to catch his attention.

Here's a quick aside. This is me your storyteller talking by the way.

Here's an aside:

Understand this:

Metro is indeed The Sheriff's name only not his last and not even really his first. His last name is *Molyboha*. His Christian name is *Dmytro*. 'Metro' is a shortening of this. The townspeople call him *Sheriff Metro* and pretend like they can't pronounce *Molyboha*.

They can't say it alright, though it ain't for a lack of pronunciative skills. They can't say it because the best they can do for tolerance is deny Sheriff the quality of being a Galician. Don't say the man's surname, there's no evidence of who he is hence there's no need to bring certain of the federal government's expectations into the rinky-dink day-to-day political affairs of Shale.

See a few years ago The Sheriff's homeland found itself a geography between two warring nations. These nations decided in complete and cordial agreement that the center of The Sheriff's homeland ought be the middle where they would meet in conquest. Half of The Sheriff's homeland was thus annexed by one conqueror, half was annexed by the other. All so they could continue fighting their war in peace.

Nobody asked the citizens of the country broke-in-two what they thought of all this, which was, to say the least, rude.

What does this matter to the people of Shale? It doesn't, save for a small faction of zealotous types who confuse patriotism with government bootlickin'. Why does it matter to the government bootlickers? Because it matters to the Amerikan Federal Government they're always lickin' the boots of, that's why. One of them conquering factions was an ally to *The Federals* the other an enemy. Because the enemy conqueror annexed half of The Sheriff's homeland, this made half of his homeland an enemy. This, due the nature of federal politics, made all of his homeland an enemy. Might just as well have said half was an *ally* and generalized in the other direction. Of course, to do that we'd have to dispatch with the broad-brush easier-to-trust-no-one-than-understand-anyone approach of The Federals. That *nature* again...

Sheriff's homeland's an enemy so all those native to his homeland are enemies. Buggy's thrown a wheel so all the passengers are cripples too? There are still many of Metro and Kate's people incarcerated in camps to the north. Men women and children. The Federals call them *enemy aliens*. Call Kate and Metro that too, make no mistake, but the Molybohas have managed to escape the camps up north. Again, could just as well have called them *like-minded allies* if we're generalizing, but that *nature* rears its head again...

For near all the people of Shale, like so many under the thumb of The Federals, it's just easier to act like the problem ain't present than to have to take up a position on it. Problem ain't present for the people of Shale if their sheriff's *Sheriff Metro*.

Sheriff don't mind it none. He has a job to do. Sheriff don't mind the townsfolk regarding his first name as his last though he does have his limits. Once and only once someone called his wife *Mrs. Metro. That* he does mind. One and only one Shale resident ever called her that where, if there ever was a bootlicker, this guy misspeaking was that! Caused Sheriff to not feel so bad whomping him across the chops with his hip pouch. Nobody knows exactly what's in that moshonka but on that day they learned whatever it is, it ain't feathers. Whomping made the point. It made it publicly. From then on Mrs. Molyboha was *Kate.*

"Sheriff Metro?" asks a Shale resident.

"Yes Mrs. Bell?"

"What'll be done of the mine presently?"

"That will be up to town hall and The Mining Council."

"Surely you must know? Your men are guarding it."

"My men?" Sheriff chuckles, taken aback. "It's just me and Dep and he's in the jail right now."

"You don't have reserves?"

"I don't even have a second pair of boots. Tell me more about these men you speak of?"

"W—well I don't rightly know. I thought you might. There are armed men standing guard at the main bag so says my husband."

Sheriff's pensive. Appears resolved to irresolution. *Nothing you can do just standing here in the street Metro.* "Thank you Mrs. Bell," he assures. "I will definitely be asking The Mayor about this."

"...My husband will inform me."

Then...

"Popa!" Metro and Kate's four-year-old shouts. Her

name's *Anya* by the way. She flies through the picket fence gate and past Hannah to greet her father. He scoops her up and kisses her on the forehead. Walks around Hannah and through the gate.

"Mayor," he greets.

Hannah smiles cordially. "Settling in nicely?"

"Very cozy," Metro says. He clears his daughter's hair from her face brushing gently. He puts his forehead to hers. Grins. She beams back at her father. He kisses her on the nose and sets her down to go back to her play. His focus is on The Mayor once again. "There are armed men down to the mine?"

Hannah furrows her brow. *Officious little usurper!*

Kate dips away excusing herself from *the business*. She rejoins her children on the sod.

"The Council's private security," Hannah assures. "Wouldn't lift a finger when Rosans were under siege yet they'll dispatch a whole platoon to protect a pot of iron soup."

"Men like those have always been quick to put the brakes on after the wagon's over the cliff. They've never been known for their prescience."

Hannah chuckles. "You're better versed in their bureaucracy than I am!"

"I had to go through the election processes."

"I didn't!" she laughs.

"Next year?"

She shakes her head, evades. "Elected or not, that mine sits on land under the joint jurisdiction of Shale council and the Rural Municipality, not Waylan Burke's daddy!" She stifles herself a little. Throws back and takes a deep breath. Looks to Metro once more—li'l apologetic. "You folk's working day's done and I'm filling your leisure time with politics..."

Kate recognizes Hannah's tone of culmination. She stands to join her husband in the goodbyes.

"...You two have a wonderful evening—" Hannah looks down to an imploring tug. "Why hello there." *Viktoriya*, Metro and Kate's eighteen-month-old, has toddled over to Hannah and's latched onto her skirt. Hannah scoops Vikki up. "What a cutey-patoot you are!" She says to the Molybo-has, "You have two beautiful little girls." She makes googly eyes at Vikki. Vikki grins then catches sight of her moma and reaches out. Hannah hands Vikki over the fence to Kate. "Have a good night," she says and recommences her stroll.

Kate sends Vikki back to play with Anya and kisses her husband hello. Her hands are on his cheeks. She doesn't pull them away completely along with her lips. She starts grooming at his mustache. She's pulling its wings outward and upward.

"You think this fuzz makes them forget where we come from?" Metro says this lightly, not thinking a second about stopping his entertaining of his wife's preening. "They have brains dove. They remember the second I open my mouth anyway." He glances down at her gumboots. "You never wore such things back home?"

"You never wore that..." she says pointing at the moshonka.

He prods at her gumboots with the toe of his everyday ordinary cowboy boots. "Protest? Farmer woman?"

"Just ensuring the anchor well-fastened as we drift."

"This can't be home?" Metro asks, gesturing all around.

She considers the girls playing a second. They're certainly happy. However, she's done talking roots out in the yard. She returns to the more trivial matter.

"I can wear these," she insists, pointing at her toes. "You need to maintain their trust." She baps him in the moshonka. He winces ever so slightly.

"You didn't answer my question," he probes.

She simpers a little then makes a wide-swathing scooping motion with her left arm. She breaks no eye contact with her husband as the children stop their play and flood into the nest she's made. She wraps her other arm around Metro's waist and leads her family into the house.

DINNER TIME. KATE'S CLEANING UP the children's dishes as Metro prods his fork disinterestedly in fried cabbage. A thump is heard outside and he lifts his head, alert. A potential for action?

"A dog! A dog knocked over one of the Carlson's planters!" Kate chides. "You are fevered over the thought of their disobedience. All week you sit in that office—just sit I know—but you should be happy to have no work. No work means your job is done."

"These people Kateryna, they do no bad yet they do no good. There's no crime as there's no life. It's all work. All iron. No zest. No spirit."

Kate scoffs. "They're certainly spirited when you're not near. Sheriff Metro *the flying Cossack*. They say that even with me around. I know it's Metro *the hunkie* when not. What do you think they'll say during their midnight mass for their English Christmas!"

"I think they'll say prayers."

Kate shakes her head. Moves toward her husband to take his plate away. It's clear his interests ain't in the cabbage no more lest that fork he's perpetually spinning in them leaves is somehow divining the thoughts preoccupying him.

She picks up the plate sighing at the limp noodly pile about to go d'bin.

He rises up and follows her to the wash basin. He puts his arms around her waist as she drops the plate in. She turns herself in those arms to face him. She simpers again. He cocks his head playful-like. "Do not worry about what happens in the north my love. It is not happening here."

"And if *The Flying Cossack* is not said of endearment?"

"Then at least their prejudices mean morality. Questionable morality but morality nonetheless. I don't want to raise my children in an amoral world."

Kate smiles. Points into their bedroom at the little girls asleep. "Come to bed philosopher. Lay with me and the children a while."

Metro looks to the children then to his bundle of envelopes on the table. He sighs. "I will be to bed in a while. I have some reading to do."

5

———

THE WEST BRANDON TRAIL

S heriff sits up poring over the contents of his bundle. He reads by lamp light starting with that letter from the US Marshal's Service. Looks like it was written by one of them aluminum automata I was telling you about earlier.

Dear Applicant

Per your request of pre-assessment for deputy-marshal-ship in Rubrum Territory: your application has been shunted to the Rubrum US Marshal's office and will be assessed by Marshal P.T. Swade. All incoming and outgoing correspondence is to be sent to/from the Rubrum office.

Signed
Fergus Gerhardt AAG
Department of Justice

Whulp! Kiss any deputy appointment goodbye Sheriff.

No way petty Swade, who's already paltry enough at what he does, is gonna stock the Marshal service with future replacements whose future performance will only amplify his absolute ineptitude by virtue of relativity. Think the shit smells bad now? Take a snort after pruning a rose like Metro Molyboha: lawbringer so mighty, Shale electorate forgot he's an enemy alien. *This* even a man like Swade knows. Though he'd sooner resort to picking out the relevant bits of brain with a knitting needle than have a fact of his inferiority be disposed of mind.

You're a victim of your own competence Sheriff.

He moves on to some newspaper clippings. First he selects is the lengthiest most recent and most local. It's from *The Carson Daily Epitaph*. Naturally, the clipping's about the capture and execution of Haidt.

YESTERDAY'S HANGING (OR WAS IT THIS MORNING'S?)
The Carson Daily Epitaph – October 27
One Man Hurled into Eternity in the Secrecy of the Night

Tumultuous as are the days of Carson, nothing ever occurred equal to the events of yesterday *cum* today. The events were precipitated by the recapturing of the convict only known as 'Haidt'. A man as notorious in deed as he was mysterious in personhood, captured by Marshal Martin Shawk (retired), remanded to Deputy Marshal Pontipool Swade (now Marshal). In the events leading to Haidt's demise, Carson rural municipality (and later Carson City proper) would see an ambush of lawmen, an ambush upon that ambush, and finally, per several reputable witnesses, an extra-judicial hanging. All this spanning a single hour on the Carson clock—

METRO PLANTS A FINGER on the clipping. Slides it along the text scanning forward for some sort of keyword. Satisfaction a few paragraphs down so he inches his finger back to the start of the passage and continues.

> The recent emergence of the fractious and now much-dreaded 'Red-Eye Gang', contestably led by Haidt, saw only short license for mayhem thanks to Shawk. Shawk's history in Burke Range runs parallel to the metastasis of the Red-Eye Gang, believed to have its origins in the West Brandon County Penitentiary riots. These weeks-long riots resulted in the complete ruin of the penitentiary in which several hundred of the inmates escaped *en masse*.
>
> Shawk followed the southern migration of the more than two hundred escapees from West Brandon to Santa Rosa city, through all two thousand miles of Amerikan frontier country. Shawk and the roving fugitives came to shape and extend a good part of that frontier (for better or worse). He and others in the Marshal service, aided by local lawmen and the provisionally deputized, managed to apprehend most of the more notorious of the runagates while still in the northern territories.
>
> Those convicted of lesser crimes posed a greater difficulty of recapture. As their initial arrests tended to be immediate to the commission of their crimes, there was never a need for manhunts, hence sketches of visage, hence they were only known by name. No other records existed. Worse, the men who managed to evade capture the longest consisted largely of more temperate ruffians and confidence men. With the confidence men teaching the ruffians methods of manipulation, and the ruffians teaching the confidence men methods of violence, a skillset developed allowing for ingratiation into communi-

ties rode upon. With their charms they gained trust. Then, once the people lay maximally vulnerable, the fugitives would turn to beasts to ransack the town. The sackings were known to be murderous to a degree of depravity biblical.

The *modus operandi* of the roughly god knows how many remaining men was thus: a quantity of smaller parties (numbered commensurate to that of cities within a day's ride of the gang's camp) would be dispatched to take up residence. A few of the party moved in at different times so as to appear to the townsfolk as men bearing no special relation to each other. At this, the ingratiation began.

The path of plunder came to be known as 'The West Brandon Trail'. Due the convicts' *modus operandi,* townsfolk south of the migration became fearful of any outsider they didn't recognize. Even women and children no more than a single community over, if not vouched for by a sufficient number of locals, were feared tools of the roving convicts. It was at this point that Marshal Shawk found himself dealing with not just the trickster Vikings, but lynch mobs attacking anyone less than two generations a resident of their municipality. Worse, the fugitives took on new members as they moved: members in the form of townsfolk grown dependent on the ways of the 'invading empire'.

It was at this point that Shawk realized if he was ever going to stop the rovers, he would have to get ahead of them on that trail. Of course, getting ahead of what you're behind, where there's no time or earth to take you around, meant going through.

Shawk, being a man of near as much mystery as Haidt himself, was a recluse when off the hunt. He was only recognizable to his wife when off due the beard he wore when on. This, he intended to use to his advantage. He informed his men of his intentions to head up the trail. He'd go alone and get at least a ten days' ride of distance between himself and the rot of the fugitives and lynch mobs. He'd make for the woods to the east on his way over. He'd shave, hunt, get fattened, then commence heading down the road. He'd pose as a traveling salesman robbed of his goods.

His men were told to carry on with the hunt as usual. Shawk intended to find them when his operation was over.

Taking a page from the runagates, he ingratiated himself into a more peaceful town ahead their trail and he waited.

"TRAVELING SALESMAN?" THE TOWNSFOLK WOULD ask early in Shawk's stay. "What did you sell?"

"Nothing anybody needed. Nothing anybody knew they even wanted until I started with my spiel," he'd answer. "Those bandits that robbed me, really, they saved me. They took my snake oil then you nice people took me in and now I'm looking to start a new ledger on the very first leaf. All I ask is meager accommodations for a hard day's work."

And that's what they gave Shawk and that's what he took. He worked hard. Washed dishes at the town cookhouse. The use of his body caused the body to tear, his muscles a need to eat to rebuild. The striations melted The Marshal's fat to flame. His body got lean like before the hunt.

Yet that beard never grew. Never grew back to hide his face to betray him.

One day, a couple weeks a resident, Marshal asked the

cookhouse boss if he could try a recipe of his, said the boss wouldn't regret it. From that day on Shawk was promoted to cook. The mean chili that got him there, the Thursday night special. It was all in the spices.

Shawk got lean and the people got plump and appreciative. The days passed.

By Shawk's watch it had to be about time for the runagates to have arrived. He had not a clue who they were. All he knew for sure of their scheme was that the convicts would recede like the tide the day before the sack. Recede the day before the night they flooded back in to take it all. He waited for the recession. He didn't know who was going to leave though he knew when they did they'd leave all at once.

The morning the recession came Shawk betrayed himself to the townsfolk. They didn't believe his story at first. However, the Marshal's erudition of the letter of the law and, better, the pragmatics of a certain of his observations got the people going: *if everything were fine why've all the telegraph lines to the north been dead for better a week? Go ahead and try them. You'll get no response.*

They knew the runagates were coming (they'd read the papers). They knew the lines were dead too. That got them going. It was the reveal of Shawk's star that got them movin'. Marshal sent the townsfolk south as he knew the convicts were camped to the north. From the point of their departure he haunted that ghost town. A ghost town of his crafting no more than a few hours prior. In that town he stood, waitin'.

The marauders returned at midnight, though with many more men than had done the ingratiating.

"They're gone," Marshal said. "You all've been making

yourselves real known for real long up that trail. They saw it."

Shawk recognized the ingratiating convicts and they recognized him.

"And you?" one of them asked.

"I couldn't do it. I came looking to do good and yet I knew I'd slip and start conning those good folk if I'd taken up with 'em. I'm restrained in calm, conniving in chaos, see."

Couple 'gratiators drew their pistols, aimed and cocked.

Shawk went down to his knees. "I can't leave and I can't fight you. I'm hopin' you can use a cook. Or at least a better one?"

One of the plumper of the 'gratiators leaned in to whisper something to who must have been the party lead. Seemed real insistent as he spoke to the leader. Was pointing at Shawk.

WITHIN THE CONVICT CAMP, SHAWK counted 85 men coming and going. He counted the men and he counted items they carried one and exactly one of or marked for propriety. Items like canteens and boots. 85 canteens with unique markings. 85 pairs of boots with the same. 85 men.

As near as Shawk could tell, about eight of the men must have come from the last village sacked as they were awkward, clumsy about procedure, and dopely reverent. Strange thing was, they weren't mistreated. They weren't distrusted. Neither their failings nor the odd mild presumption was ever met with violence. In fact, the only time violence ever occurred in any way associated with the neophytes was as punishment to a runagate. For a clumsy latter stumbling and toppling an unsuspecting former onto some rocks.

The new men were even trusted to carry guns which was strange considering they weren't exactly capable. They were too warped by their recent trauma to be cunning and they were kept from any kind of strenuous physical activity ensuring a lack of strength and spirit. Curious indeed.

Shawk was treated much the same though not permitted use of firearms. He thought he'd meet the convicts halfway, only pilfering a single .30-30 repeater from the camp's make-shift armory. Hey, they said 'firearms' plural...

He had stolen the gun mid-afternoon of day one. He had been there a full day since then and was told it would be roughly three and a half more days before the next sack. He'd know it was about to commence, they said, when all parties returned at once. Until then the camp would be sparse of people. Each party only checked in once a day at staggered intervals. He had to make the most of his time.

He got to work picking flowers.

The flowers he was interested in had a large carrot-like root. The root wasn't orange, it was black and oozing. He spent the first morning of his first day in camp picking and pulping a saddlebag's worth of the root. Before picking, he made sure to empty that saddlebag's worth of the camp's rotting vegetables around a creek bank. He also stashed the .30-30 in the hollow of a tree. In the early afternoon, he laid the pulp out to dry by the cook fire. He dried other plants for spice too so as to not draw suspicion.

While the spice was drying he headed back into the woods and toward the river. As he neared the bank, his steps slowed and softened. He retrieved the .30-30 as he passed its stash. Getting to the bank the Marshal came upon three wild pigs. They had just finished gorging on the rotting vegetables and were rooting around for anything they may had missed. The Marshal raised the rifle and shot two of three stone dead.

"Sorry fellas," he said as he approached his quarry. "Got a lot of men to serve."

A couple of the convicts came running to the river bed, guns drawn, looking for those shots. Coming upon Shawk commencing to dressing out the hogs, they calmed a little if not completely.

"Where'd you get that?" asked one of the convicts. He was pointing at the rifle lying next to the half-dressed animal.

Marshal chuckled "You two're worried about a short-shootin' .22 when you're about to eat like kings?" He pointed his knife at the meat in order to reiterate with ostensive gesture, then he continued on dressing out the animals.

"We don't need no—"

WHACK! The other convict stopped the first's talking with a smack to the gut. "Gun's got a lot more caliber than that," he said, incredulous.

The lawman slipped at these words and accidentally punctured the bladder of the pig. Urine spilled out onto the meat as Marshal kept his focus on the convicts.

"Then take it," he offered, pointing his knife at the rifle. "I'm done with it anyway."

The first convict reached for it. As he got just close enough Shawk snatched him up by the wrist, startling him. Instinctively, the convict wrenched back but Shawk had him fast. The other convict moved in to help his partner.

"While you're down here..." Shawk defused, releasing his grasp. "Help me skin it."

Convicts were apprehensive.

"Wanna eat or not?" Shawk reminded. "Just hold it inside the front tendons." He grabbed the convict's wrist again and guided it to the front cloves of the beast. The convict slipped his fingers between the leg bone and heel tendon (where they meet the cloven foot). The convict held the pig up like a wheelbarrow as Shawk grabbed the slit of skin at its collar. He wrenched as the convict pulled back in the opposite direction. The hide peeled off like a sheet of a whorehouse mattress in a town without a laundry.

"One more and you're done," Shawk gibed.

THE SECOND THE CONVICTS RETREATED from the al fresco abattoir (taking Shawk's .30-30 with them) the Marshal got to honing the kitchen knife he'd been working with. He needed it as sharp as he could get it for as long as he could get it and butchering dulls even the best hunting knife faster than sawing at a train track. A dinky kitchen knife didn't stand a chance.

After a good several minutes of grinding he got off the whet-stone and laid into the strop. He slapped the knife's edge against the leather a few times until a sense of closure washed over him, an intuition. He ran his finger perpendicular to the edge and felt the anticipated grit. Any finer an edge and the damn thing might fold over onto itself leaving the knife duller than when he'd started (it's been known to happen).

He got back to the hides not missing a beat. He started slashing them into strips half-inch wide. He went from the first hide, cutting those strips up and down the length of it, working his way to the right all the way across the width of the second hide. The knife's edge got the job done but the last half dozen strips felt like cutting jerky with a trowel. By the time he finished he had filled both his saddlebags with the porky ribbons.

He went down to the water and added about ten pounds of rocks to each pouch apiece. He looked back over the ridge toward the camp. Satisfied that no one was watching, he waded out into the river toward a lone protruding rock. There, he buried the weighted saddlebags to the north side of the rock, the side facing upstream.

HE RETURNED TO THE CAMP, a side of hog across his shoulders like a yoke, his arms resting on either side of it for balance. "Three more at the riverbank!" he shouted at those in camp. They roused at this though lethargically.

THE NEXT MORNING SHAWK MORTARED the dried root pulp and put it into an empty salt pouch. Two and a half cups would do and he figured he had that and a little better. Now he waited.

SURE ENOUGH, ON THE MORNING of Shawk's fourth day in camp each member of each party returned to prepare for the night's plundering. Shawk made them a small breakfast with the provisions they had brought back. Before the men commenced to getting their rest for the long night ahead, they ordered him to prepare a sizable enough lunch that they be well-nourished. They told him to use their salted meat though otherwise cook *ad libitum*. He did just that, making one of his chilis. Only, this time he added about four times the required measure of salt.

THE MEN SLEPT AND LOUNGED until about eleven that morning. They then roused and gorged on the chili. As far as the Marshal could tell, they had no care about the excess salt. The men then commenced to some last-minute strategizing.

It wasn't long before they were filing into the kitchen tent with empty canteens acting as though dying of thirst.

"Fill my canteen again cookie!"

"Sure thing!"

"Where's the coffee?"

"Right here!"

"Anything tea'd?"

"I'll get *t'* brewin'!"

BEET-BOIL OF THOSE FLOWER roots is red as hell but it has no taste. As long as you keep it in the canteen, the coffee, or a black tea, no one will notice the color. Unless…

By suppertime the convicts looked like drunks bleeding from their maws. By nightfall they had lost all possible wits about them. As they stumbled aimlessly around the camp, Shawk headed to the river to retrieve the saddlebags full of pig strip.

Arriving back at the periphery of the camp, he took one last look at the West Brandon Runagates, in all their stumblin' cohesion, then let loose with some howls and hoots that sent them terrified marauding intoxicants running and screaming in all directions and finally off into the woods.

From here, all the Marshal needed to do was stalk and hunt those crazy dazy flesh automata one-by-one. He counted as he went, repeating the number he was on over and over until he caught another.

"Fifteen fifteen fifteen…"

"Twenty-eight twenty-eight twenty-eight..."

"Forty-five forty-five forty-five..."

A hit to the head, choke of the windpipe, letting them succumb to their own paranoid exhaustion. Whatever it took, he kept putting them to sleep. Then he'd drag them to a tree, extend their arms out behind themselves on either side of the trunk, and bind their wrists with that wet hide. By morning the hide would have dried like a cast around those wrists and they wouldn't be going anywhere until someone cut them loose.

"Fifty-six fifty-six fifty-six..."

"Sixty-two sixty-two sixty-two..."

"Seventy seventy seventy..."

THUMP!

Marshal took a hard shot to the back of the head. Everything was spinning and silver-edged. What the hell got the drop on him? Not one of them automaton convicts coulda... Then...

"I knew you were up to something the second I saw you ruining that hog meat, worrying more about them hides." A figure was standing over the woozy Shawk, holding a gun on him. It was the second convict of the two who'd stumbled upon him at the river. "Then I saw you fillin' them bags with pig strips only good for one thing."

"So you decided to let me capture your entire crew and put ya'll out of business?"

"I decided to let you capture these shitheads so I could get out of this toil and make *ours* mine in the process."

Shawk scoffed. "Think you're going to carry a hundred stone of treasure out on your back? Might as well have drank the beet-boil."

"Too bad about that." Convict cocked the revolver.

"Ate the chili though..."

Convict's eyes widened a mite. He tried maintaining his composure. "Feel fine," he assured.

"Don't smell it."

Instinctively, the convict started sniffing.

"Them flowers weren't the only dose," said Shawk.

The convict was still sniffing. He lifted his arm slightly to smell at a sweatier more pungent region. In his haste, he let his gun sights sway just far enough. Second the sights were off him Shawk let out with another howl, only this time it sounded like a wounded animal.

Convict looked confused just an instant before...

Automata emerged out the darkness. The arms of what must have been all of the remaining fourteen burst out from behind him, wrapping around him and dragging him off into the night. Screams were heard. Then silence.

"SEVENTY-FIVE SEVENTY-FIVE SEVENTY-five..."

"Seventy-nine seventy-nine seventy-nine..."

"Eighty-four eighty-four eighty-four..."

It took Marshal a bit more time to find the eighty-fifth man, our 'cunning convict'. Eventually he stumbled upon him curled up in a fetal position, back against the trunk of a fallen tree. The convict was very much alive, his clothes torn, though none more the worse for wear. The substance Shawk put in that chili didn't cause the automata to kill a man. Nah. Strangely, the dose caused a beet-boil automaton to more 'mother' him. It's not painful. It's not harmful. It's just weird. A dozen drugged men all forcibly hugging, holding, caressing, even trying to suckle a chili man. Just weird. Confusing.

Marshal puts this one to sleep too (a sleep the convict was likely welcoming).

BY MORNING IT WAS EIGHTY-five men bound to eighty-five trees.

SHAWK'S MEN HAD CAUGHT UP to the ghost town and were surveying it. Much had been taken. Where were the people? The bodies? That's when Shawk came strolling in from the north, whiskers coming back in.

He informed his men of the townsfolk holed up one municipality to the south. Needing rest, he sent his men back to the camp to apprehend the fugitives.

They came back with exactly 84 men.

IT WAS A YEAR AND three months of peace all along and south of the end of the trail. Shawk had decided to stay on as Marshal of the territory and sent for his family. Everything seemed in equilibrium. Then...

Strange things started to happen in Santa Rosa City. People claimed they saw ghostly apparition-like figures on the edge of town late at night. They had red dripping from their eyes like blood, and leather straps hanging from their wrists as though—

THUMP!

Metro looks up from the article with that same anticipation his wife reproached him for earlier. It's not anticipation for any dog knocking over any planter though. He's exercised different. As if by some unearthly intuition. He turns the lantern light down to near darkness.

COUPLE'A' DRUNK MINERS CLAMOR ABOUT the outside of The Mayor's office trying to find a way in. One carries a bucket of something and the other a puffed-out pillowcase along with some paint brushes.

"Find a rock," whispers *Drunk One*.

"Think of tryin' the doorknob dumbass?" says *Drunk Two*.

"I'm the dumbass? Think the highest authority in town's just gonna leave the door unlocked?"

"Highest authority in *Shale*..."

"Be that as it may—"

CREEEEEEK.

The office door swings open seemingly of its own accord. Drunks just stare at it quizzically. Being drunk they don't question the convenience in all this. They just continue on with whatever stuporous task they've laid out for themselves.

They enter The Mayor's office.

"Find something to set the tar onta."

"You!"

"I'm holding it ya cur! If I could set it down to find something to set it onta I'd have something to set it onta and wouldn't... need ta find..." Drunk Two's reasoning peters to a stop.

"What?" asks Drunk One.

"What the fuck was I arguing about?"

"Just throw it on the wall!"

"Which?"

Drunk One looks around trying to catch sight of anything worth the tar. He can't see much in the moonlight when...

"There! That picture. One of that fillybuster's paintins!" He points to Hannah's sketch of the office.

"I think it's charcoal."

"It's tar!"

"No the paintin'."

"Just throw the goddamn tar!"

Then another voice.

"Time to sleep *eh-tuff* boys."

The two drunks spin to the front of the office. Nothing at the front door. There ain't no backdoor. Then...

The lantern sitting on the back desk ratchets up to full illumination. The Sheriff walks out from behind it, dropping the clipping he was reading onto a pile of papers and envelopes. He picks up the lantern. The drunks recognize the law immediately.

"Shit! It's the flyin' coss—"

WHOMP!

"Shut!" says Drunk One to Drunk Two whipping a tar brush into his gut.

Sheriff moves toward the men. He lifts the lantern up to their faces. The men are frozen.

"Jimmy Lynch and Bill Phipps. Both miners. Both married. Both fathers. I'm here to offer you the jail. Sleep *eh-tuff*. Stumble home tomorrow at first light." Drunk Two looks to Drunk One using his tilting face to gesture at the bucket he's still holding. Drunk One looks to be mulling something. Sheriff notices. "Nobody need know what you did here. You do anything else you do what is stupid. You have tar all over your hands. You will also when they start searching for whoever emptied that bucket. You empty it your name is *Dr. Mudd* in this town. It will be worse across The Belt. You'll never work a mine again. Your wives will despise you. Your children will never know you because your wives who despise you will leave you and the children will go too. Children need fathers. Fathers show sons how to be good men. Fathers show daughters what a good man is.

You both have sons and daughters correct? You throw that tar you are finished."

The drunks' postures falter.

"Or!" Metro shouts startling the men back to attention. "You go down to the jail and sleep *eh-tuff*. You let your sons and daughters know you. The drink has made you sentimental and that has made you teary-eyed. I can see you cry for your children already. No need. You're good men and better fathers. You want to do what is right for them?" The men lower their heads. "We go. Comfy beds await you."

The pair set their belongings onto the floor and stretch out their wrists for the shackles. Sheriff drops the office keys into Drunk One's hands and puts his lantern into the hands of Drunk Two.

"You lock up," he says to One. "You carry my things," he says to Two. "The least you can do." Sheriff grabs his papers off the desk and moves for the door. "Don't forget your supplies."

Sheriff moves toward the cop shop as lantern-drunk follows with the sack of feathers and brushes in-hand. Key-drunk fumbles to lock the door trying to not fall behind.

HE FLIES INTO THE JAIL startling his deputy.

"You not hear any commotion?" Sheriff unlocks the key box.

"Whah?" grumbles Dep.

The two miners amble in and head toward the cages in back. Key-drunk drops the office key into The Sheriff's outstretched hand as he goes. Sheriff hangs the key back up on a hook under the label *Mayor's Office*.

"What's the frequency of your rounds?" he asks Dep. "Be honest."

"U—usually—"

"Tonight. Bearing in mind I've been in The Mayor's office for the last three hours. I see everything across the street."

"Fell asleep!" Deputy says in a punctuated manner. Not angrily or in any way emotionally. More like he knows The Sheriff will appreciate the directness.

Sheriff does. Goes easy. "Then you'll be alert and rested until well after I return from church tomorrow. You will work overtime and I will take those hours to spend with my wife and children."

"L—least I can do."

"I know."

The two drunks can be heard slamming themselves into their cells in back the jail.

6

SOIREE

I t requires no great skill or sweat of deliberation to understand why the quarterly meetings of the Mining Council and Mayors take place in Carson. Hangin' hub of The Belt is such because it's the hub of the law too, naturally, and there's never been any better bedfellows than the law and the leisurely. Marshal's office was here. A ranger station in the RM. Fifty jailers taking up residence. A sheriff's office with one deputy for every 30 residents—unlike Shale's ratio of one to all in perpetuity.

Considering the decisions of the aforementioned leisurely of late, cozying up to the law has never been more of a necessity. At least according to traditional political wisdom—or something less oxymoronic? Traditional wisdom suggests if you're gonna be pushing people around you best protect yourself from those don't wanna be pushed. And if you're gonna be drastically scaling up your pushing, you better be drastically scaling up your protection.

Aw, but traditional wisdom never really applied much around here.

See, Belt folk ain't exactly the kind for defiance in the

face of that special brand of you-asked-for-it persecution that comes with believing a tiny body of know-nothing laypeople ought be making the most important decisions of your life for you for no other reason than the tiniest subset of the tiniest subset of the population said *Aw hell, why not! Go ahead Dale. Go ahead and write all them laws for us! You got a lot of time on your hands what with you not being able to do anything anyone would ever pay ya money for. Go ahead on!*

Naw. As you've seen, Belt folk are more the kind to just fumfer and jeer and blow hot air in the face of such insidiousness. Politicians around here ain't got much to worry about by way of personal attack therefore. Course, politicians ain't much for understanding the character of the people nearest them... or their will... concerns... sentiments... ideals... hopes... dreams... Which explains an awful lot about their reacting to these docile folk as though militants.

It requires no great skill or sweat to figure out the *why* of the meeting location. It does require such to address the *why* of the why. That lifelong mystery of the powerful. Eye Eee:

If you, the person who trades exclusively in coercing the starting and stopping of those of ingenuity and skill (seemingly of your whims and little else), feel you can't walk safely among those of ingenuity and skill (and kin) to the point that you need a town's worth of lawmen beside you to make you feel secure, why persist?

Wanna know why they persist? Here's a clue,

"I must commend you Madam Mayor on your defusing any civil unfortunateness that spill-over may have caused. Simply Platonic the nobility in your amelioration of the more sentimentalist of your lot. It takes a firm hand with them."

POP!

"Pardon?" Hannah says to the Carson Mayor.

The Mayor, *Mayor Dalton Pettimore* to be precise, smirks. He angles that smirk at the other men of the circle in which he and Hannah converse. "Oh yes, I forgot. You and Tom were Shale born-and-raised..." He puts his right hand in his right coat pocket and extends his left in some sort of faux-offering. Handing out the condescension I guess? "You see, Plato—"

"No, I meant there was nothing noble in my lie nor were the citizens of Shale ameliorated by it."

"Ha! Yes! I was told you were quite the firecracker as well! Simply stated madam, the people are calm now, you attempted amelioration shortly before they calmed—"

"Over a week before..."

"*Hmmmph*, allow me to finish my dear lady. You attempted amelioration shortly before and now they're ameliorated. I'd say we have our efficient cause. Wouldn't you agree gentlemen?"

POP!

The soiree circle nod. All except Hannah.

Why Dalton Pettimore ya scoundrel! You're the kind who'd shout 'rise' at the dawn horizon and take credit for the sun coming up. And these toads would applaud ya for it all along!

"I'd say we have our *post hoc ergo propter hoc*," Hannah says, deadpan.

"Pardon?"

"If you'll excuse me gentlemen." She bows slightly as the men raise their snifters her way. All except the confused Mayor Pettimore.

POP!

Let it Breathe! The oxygen brings out the bouquet!
Pour it quick! The oxygen will ruin the bouquet!
Does French Champagne have a bouquet?

A white-gloved server gestures his silver salver at Hannah as she approaches. She waves off the bubbly and twists into another circle of soiree guests, gives the fella adequate clearance to pass. Currently she has no taste for any delicacy on any serving tray. Though she has been scanning the crowd no higher than those trays. The servant she's attempting to eyeball is only of the *civil* variety, a little intermediary of a man. Through the attendees she sees the little man's head among the salvers. And it is kinda flat. However, a comb-over of Bear Grease ain't exactly a delicacy.

"Ah! Hannah!" Burke booms as he catches her approaching, raw oyster queued up to his gums. *SLURP!* "Have you had a chance to talk to Mayor Dalton?"

"Yes and now I know how you feel dealing with the Mining Council." Hannah says this as she non-consciously lifts herself on her tippy-toes. She stares down at Burke's head from greater altitude.

"Ahem! What was that?"

She realizes what she's doing and catches herself. *Damnit woman stop the mockin'! He's your only real ally here! Not much of an ally and a pale of the politician his father is... so not a complete scoundrel either... yet go easy on the shrub!*

"Oh just commenting on the regard Carson folk have for Shale."

"*Hmmm*, yes. Well, the Burkes are from Washington originally, so..."

"Yes I know Burke. Further down the road from Carson even."

He looks like he wants a pat on the head for the origins

of the dirt between his toes. He and everyone else in this room.

"Mayor Pettimore was very pleased with how you handled the mine issue," Burke parrots.

"Right. Everyone's acting like it's been handled."

"Well the townsfolk *are* happy."

"And two-thirds jobless..."

"*And* they have every faith in the world you'll fix that. But the important thing is, at present they're happy."

Happiness: Never forget Hannah, that ace in the hole of every leader of men. Never forget: a single ant can live a lifetime off the last nectar of the last raisin of the last grape of a once great vineyard. He need only stand on the backs of his brethren to suckle it. You'll know you've crossed the threshold of Shale's irredeemability when all the politicians care about is keeping the people docile as those people fade away. They'll call this docility 'happiness' as they bleed them dry.

"Will your father be in attendance tonight?" Hannah asks.

"Speaking of Washington Madam..."

"Lie?"

"Precisely."

"I want those armed men out of the mine."

"Why Hannah that's not up to me."

"I know. It's up to the Reeve and myself. But since your father put them there I thought I'd extend the courtesy. Make no mistake, if they're still there in a week I will remove them. You can tell your father that."

"*With the cooperation of the Reeve.* As you know, we don't invite members of rural municipality councils to these get-togethers. And yet if the Reeve were here I think you'd find he was very much in favor of the extra security. As should you be..." Burke pauses and smirks. It's a real Burke Brand Smirk. "...What with the recent break-in to your office."

Why you king toad! I gave you the benefit of the doubt treatin' you like you weren't your father ya toad! And what do ya do? You go ahead and croak!

"Well then, I'll have to talk to the Ree—"

"My god! He showed!" Burke says this turning away from Hannah. He says this in fake-hush too. *Like Burke'd know anything about discretion.* He's not the only one surprised.

There's a general gaspiness to the parlor room as The Mayor of Santa Rosa enters. He's unsteady. Furtive. As most people would be surviving the kind of warfare Rosa did. A warfare no one, especially Rosans, knows much about to this day. You can see the remains of the beet-boil around his chin. He had obviously attempted several good scrubs and yet the boil was still remindin'. Like a chafing.

"Morgan!" Mayor Pettimore moves in haste toward *Mayor Morgan 'Morg' Munsen.* It's all smiles on Pettimore but they're smiles of blue mud. He wraps an arm around Morg and leads him back out of the parlor. He's whispering something in Morg's ear as he goes.

"Morg's just not ready for his debut. That could have been quite the scene had Dalt not handled things." Burke says this in proxy relief.

"Oh that was a scene," Hannah says.

"Poor Dalt." Burke shakes his head in the least genuine lament anyone's ever seen.

"*Dalt*? Dalton Pettimore strikes you as the person to sympathize with?" Burke stares at Hannah in genuine puzzlement. Hannah frowns. "I'm getting some air."

. . .

SHE LEANS ON THE VERANDA rail of the Pettimore mansion. Only part of the complex she feels at home. It's just a much bigger Queen Anne facing a much bigger Shale. She can hear faint Byzantine chanting coming from a church somewhere near the end of Main Street. *I bet Pettimore's been trying his damnedest to—*

"Pettimore's been trying his damnedest to shut that church down."

Hannah turns to see Morg Munsen approach. He has his tobacco pouch and a rolling paper in hand.

"Can barely hear it," she says.

"Don't matter to ol' Dalt when conformity's on the line. You remember his *molded-out-of-clay* speech last year?" Hannah grins at what's to come. Morg affects a mocking tone. "*Every new leader must get his hands dirty! You only get one go at the kiln. You better be darn sure the community you've set your hands upon, that you've kneaded and shaped with those hands, meets your mold. Because when your term's up, your work's gone to kiln.*"

He starts pulling the drawstring on the tobacco pouch. There's a noticeable tremor in his hands that only gets worse the more he tries to concentrate on the rolling. He manages to get a pinch between fingers but it's in the wind before them digits reach the paper.

"Damn it!" he says louder than he'd wished. He smashes his fist onto the veranda rail like that'll work the shakes out. Hannah takes the smoke fixins away delicately. Morg hands them over. She starts the rolling process anew.

"Thanks," he relents. Looks back down the road. "That church's a gem of a different Mohs. Something Dalt can't shape."

"Kinda like *you* in that parlor room?" She strikes a match and lights up the tobacco with a quick puff. She takes a second draw on the cigarette, a deep one, then hands it over to Morg as the stimulant starts nipping at her lungs. "These soirees are just another little lump for him to fire for the mantle."

"Couldn't give him the satisfaction. No mantelpiece this year." Morg flicks at the cigarette despite his tremor already doing the job. His hint of contentment provoked at the thought of not giving ol' Dalt the satisfaction fades. "He's coming for the whole Belt you know. He and Waylan Burke Sr in cahoots so obvious you can smell it. Once the iron's dwindled that's when you'll see their diverging interests come to the fore. It'll be blood between 'em before The Belt's taken. Mark my words Hannah."

"I know it," she says. "Tom had the same suspicions." Morg nods. He starts rubbing at his rosy chin with that trembling hand. Hannah notices. "What happened in that town of yours Morg?"

He looks her in the eye like she need know right here and now he ain't for allegory. Like she need know what he's about to say ain't anything close. "Baptism Hannah." His hand goes perfectly still. "One that took us to hell. One that delivered us."

He turns back to the rail and leans. The cigarette smolders while the hand holding it remains steady. He's as contemplative as Hannah is. Church chanting's ended so the two Mayors just enjoy the silence and the mid-afternoon sun a minute, then...

"Speaking of deliverance..." Something's caught Hannah's attention. Morg attends to her, curious. "I ain't Irish Morg but this is an Irish goodbye." She bolts off the veranda and toward the church.

"Not to me it ain't," Morg shouts after her. "Yer biddin' *adieu* as ya fly!" He laughs.

"Tell them snobs I got caught up in the wind!" she calls back as she goes. "And best of luck with Rosa!"

He waves goodbye.

HANNAH APPROACHES FAMILIAR FACES DOWN to the church.

"Fancy meeting you here!" she says in platitude but all due warmth. The implicature of *welcome* is as heartfelt as it gets. She gazes past the current object of her interest to a Hungarian Orthodox Church. It was the source of the chanting. It's situated in a defunct post office. She puzzles a bit.

Metro's finishing lifting Kate up into the buggy. He turns toward Hannah scooping Vikki into his arms in the process. He greets his mayor. "*Fancy* isn't enough a word ma'am." He gestures across the sodded expanse toward Pettimore mansion.

"Every goddamn three months," Hannah laments. "Superciliousness is a language I hope to never speak!"

Kate finishes fastening Anya in and leans into the conversation. "And we don't speak Hungarian ma'am," she smiles pointing at the church.

"We don't speak Slavonic either," Metro reminds. "And yet we've always indulged our priests their use of that. The powers that be love such adornments."

"Ever notice," Hannah says, "the powers that be are the first to call themselves *servants*?"

"How's that ma'am?"

"The servants of *god*. The servants of *the civil*. Any of 'em do any serving of either?"

"The priest here seems sufficiently humble."

"He's a cloistered-up Jesuit delivering sermons from an old post office. He ain't the powerful." She glances over to

The Father coming out of the post-office-cum-church. He waves goodbye to the Molybohas as the local congregants swarm him for last-minute blessings. "He's been railroaded like ol' Morg Munson."

"I see," says Metro. "And where do *we* fall in this game of power ma'am?"

"Ha! Let our adornments be our first clue. Hard to see them under all this red mud!" She chuckles. The Molybohas laugh a Sunday laugh. "Spare a ride back to Shale?"

HANNAH HOLDS ONTO VIKKI AND **Anya** in the backseat of the carriage. She sways them back and forth as she sings:

> *There's a hole in the bucket dear Henry dear Henry.*
> *There's a hole in the bucket dear Henry a hole.*

> *Then mend it dear Liza dear Liza dear Liza.*
> *Then mend it dear Liza dear Liza mend it.*

Kate looks over to Metro as he drives. She nudges him. He shrugs. Kate shrugs back. Then... She joins in the singing much to Anya's joy and surprise.

> *With what shall I mend it dear Henry dear Henry?*
> *With what shall I mend it dear Henry with what?*

> *With straw dear Liza dear Liza dear Liza.*
> *With straw dear Liza dear Liza with straw.*

To the backs of the riders the setting Carson sun barely clings to the horizon.

· · ·

IT'S A MASS OF WAVERING orange emerging to the east. It's been an hour and a half the carriage's been heading that direction and the sun don't rise so quick in The Belt. Metro whips the reins and *yips!* the horses into a canter toward the glow. He'd get them to a gallop but not with his babies in the cart. Kate, the kids, and Hannah startle back awake.

"What is it?" Hannah demands as she soothes Vikki.

"Church. Must be."

IT IS THE CHURCH. BY the time the carriage pulls up, the roar of the flames has died though the tower's been burned unsalvageable. The bucket brigade's in full effect stretching arm-in-arm to the well out back.

Metro halts the carriage and Hannah hoists Vikki to her mom. She runs down to the crowd gathered out front.

Metro strokes Kate's cheek. "You stay with the girls," he says then bursts away.

He gets to the well and offers to relieve the bucket filler. Filler's obliged and leaves to squeeze into the line of passers.

Hannah scans through the crowd of observers. She homes in on *The Pastor*. "What's happened?" she asks.

"Hell's come to Shale Madam Mayor!" Pastor responds as though there's always time for melodrama. "Hell is here!" He stomps off toward the well.

Metro's pumping that pump and filling them buckets as fast as they return. You don't work the handle quick you work it in rhythm otherwise you lose the prime and then the flow. He's got the rhythm but something about the performance has irked The Pastor. Metro feels a tension on the bucket handle as he tries handing it off to the lead passer. Pastor's tugging back on it.

"Give me that you heathen!" The Pastor yanks. Metro

pulls back and the well water sloshes all over his Sunday finest. He has a look of some surprise.

Lead passer's confused himself. "Let it go Rev!"

"Unholy pagans!" yells The Pastor not relenting.

Hannah and the crowd hear the confrontation. She starts to move toward the well as certain of The Pastor's congregants break away from the crowd too and move in the opposite direction. *Lumbering* would be the better way to describe the congregation's movement. They're heading toward Kate and the girls watching the fire from the carriage. Hannah catches this in her periphery and changes course.

Sheriff!

Metro looks in the direction of Hannah's shout to see the clumsy mob bearing down on his family. He lets go of the bucket, toppling The Pastor and dowsing his cassock in the well water. Sheriff runs to his wife and kids.

Hannah's gotten between the carriage and the congregants still shuffling. They aren't saying anything just fixating on the carriage. By now Kate has noticed what's happening and is sheltering her girls. Hannah extends her arms though it ain't gonna do much good. The automata keep on lumbering as Metro jumps in front of them to join her. He's got a flaming one-by-four and is waving it at the deranged church-goers. He's stifled them more though they ain't stopped. He's backing up to Hannah and taking her with him toward the cart. Space between cart and mob is less and less, when...

CRANCH!

S'it's goin'!

Church bell breaks free and hammers down through the tower to the antechamber. *GONG! GONG! GONG!* it goes as it catches material all the way down. Firefighters have jumped off their ladders and are scattering as the bell starts rolling down the porch and out the churchyard. The remains of the tower topple after the bell. The front third of the church falls outward and crumbles downward with a rumbling thumping series of crashes.

The commotion appears to have shaken the automaton congregants out of their daze. They glance around a second, find their bearings, then disperse—all to Metro Kate and Hannah's confusion.

Besides snapping the mob out of their stupor, the sliveriest of silver linings to that bell leaving is this: the porch collapsing took the bulk of the flames along with it saving the church proper.

ANOTHER DAY ANOTHER EMERGENCY TOWN hall meeting. The Pastor's been monopolizing the bulk of the minutes which ain't so difficult considering he's on town council besides. He's whooped his more zealotous congregants back into the same frenzy he had them in yesterday night. The difference is they aren't acting the same stumblin' fools just a mob searching for a scapegoat.

"Every single one of us depends on that church 'cept them!" a congregant raves.

"Justice must be done!" shouts another.

Kate's in attendance. First time ever, though she had an inkling she should accompany her husband today. She was right. "They not know we were two towns over?" she whispers to her Metro.

"Why would they? All they know about Catholics is where we're *not* on Sundays."

"They sound like they want us interned."

A blasphemy!

"This isn't Ottawa my love. We were two towns over and on our church's registry. Plus, The Mayor. They'll only embarrass themselves."

"Well I won't put up with it! You put out more fire than that priest!"

"Pastor."

"Even better!" She nudges her husband. "They scare the children. That's sufficient for putting an end to this!"

Justice be done!

"Well speak up then woman!"

And with that, Kate does.

"We've no reason to harm your church," she says rising. She talks to the sitting Pastor not his sycophants. She talks to the ringleader.

A congregant jumps in front of the rhetorical bullet, so to speak. Tries speaking for The Pastor one last time. "It ain't that you have no reason—"

"Bless you brother Clemmens," says The Pastor now rising. "But a man of god is *still* a man and a man must fight his own battles—"

"When the battle's 'gainst a housewife!" heckles an attendee from the back.

Many laugh. The congregants hiss. Pastor flushes.

He tries getting back some composure. "Mrs. Met—Kate. It ain't that you have no reason to burn down the church. It's that you have no reason *not to*. You and your husband are the only Shale folk for whom the church ain't a necessity."

Kate ain't having it. "You think people destroy what to them isn't needed?" she speaks to the crowd in general now. "How hard did you look before you and your congregants assured yourselves we were the only people unburdened by all this? Because we are certainly burdened now."

"Now ma'am—" Pastor says as though he's a calming presence all of a sudden.

Mayor intercepts. "I remind you Reverend, I was with the Molybohas over the time the fire started. Two towns away."

"Justice must be done mayor!" Pastor affects a hush. "Even if you were in on it…"

Gasps emit from the town hall crowd at this presumption.

Hannah quiets everyone. She sets her focus back on The Pastor. "You know the law, being on council yourself."

"The two a' you *are* the law!" The Pastor protests, pointing to The Sheriff then Mayor then back to The Sheriff.

"Not above it." Hannah turns her attention to the crowd for what follows. "If you want to press this then you ride out to Carson and make your case at the Marshal's office. Against the Molybohas, myself while you're at it." She pauses a second. Resolve. She turns back to The Pastor. "Though before you do that Reverend, I would take stock of how much communion wine you have in reserve now and consider where it was prior to the evening's fire. Don't forget, in all your accounting, to consider your penchant for leaving the prayer candles burning on the occasion too much of that wine turns to water and not the blood of the Messiah."

There's some snickering and chuckling among the attendees. The Pastor gets a look of embarrassment. He sits, waving away any further attention.

Then…

Another tremor.

Another freezing wind.

The dam has burst.

7

———

THE SHIFT

They didn't lose the use of the mine when the dam burst—*collapsed* being the more precise term.

As Hannah had predicted, that trickle from the first plate filled the pit up to the sleeper level in a day. Complex had been good for nothing other than a buried earthen flophouse for the last month-and-a-half before the collapse. First five floors consisting of iron soup, penthouse consisting of utility rooms and sleepers of rotted-out bunk beds of moldy straw mattresses. All a half-mile outta town for no one's added convenience.

If you were unlucky enough to have a need to sleep there when the mine was operating then if you were unluckier enough to find a miner's mint on the pillah, I sincerely hope it was your touch not your taste letting you know ya found nothing more than a gummed up and processed gob of chewing tobacco of a forgetful sleeper the night before.

Nah, it wasn't the dam giving out that rendered the mine useless. It wasn't even the dam giving out that rendered the uselessness permanent—if we're to be honest with ourselves. The dam giving out just made that irreversible obsolescence *knowledge.* A proposition every Shale resident now believed. Something they couldn't not believe. A proposition as true as any proposition needing proof by appeal to fact could be. A truth as justified as *I think therefore I am.* The city logicians call a claim a *tautology* if it's so true it can never be false, or something like that. Well, *that mine ain't ever coming back* is the next closest thing to a tautology after *whatever will be will be.*

Mine's been gone since end of summer. Shale's hope's been gone with the dam.

Now the good of the bad...

With all hope lost, Shale citizens had nothing left to keep them from getting back to work. Seems people holding on for dear life to the conviction that *things will change for the better* tend to add the amendment *all on their own—* whether they realize they're operating under this assumption or not. Hope's stifling that way.

Of course, the last thing you're ever going to do when you know for a fact things won't get better without your doing is sit around waiting for things to get better without your doing. Sure, Shale saw a week or so of moping, then an exodus of half its miners to Santa Rosa—welcomed miners too as Santa Rosa lost miners in Haidt's attack but not the mine, and Shale lost the mine in the collapse but not the miners—but after all that there was a reckoning, a taking-stock of bankable talents the citizens of Shale'd been neglecting due the lull of the iron.

Citizens had a variety of talents and many of them talents bore fruit boy! Fruit's a bit ironical a metaphor considering the lack of arable land in southern iron country. Angering metaphor too as it became readily apparent to Shale folk, short of any infrastructure for growing and raising, out-of-county bartering would be essential just for Shalers to trade with each other *letalone* all the people across The Belt they'd have to to make ends meet. And, how exactly were they going to barter at a distance? Money, goods, and terms would have to travel. They'd have to travel in a town where importing and exporting had only ever been left to trains haulin' iron *out* and general goods *in*!

Shale may be able to survive without the iron but it certainly won't survive as a closed system. A world-class baker could intend to trade ten loaves of bread for a pair of shoes from a world-class shoemaker just next door but without the leathers and the grains to produce the subjects of the terms of the barter, they'd only be trading IOUs. And we all know what happens when you print IOUs in an economy with no resources to cash 'em in for.

We know what happens because The Federals do it all the time. They just write them IOUs with more generality. Slips of paper that say tacit-like:

> I, *any producer*, for any of my products and for some number x, owe you $1/x$th of that product to be purchased per unit in return for this slip.

Federals print these 'universal IOUs' and call any one a *dollar*. They print as many as they please telling folk anyone but them owes some fraction of any good or service available for sale. They don't consult the people providing these items about the deal of course. Doesn't matter. As soon as that Monopoly money comes flooding into town them producers know of the contract they're bound to yet didn't sign.

Producers also know roughly what they owe, and are owed, so they raise their prices to not give away goods and services ain't owed. Say a baker owes me a single loaf of bread so he writes me an IOU then a Federal writes me another—where as we all know it ain't that Federal gonna be doing any baking—guess what? That baker's loaf now costs me two Federal IOUs! Of course it does. All I was ever entitled to was that one loaf and that's all my IOUs are gonna get me! Federals could write me a million *IOUs* and I'll still get the one loaf for 'em should everything be kept fair.

Costs all start going up—and balances coming out in the wash—the second that funny money hits the market. Just remember, the price of the labor you sell if you a working guy or gal has got to go up too. Otherwise that loaf of bread you laboring an hour for gets cut in two. Literally.

Can't eat an IOU. Can't shelter under it. Can't clothe yourself in it. At least not without danglin' yer shames... Town needs resources from without plain and simple and they can't afford any fancy parcel service to bring them.

There wasn't any parcel services available to patronize to begin with, fancy or otherwise! Now, it ought be noted, any parcel service in The Belt would be a fancy parcel service if it were, as it'd be the *only* parcel service. Anything everybody wants that is the only one of its kind is more elaborate and novel than any other of its kind, hence fancy I reckon. What I'm saying is, it's redundant to say *The Belt didn't have any non-fancy parcel services* since we only need one and its uniqueness of function would make it fancy by default.

Naw. All The Belt had was the bi-weekly pick-ups and drop-offs of the Mail Express Service by way of the iron trains. Mail drops were unreliable as hell too. The train would just toss the bag of letters at the station hook in Clunch—the first Belt town the train passed in the morning —then if the bag were lucky enough to have hit the hook, the post office would filter out all the Clunch letters and leave the rest for pickup from the next town over. A postal worker would come from the next town, collect the bag, then repeat the same sorting procedure as Clunch. Apply this recursion for all fifteen Belt towns and I bet you wouldn't be surprised to learn Shale was lucky to get its mail by end of day-two of the sorting. That ain't so bad considering Rosa—being the furthest from Clunch—was lucky to get its mail by end of first week. And that's if the bag were lucky enough to have hit the station hook in Clunch in the first place.

Dealing with the problem of importing and exporting was where Hannah came in. By her schoolmarming she calculated that Shale, being smack in the middle of the fifteen mining towns, could get to the greatest number of towns faster than any other in The Belt. Being smack in the middle, with just two teams of horses, one moving east and one moving west, Shale could touch all towns in The Belt in a day and have both teams home before dinner.

Town had the horses and the wagons for a teamster operation and now that it had near half the mining men out of work, the teamsters too. They just had to learn to drive a team. Some of the men took to it more quickly than others. The more competent drivers drove and the less competent drivers became shotgun riders. Through the bottom-up, drivers came to manage their own teamster operation entrepreneurial-like. They hauled whatever it was they had the best ability to haul. They'd collect an agreed-upon fee for the importing or exporting, then they'd pay an agreed-upon portion to a rider competent with a coach gun. Now, you might be asking *what would a driver need with a shotgun rider in a crimeless society like The Belt?* Well, the birdshot would often provide a nice partridge lunch and the rider was great help with carriage repairs and heavy lifting.

With the teamster operation in full swing, new businesses could form and established businesses could expand. Will and Rosey saw an opportunity to sell boutique furniture to the snobs of Carson as well as simpler furniture to the people of Rosa rebuilding. Will and Rosey paid a good price to a Shale driver bringing timber from one county over and a good price to another to move the furniture to Carson and Rosa. They were paid an even better price for their furniture.

Kate pointed out to Metro that if that strange alien sod could take root in the red mud, so too could the fruit of the chornyy. Just because the soil didn't have an arable component that didn't mean it couldn't. Kate ordered a few wagon's worth of earth from the grasslands of Karn County—the only county within driving distance with arable soils. She started a little horticulture operation in her backyard. She sold the produce from the backyard out a stand set up in the front yard.

Hannah'd also arranged to run mail all across The Belt. Mail Express could do their standard bi-weekly drop in Shale instead of Clunch and Shale'd sort those letters for delivery in two team-driven wagons. Using Hannah's east-*n*-west formula the mail would get to every belt town on the same day Mail Express got it to Shale. She brokered the bidding between the Shale teamsters and Mail Express and after Express representatives realized they couldn't take the lowest offer when it meant hiring a bidder incapable of doing the job, the right combination of merit and price won out. Bottom-up.

Another short-lived though happy accident was Shale's economy benefiting as much from the mining men's exodus as Rosa's did. The families of the emigrated mining men remained in Shale receiving two-thirds of the men's earnings to spend *in* Shale.

As alluded, this accident wouldn't stay a happy one. Affairs were all well and good but only while Shale men's incomes remained commensurate the Rosa men's. See, the Rosa mine could accommodate exactly half the miners of Shale and that's what they got. That meant all of the Shale miners vying for positions that only half could fill. Ol' Morg Munson, to his credit, refused to nickel and dime the Shale immigrants he knew desperate for work—men he also knew were well aware their perishable supply of labor out-met Rosa's demand by exactly one hundred percent. Ol' Morg paid them men equal wages at first and Ol' Morg even protested when Waylan Burke Sr vetoed Morg's decision to not commence with any nickel and dimin'.

Burke Sr refused to pay a Rosa man's wage to a Shale man so desperate for work he'd take anything that wernt nothing. It was a race to the bottom among the men of Shale bidding for Rosa jobs. One Shale man'd offer to do it for a half of what a Rosa man'd take and another Shale man'd offer to do it for a half of that. Then another man'd take the bid to an eighth of what a Rosa man-made. Then yet another'd take it to a sixteenth. Then rock bottom.

When every man'll take what's next-to-nothing for his labor, knowing there's a man for every one of him willing to take half that, what leverage does he have? There certainly wasn't any leverage in his skill. Iron mining's so rote—and The Belt's been filtering in the iron-blooded for so long—a toddler could do the job in his sleep. Nah. Burke Sr knew they had no leverage so Burke Sr bilked the hell outta those Shale men. Then when he realized any Shale man who didn't get the job would happily replace any Rosa man for a sixteenth the pay, he leveraged that against the Rosa men and bilked them too.

An enmity formed between Rosa and Shale the day Burke Sr started messing with the mens' wages. Rosa miners saw the Shale miners as opportunists and scabs. Shale miners held firm suggesting the Rosa miners were no different in disposition, that they'll be the same scabs the second the Rosa mine goes dry. Back and forth the two factions went getting to all manner of quarreling once out the bag for the day.

Yet, in all their accusations and blame, neither party ever thought to question their bipartisan facilitating of Burke Sr's confiscation and redistribution of the spoils. After all, Burke Sr was no businessman. He didn't own the land on which those mines sat nor did he work for anyone who did. He didn't purchase or tend to the materials necessary of any infrastructure. He had no greater stake or claim to The Belt than any miner. He certainly had less skill of maintenance than any mining man. Of any mining procedure from pick to pack from raw to refined. He was neither necessary nor sufficient for any outcome anyone of that belt had ever admitted to desiring. Yet everyone acted like by some divine right he and his stooges ought be making every decision.

The best you'd ever get outta the folk under his thumb was *get rid of Burke Sr and someone else will just take his place.* Of course, no one ever asked why the hell they even needed a Council. People of The Belt seemed to treat bureaucracy as a fundamental element of the universe. Something that could neither be created nor destroyed. An eighth-day substance ready to possess any man where there dwelled more than one. Possess him and drive him to take control of everything while assuming accountability for nothing.

Enmity or not, the men still mined shoulder to shoulder

as cooperative as could be, thankful for an iron only slightly less indifferent to their plight than the men of the Council. They were thankful for the habit really. A habit that didn't pay the bills.

Maybe The Council does what it does out of habit too? Maybe the whole world? Just serving some assumed master, that master itself doing the same? Is there a top to all this or only a circle? A world of people serving cuz their story mistakes the latter for the former? Just blind function and feedback? Either way, mining was all anybody around here knew and at least they were doing what they knew, they reckoned. And not quite for nothing.

ALL *THEY THOUGHT* THEY KNEW more like it! Goddamnit! The unemployed miners that stayed in Shale learned quick enough that picking and packing wasn't their only skill! They learned their other skills were in far greater demand. They also got to plying them skills.

Why is it that any seller of anything knows you never sell what you can hold in one hand what everybody else is holding in two unless that seller's a working man? If labor were wind, the workin' man'd demand a living whistling in a hurricane acting like all he had in the world was a pair a' lips! You don't sell sand in the desert and you don't sell labor a million other men are selling for less. In fact, you don't sell labor at all until you've proven beyond a shadow you don't have something:

1. the whole world wants,
2. is willing to pay for in perpetuity, and
3. only you can provide.

If you meet these three conditions in conjunction then what the hell are ya doing diluting the labor pool denying any leverage to the people who do that labor and only that labor best? Go into business for crying out loud and make more jobs for the type of laborer you never shoulda been! Just remember to keep bureaucrats like The Federals and the men of the Mining Council from stifling you, because they'll try.

I rant. I rant. However, the lesson stands and the mining men of Shale gone to Rosa will learn it soon enough.

WITH ALL THE CHANGES, SHALE wasn't exactly thriving. In truth, the people were barely subsistin' though they were subsistin'. For every *Kate's Farmer's Market* or *Rosey and Will's Furniture* there were a half-dozen teamsters who couldn't drive for shit. Some literally.

One teamster took a shortcut and rattled two-thirds a load of manure off his wagon not even noticing. By the time he got to Karn County he couldn't even sell enough shit to feed his horses letalone pay his rider. Rider quit and driver had to sell the horses and wagon for hotel accommodations just to wait to hitch a ride back to Shale, destitute. I guess nobody told him to sell three horses and the wagon and ride the fourth home. Oh well.

That was one failed teamster of a half-dozen. A half-dozen failed teams meant a dozen failed drivers and shotgun riders combined, all looking to ride shotgun for drivers who already had the service. Needless to say, the problem of too many miners was now the problem of too many riders. Remaining drivers knew they could replace their hired rider with a perfectly competent out-of-work rider offering a cheaper price. With this, the race to the bottom for riders' wages began.

Ebbs and flows. Ups and downs. That's the best way to look at things.

Flow. Will and Rosey realized much of the more basic furniture assembly was rote. They offered failed teamsters the opportunity to build in the empty barns that used to house their horses-sold. This employed a third of those men and increased efficiency of the furniture operation enough that Rosey and Will could focus exclusively on building more ornate boutique items. *Ebb.* Then the mining men came home from Santa Rosa. This meant more unemployed in Shale. *Flow.* It also meant more men with an aptitude for driving a team and more reemployment of the fired shotgun riders.

Ebbs and flows.

Ups and downs.

You could call the recent shift of Shale a reprieve without a pardon.

8

EBB

"Christmas in January! Now I've heard everything." Mr. Partridge says this holding a summer squash.

"It's not January," Kate insists. She's leaning under the too-low banner of her produce stand. She's doing this in order to look Mr. Partridge in the eye. She and Metro thought it a good idea to place the banner at the customer's eye level for promotion's sake. Sort of a subliminal marketing thing. It wasn't until the grand-opening that they realized a banner at eye-level for the customer is a banner at eye-level for the proprietor. She puts her elbows down on the counter and stares up at her neighbor, says matter-of-factly, "It's December twenty-fourth."

"Now... Now yer mistaken Miss Kate—"

"I can get my calendar."

"It's a week after New Year!" She just stares, deadpan. "Don't tell me you ain't in the new year yet either!" he gasps.

"Any day can be first of new year," she insists. "As long as you wait three-hundred-sixty-five and a quarter days before you say it's new year again. Nothing special about new year.

New year can start anywhere like anywhere can be North Pole."

"You got a different Santa too!"

"*Didukh.*"

"*Guh*-what?"

Kate's growing impatient. She's come to enjoy the culture shock she elicits in her fellow Shalers, as have they. A fascination for all involved though it's getting late. "We will be leaving soon Mr. Partridge."

"Really need them tomaters for supper tomorra. Best if I could pick 'em fresh."

"We'll be gone all day for mass. You really should just grow your own."

"I don't want to take yer business away…"

"I can't meet demand as it is and I not expand."

"I wouldn't know where to begin."

"Ask for dirt. Three carts. Cultivate half of lawn and dump. Drop seeds. Hardest part is *mayb-yee* digging a deeper well in case of drought."

"What about bugs?"

"Put cayenne pepper in water and dowse."

"Where do I get the pepper?"

"Grow peppers."

"Now… Now this is getting a bit paradoxical. I could come back with my notepad?"

"Maybe I expand." She sighs.

KATE ENTERS THE HOUSE COUNTING a wad of The Federals' IOUs. Metro hears her as he rummages through the chest of drawers in the bedroom. The girls jump up and down on the bed as he rummages.

"Where's my white collared shirt?" he shouts into the kitchen.

"Which?" Kate says popping her head through the bedroom door.

"One of the four," he shrugs. "It has no distinction. Just a church shirt."

"Is it this?" she says as she walks back into the kitchen. Her tone hints that Metro should follow.

She opens a cupboard next to the wash basin and starts searching through some scrub clothes torn up for wash rags.

Metro watches her and the dollar bills poking out of her vest pocket. He grins. He's grinning about something other than the matters at hand though these matters are what triggered the expression. He grins at her. Grins for himself.

"Heard you educating Mr. Partridge out there," he says with all due intimation.

She stops rummaging for a second. She smiles without him seeing it, rehearses her line. "I can talk about life back home. You work. You need to maintain their trust." She goes back to her rummaging.

"Oh really agrarian? I guess that stand outside is for Anya to sell lemonade?"

She pulls out the rag she was looking for.

"You work for them. I have hobby for me." She says this standing and spinning to face him. "They just pay me for that hobby." She unfurls the rag in her hand showing her husband. It's a four-inch wide strip of shirt with the left breast pocket still attached. "This?" she asks wincing preemptively and exaggeratedly. A gesture intended to say,

Dearest husband, my destroying your shirt pains me more than you could ever know. Thankfully for you, I've already been

punished enough having had to live with the guilt my actions have caused. There is no point in you expressing any further disappointment therefore, as it would only compound my guilty feelings where, as you can plainly see, I've already suffered enough.

Metro's allayed by the gesture. Hell, he's downright charmed by these Raskolnikovian maneuvers of Kate's in trying to defuse any frustration she's caused. Always has found them charming. He stands faux-firm however so as to not let the charming though mildly deceptive nature of her faux-pain go unaddressed. He does this for both the ethics of the matter and the fun of it *though* really just the fun of it.

Two wrongs make a right as Metro affects his own pretend dismay.

"That is part of it," he laments. "What did you do to it?"

"I could not wash the fire out of it," she insists.

"*The fire out of it*?" he mimics in confusion.

"The red. The fire red."

"Fire doesn't burn red woman!"

"Well it was red after you put out that church fire!" She goes back to the rags in the cupboard and starts sorting through them again. She finds what she's looking for. It's another part of the shirt. The right sleeve. "Here." Sleeve's a little pink. "It's faded but now you see. You could never wear that in front of God."

"I don't remember any injury." He examines his arms.

"*Fire doesn't burn red! Fire doesn't burn red!*" she mocks. "Neither does blood dry red. It dries brown like rust. This dries like a poppy pedal." Metro takes it in hand. Eyes it quizzically. A serious change of demeanor. Kate notices. "Are you really that upset?" She reaches into her pocket and pulls out them Federals. "I can buy you an even better one—"

"No. No no dove," he intercepts. "I am not disappointed. This red, I just... I remember reading something about it." He shakes his head like he's trying to knock that idea out of it for the time-being. He looks to his wife with a different kind of semi-seriousness. "We must go. We are already running late."

JON APPROACHES HANNAH WITH A piece of newsprint in hand. She looks up at him from her desk. Immediately registers the expression on his face. He's looking about a quarter past dire. She reaches out for the print, gesturing as though to say *it's ok Jon just give it to me.*

"He wants me to put it on *der* office door," he says.

Hannah scans what turns out to be a notice of the Mining Council's. It reads,

Vote 'Yes' on Proposition 26!
Date: January 15th

Proposition Title: "A Fee on Purchases and Sales
Conducted by Non-Residents,"

A Vote January 15th will decide the addition of a 35% fee
on the price of goods purchased by or sold by any Burke
Range resident within any Burke Range community he or
she is not a resident of. The measure is intended to stem
the migration (and concentration) of working men to
certain locations of The Range. This migration poses a
great threat to the lifeblood of Burke Range, i.e. the
taconite mines that have sustained each municipality for
the past 37 years. With mining men tempted to leave in
hopes of finding more lucrative careers in just a small

number of Burke Range communities, there will be insufficient numbers to work our mines. The proposed fee will keep a portion of business profits in all our communities, where keeping a portion of these profits in our communities, because they will be redistributed to our mining men and families, means keeping our mining men in these communities.

A 'Yes' vote is a vote in support of our hard-working mining men as well as support for The Burke Range Mining Council!

"*Small number of communities,*" Hannah says. "Guess one *is* a small number."

"Maria's brother's started mining in Clunch. Word out there is any miner caught voting *No* loses a week's pay."

Hannah hears Jon. She's too exasperated to respond.

"Mail is three days late," he adds.

She raises her head up from her hands. "Are you enjoying this or something?"

Jon appears almost hurt. "I—I'm sorry ma'am. I forget your attachment."

He's right not to pull any punches Hannah. You're who they come to for fixin'. That's the essence of the occupation. Now you know why doctors don't treat their kin.

She takes a deep breath.

"Mail's in Carson."

SHALE'S COOL IN JANUARY. WINDS shift to the north dropping the temperature significantly. Yet, it's a big drop in a hot place. The Belt's southerly enough you rarely get even an overnight frost. However, the wind's extra bitter to the Molybohas in that wide-open conveyance of theirs, they having set out for Carson to attend midnight mass.

Metro's driving the carriage with one hand and pulling his coat collar up over his ears with the other. Kate's in the backseat huddling under blankets with the girls. It's bitter and they've only just left town. Driving into the wind!

Weather isn't keeping little Anya still though. She's begun to twist and squirm under her mother's arms. Something's got her attention cold be damned.

"What. Are. You. Doing. Child?" Kate asks with all due curiosity as Anya ups the intensity of the squirmin'. Moma finally relents and lets the girl up to stand. Anya leans in closer to her father, hanging onto the back of his bench and peering out the front of the carriage.

"Popa what's that?" She's pointing to the northeast.

Metro leans his head down and into his daughter's arm so he can see along it. He lets her tiny finger act the sites guiding him to the object of her curiosity. He catches it. Something being built up on the hill almost due north of Shale.

"I don't know what that is," he relents.

He don't know what it is though it's sure somethin'. A complex bigger than anything The Belt's ever founded and floored. It's gotta be ten-thousand-square-feet in area. Not much of it's built beyond that foundation, yet you can already tell it's as futuristic as a jet-powered backhouse. Structure's all concrete and steel in a county where everything's built outta wood or stone. Next to the concrete slab of a foundation sits a stack of girders already higher and wider than any building of Shale. Girders sit like interlocking upper-case 'I's. The 'I' between any two others betrays the appearance of a steel man trying to hoist himself up over the shoulders of those others.

"I don't know what that is."

"Maybe you should ask Hannah?" Kate offers.

"It's rural municipality. Though very close. It's still RM's jurisdiction so I should ask the Reeve. I'll ask after boxing day."

"That hill was completely bare not even a week ago. By Boxing Day there will be no need to ask as Mayor Dep and everyone else will be seeing it from half the windows in town."

"Then leave them to it. I stay home and help you hill potatoes."

Kate baps Metro playfully then grabs onto Anya. She tickles her while pulling her back under the blankets. Anya chuckles and leans in closer to moma.

HANNAH'S LEANING ON HER OFFICE desk with both arms splayed. Arms support her torso tripod-like. Same as Kate in her stumpy produce stand. Hannah ain't doing it to look anyone in the eye. She's doing it for the loom. For the imposing nature of it. Whether she realizes it or not.

"You get your daddy to back off Burke!" She insists this in Jr's diminutive li'l direction.

"Oh my dear—" he begins to condescend.

"Not in any mood! He's head of the Mining Council. Shale ain't got a mine anymore. He ain't got warrant to tell us how to conduct our business anymore."

"He is doing no such thing Hannah." Burke's patronizing tone lingers a little in this statement. Best he can do. He appears to be trying.

"What's the message he's sending then Burke? Having the mining train drop the mail in Carson all a sudden?

Every single mining man voting for every single Labor Chair's tariffs?"

"Now you can't prove that daddy—"

"All the mayors and councilmen in The Belt been thankful for our operation 'cept for the single member of those councils happen to be in your father's employ?"

"One could also frame it thus Hannah. All councilmen save for those Labor Chairs have been neglecting our mining men—"

"Miners like getting their mail on time same as everybody else."

"Be that as it may—"

"Dalton Pettimore's been aiming to take money out of his coffers as grants for our teamsters," she adds. "Last thing a promising business needs is money that comes either way but it means Dalt sees the value in us." Her tone turns suggestive. "Your father really want a rift developing between Dalt Pettimore and himself?"

Burke relents a little. If what Hannah's said is true then she and Dalt have put him in a real spot with his daddy. That, there's no denying. He don't know much about his father's desires for The Belt but what he can infer from the man's actions. That and a few offhand remarks made to his confidants. Made just before shutting the door on Jr shutting him out. He's only ever really known that keeping Shale folk working means he and his father keeping on good terms. That's about it. Well, Shale folk have never been working harder and daddy's never been angrier.

Burke indeed relents. Draws the only inference he can "It's just... Hannah it's just that nothing's going to rejuvenate that mine. Eighty mining men are a horrible thing to waste."

"No such thing as a mining man Burke, just a man who works a mine. This belt's already got enough of the latter.

Any more and we're back to there not being a living in it. Or was that your intent all along?"

"How dare you!"

No theatrics from Burke. No condescension. You can say a lot about him that's unfavorable but you can't say he's never cared about keeping the people of Shale working.

Hannah feels a pinch in her chest at her hurting this little man. It was cheap. She's on a mission though, for Burke and everyone else. She keeps pushing, hating herself for only having a utilitarianism as cheap as her digging away at Burke to move her forward.

"Your father's then?"

"Now madam! Daddy lives for mining and those mining men!"

Something about the shift from accusing Burke Jr to accusing Burke Sr has brought back some of Jr's theatrics. Catharsis for him? Hannah pushes further in this direction.

"In Belt terms your dad just got here! Just because iron's been your whole life that don't make it his."

"W—What are you implying?"

"Daddy's a dilettante. You think he's all iron because it's all you've ever known of him but it takes only a little more than your life-lived to empty a belt. You act like that taconite's limitless. Your father sure don't." Burke stares blankly. "Are you really this naïve?" Burke shakes his head. Shakes away at something other than that charge of naiveté. Hannah rolls on. "He's gonna bleed this belt dry and he wants those mens' slave labor to maximize his profits doing it."

"Never!"

"And then what happens once he's bled it dry? No iron, Council dissolves."

Burke's gone from condescending to indignant to near-pleading. "He'd lose everything he's worked for Hannah!"

"He worked for the taconite. He'll follow the last of it out of here on the same train. Why do you think he's been spending so much time courting Washington of late?"

"The—"

"The lie? The same lie that got you to put that geologist on the train for him?"

Head low. "I'm sure daddy has his reasons—"

"For lying to you me and everyone else? If he cared at all about the prosperity of this belt he'd tell those mining men the truth about the dwindling taconite and condemn those tariffs. He'd stop stifling our innovations and his insuring all but a strip of ghost towns once the iron's gone."

"I can assure you our iron supply—"

"I caught that geologist before you could hustle him off on that train remember?" Burke sighs. Hannah culminates. "Dalton Pettimore may want all of us under his thumb but at least he's got his sights set on developing The Belt beyond the mines." She pauses a beat. Then... "Quite frankly Burke, so did you. *Buying time for another form of commerce.* That was the only initiative you and I ever agreed on. You were right and that proposal was the first natural and honest thing I've ever heard flap outta those cagey gums of yours. I'll be damned if I'm gonna let you abandon it just to appease a daddy with less concern for these people than those mines drying up on 'em."

Burke may have had his head low the last few of Hannah's remarks but it's rising now. He lifts it to reveal some shaky though honest-to-goodness resolve. "What do you wish of me Hannah?"

"I want you to do the job you've been lying to yourself about doing all along. For The Belt not your father."

· · ·

IT'S THE DAY AFTER BOXING Day and Metro ain't investigating that complex. Kate was right. Its massive steel frame is already up and it's got everybody's attention. It's day after Boxing Day and Metro ain't hilling any potatoes either. He's at the church. Not going to church. Not even his church. He's back at Shale Baptist, all done being rebuilt but the doors. Doors need to be hand-crafted to match the originals with a cross routered into each. A large wool blanket hangs in their place.

Sheriff's skulking around the churchyard in the dark of early morn. His lantern wick's no brighter than a lightning bug—near snuffed. He sneaks up to the outside of The Pastor's small apartment at the rear. Hears nothing but loud snoring coming through the open window. He carries on. Moves to the well at the edge of the backyard shelter belt.

Over the pump, he pulls another of Kate's wash rags from out his pocket. He lays it flat under the well's spout. As gingerly as possible he pumps about a gallon's worth of water out onto it. Satisfied, he turns up his lantern wick just high enough and just long enough to fully illuminate the cloth. Intensity lasts only a second or two but the result is unassailable: a white, albeit drenched, rag.

Sheriff grimaces. He rings out the cloth and pockets it. Well that was for nothing... He scans across the yard toward The Pastor's apartment. Doesn't seem to be any light or movement coming from the window, however the bright of that lantern's left a wash of afterimage in his view. He squats down to wait for the dark to return so he can confirm the coast's clear.

As it does, and form returns to the objects nearby, something else takes shape. It's the pile of burned-out siding from the church fire.

Metro grins.

AS THE SHERIFF SIDLES ALONG the edge of the church again, lantern and a couple of those charred wooden slats in his arms, he feels a flickering in his peripheral vision. Through the window he sees there's a candle still burning at the alter hissing periodically spitting hot wax at various trajectories. One of the candle's targets is a doily of fine lace, another's the dried-out pages of an open hymnal. He frowns. Starts sidling back in the opposite direction.

Back under The Pastor's bedroom window he belts the wall a few times with his left arm. *BAP! BAP! BAP!*

A couple seconds then...

"Whuhs that? Who's there," says a groggy voice.

Metro affects his best townie tone as low and gruff as he can make it. "Blow out them candles ya curr! Wanna burn the church down fer good this time?"

He turns the lantern wick down as far as it'll go then rebundles it in arms. He bolts for the church's shelter belt and disappears into the bushes a good fifteen seconds before the reverend's head pops out the window. Would that old drunk have even remembered seeing Metro if he did?

SHERIFF HAS RUSHED HOME JOGGING the whole way anxious and excited, feeling like a child playing Pinkerton man.

He enters the little shop at the corner of his backyard. He sets his slats down on the workbench carefully. It's pitch-black in the shop so Metro isn't sure if there's anything on the bench to knock over. Didn't feel like it. He twists the lantern wick up full and lights it with a match. Illumination shows he missed dumping a near-full can of wood stain by a half-inch of where the slat settled. Oh well...

He sets the lantern down on the bench and puts one of his slats edgewise in the vice. He cranks the vice tight as it'll go, crimping it an eighth-way into the broad side of the singed timber.

Sheriff picks up a mallet. He glances back at the house like he can see anything through the wall of his shed. He's thinking about the sound he's about to make and the girls sleeping. *Just one solid strike should do it* he thinks. *Even if the sound wakes them they won't be disturbed and they drift right off again.*

Who's he kiddin'? He's come this far already. Of course he's going to finish the job. He lifts the mallet and arcs it back in a side-handed gesture. He arcs the mallet back-and-forth a couple of times delicately. Motions the tool into the side of the slat poking out the vice. Does it practice-like in order to ensure he's got the right line on it. He pulls back for real this time and... *CRACK!*

Just as he intended: board's split in two all the way along its length at the top of the vice.

Sheriff sets down the mallet and grabs the lantern. He moves it as close as it'll go to what remains of the timber bound in vice. He examines the wood along the inside of the slat.

Eyes widen at the sight.

9

FLOW

The foundation up on the hill is completely enclosed in steel and concrete. Wires extend from it in all directions save for the side facing Shale. The wires are carried off in all those other directions by telegraph poles staked out every fifty meters. The poles extend out and disappear over the hills dropping off their stark curvatures aided by the gentler curvature of the extending horizon.

Has that complex been completed? That's a question of purpose. For the answer to that you'd have to know the complex's intended function. If whoever commissioned its erection intended a black box of a curiosity generator then that concrete beast's as complete as a theory of arithmetic with just one number and an equal sign. Otherwise who the hell knows?

Sheriff and Mayor investigated independently at first and to no avail. Then they tried pooling their authority to get answers. Problem regardless of collaboration is, it's only ever been workers up there who either have too little information or aren't at liberty to discuss matters. Authoritarianism's no use anyway as the complex is in the Rural Municipality of Shale, meaning neither The Sheriff nor The Mayor have any formal warrant to compel answers. *Talk to the Reeve* was the response the workers would give.

Talk to the Reeve yet nobody's seen that man in months.

See, RM's populated by just a few dozen. All eccentric and reclusive as hell. Most are on the Reeve's council too so no one needs the Reeve to decide what they can just decide for themselves. For this, there ain't exactly council meetings to attend to get answers. It's the RM's party out there and I mean party. RM's only two-hundred yards outta Shale City but it's a different country out there. Different world.

What they get up to who the hell knows?

"I'VE GOT TWO PIECES OF good news for you!" little man says to Hannah in all boisterousness.

She's as receptive as she should be to a Burke Jr attempting a new leaf, yet her body language betrays a standoffishness of a more primitive source of judgement. Betrays her essence too. Burke notices.

"I see. Had that comin'. Well here's the first piece of good news..." He goes to the office door, pops it open and reaches down for something. It's a sack. It's a symbolic sack because it ain't exactly the official version of what it's meant to represent. Exactly why Hannah don't recognize it. Burke brings it over. Tugs open the drawstring and dumps a pile of letters all over the desk.

Hannah brightens. "This what I think it is?"

"Talked to Dalt myself. Mail Express is once again delivering to shale. Three times a week!"

Hannah laughs of joy. "How?"

"Dalt and I arranged for the prison train to Carson to carry the mail. Mining Council can't touch it."

Dalt and 'you' huh? Fair enough Mr. Burke. You did good.

Burke's beaming at Hannah. She can't help but beam too. Though a thought creeps in.

"What about your father?"

Beam fades a little, though Burke holds onto the smile it birthed. His eyes glisten. Attention drifts.

"I... Um..." A change in tone. "Are you not going to ask what the second piece of good news is?"

"What's the second piece of good news Burke?" Hannah's genuinely curious.

"I thought you would never ask. That's why I asked you to ask! Indulge me Hannah. Let this first piece of news be the goodwill sufficient for me to present the second at this afternoon's council meeting. So the whole town can be present."

"I can't coerce that information out of you Burke. It's yours to tell or not. Let me ask ya, would you tell me right now if I demanded it?"

"Alright Hannah, it all has to do with that form of commerce we've been talking about—"

"Whoa! I didn't ask you to tell me. I asked if you would. And obviously you would. Save it for the meeting!"

Burke claps his hands. "Ha ha! You just wait!" he says in excitement-reinvigorated. He's out the door.

OUGHTTA SET UP A TOLL booth for these ceaseless meetings if they wanna bail out the town.

We'd just be payin' our own money which we don't have any more y' fool!

Least we got the mail delivery back.

So you want to spend that cash just to get through a door—

Quiet! Jr's about to make that announcement a' his he's been inti-matin' all over town!

HANNAH'S TURNED PROCEEDINGS OVER TO Burke who stands solemn. Hands on lapels.

"Mayor Price, good people of Shale, I stand here today the bearer of good tidings. Oh, but it will not be me who tells you. It won't be anyone who tells you!" He gets into a slight twisting hunch like he's about to unleash something from his suit jacket. "Why tell you..." He does unleash something: theatrics. "...When I can show you!" He leaps upward and openward, standing on tippy-toes. Both arms are directed at the back of the hall.

Instinctively, attendees twist to see what he's gesturing at.

A slender woman rises from the back corner.

"I would like to introduce you to—"

BOOM!

French doors of the meeting hall burst open and in struts Reeve Capable 'Cap' Johnson all six-foot-four inches and three-hundred-fifty pounds of him wearing his coat and tails and a ten-inch-tall derby in place of a top hat. He moves like a real peacock dipping and weaving up the aisle. Several of his fellow RM bohemians follow him, all fanning out huge stacks of Federals in their hands waving them temptingly at the attendees as they sashay along.

Metro, who's sitting next to Jon and Maria, turns to the couple for an explanation.

"I'll tell you some time," Jon says. "For now just watch. This will be good."

Hannah's staring daggers at a Burke trying to wave off any responsibility. He seems just as surprised as she is. Cap's bohemians have settled onto the floor in front of the bench closest the stage. They sit crisscross-applesauce and rapt. Cap stands enthusiastic, staring up at The Mayor on stage. Top of that monster of a derby of his's higher than Hannah's lectern.

"Hannie Price!" he shouts. "Waylan Junior!" he says spinning. He tips his hat to Burke. "Tell her the good news?"

Burke inches forward to get between Hannah and Cap. He's dwarfed between Reeve and stage. "I was just about to introduce everyone to—"

"Dotty Lamour!" Cap spins a dancing spin back toward the crowd. Spinning and opening his arms across the whole of the hall at the slender woman at the back corner. She's been standing meekly, seemingly biding her time. She raises a hand to Cap and his folk. Waves a *hello* doing double duty. Gesture's meant to get them to settle too. Pomp has left her not quite sure how to proceed? *Pomp*? Maybe ingenuousness? She gives off the air of a neophyte. At what she's new to, who can tell just yet. "Say hello to your savior, Shale!" Cap shouts.

Burke leans around Hannah's lectern to look her in the eye. "Hannah you've got to believe this was not my doin'!"

She waves an absolving wave. She's attending to the slender woman across the hall, curious. *It's ok Burke. Cap's just beat us to the punch is all. He's known for that.*

"OK everyone. Let's calm a little," Hannah says. "I'd like to welcome The Reeve and our other guests of the RM." She waves across Cap's people all along the front row then gestures back up to their guileful leader. "Reeve Johnson," she greets. Cap tips his hat and grins. "You've arrived just in time for Mr. Burke to share some important news." Hannah motions as though The Reeve should sit.

Cap nods then gives a little bow to the attendees. He hops his ass up onto the proscenium of the stage. His legs would dangle if they weren't so damn long. Cap's waist seems to start at his ribs allowing him to sit on the edge of the stage and keep his feet firm on the floor. Despite his height, being two-thirds leg means he appears short near-childlike when sitting.

"Mr. Burke," Hannah recommences. "I believe you had an announcement?"

Burke snaps back into councilman-at-large. "Thank you Mayor. Good people of Shale, if you'll direct your attention to the rear of the hall, I'd like to introduce—"

"Ms. Dotty Lamour!" The Reeve shouts once more.

"God dammit Cap!" Burke barks as the attendees snicker. Then...

"It's alright Mr. Burke." The slender woman says this in a voice as meek as gesture. She's sidling up along the wall to Hannah's left. "Mrs. Mayor," she acknowledges as she nears the lectern. She stops and motions to Hannah as though seeking permission to speak.

Hannah bows in assent.

The slender woman turns to the crowd. "W—Well hello good people of Shale City." Her voice is soft—airy. "As Mr. J —Johnson has said my name is Dorothy Lamour... Well, he said *Dotty* which is fine. Please call me that. Call me *Dotty* everyone." She pauses a second taking a breath.

She speaks with a nervousness further attesting to the fact that she's new to whatever it is she's endeavoring. This and her slender meekness grant her a dignity as well as sympathy from the townsfolk. Sympathy's tempered slightly as, despite the muted colors of Dotty's riding skirt and vest, the silk bonnet atop her with its visor of lace and its ornate bow knotted down around her cheeks hugging onto her chin betrays money. Money that's known generation upon generation of leveraging itself for more. The townsfolk recognize this. They've seen such affluence in The Council men before her. They grant her their sympathies and cautious ears.

"I'm Dotty and, well, I'm in communications. My whole family is in communications as a matter of fact." Despite that bonnet hiding so much of her, she says what she says looking away from the people at an angle down and to the floor. This buys her more of that sympathy and so the people sit attentive. Not a grumble from any.

"My father was Clayton Lamour and he's in part responsible for your telegraph services here. Telegraph services everywhere really. You've probably never heard his name but h—he invented the frequency modulators for quadruplex, later, octuplex telegraphy."

The crowd in all their decorum are trying to hang in there with this talk of telegraphy though it's clearly going over their heads. Dotty notices.

"The technical aspects don't matter really. With these technologies we can send four different telegraph messages at once from just a single terminal. The patent made my father a—a significant sum of money and it was always his dream to use it to *start the whole world talking* as he put it. To allow people to communicate with anyone they wished at near the speed of light. Even across oceans."

At this there're some scoffs.

Dotty smiles anticipating the response. "No really, I say

this in all seriousness. You send signals through the tele-graph wires along your rail systems, why can't similar signals be sent through a cable buried in, say, the Atlantic Ocean?"

"It'd take forever!" shouts a voice from the back.

"*Hmmm.*" Dotty's thinking a second. "Who here has ever seen electric light? In a filament in a vacuum tube?"

"We've seen a light bulb before!" A different voice.

"Well then, how long did that take to illuminate after flipping the switch?" Dotty entertains.

"Lightbulb wasn't underwater!" The first voice answers.

Dumbasses says a chorus of crowd members in regards the two naysayers. Two naysayers don't like this. Dotty tries to diffuse the tension.

"Ok ok. Intercontinental communication can wait. Let's talk about Rubrum Territory. In fact, let's not. Mr. Burke mentioned showing not telling and I'd like to do just that. You've all probably been wondering what that big grey building is to the north of town."

There's a collective leaning forward among the atten-dees. Even their breathing gets quieter at this. Dotty continues.

"In brief, it's a state-of-the-art communications relay that —with the help of Reeve Johnson and the Shale RM— Lamour Communications has built. That complex is the first step in revolutionizing the sharing of information all over the world and it all starts in this territory. To put it in even briefer terms, it's a business opportunity for you the good people of Shale City."

Cap lifts his hands from the stage and starts fluttering the fingers of his upward-facing palms at his constituents. It's as though the fingers are saying *rise*. The bohemians do just that and start fanning out them dollar bills again real decadent-like.

"Yes thank you Mr. Reeve." Dotty says this in response to the display, a little embarrassed by its garishness. "Y—yes as the people of the RM have indicated, there will be money to be made. However, I don't want to get ahead of myself. I want you all to fully understand the nature of the proposition before I make it, and for that I want you to see the tools of the communications trade." She turns to speak to Hannah directly. "Miss Mayor, I cordially invite you and the citizens of Shale to a picnic luncheon up at our relay facility tomorrow at noon. We will conduct a brief tour of the facility then dine."

Hannah nods reciprocating cordiality. She mulls, though favorability is winning out. *Goddammit Hannah, Shale's hit rock bottom so many times these last few months what difference does it make if we hit it once more! Maybe we won't? Burke's earned a little of our trust after all.* She speaks to the crowd, "Well, what do you think ladies and gentlemen?"

M—Might be alright...

Couldn't hurt I guess...

Heard these types of proposals before...

FUMFER FUMFER...

"Oh come on!" Hannah shouts playfully. "It's a free lunch! You know how you're always left scramblin' after church!"

Yeah... Yeah that sounds alright.

Hell why not!

Sure!

Hannah looks down to Dotty. "See you at noon Miss Lamour?"

Dotty smiles "See you then."

· · ·

IT'S A WEB OF COPPER wires and junction boxes: millions of strands of those wires like capillaries feeding in from all over gradually braiding into veins clamped to arteries spiraling in increasing complexity inward to a heart-like center. A shiny spider's heart in a shiny spider's web of electrical inputs and outputs seemingly suspended by itself *ex nihilo* which is what the dead Latins say for *by the bootstraps*. Pumping ceaselessly yet silently. A mass of copper-pure.

The whole town has fit into the Lamour complex along with the Reeve and the RM. All those Shalefolk just stare up at that monstrous form of wires bigger than the Carson post office. Then...

"Why're there no sparks?" asks a guest.

Burke intercepts. "I think what Mrs. Garrett is asking Miss Lamour, is what insulates these wires? What keeps them from not interfering with one another?"

Dotty smiles obligingly. "That's due to a number of factors. Namely, my father's transducers ensuring no two wires of any bundle carry the same octuples of frequencies. More, variation in tensile strengths across strands as well as a near-imperceptible anti-galvanic coating prevents these signals from meshing." Dotty chuckles. "I say this of course knowing I can't do my father's theories any real justice. I'm not saying *you'll just have to take my word for it*—as we fully intend our engineers to brief you on the more technical details as well as any anticipated changes to our infrastructure prior to any decisions—but for now, since this is more a social affair and I've always favored function over form... *You'll just have to take my word for it!*" She bookends her explanation with another smile. This time a smile of good humor.

Most in the crowd laugh. Burke doesn't. Hannah doesn't either though it's because she's lost in a world of assessment and prediction, cost-benefit analyses, the good and the bad of all she's observed so far and what she is prepared to amend with every fact revealed.

Burke's not laughing because of all that copper.

"Miss Lamour," he begins. "Why the copper? Isn't iron the preferred metal for telegraphy due its durability and affordability? Especially affordable considering where you've built?"

This observation snaps Hannah out of her deliberations. She wants to hear any explanation too.

Dotty's grimacing slightly. Her otherwise porcelain face flushes. Then... Composure. "Y—Yes. The simple explanation for this is the variability in tensile strength. Iron isn't always strongest where varied tensility is concerned. Copper is a necessity therefore, should we endeavor to move the sheer amount of information we'd have to to achieve our vision."

Burke nods half-satisfied at Dotty. He nods more vigorously at the members of the crowd surrounding him as though they should act more than satisfied. They all start nodding maximally vigorously at Dotty.

Hannah remains probative. "You mean your father's vision of bringing people together through communication, Miss Lamour?"

"Exactly Mayor. That was always my father's dream and now mine as I follow in his footsteps. Like a journey of a thousand miles begins with a single step, the bringing together of nine billion voices begins with a single copper wire. We've taken a substantial number of steps since then and now it's time for a leap. *Why Shale?* you may be asking. Three reasons. Three reasons for my father's dream. For a proof of his concept. He needed *first* a steady supply of moving water to power his hydro generators. With these generators we'll never run out of electricity to charge our power cells and never lose a single message. *Second* he needed a location central to where communication was essential to feature as our hub. *Third* he needed people ready willing and able to make that hub work.

"With the recent and unfortunate collapse of the Rubrum River Dam we have the currents to run our generators. Shale is smack in the middle of an iron belt that thrives on communication for your iron industry and your legal institutions in Carson. Last, with the loss of your mine, I'm sure the opportunity for work is welcome."

"You're taking an awful big risk building this *my God* I can't even imagine how costly a facility," Hannah reminds. "While banking on our residents to work it for you."

Dotty goes austere. "I'm not going to mince words with you Hannah. We already have a hundred people moved to the Shale RM to work our terminals."

She steps out of the crowd of residents to speak to them as a body. She's still in that mask of a bonnet and she still favors staring at the floor the bulk of the time she spends speaking but there's a fluency in her words now—a confidence. Warming up to the people of Shale? The role her father's death's forced on her? She continues.

"This means a hundred additional Shale residents earning the same as Belt miners, maybe more. In fact, right now about a dozen of The Reeve's folk, the ones with the right amount of gumption, have been earning a day's worth of mining wages in just a few hours working our terminals—"

"And don't forget their sign-on bonuses!" Cap shouts.
Could use that money...
"Yes of course Mr. Reeve," Dotty agrees. "Although I

must say I prefer a more subdued approach to incentives. No offense."

"Ha ha! None ever taken!" Cap guffaws.

"Well y—yes," Dotty continues. "Well we can't offer much by way of a bonus. However, we hope it's enough to show you we operate in good faith. Faith in you. Faith in this endeavor. Faith in The Belt. Though I digress. And I was just getting to the good part before that digression. The part about how Shale City wins either way.

"That's a hundred residents moving in making very good money and spending the bulk of it in Shale City. Of course, that doesn't mean there won't be room for all of you at Lamour Communications. To exhaust the potential of our facility we would need four Shale Cities' worth of telegraphers working around the clock. So, come to work for us and your economy grows. Don't come to work for us and your economy still grows because others will come to work for us and spend in Shale.

"But we really hope you'll consider working with us. Since meeting all of you I've come to realize a fourth condition's been met. One my father never considered. The condition is thus. You fine people in so many ways share my father's mindset. With the loss of your iron mine you seized the opportunity to bring mail to every town of The Belt. You recognized the significance of your connection to the surrounding cities and the power of communication. You all and my father... a—and I... we're kindred spirits."

The more shrewd of the crowd stand pensive considering things. The less shrewd at the very least know enough to not get in the way of the more shrewd considering things.

"What's the job entail?" a resident musters.

"Simple. You receive and decode messages sent to your

terminal coming in from all over Amerika then send them along to your assigned terminal somewhere in The Belt."

"Like a middleman?" is the follow-up.

"In a sense. Without our hub's ability to handle volume, there would be too much of a bottleneck at each community and the bulk of the messages sent would never be received. Instead of a bottleneck think of it like a funnel with too small a spout. Too many messages sent to any one town is like too much water flowing into that funnel. If water pours in faster than the spout can drain, the bulk of the water just flows over the edge and goes to waste. Same thing happens when everyone needing-to tries wiring The Belt. This is why you currently have restrictions on who can and can't send telegraphs into the territory.

"Since we can't increase the size of the funnel and the whole point of our operation is to maximize flow, we'll use our hub..." Dotty points at the copper heart. "...as a 'reservoir'. The messages will pour into our hub to be divvied up and diverted to your terminals where, as I said, you will receive these messages to send on their way to another terminal in The Belt. We'll never overflow the 'funnel' because our hub has the capacity to receive far more messages than can ever be transmitted into this territory in a day. Theoretically, even if that limit were reached, worst-case scenario is all those messages are received by your terminals and printed. *Archived.* You'll date any incoming message to be held in your 'reservoir' until you can recode them into your terminals sending them later. And thanks to our octuplex technology you'll be able to do that in a quarter of the time it takes any other telegrapher. It will be a steady stream of information flowing out where none of your incoming stream will ever flow over the funnel so to speak."

"What're our required qualifications?"

"You'll have to learn to do this…" Dotty moves her index finger up and down mimicking a person hitting a transmitter key.

There's some scattered laughter.

"Won't we need to know Morse Code?"

"No. Just the correct technique for keying in the dits and dashes. Since you'll only be resending incoming messages, your only additional responsibility will be to date them so that they're resent in the proper sequence. You'll also amalgamate them."

"Amalgamate?"

"Yes. You will be using our octuplex technology to send four messages at once. That means sending the first dit or dash of each of your four messages ordered oldest to fourth-from-oldest… then the second dit or dash… then the third… and on."

This explanation appears to have gone over the heads of many in attendance.

Dotty adjusts to a tone of assurance. "A—admittedly it sounds like it will be the hardest part of your job, but it's no more complicated than lining up four message slips side-by-side and tapping out the symbols left-to-right top-to-bottom. We'll teach you, rest assured."

A little mulling, then…

"What's the cost for a terminal?"

"Nothing," Dotty says once more assuredly. "We wire your house up with a terminal and as soon as it's installed you can get to receiving and sending messages all from the comfort of your own homes."

Ya obviously ain't seen the bulk of our homes!

Some laughter.

"Fair enough." Dotty chuckles. "From … your own

homes. There's no maintenance either. If something stops working let us know and our technologists will repair the terminal equipment. You'll only ever have to touch a transmitter key. Easy."

Many tilt their heads and shrug agreeably. Hannah is still steely and discerning. Burke's still got a bug about that lack of iron. Cap Johnson is dancing with some ladies of the RM gesturing for some ladies of Shale to join in. Shale ladies feign their best look of disgust in Cap's direction.

Hannah remains lost in that copper heart. *Oh God Tom is this monstrosity really our savior? With goddamn Cap Johnson vouching for it!* She examines it as though she's counting the inputs and outputs following every line in trying to catch the same line coming out like she'll discern a flaw. How could such a vast complexity ever work?

"...you think Miss Mayor?" ... "Hannah?"

Hannah's feeling a nudge at her shoulder. It's Dotty snapping her out of the daydream. She gives the heiress her full attention.

"What do you think Hannah?" Dotty's all alight in anticipation.

Hannah hesitates a second. "Um..."

"I'm thinking maybe it best to continue this discussion on fuller stomachs?" Dotty intercepts.

Hannah dips her head in agreement—and relief. Dotty continues.

"Then—"

"Then let us dine fair people of Shale!" Cap shouts. "That's you too Dotty," he says suggestively.

10

UP

B y Valentine's Day all of Main was lined with monster telegraph poles and two-thirds of Shale homes were wired up with Dotty's terminals. Infrastructure would be welcome if it weren't for the fact that less than one-third of terminalled homes had a resident who'd learned the amalgamation process. At least one resident of any wired-up residence required such a competency though it was taking longer than expected. Dotty chalked it up to the octuplex technology requiring telegraphers to use parts of their brains other than the bits meant for language.

Although we read code and decode messages in the standard manner, we send them differently with the Lamour system. As hinted, the amalgamation process requires Shale's telegraphy students set the messages across four columns, one message per column, then start keying in the symbols of the top row, left-to-right moving top-to-bottom.

If you were sending two messages, say the lyrics to *Happy Birthday* and *Hail to The Chief,* the message would be written like this:

H H

A A

P I

P L

Y T

... ...

And while moving left to right from key to key you would write:

Hhaapiplyt...

Given up to four messages could be sent using up to four keys, sending these messages was cumbersome out of bed in the morning and taxing as hell. Needless to say, it wasn't like writing cursive. People were struggling with it.

MR. GARRETT AND MRS. GARRETT watch as a Lamour technologist installs their terminal. Tech's sliding a shiny metal cylinder into what appears to be a large lockbox turned on its side. Real delicate about it too. The cylinder has two iron posts on each end about a half-inch in diameter. Each taper at the center like an hourglass. Like a coupl'a groovy iron nipples. The technologist slides the cylinder vertical into the lockbox. The grooves of the nipples fit into the notches of two metal strips bolted perpendicular to the back of the box.

Grooves slide into those notches with a *CHUNK!*

Mr. Garrett leans a little closer to the box to get a better look. The tech's hand goes up swift as anything in a gesture universal. Mr. Garrett halts. Backs up. Backs up a little more. Tech lowers his hand wavering it as soon as Mr. Garrett's a safe distance away. Mister still watches on in curiosity only he squints.

"Dawny and I," he gestures to the missus, "we're quite good with the Morse Code should you need more inter-preters up at your complex."

"We'll keep that in mind Mr. Garrett," tech says noncommittally. "However, we've already got more techs than we need due Miss Lamour's prudence." Mr. and Mrs. Garrett are reasonably disappointed. Tech notices. "As I said, it's appreciated. Rest assured we will keep it in mind."

Tech stands himself up to examine the machinery atop the terminal pedestal. Setup's like this... Four embossers running along the top half of the pedestal and four keys running along the bottom half. Keys and embossers lay aligned two-by-two. 'Bossers have a strip of paper fed out under a wooden armature with a pencil lead held at the end of it. Keys look like little teeter-totters with a round iron petal on one end and a tapered iron tooth at the other. Tooth connects and disconnects with a conductive metal plate when the petal's tapped. Tap the right key somewhere in Amerika and the respective embosser armature in the Garrett's living room starts feeding the paper along the pencil lead. Lead bobs up and down to the rhythm of the tapping on the other end, writing out the dits and the dashes. That's the mechanics of it.

To the right of the four pairs of keys and embossers is a four-inch by eight-inch wooden box. Tech lifts the box off the pedestal to reveal another key and embosser pair. Mr. Garrett's eyes narrow at this. Tech taps .. -. / - .... . / .--. .. -.- . on that key petal a few times and waits. Then...

..... -..- .....

is returned through the embosser next to that special key. Tech kneels again. Slams the lockbox door and puts a padlock on it.

Mr. Garrett's curiosity is piqued. "Any chance I can get a key to that?" I'm quite handy with machinery."

"No chance sir." Tech says in all due seriousness.

"I repaired our conveyors for twenty years."

"I respect that I do. But this terminal isn't a mule-drawn conveyor belt—"

"It was steam."

"Lookit, a mule'll kick ya. Steam'll blister ya. The electricity in the power cell you just watched me put in here." He taps the box. "It'll stop your heart."

"Well I—"

"It'll stop your heart and the arcing will set your new widow's house afire. No offense ma'am." Tech stares sincere yet dead serious at Mrs. Garrett. Missus grabs onto her husband's arm with both hands and digs in. Mr. Garrett winces. "Listen," tech says, now reassuring. "That box is well insulated. Nothing to worry about there. All you two need worry about are the messages coming out of here." He moves his hand over the four embossers. "And sending them along through the keys here." He moves the same over the four keys.

"And what do we use the other one for?" Mrs. Garrett asks pointing to the box-covered key.

"Nothing. Unless something goes wrong. Let's call the key under the box *Box Key* and the embosser *Box Boss*. If your terminal's stopped working properly tap any message into Box Key and someone like me will be sent down to do any repairs. If for some reason your messages aren't being received a message will be sent to Box Boss. If that happens, follow the same procedure you would if your terminal stopped working by tapping the Box Key." He points at Box Key and Box Boss one more time then covers them back up. "Unless you've received a message from Box Boss..." he puts some needle-nosed pliers into a slit out the front of the wooden box pulling a short length of ribbon out. "...Your only responsibilities are to receive amalgamate and resend."

"That's it?"

"And occasionally replace the lead in the 'bossers." He hands Mrs. Garrett a box of 1.5mm lead lengths.

"And who're we sending the messages to again?" she asks. A bit of suggestion in her tone.

"No *again* about it," the technologist grins. "To ensure objectivity we do not tell our employees which of our clients are on the other ends of these terminals."

"Objectivity?"

"Consider it like this. Say for instance—not you fine people mind you— maybe a miner in Carson. Say he loses his job, moves out to Shale to work our terminals. What do you think would happen if he found out he was sending highly sensitive information to the foreman in Carson who gave him the boot?"

"We ain't a miner from Carson."

"Process of elimination then. What if you all know who you're sending to and the Carson miner don't? What if he knows one of the receivers is his foreman and he knows all of you aren't sending to that foreman? Pretty easy to figure out he's gotta be the one messaging the dingbat who fired him, right?"

Mr. and Mrs. Garrett look at each other and do one of those noddy-shrugs like either's body language means to say, *makes sense to me.*

Tech gives the padlock a final tug. *RUNCH!* He attends to

the couple once more. "Receive amalgamate resend. That's it."

WEEKS PASS. TRAINING HAS BROUGHT the numbers of qualified telegraphers up significantly. Not all the houses with terminals have a qualified operator but many of the houses that do, have two or more. Dotty figures the increased transmission of multi-user houses more than makes up for the terminals in disuse. For that, she's granted the holders of disused terminals an additional month to learn the amalgamation process.

In the passing weeks, Shale's population's increased by more than a hundred. Most are spread out across the RM, though a few have moved into Shale City proper. Requests for city lots are numerous. Many more intend to relocate to the city as soon as building a home is feasible. All of the new residents work the telegraphs. Town's growing and so's the economy thanks to that copper heart.

Heart beats like a champion. Eerily immaterial nudging of electrons sent pulsing down the barrel. I weigh a fifth my favorite horse and I can't nudge that old nag with a running start but an electron, weighing nothing apparently, moves them armatures all day long all across the land. Messages are pouring into the collective of working households from everywhere in the world reachable by telegraph wire.

Shalers who understand Morse Code say the messages are mostly business-speak that reads like shopping lists for the suited and booted. Triteness is immaterial really. As long as those messages are pouring in, keeping the money coming, ain't gotta be literature.

Transmission quotas and then some are met. Outputs are adequate—realizers of those outputs notwithstanding—

but all this means desirable outcomes have been achieved and achieved on time. That copper heart is beating like the champion of Marathon's.

THE CHAMBER OF COMMERCE HOLDS its monthly meeting in Hannah's office. A momentous occasion as it's the first since the Lamour facility got up and running. A representative from each business of Shale is in attendance. They all sit around a large makeshift table formed of three pallets. Jon's laid them across three sawhorses. He drags everything in then drags everything out happy to do it all as he's the office allman.

Sally McSween reports on business the general store's been doing.

"It's interesting," she says. "Had a huge run on tobacco and coffee the first few weeks of the month. Double the coffee sales triple the tobacco. Both the kinds fer chawin' and smokin'. Then everything went back to normal by end of last week."

"Burning the midnight oil getting used to them 'graphs," Rosey conjectures. It's her turn to attend the chamber meeting. Will's turn next month.

All in attendance nod except Dotty. She appears a little perturbed.

"And you accounted for the recent influx?" Hannah asks.

"Adults of Shale buy about a pound a coffee a month a person average. First three weeks of last month we were selling two pounds per. Now back to one."

"Rosey's likely right then," Hannah agrees. "Folk working the telegraphs had a bit of a time adjusting. Seems like they've caught the right groove now. Speaking of the good and the bad of Shale... How's that barometer looking Bob?"

"Huh?"

"How are liquor sales Bob?"

"Horrible!" Bob grimaces. "Everybody's too busy workin' those damn terminals t' patronate my saloon!"

"This all provokes an important dubiety," Dotty interjects.

"Well I'm sure t' shit provoked Miss Lamour and I appreciate you noticin'," Bob says assuredly. "In all due humility I'll even grant I am quite important around here. Yet I don't know that I'm a *dubiety* strictly speaking. Maybe a little on my mama's side—"

"She's not talkin' about you y' shit!" shouts Harp, owner of the hotel above Bob's saloon and default roommate of Bob's.

"Well who the hell else is provoked around here?"

"Yer starting t' provoke me y' slug in a ditch!"

"I got a slug fer y', y' coot! A lead slug!"

"Why I ought—"

"Please!" Hannah shouts, shutting Bob and Carp up a second. She turns back to Dotty. "Miss Lamour, if you could elaborate?"

"Certainly Mayor. If you good people will allow me an observation. I've seen what happens when working folk are largely responsible for determining their own pay. Be it through self-employment or, like our staff, working according to an unbounded quota. Now understand, I—I bring up what I'm about to for purely instrumentalist purposes, it being bad for business to get sentimental over business doings—"

It's me again everyone, your narrator. I feel I gotta interrupt a second to acknowledge a potential disingenuity.

Maybe what Dotty's saying is true and she ain't a sentimentalist on the job. Maybe, but it's important to remember that she's also an heiress and so may just be putting on airs... heiress airs... about concerning herself solely with the bottom line. See, people who have operations like Clayton Lamour's simply dropped into their laps tend to not be trusted to run 'em right. People tend to treat a business as something competent businessfolk have built themselves *not* been gifted. So she may just be taking a hard-ass approach to business to allay any such concerns. I guess we shall see.

"—I recommend this purely for instrumentalist purposes as burnout brings productivity to a standstill. We need to make sure the people working those terminals aren't pushing themselves too hard."

"The coffee and tobacco sales have gone back to normal," Hannah assures.

"There are more stimulants than those out there and much more effective stimulants at that. With Lamour operators often meeting a quota-and-a-half in a day—sometimes two—we need be absolutely sure they haven't turned to something stronger to keep awake."

"Shale folk ain't exactly the type—"

"Trust me Hannah," Dotty's up on her feet. Almost so as to better leverage the insistence. "I've seen my share of people destroy themselves when allowed to determine their own successes. It's a very comforting idea to tell yourself *I'll make my money for the week by Tuesday, Wednesday at the latest, then it's five days of rest... I'll make my money for the month by some sort of Tuesday. A year. A lifetime... Just gotta keep awake... Just gotta waste no time...* I've seen people destroy themselves realizing a quota. A dream!"

There's a silence around the table.

Dream?

"I—I'm sorry. I got a little c—carried away." Dotty sits.

Burke puts a comforting hand on the heiress' shoulder. "That's ok Miss Dotty," he says as he rises. What's he up to? "Your concerns are anything but unfounded." He scans around the room. "Ladies and gentlemen, please permit me the recounting of a little bit of Belt history?"

No one objects. Well, Bob and Harp *do* grumble, but they grumble at everything. They'd grumble at a Christmas present.

Burke begins.

"As some of you may remember and as some of you may only know from men like my daddy's s—stories." He pauses a second. "Before the Mining Council put a stop to it, some of the mines used to pay men by the quarter-ton instead of an hourly wage. Some of the men could, by natural disposition, haul a ton a day. Most men could not. Those latter men *could* haul a ton in a day and a night, just never a single day. They'd put in as many hours into the night as they had to to get that ton. Now, back then there was so much taconite and so much untapped earth nobody cared if a man went off and forged his own drift. There were two, often three shifts worth of men in those mines diggin' all day and night!

"Nobody paid any mind. Not until they started finding the odd mining man dead at the end of his drift. Everybody just assumed the man'd pushed himself too hard. Worked himself till his heart gave out. It was a natural deduction given how hard the men had been pushing themselves to make that ton. Strange thing was, all those men they found down there, supposedly dead of working their hearts out, all those men had the same feature: a tint of blue to their gums. Barely noticeable. Coroner had to shine a light on them to see it, yet it was there all the same. A little tint of blue. Always there.

"Well no one thought anything more about it due the convincing nature of that deduction. Those men just worked themselves to death. Council ended the quota system and left it at that. Nobody thought a thing more of it until they found another mining man dead. Same tint of blue at his maw. Then they found another. Then another. All of them with that tint of blue. Only, they weren't finding those men in the mines. They were finding those men in the beds they shared with their wives. In their easy chairs. One man even keeled over in the middle of a church service. Then men started dying who didn't even work a mine!" Burke pauses. Glances around. Makes sure everyone's rapt. They are. He goes on.

"They weren't dying from hard work. They weren't dying from any kind of work. They were dying of a bark. The bark of a tree called a *Toh-Him-Hay*. Few grow naturally in the region though they're easily farmed if you know where to find the seeds. In fact, that's exactly what was doin' out at the very edges of the RMs of this belt. Out in the wildlands where not even Cap Johnson would dare tread. *The Bark* knew not the same fear. It traveled handily. It wasn't like ordering out of a catalog, however. Once those Wildlander pharmacists caught wind a good portion of belt men were working a quota, you could buy Bark in any town. Just look for a blonde-bearded tree trunk of a man nursing a cordial glass of the cheapest gut-punch hooch in any Belt saloon. Mining men knew 'em by the cordial glass. Men'd throw their money down to chew that Bark like shredded tobacco.

"Bark'll crank yer engine that's for sure. Keep ya up for as long as you want it too. It also rips the oxygen right out your blood! Choke ya without even putting a hand to yer throat! Those men were suffocating themselves to death and not even knowing it. That's why that blue.

"It was easy enough to spot once ya knew what you were looking for. Couldn't stop the market though. Wildlanders were too wily about their methods. Though a wife could tell if her husband wasn't ever coming to bed. A foreman could read a punch card and see a miner was triple-dippin'. Most obviously of course, everyone could see that blue tint in a smile if they looked close enough. Once people knew what to look for, you couldn't get away with it. And once you couldn't get away with it, you didn't. It stopped."

Silence for a second.

Then...

"Bah!" Bob grumbles. "You don't seriously believe that blue bark wives tale?"

"I do. Do you wish to adjourn to your saloon and debate the matter further sir? Say, over two cordial glasses of your finest sherry?"

"I don't serve anything in anything so sissified as a cordial glass. Sherry or otherwise."

"Then what explains that bearded ruffian sitting in the back corner of your saloon? Sipping rotgut out of such a glass the last five nights?"

Bob goes red.

"I bet he's there right now," Burke adds. "Should be easy enough to spot, seeing as everyone else is too busy to 'patronate' your establishment..."

Bob goes redder.

"Walked right into that one y' dummy!" Laughs Carp.

"I'll walk my foot right into your ass!"

"Better serve it in a cordial glass then!"

"That don't even make no sense—"

"Gentlemen!" Hannah shouts. "Settle." The two

curmudgeons do, begrudgingly. Hannah gets back to task. "What's the upshot Burke?"

"What this all means Mayor Price, Miss Lamour, is that no one has to cap any quotas. No one has to stifle the spirit of your workers, my neighbors, though we will have to keep an eye out for signs of The Bark. However, we know what we're dealing with and we know what to look for. We need only spread the word."

Dotty sighs. "I can't say I'm happy to hear my worst fears realized, yet I appreciate your investigating the matter Mr. Burke. As well as your prescriptions for how to resolve it."

"My dear, don't ever deign to mention it! It was my pleasure."

"Well!" Hannah says in that kind of mock relief meant to inform of a pending culmination. "I think that's it. I think we're closer to an even-keel than further. We need only be cautiously optimistic about keeping Miss Lamour's opera-tors motivated. Without 'em turning blue! First thing I will do is inform The Sheriff about our bearded bearers of cordial glasses. And Burke, can I count on you to get the word out about that Bark?"

"Consider it..."

Burke snaps his fingers and points one of 'em at a bunch of kids peeking into the office window. They catch his *go-ahead* sign and scramble off in all directions holding onto something like flyers. They hand one of those flyers to anyone they happen to pass.

"...Done! Because it is!" Burke's really in his element here! "My people have been disseminating Bark informa-tional pamphlets since the snap of my finger!"

Your 'people'? Well done Mr. Burke.

"Well done Mr. Burke. Meeting adjourned."

· · ·

BOB'S ALREADY HALFWAY TO THE door by the time Hannah calls the meeting adjourned. He opens it and a sudden gust of icy wind hits everyone in the office. Then he walks out barely closing a door that just blows back open in said wind.

"Insensitive cretin!" Carp moves toward the door to latch it.

BOOM!

A clap of thunder! Everyone hustles toward Carp to meet him at the clamor. Wind intensifies. All are at the front windows of the office in time for the clouds to let loose with a monstrous hail.

"Stay inside!" Hannah shouts. She sees Jon and Maria ushering Burke's flyer kids into town hall. She exhales in relief at that. Doesn't look like anyone else—

"Bob!"

Hannah leans closer to the window to get a better view of what's to her left. It *is* Bob. Lumbering as fast as he can back toward the office. Hail's pelting him as he goes. Hailstones are huge. 'Bout shot glass size. Some bigger.

Carp opens the door and shouts, "Hurry y' fool!" as Bob continues. His lumbering's slowed more and more by the pelting. He's already covered in welts.

Just now a hailstone that's gotta be the size of a cow heart ricochets off the back of a carriage parked out front. Ricocheting stone cracks Bob in the ankle hobbling him. He goes down, instinctively curling into a fetal position trying to cover his face and head.

"Oh god!"

What can anyone do? They'd be ground to a pulp too if they ran out there. Someone's gotta do something. It's a horror show. Gotta do something and yet they all just stand there frozen, hating themselves. All except...

"I've got y', y' old coot!"

It's Carp! He's holding one of Jon's table pallets over his head, running toward the door. He bursts out into the storm, shield in arms overhead.

CARP'S MANAGED TO GET TO Bob. He crouches down holding the pallet over him. Just his boots poke out the back of the slanted pallet. Hunkering over the beat-down barman, Carp starts barking orders. "Gotta stand with me Bob! Gotta get under these boards and move! It's just a few yards. Y' hear me? Bob? Bob!" Bob's perfectly still. "Oh Bobby..."

The hail's making short work of that rickety pallet but that don't stop Carp's head from lowering in his grief.

Man's broken.

Then...

A whisper, "I hear y', y' varmint."

Carp doesn't miss a beat! "Gotta stand with me Bobby! Boards won't last much longer. Put your arms around my neck and hold on. I can carry your weight. Do it!"

Bob tries his best. He wraps his arms around Carp's neck and Carp heaves him upward keeping he and Bob centered under the pallet as they rise.

They're up.

Carp starts lumbering Bob toward the office door.

"Just a few more feet Bobby."

The two men keep moving. Moving onward. Then...

A shot glass worth of ice whacks Carp in the calf. He stumbles though doesn't fall.

Another of Bob's whispers "What is it?"

Hail's broken through near all of the top slats of the pallet and is shredding the second layer pulverizing Carp's fingers.

"Nothing Bobby nothing. We're almost there."

Another hailstone hits Carp in the thigh taking him down to a knee. He tries to rise. He's struggling.

"Almost... There... Bobby..."

More hail.

Carp's down on both knees. Grimaces of pain.

More pulverizing.

Still trying...

When...

THE TWO CURMUDGEONS SMASH THROUGH the office door, tore up but alive. Carp lets go of the pallet and it drops to the floor. Last of it crumbles to splinters the second it lands. He sits Bob down on the floor and cradles him. Lotta bumps and bruises on 'ol Bob about now.

"Should we get him some ice for those welts?" Burke asks.

"No!" shouts Bob.

"Oh, right..."

Carp looks like he's gonna cry. "I don't know what I woulda done if I lost y', y' ole fool!"

"I do! Weasel your way into runnin' my saloon!"

"Now what would I want with a broke-down old honky-tonk with more water in the whiskey than juice in the spittoon!"

"It's yer varmintin' pilferin' of that hooch that nessa-tates my hydratin' it down every morning!"

"*Nessa-tittin'*? *Hydra-tittin'*? Aw, there y' go again with them ten-dollar words! Always lordin' yer erudition over all of us! Making everyone feel stupid! Mr. Burke especially!" Carp tugs Burke's pant-leg toward Bob to better make the point. Burke appears confused and *not* over any erudition.

Bob gets contrite. "He's right. Sorry if I made you t' feel the lesser Mr. Burke."

Burke is utterly at a loss, when...

"Oh you ain't sorry Mr. MegaMind! You looooove to intimidate with that intellect of yours!"

"Why I'll timmy-date you!"

AND WITH THAT THE TWO roommates argued throughout the entirety of the hailstorm keeping everyone holed up... Then argued on into its subsiding... Then argued some more.

11

———

DOWN

‑‑‑ ‑‑‑ ‑‑‑ .. ‑‑.. .‑ ‑‑‑... .. ..‑‑.. ..‑.. .‑.‑. ...

AND ON...

MESSAGES ARE NONSENSE BUT THEY'RE all coming in through Box Boss. *So* trouble. Boss is speaking that gibberish across better than half the terminals of Shale so that means better than half of Lamour's lines are down! Boss Key jawed back to the Lamour complex at first. Jawing back to the Lamour facility where there wasn't anywhere near the number of techs required to mitigate the situation. Boss Key jawed on as proxy for in-home operators at first, then those operators took to the Lamour facility to speak for themselves. Couldn't get any satisfaction either way so now they've taken to town hall, clustered up onto the steps.

The Sheriff minds the telegraphers. Jon helps. Telegraphers are still just grumbling so all's fine for the time-being.

How much longer this will last is a different concern altogether. Grumbling had only ever led to more grumbling before the dam collapsed. Grumbling had only ever led to more grumbling *after* the dam collapsed too. Difference with this latter case was, another carrot dangling from another stick would come along to quell them bad humors driving them grumbles. Shale folk would even get to take the odd bite here and there before the snapping of the stick. Snapping was unceremonious. Uncalled for even. Malicious at times. Think those tariffs. And yet there was always some other stick with a shiny new carrot hanging. That telegraphing operation's the last root I reckon.

What happens now?

"All iron now all copper," says Metro. "Deprive us of one we grumble for the other. Deprive us of the other we grumble for the one?"

"Be thankful Metro," Jon nudges. "No real leisure to get us into any trouble this way. Grumbling is honest toil."

"What do you think we'd do in leisure?"

"Dream of work."

"You know how many arrests I've made since the mine closed?"

"Two."

"None," Metro chuckles.

"Rumors of tarring and feathering unfounded?"

"True though only attempted. Plead down to a night in the drunk tank. Good men in a bad place."

The grumbling lessens. The rigid indignant posturing of the masses turns to listless milling. Jon notices.

"There are worse things than apathy Metro. Makes the job easier. Like I said, be thankful."

Metro chuckles again at Jon's observation. "You sound

like my wife." He glances back at the assembly. He sighs as a few of the townsfolk set themselves upon the steps, elbows on their knees and faces in palms. They still let out the odd grumble though. "I think a worthy lawman establishes the boundaries one must butt up against from time-to-time in order that life be well-lived. Without boundaries some fall off a cliff of excess. Of decadence. Of all kinds of corruption. *And from what heights do they fall* we like to say. Others who see this fall fear to even move out from the center. In this town there isn't even the fall. For every one person moving in *this* direction there's another to pull him in the direction of *that*. They not move. It's like they are chained together by —pardon the poetry—shackles of iron. I'm not needed here."

"Boundaries are the law," Jon reminds. "Good laws, well understood, provide the right incentives and disincentives. You've *yust* informed the people of the law. You did your job, well ahead of time."

"They don't know law and I not tell them. They don't know good or bad. Not on theory not by impulse. They just know iron. What if I told you the lawman's boundaries are defined by what is *just* not what is law?"

"Don't tell the writers of those laws that."

"Writers of laws don't enforce laws—"

"Or follow them!"

A bit of laughter.

"Right! Regardless, I only mention as hypothetical. Food for thought. Personally I have no problem... hypothetically mind you... extending the bounds of what is permissible beyond the law given injustice does not result. If expected of me, I not enforce tariffs for example. For another, I not enforce lack of commerce on Sunday. Good or bad. Day of rest or no. Dilemmas like this are why God gave free will."

"What about reducing those bounds before the law? There's nothing illegal about those tariffs though they're certainly unjust. Would you end tariffs if you could?"

"How can you be sure what you deem just or unjust are truly that?"

"Do I need to be sure? You're The Sheriff. The setter of the bounds," Jon chuckles. "How do *you* assess such moral judgments?"

"Ha! I could say fair enough to you. I could also say you are being evasive. If what you say is fair I am obligated to answer. If you evade I have no choice but to answer or else we both evade and stifle this wonderful conversation." Metro smirks slightly. "In all honesty I never let the higher-order questions of justice bother me. Is my metric for what is and isn't just *just itself*? This I never considered. I only possessed a sense of justice and I felt I could trust it." A wistful look a second… He shakes his head. "No longer."

"You no longer trust your sense of justice?"

"No longer have a sense of justice to trust…"

"Ah Metro!" Jon says in all boisterousness like he's found a contradiction. "If not for this sense, how could you conclude letting the people break the laws you mention *not* unjust?"

No hesitation. "Intuition? Habit maybe? It's just a judgment that is there though I don't *feel* avoiding tariffs wrong. I don't *feel* avoiding them unjust. I imagine I could reason to these conclusions by manipulation of moral and ethical principles too. According to some logic. There just won't be any spark. No *ah ha!* or *eureka!* for coming to understand the good like I have when coming to understand the facts. I fear I am succumbing to the apathy of The Belt."

"That sounds horrible."

"There are worse things than apathy Jon," Metro mocks.

"I may have spoken too soon."

"It's not as dire as it seems. I lack feeling for what grounds my moral judgments. I don't lack the moral judgments themselves. The justification of which I do lack the grounding for, granted, though otherwise I am a feeling man. I couldn't be happier. I'm full of love for my wife and daughters. I feel esteem and admiration for many in this world worth feeling esteem and admiration for. I even feel sentiments that ground my feelings of love and happiness and esteem. For these emotions there is no question of their righteousness. I'd like to think I have all the qualities of a well-rounded man just not all the qualities of a well-rounded lawman."

"And you're *my* sheriff," Jon says in mock alarm.

"I am *everybody's* Sheriff!" Metro jokes, upping the ante. "But it's fine Jon. If my lack of moral sensibility is a product of the amorality of The Belt, then when this town needs a well-rounded lawman again, amorality no longer prevails and I no longer lack in moral sensibility. I no longer lack the requisite qualities for being a proper lawman therefore."

"As simple as that?"

"As simple as that. However, it's not for me that I dread a growing amorality in the world. I'm a family man now. I live for the well-being of my wife and daughters. That is a good I long ago learned to set my watch too. It is for my daughters that I want a moral world. Whether there is good to be made or good to be sought, there must be motivation for the good. The Mayor wants progress so do I. I want a world for my daughters better than this one but don't we all. What I really want is for them to feel they can take hold of what of the world is theirs and make it—ideally, keep it—one that is better. To whatever degree they are able to of course. For this they need motivation for the good. Without it they just grumble.

"But! To answer your question, I think I'd be obligated to end tariffs as justness is my measure after all. Ending tariffs by fiat would give away the game however. Powers that be would replace me faster than any commerce could be made freer. My dilemma is this then... *I attempt to end tariffs, as is my duty, and a more officious Sheriff takes my place leaving Shale less free. Or, I allow tariffs and only avoid this injustice by extending the bounds of permissibility beyond the law ensuring no one punished for not paying or not collecting. However, I betray my duty to abolish in so doing.*"

"What will you choose Metro?"

"It's hypothetical remember?"

"Ah, yet there is nothing hypothetical about your assumed duty to draw boundaries along the lines of justice *not* law?" Metro grumbles but in a decided playfulness. He knows what comes next. "And..." Jon continues. "...That the tariffs are unjust is no hypothetical either. Are you not now obligated to act by these two non-hypotheticals? These facts?"

"Fine." Metro snaps in decisiveness. "I choose to be utilitarian. I leave the tariffs as is, though I do not enforce them."

"That was a quick calculus. Not a moral sentiment helping you decide?"

"Rational processes."

"Metro! The world's fastest thinker!"

"No. I think quite slowly. This is just not the first I've thought on the matter." Jon laughs. Metro continues. "Even if not hypothetical, there should be no need to defy law to maintain justice. There are forces at work beyond lawmakers and lawmen that ought be ensuring the lines of the law drawn along the lines of justice."

"What force is this?"

"A people who do more than grumble."

THEY SAY THE LINES WERE taken out by the storm. They say this but...

"We need to take seriously the possibility of sabotage Miss Lamour!"

Burke's imploring Dotty and Hannah as the three of them conduct an impromptu pre-meeting at The Mayor's office before the impromptu town hall meeting to follow.

Dotty's hesitant as per her usual. "I don't want to be alarmist about this Mr. Burke—"

"Now," Burke interrupts. "Miss Lamour, you know about people working themselves too hard. *I know* about the sleazy business tactics of The Belt."

"This seems premature. It was almost certainly the hail," Dotty assures.

"Council's proprietary lines are right as rain!"

"You said yourself Burke, the iron they use is more durable," Hannah reminds.

"And I stand by that! I absolutely do! But it's them ceramic insulators that are the cause and we all use the same insulators. Council and Dotty's lines got the same hail and only her insulators are smashed? In those numbers?"

"Well we can't just go ahead and accuse... I don't even know... The Council? Your Father?" Hannah looks to Burke, implores.

He thinks a second. "Permit me a proposal?"

"Of course."

"In the immediate we cut our losses and just repair them poles. Don't accuse anyone of anything. In the midterm and the long-term I recommend we protect our lines from further harm. In the long-term Miss Lamour, might I recommend, due the necessity though weakness of that copper, we start construction on a trench system to bury those lines? I've been talking to an engineer friend of mine in Carson and he says that although the procedure costly, buried lines will be better protected from the elements. Additionally, since only you and your technologists will know where those lines are buried, they'll be protected from saboteurs."

Dotty bows in understanding *not* commitment. "We considered that too Mr. Burke, but we barely had the financing to run the lines by pole. We'll need two years of revenue generation—likely three—just to start turning a profit."

"Buried lines will reduce operations costs by 25%."

"We'd still need money we don't have, up front."

He barrels on. "Though decimated, the remaining Teamsters of Shale are profiting now in spite of the tariffs. Thanks largely to the population increase Lamour Communications has hastened. They know it. They've already agreed to run the construction materials for free. I know a contractor, owes me a favor we'll just say, willing to do the trenching and put the adapters into our homes at 60% of cost. Your techs can lay the cable on the salaries they're already making." Burke's really gone for broke here. Pardon the poetry...

"Alright alright!" Dotty laughs, giving in to the bravura. "You've made a very good case. Allow me to Friday to consider your proposal?"

"Absolutely!"

"And the midterm solution?" Hannah asks.

"I'm going to talk to Dalt Pettimore about putting some Carson lawmen along our lines. With present company's permissions of course." The two ladies give a *by all means* hand sweep as Burke continues. "Ol' Dalt's been benefitting more than anyone from our teamsters. Set to benefit the same from Dotty's services. Least he can do. Now, I'd prefer to head out to Carson immediately. I'm formally requesting you permit my absence at today's meeting Hannah."

"I'm fine with that Burke and I'm fine with your vigor and priorities of late—"

"But?"

"*But*, you're taking an awful lot of steps you know your father won't approve of. Especially... Accusals of sabotage?"

Burke's eyes glaze again. Right hand trembles. Hannah realizes she shouldn't have broached the subject the way she did.

"M—my fath—"

"You know what?" The Mayor says. "I think those towns-folk are about to pop. We better head over there before The Sheriff and Jon get bulldozed!"

"You're absolutely right Ma'am! You finish up here and I'll escort Miss Lamour across to the hall before I set out myself." Burke opens an airy arm gesturing that Dotty join him in leaving. She does just that.

He lets Dotty out the door before him. He's about to leave too when he decides to linger a second, hand propping open the door a few inches.

"On second thought," he says to Dotty from the other side of the door. "I have just one more triviality to discuss with Hannah. You go on ahead and we'll speak upon my return!" Dotty nods at this and continues on her way. Burke shuts the door. Puts his back to it. "Hannah he's disowned me."

Hannah knows to just listen.

"I—I know. Sounds silly," he continues. "Ya disown an impetuous rebellious adolescent for a betrayal or the like and I'm a thirty-two-year-old man!" He chuckles this out as a solemn tear collects under his left eye. "I'm out the will. Barred from Council affairs. I'm barred from daddy's estate. That's a disownment if there ever were." Voice is breaking. "Gave me an ultimatum. Aw, you were right. It was always about what you said it was. Gave me an ultimatum I didn't heed. Ain't seen mama in a month, maybe a month and a week. Damn that old man to hell. Fuck 'em! Oughta disown *him* for his betrayal. But mama?"

Hannah rises from her seat.

Burke puts up a hand. *No! Don't need it.*

He collects himself. Stretches his neck out by lifting and rotating his head. Wrings the tears out that way. Resolve. "Now, I'm still a member of your fine council ma'am, as well as Labor Chair. I will be until the next election at least." His voice goes sober. He musters all dignity in The Belt all-a-sudden. "I am at your service. I am at the service of the people of Shale. I am honored to be."

With that, he exits.

With his exit, Hannah bursts into tears.

"NO!" SHE SCREAMS, HER BACK turning to Jon and Metro. She smashes her fist against the newel post at the start of her staircase.

A gust of wind blows through the door Metro's left ajar. It hits him full-on. Jon barely registers it thanks to the lawman's occlusion. Wouldn't have anyway as he's rushing to stop Hannah from any more grief-induced pugilism. The air has sent a shocked chill up Metro's back. It's less the cold more the suddenness. He moves to shut the door. Hannah sobs in Jon's arms.

"It'll be alright ma'am. It's ok."

Metro sits down on Hannah's little ornate chair next the door. He holds the letter in both hands, his fingertips non-consciously kneading the ends of its envelope. He realizes he's deforming it, so sets it on the table next his chair. Kneads his hip pouch instead. A soothing mechanism.

Envelope sits the betrayer. Written on the envelope is,

Madam Mayor

12

THE BOTTOM

Hannah didn't believe the cause. Didn't believe it the second Metro put it out there holding that note like he did. *Madam Mayor!* Burke, though a self-admitted and since repentant culprit of this condescending address was also instrumental in ending it. Hannah'd granted him the dignity of a man not just capable of stepping outside his father's shadow but of a man better than Sr in every way and Burke returned a dignity to her ten-fold for it. Not a chance he'd address that letter that way. Thanks to him, no single person in The Belt would dare.

Burke was dead by hanging. Hannah didn't contest this. What she contested was the stated cause. The scene of his end suggested he'd torn down the iron lines of the Council's telegraph poles, first pole standing outside Shale RM, and hanged himself by a braid of wire.

None of this sums! None and that goddamn Sheriff... Metro sits across from Hannah at her dinner table. The note sits on the table address up and equidistant Hannah and him. *He just sits there... He just...* Hannah feels a wave of pain in her solar plexus. A half-vomitous pang of guilt. *Ah Jesus Hannah!*

He's here for you ya ungrateful... So was Jon. They're not here to solve anything. That's your machination! Goddamn-it they're here of the humanity in this.

Jon's since left to get Maria. The allman and allwoman agreed to stay with Hannah for the time being. It's not like in a vacuum Hannah couldn't grieve a man she'd come to depend on and respect. A man she'd come to call a friend. Though it made sense now given the winching stress she's been under. Made sense to have people near.

Hannah needs this yet she doesn't even remember agreeing to the help. It was all a daze for her when she nodded away like a hobby horse—as though the same measure of wood were in her head. It was all a daze, which is why she needs this.

"Do you want to read the note?" he asks. "There are protocols for such materials given the nature of the scene they were found in. However, there is another concern—"

"*Protocols*, like evidence?"

"Man is found dead. It helps tell the story. If there's foul play it features as evidence. Letter's also addressed to you. You have a right to read it. There are ways of handling it such that nothing is contaminated. It was Burke's last wish—"

"Why do you have it?"

"I found him."

"How?"

"Mr. Garrett. Came running to my office. Apparently, passing train saw and engineer sent a message on one of the last telegraph lines working. That was Mr. and Mrs. Garrett's. *Boss Boss* I think he said."

"Box Boss?"

"Could be."

"And there Burke was, just dangling by his lonesome. Note in hand?"

"In pocket. Do you want to read it?"

"He didn't write it."

Metro hesitates a second... "I know you think Mr. Burke turned over a new leaf and I believe he did too. However, sometimes the imprint of the previous page is impressed in the new—"

"Not the goddamn *Madam Mayor* bullshit!" She immediately stifles herself. She puts a hand to her chest, inhales. "Though it's part... No, it's not the idea that Burke would go out insulting me one last time. Trust me, he wouldn't. It's not even the idea he killed himself just inches outside of *his* Shale that makes this so implausible." She shakes her head in agitation again. Guilty over it again. "Y—You don't find anything strange about the circumstances of his death?"

"Besides what you mention?"

"The poles Metro! The council's proprietary lines go down they know immediately. They got that duplex or quadruplex technology too! Every line sends a signal at some special frequency. Line goes down the embosser stops and they know. Thanks to Burke I know all about it!"

Sheriff gets the implication. He's pondering. "Maybe," he says, talking his way through his inferences. "The distance from Carson? It takes plenty of time for Council techs to get here—"

"Two relays in every town. Takes twenty minutes to sweep the whole of those lines."

"Council man asleep at the switch?"

"One man goes east. One man goes west. If they don't meet the man riding opposite from the next RM they keep going. You would have had to meet up with someone from the Council."

He bows as though what he hears is plausible. "What are you thinking Mayor?"

Hannah's considering her next words carefully. *You've always been able to trust him Hannah but he wouldn't be a Sheriff of anything around here if he wasn't a value to 'em. Then again, Burke was a value too. Hell, Tom wouldn't have been mayor if he wasn't the same. Even you persistin'*—

"Ma'am?" Metro interjects, snapping Hannah out of her deliberating. "If what you're intending can't be done alone, then if you can't trust anyone maybe beholden to the Council and that means not working with any of us with such a disposition, that's all of us. You work alone therefore. If what you're intending can't be done alone then you must work with one of us so-disposed. What are you thinking Mayor?"

Hannah takes the letter. She starts running a finger along the cursive of the address. *Alright girl, let him have it...*

"He was killed."

Sheriff leans back, calm. "Hannah we've had the same three criteria for deciding suspects for years. A murderer needs a *means* first and foremost. The tools to do the job. He also needs the *opportunity*. An acquaintance with the victim must be facilitated sufficient for 'applying' the means. Lastly, and this one doesn't always hold as some commit murder without a thought in their heads letalone intentions... however, it helps statistically... we consider those with murderous intentions: a *motive*."

"We can start and end with motive because there's only *one* with any motive. From this follows all the opportunities in the world as well as means. The Council."

"The Council consists of a multitude—"

"One man moves The Council. Anyone on The Council

acts, he tells him. He tells any man on The Council to act, man acts."

Sheriff's a little less calm though barely. It's the slight tilting of his head that's the giveaway. "Burke Sr?"

Hannah leans back in her chair. Tosses the letter back onto the table. "What now?"

"If you are correct, formal investigation is a matter for The Sheriff in the RM Burke was found. Clemoines. Possibly US Marshal's office too. Marshal is beholden as well, though not to Council. To Department of Justice."

"Sr's bigger in Washington than he is in The Belt!"

"That's—"

"That is a fact!"

"Hmmm. It doesn't matter anyway," Metro laments. He's realized something in addition. "Marshal's office is headed by Pontipool Swade now."

"Shit. S'what now?"

"If no foul play everything is fine justice-wise. We grieve a man redeemed. If murder, it's just you and me Hannah."

"Then let's get it declared a suicide in the eyes of the law. Get 'em off the case and you and me'll push this as far as it'll go!"

"Investigate Burke Sr?"

"I know about that damn-near Euclidean *Lines of Justice* of yours."

Metro sighs. Jon! "OK. First things. We make sure that letter says what we need it to say and it says it in Burke Jr's voice. I'll ride our letter out to Clemoines' sheriff in the morning."

"Good."

Metro has a last realization. "One more thing. Mr. Burke was very helpful right before the end. He was also very open about his desire to help. If you are correct, then for my family tell no one about my investigation."

SHALE CITY CEMETERY SITS EAST of town on a hill. They always seem to sit on a hill. Shale's is no different. All on that hill stand row upon row as community members pay their final respects to Waylan Burke Jr.

Many have turned out. Burke's turn-for-the-town brought swift and widespread purchase with those who cared about Shale. Those who cared about The Belt in general. Ol' Dalt's come out. Ol' Morg too, standing next to Dalt. Morg must have got one good scrubbing in cuz that boil's all gone. Many have turned out. There's one in attendance Hannah's especially happy to see: Burke's mama. No sign of daddy though. Hannah ain't so upset about that. Not for her machinations on Sr's guilt mind you, but because she's sure Burke Jr wouldn't have wanted him here. Though who knows for sure? Death changes much. Priorities especially. Had Burke left this world in front of someone to hear his last wishes, who knows?

Had Burke?

Dotty's asked to say a few words and speaks currently. She began by pointing out how she only recently came to know Waylan. About how she quickly came to admire his devotion to the people of Shale. His ingenuity too. At this, many smirked. As well they should have. There were even a few chuckles all in warmth and good humor. Dotty took it as such, imagining that the Burke she knew would have been the first to admit he had it coming.

"In honor of Waylan I'd like to draw your attention to the bustle behind me." Dotty points a finger to the northwest to a set of gouged-out strips of earth spanning outward in all directions of the Lamour Complex. Team-driven culti-vators made the enormous grooves while working men's spades hurriedly dug out the flaps of earth left behind. Those men continue to work away as Dotty speaks.

"What you see are telegraph trenches being dug. In those trenches we will bury all Lamour lines. This will safe-guard them from the elements, as Waylan proposed. You have my pledge to see his proposal through. Consider this one of Waylan's last gifts to The Belt." She bows solemn-like at the folk then turns to Burke's closed casket. She puts a hand on it.

HANNAH UNFURLS A PIECE OF Bristol paper to lay on Burke's casket. The second she pulls the ribbon the coiled-up parch-ment bursts from scroll due its rigidity. It's a sketch of Burke Jr. A portrait of him to be exact. He's looking dignified in his inimitable way. Got an ingot of iron held in his right hand. She lays the sketch down and lets its convex curvature hug the concave of the casket's. She's about to move along and allow the remainder of the procession their goodbyes when...

"This isn't right! He can't be interned here!" It's Burke Sr come storming across the hill walking over graves and shouting. "My boy needs to come home. To his rest and reward!"

He pushes up between Hannah and the others of the procession. He leans onto his son's casket. Mrs. Burke has come up behind and is holding onto his shoulders massaging them, trying to pull him away at the same time.

Hannah eyes Sr with a concealed skepticism. He stares back in crisis. He breaks into tears. Collapses onto the casket, wailing.

. . .

"IT WAS MISDIRECTION!" SHE SHOUTS. We're back in Hannah's office. Couple days after the funeral service. "He's distancing himself from what he did. We just gotta find one of his scoundrels he had do the deed—"

"Hannah stop!" Sheriff demands. She's taken aback yet can't figure as to why she's entitled to be. In her deliberation, The Sheriff prepares words. He removes his hat, "Burke Sr had a bleed the night of the funeral. Jon's sister-in-law works as servant. Rumor is there'll be no recovery. He can't talk. Can't move. Just one eye. He communicates through *yes* and *no* with that eye, or so they say. It's all gibberish."

Hannah don't flinch. "Carry on."

"Ma'am?"

"Carry on with your investigation!"

"A no good man is still a man, Hannah."

"You humanizin' him?"

"He *is* human."

"You defendin' him?"

Metro stands a beat folding the brim of his hat in his hands. Then... "I'm defending you."

She's at a loss.

SHERIFF RIDES OUT ALONG THE rails of Shale. His destination's the telegraph pole where he recovered Burke.

Finding it, he lashes a rein to one of those pieces of bent reinforced steel coming out the pole. Kind meant for climbing. He assesses things. Pole's since had its lines replaced but other than that, nothing out of the ordinary? Well how the hell would The Sheriff know? Pole's a pole as far as he can tell. Best he can do is make a few comparisons, find a few controls. A control pole. See if any glaring differences jump out at him.

He rides out to the next one down the line. Before even dismounting he notices an anomaly. There's a pair of brackets bolted up near the top. Up where the pole meets the crossarms. Nothing's in them brackets at present. He pries one off with his hunting knife.

As he peruses, I figure I might as well ask *which pole's the anomaly?* Considering the relative nature of things, is the anomaly inhering in the pole having them brackets or the pole not? If them brackets stick in every pole except the one from which Burke hanged, why? If them brackets stick only in the pole next to that pole, why?

Sheriff decides to examine a few more controls. He yips his standardbred into motion.

FOUR OF THEM BRACKETS DUMP onto Hannah's desk.

"You know what these are?" he asks.

"Seem familiar." She peers closer. "Telegraph equipment?"

"Brackets for power cells," The Sheriff says. "I found a pair of these at each pole opposite one Burke hanged. None on any others for half mile in both directions."

"What are you thinking?"

"Electricity from power cells could allow for no disruption of warning signal to Council. Council would have no idea lines were down. That's why they not come."

"That's how Sr kept his men from knowing."

"Except he didn't..." Sheriff picks up a bracket. Hannah watches on in cautious curiosity. He draws her attention to a little circled 'L' in cursive. "...This is a Lamour proprietary instrument."

Hannah grimaces. "Forgeries."

"Hannah, maybe. Though it still betrays a fact we over-looked. Dotty is a suspect. She has the same means. Same opportunity. A mo—"

"What?" Hannah chuckles, shaking her head. "That rift over copper *n'* iron?"

"*Everything* between her and Burke."

Hannah shakes that head of hers any more vigorously, centripetal force is gonna pull the incredulity right out her ears. "She's implementing Burke's goddamn trench system as we speak!" Her tone gets a bit pleading. "For Christ's sake!"

"What you say is exactly the problem. Burke had an alternative to every one of Dotty's proposals. Some propos-als, as you admit, were better. An inheritor of a business like Lamour, desperately needing to prove herself, is not going to appreciate all her decisions second-guessed. Especially when some of her decisions are proven wrong by the second-guesser."

"I don't believe it!"

"I don't either and yet it's there. We wouldn't bet on it but we can't rule her out."

Hannah just shakes on...

"You said you wanted to push this as far as it would go," The Sheriff reminds.

Then...

THUMP! THUMP! THUMP! THUMP! THUMP!

"Sheriff! There you are!" Dep's already let himself in at the doorway of the office front. "It's the Garret's."

THUMP! THUMP! THUMP! THUMP! THUMP!

Sheriff hammers on the front door of the Garret's place.

"What is happening?" he asks Dep realizing he doesn't even know why he's all but barging in on the couple.

"Dotty says their terminal's been dead for a day and a half. Came calling an hour ago and no one answered."

"Not possible they take trip?"

"They've been shut-ins since the bulk of our lines went down," urges a voice from behind the lawmen. It's Dotty. She's brought Doc Smart, the town's physician. "My techs told me this morning that messages from their terminal have been going out nonstop for over a week now nothing. I shoulda been keeping a closer eye... With Mr. Burke... I—"

"Miss Lamour!" A few Shale residents have caught sight of Dotty in the street and approach angry. She moves to intercept them.

"Why're our messages not going out?" one of them demands.

Metro leans into Dep to hush. "Keep the doctor here." Dep moves down the steps to the Doc and hustles him up while Metro moves to join Dotty and the townsfolk.

"I—I..." Dotty fumfers at the folk. "I made the difficult decision t—to close down our remaining terminals. Just temporarily... Suspending our services until we can get the lines repaired."

"Why the hell would you do that?" a resident demands.

"Quite frankly, you've been overworked. We don't have enough terminals to cover—"

"With all due respect Miss Lamour," another resident begins. "And there is a lot of respect due thanks your doin'. We can look out for our own well-being—"

At this point a couple of the townsfolk notice Doc Smart having headed up the Garrett's steps.

What's happening with Dawny and Brett?

Why's Doc callin' on them?

What's wrong?

Out of concern, the crowd attempts moving after the Doc. Metro puts his hands up.

"Please. For the Garrett's. Please stand back and let us do our job."

Crowd halts. Sheriff nods obligingly.

HE JOINS DEP AND THE Doc at the Garrett's door.

THUMP! THUMP! THUMP! THUMP! THUMP! Again.

"Mr. and Mrs. Garrett! Are you home?"

Nothing.

"Mr. and Mrs. Garrett! We are coming in!"

Metro backs the Doc down the steps and gestures for him to wait. He lifts his leg up and rears back... *SMASH!* Leg's snapped forward boot to door bursting it ajar.

He moves carefully into the small foyer. He tilts his head to see up the stairs to his left then back down to see into a small guest bedroom. His pistol stays holstered. There's a smell though it's early. Could just be the Garrett's cloistered nature the last few weeks.

It's the living room up and to Metro's right where he knows whatever will be will be. Where that terminal is. He's not ready yet.

"Mr. and Mrs. Garrett! If you are unable to speak make any sound at all. Knock something over!"

Nothing.

He's not ready yet.

Shale's not the town for this. Death happens all the time in big cities and small. In the mines at the periphery of towns like this. After that periphery too. In instances he knows too well. But this is to be his first glimpse of it here in the place he thought he'd grow old with Kateryna.

Where he wanted his girls to mature into women as fearless as his beloved. In a town like this. In a house like this. He bought into the tale of the idyllic. Some ups and downs in a town like Shale though nothing like this. Fool. Mortality rears no matter the force of the idyll. Mortality always rears. Even... In a town like this... In a house like this...

He's not ready but it's the job. He moves to the living room entrance. Beholds.

"Doctor!"

THE PHYSICIAN HUNKERS DOWN TENDING to the Garrett's. Metro leans against the left side of the archway leading into the living room. His arms are crossed. He's rarely the type to hold onto himself like this and yet he does it now. Brett must have died first as Dawny's lying over him from above. She's looking down on him as though before she went over herself she was in the same position as the doc currently. Where after that she went rolling up and over Brett's right shoulder. Her arms ended up draped over him after she settled, dying trying.

There's a sudden commotion heard at the entrance of the house. Sheriff can barely react when...

Dotty flies in. Halts herself in the living room archway. "No! I begged them!"

Sheriff grabs her—holds her. *Damnit! My fault! Dep can't police that crowd alone.*

"Exhaustion," says the Doc. "Worked themselves to death on that machine of yours Miss Lamour..."

"No!" She breaks away from Metro and pushes the doc away. She kneels down to the Garrett's as though to examine them herself. Sheriff and Doc pull her off immediately.

"Look at their mouths!" she wails. "Oh daddy!" Sheriff lets go as Dotty struggles in Doc's arms. "Look!" she pleads.

Doc shakes his head in condescension, holding Dotty tighter. Turns to Metro. "Death is more traumatizing to some."

Metro's eyebrow raises at the Doc. He frowns, hunkers down to Mr. Garrett. He carefully reverently reaches out to the man's upper lip. Rigor's long past so there's a malleability there. He lifts Mr. Garrett's gums to reveal a steel blue.

"I'll be..." says the Doc in confusion.

I'm sorry. There's a strange focus coming from Dotty as she laments. Her attention's given to Mr. Garrett exclusively. Transfixion.

13

THE DEPRESSION

Near the whole of Lamour's telegraph service has been suspended. This is going back a little better than three weeks now. While Dotty's techs work on getting those lines back up only a redundancy system is sending messages and that system is operated exclusively out of the complex. No Shale folk are permitted to work the terminals out their homes.

It's taking more time to get the lines up too as the trenching system can't be left to stagnate. Something about susceptibility to the elements. Problem is, until the conduit to protect those copper wires is fitted, those wires don't go in the ground. Until those copper wires go in the ground, those trenches don't get filled. *Should be fitted by end of week* is the promise. That's the good news. That still means a month before the trenching is finished and a week after that before the above-ground lines are up.

Needless to say...

Townsfolk've never been more dispirited. They've every right to be. To a maximum too given their tribulations. Folk ain't just drinkin' *t' get t' bed* no more either. They're drinking for something anything to keep them occupied in a town half-destitute. They drink then sober up then hate themselves so drink to relieve that sentiment then drink some more to fill the time not spent hating themselves.

Shale's a town half-destitute where the better-off now pay a second tax. They pay those tariffs to The Council as they had been, but they also pay a subsidy of charity to sustain the destitute. The latter payments are voluntary so they ain't a tax strictly speaking, yet damn if they ain't taxin'!

There're also Wildlanders in every place a Wildlander can sit nursing a cordial glass and that means the chewing of The Bark has never been more rampant. Bark gets ya wound like a spring and the hooch stops ya caring where ya pop.

Town's seen an incalculable increase in violence and vandalism. Incalculable because crime never happened before so how do you determine a rate of increase dividing from zero? It's bad though. Week two after the crime commenced saw a 200% increase from week one. Sheriff and Dep have never been busier. Jail never fuller and for longer. Can't hire any more deputies either as all money in the coffers has gone to repairing them lines.

Even with the nightly brawling in the streets and the morning scrubbing of defacement off the businesses and houses of people still able to make a living, Mayor Hannah was still trying. Bless her, she's had to reduce herself to getting political in order to save Shale. Speaking of hating yourself...

HANNAH SITS ON THE RECEIVING end of the desk in Burke Sr's study. It's Mrs. Burke at the dishing end—the helm. We join them mid-conversation.

"This isn't Shale Mrs. Price. I don't get to take over The Council just because my husband's passed."

Keep pushing her girl. "Your husband." *Don't get riled.* "They haven't established interim leadership yet. He's not—"

"One widow to another Mrs. Price… If some entity, some ethereal being we'll say were to descend from the heavens and offer to re-imbue your husband with life only to grant the last vestiges of his earthly remains a single twitching eyeball, would this bring you any solace? Or would this be some cruel demonic trick? You certainly wouldn't call it a resurrection." Mrs. Burke glances over to the wall separating her from where Burke Sr lays. "I can't even call my husband a *man* in his current state letalone a leader of them."

Hannah won't miss a beat. Keeps pushing. *Don't think about Tom. Sorry love but you'd do the same in the situation. Keep pushing.* "They're still obligated to recognize his authority."

"And what would he authorize dear? We're talking about a man who communicates entirely through *yes*'s and *no*'s who can't even request a spoonful of soup without telling you to leave it in the bowl. It's all contradiction. *Yes* to everything and a *no* at the same time. Nonsense."

"Do you love your son?" An eyebrow raises at Hannah. She continues undeterred. "That trenching system was his desire and he abhorred those tariffs. He loved Shale and I wish more people than myself come to see it before his passing. The last thing he ever said to me was *I am at the service of the people of Shale.* What he expressed immediately before was his love for you."

The woman stirs. She's a hard woman though not unfeeling. She's a hard woman, but near-best you'll get for feeling is *feeling betrayed in behavior* and best you'll get for that is a slight shifting in her seat.

"I would have to assemble the whole of the body of council executives," Mrs. Burke suggests. "In my bedroom. In the desperate hopes that a man without a mind will push for the abrogation of a tax law!"

"Why not? Men without minds pass those laws." Hannah says this matter-of-factly. She lets the potential and potentially inopportune jest sit unqualified a second. Then... She raises both eyebrows at Mrs. Burke two times fast!

Mrs. Burke lets out a wry smile. "Have you ever known a politician to repeal a tax, even at the best of times?"

"Never known a politician at the best of times..."

"That's why they were the best of times!" The ladies say this in unison.

"Ha!"

"For Waylan Jr?"

Mrs. Burke exhales. Not a sigh but something's purged. She pushes herself in-chair from out her desk. She rises. Hannah mirrors this. Mrs. Burke collects something from the left-hand drawer and moves to our now-standing Hannah. She looks her up and down. She embraces her. It's punctuated and quick though heartfelt. Missus slips the object in-hand into the pocket of Hannah's riding vest.

"He would want you to have it dear."

IT'S A LITTLE BLACK BOOK of Burke's. Full of names and contact information of the man's many connections inside and out The Belt. Hannah peruses it as she rides back to Shale. It's a leisurely ride save the odd pothole or yip from Jon keeping the team moving. There are minimal interruptions otherwise. However, Hannah's been so singularly fixated on her mission the last few months she'd have found adequate concentration in a bathtub in the middle of Main Street in that hail storm.

The book's organized according to role first, then alphabetically. For the reader's convenience, each name is indexed according to a ratio of *accessibility* and *effectiveness*. She's turned to the following section:

Economists

Broiltman, Malcolm: 10/10 for effectiveness—predictions and models never fail!; 2/10 for accessibility—currently living in London (not Ontario).
…
Spreet, Tyrell: 9/10 for effectiveness—Coulda been an iron man!; 0/10 for accessibility—Rumor has it he's a Wildlander now.
…
Summers, Shep: 7/10 for effectiveness—competent but tells you what you want to hear (tip him well to tell you what you need to hear); 7/10 for accessibility —lives a county over but will serve Burke Range (receives correspondence in Clunch). Address…

"Jon?"

"Yes ma'am?"

"Can we stop at the next station? I need to send a wire."

"*Fer* sure."

DEPUTY DEP ENTERS THE SALOON do-si-doing to make his way through the bustling crowd. He finds himself a table next the center of the bar. Seats himself in a chair facing it. Bob, looking uncharacteristically stiff and concentrative, moves out from behind the bar carrying a rye bottle and rocks glass. He sets the glass and rye onto Dep's table. He moves his head funny at the officer. It's like he's trying to nod but can only get a half-inch in before his neck pulls his face back to default. His jittery nodding lists a little to the left. Old curmudgeon's definitely signaling something to The Deputy who's desperately, though motionlessly, trying to get the curmudgeon to stop.

Dep finally resorts to turning his head to the start of the bar opposite Bob's gesturing and bears teeth. Bob understands the signal telling him to *cut the shit* only now he's doing that jittery nod to let Dep know he understands the signal. Dep grabs the bottle and glass and grimaces a *thank you* through clenched teeth. Bob leaves, though not before making a squeaky *oooh* sound and breaking into a scurry like he's late to meet his mark.

Dep sighs. He pours a half glass of rye. He lifts it to his right cheek, not his lips. Turns his face to meet it. As he does, the man with the cordial glass comes into view. He's a *Wildlander* alright. Blonde beard about down to tits. Same colored mop of light hair drapes his forehead and cheeks.

DEP MAKES AND WILL NOT break eye contact with him. At least not until...

He raises his eyebrows at the Wilder. Wilder's gaze stays fixed on Dep though eyes narrow. Dep glances up and to the left. Wilder turns. Metro looms at Wilder's right shoulder. Entered through the backdoor.

"Care if I sit awhile?"

Wilder grunts a relenting grunt.

Metro sits. He sits for as long as he'll have to. Next to that Bark dealing Wildlander for as long as he'll have to.

AS THE EVENING HOURS WHILE away, Dep Metro and the Wilder lounge in passive stand-off. All watch as the odd Shale resident enters the saloon, heads toward the dealer, catches sight of the lawmen, then U-turns his way back to the street.

The game goes on among the bustle of drinkers in earnest until...

"Fuck you Bilker Bob!" shouts a *Drunk* patron pulling a bottle of whiskey out of Bob's weak covetous little hands. "I'm owed this hooch as it's commensurate to all the water I paid for in them watered-down bottles ya call whiskey!" Drunk picks up a beer mug and tosses it at the back of the bar laughing as it smashes. He storms out with the stolen bottle as Bob gives chase.

Sheriff has no choice. Duty calls. He bolts upright and moves for the front exit. Dep rises to join him as he passes. Sheriff stops at the door and turns back. Gestures for The Deputy to keep watching the Wilder when...

SMASH!

Sounds like the Drunk destroyed that bottle. From the sounds of Bob crying over the lost inventory, drunk didn't smash it over the curmudgeon's head. However, something tells me you could take ol' Bob's head clean off with a smashing whiskey bottle and the head you severed would go on lamenting the lost inventory for a time.

At the sound of the smashing, Sheriff spins back toward the exit and heads out. Dep spins similar, only to where the Wildlander sits. Wilder's gone.

Shit! Dep's already running down the hall to the backdoor. He bursts out of it and into the back road behind the saloon. Nothing. Just the vacant road running left-to-right. Rears of stores are to Dep's back and an eight-foot-high slat fence is to his front. Wildlander had to dash through either of the side alleyways of the saloon. Didn't have time to get any further down that back road. Which alley'd he take?

Dep goes with his first intuition and heads right.

Wrong!

No Wilder down there. Oh well, it was a fifty-fifty shot. Better head up the rest of the alley, he thinks, as that's almost certainly what the Wilder's doing in the opposite.

Deputy gets to the street. Still no Wilder just the thieving drunk, Bob, and Metro. Drunk's waving the neck of his broken bottle around while Metro and Bob try to talk him down. To be precise, Metro's trying to talk the drunk out of any further disorderly conduct. Bob's trying to talk him into paying for the whiskey. Dep scans the area.

"Go on cut me y' rascal!" Bob laments. "Y' already spilled my lifeblood onta that ground when y' smashed my inventory! Why not spill s'more." Bob holds out his wrists in the most melodramatic gesture anyone's ever seen.

"Shut. Up. Bob!" Metro barks while maintaining a calming motion meant for the drunk.

Wasn't just any whiskey. Was Dauphin Rye. The good stuff!

Bob's whining fades out of Dep's perception as he finishes scanning the saloon front. He can tell despite ol' curmudgeon Bob obstructing justice with his cheapskating that The Sheriff can handle the situa—

"Sheriff!" Dep shouts, drawing his pistol.

What Dep first took to be a trash heap is a figure rising, extending some sort of sawed-off in arms. Metro turns toward Dep's shout and...

BANG!

Dep gets a shot off. Hits the figure in the shoulder as *BOOM!* goes the sawed-off!

The lurch of Dep's lead sends figure's aim off. Buck scatters into the gravel equidistant Metro and Drunk.

Metro was half-spun to face Dep by the firing of the sawed-off so he halts where he is. Colt's drawn. He attends to where his deputy fired. Sees the right shoulder of the figure loping down the side alley, disappearing.

Drunk's spooked and so's Bob. They run back into the saloon forgetting about that disputed Dauphin Rye.

Metro waves his pistol in a chopping gesture toward the back road. Dep makes the right interpretation and moves back down the side alley, pistol still drawn. Lawmen remain wary. Wilder could zip across either alley exit but...

Nothing.

Then...

AHHHHHURRRGGGLLLLURRRG! A scream at the back road, cut off by what sounds like drownin'.

Metro breaks into a sprint. He and Dep fly out of the parallel alleyways in time to see a *Shadow* hovering over the convulsing Wilder. It's almost like the Shadow's cradling the Wilder's head in one hand and tending to his face with his other. Can't exactly see what kinda tending it is...

"Don't move!" Metro shouts. Lawmen's pistols are on the Wilder's shadow.

Like inertia ain't nothing, Shadow leaps sideways through the slat fence. Busts through the bottom half of it and out of sight. Lawmen run to the Wilder still writhing.

"See to him," Metro orders as he moves to the bust-out. He ducks down. Pistol barrel points through the opening. Can't see anything and the moonlight's more than enough to illuminate anything running off to the east. After the fence is the same wide swath of yellow grit we saw in Santa Rosa.

There's nothing other than that grit in Metro's view. Pistol's too. By his inference he assumes Shadow's got to be sidling along the slats. Worse, he might be waiting next the opening hoping for a curious pursuer to poke a head out. If he's sidling he's been so for a while. Time's of the essence... *What if he's waiting to take my head off?*

CRASH!

Time *was* of the essence so Metro smashes through the top half of the bust-out. He flies backward through to the other side landing on his back sliding whipping his pistol sights in every direction around the broke-tooth barrier. Grit stops the slide near instantly but he got enough clearance between himself and any Shadow looming.

Eyes dart.

Barrel sways.

Nothing.

Shadow's gone.

WHAT THE HELL'D I WITNESS? he thinks getting up off that grit. Through the gap in the fence he sees Dep's boots, heels up. He sees the Wilder's boots, toes up. Dep starts rising so Sheriff draws another inference: couldn't do anything for the Wilder. Despite only formality to follow, he acts like there ain't time for a dust-off. He hustles back to the scene.

"Got him in both lungs," The Deputy says. "Choked on his blood." Dep appears to be feeling a world of feelings at this, all surely to settle to trauma later on. His voice sounds of one thing: pity. He catches this. "I—I'm sorry Metro. Me lamenting his dyin' after he tried insurin' the same for you."

Metro puts his gun in its holster. "Without success

thanks to your action. There would be a disproportion of iniquity, my reproaching you your empathy in the face of that action." He fastens his pistol back into its holster. Eyes the Wilder, pensive. "I think there would be a disproportion in my reproaching your empathy regardless of heroism. He is a man dead too soon. That we lament."

"What a way to go though. Just kept yakkin' up blood." Dep starts gagging a little himself. Puts a hand to his mouth to stifle it. Metro pats him on the back.

"You go now. I see you tomorrow."

Dep nods at The Sheriff. Wabbles off in the direction of a side alleyway. His index finger's still held firm against his lips.

Metro crouches down to get a better look at the Wildlander. He puts a palm onto the man's forehead and tilts the face to look his way. The Wilder's blonde beard is dyed red all the way down its seven-inch length. Sheriff takes something hankie-like out of his pocket. Turns out to be another of Kate's wash rags. Girl's gonna be scrubbing with the curtains if Metro keeps this up... He dabs a little at the Wilder's mouth.

Blood dries like rust.

From the side alleyway we hear the sound of Dep retching.

AS SOON AS THAT SHADOW killed the Wildlander the men who sat in the corners of Shale nursing all worlds of putrid out those cordial glasses vanished. Shortly after the vanishing the habit broke. Blue smiles turned to sober frowns. There were hard feelings against The Sheriff, he being instrumental in ending the townsfolk's access to their favorite intoxicant. This came naturally.

What weren't any *naturally*—and was one of those disproportions of iniquity—was Kate getting caught between her husband and a town directing resentment at him.

Why'd Kate get dragged into this? That old drunk of a chauvinist of a pastor latched onto all them habitual Bark chewers as *a matter of grace and renewal* as he put it. Took to filling their heads with his fundamentalist nonsense all while calling it a *rescue.* It was no coincidence then that the Pastor's new core of sycophants... sycophants of a man who once lit his own church on fire and tried to pin it on Metro and Kate's Ukrainian Catholicism... sycophants who ain't got their minds right yet... are bent on making trouble for *both* our Molybohas.

Truth be told, if it weren't for Kate getting dragged into all this Metro wouldn't be so sure the townsfolk were wrong to resent him. Who's he or anyone to tell folk they can't find what little joy they can in a town on its last legs? No matter how artificial the joy? Because the joy's dangerous? People are allowed to harm themselves. Hell, people are allowed to kill themselves. They wanna choke up a cyan death in the comfort of their own homes that's their right. Dragging Kate into all this certainly was not.

If I were a lesser man Metro thinks to himself quite often these days *I'd bring that Bark back myself and shove it right down everyone's throats to save Kate the trouble.*

But...

That Bark was gone and so were the Wildlanders. Only evidence of them ever returning was the grave robbin'. No one knew the dead Wilder's identity, even after Doc Smart's investigation. In case you're wondering *why Doc Smart?* Doc also features as Shale's coroner. He had to look into the Wilder's death and—because the Reverend and his trucklers kicked up such a fuss—Sheriff and Dep's role in it too. Sheriff and Dep were determined justified in the incident, though Doc admitted he couldn't prove by evidence alone it wasn't either of the two lawmen who'd pierced the Wilder's lungs.

The pair were deemed justified nonetheless and after all was said and done the Wilder was deemed a nobody. He was buried in an unmarked grave up on the hill. Two days later the grave was found tore up and his body gone. Everyone just assumed the Wildlanders swooped in by dark of night to take their brother home.

LAMP WICK'S RECEDED TO JUST about dark when it halts. Faint flicker hangs on. Sheriff's about to call it a night when... He turns that lamp back up and opens his desk drawer. He pulls out a little paper box with a little paper lid. He sets it down on the desk, removes the lid and unfurls what's inside.

The fabric he used to cleanse the Wilder's beard lay flat.

This dries like a poppy pedal.

14

THE PRESCRIPTION, PART I

S heriff leaves that bundle of his at Hannah's doorstep. He does this while...

...HANNAH MEETS in her office with *The Economist*. Chalk figures feature on a slate board behind him. Real arcane. Lotta Greek. Literal Greek. Like ϕ ψ λ and similar. I think the point is yer supposed to plunk an x or a y into them Greeks like they're a slot machine. Like putting a coin into a kinetoscope. Only it's a kinetoscope where the story's always about money...

Economist is sitting. He's across from Hannah at her desk speaking as though recapitulating. Is he really summing anything up though? I heard study on matters of human understanding—especially the understanding of technical information—suggests even when a sufficiently articulate expert explains something to another of his vocation, if it's explained for the first time, *only* a scantilla or less of that information is understood. I ain't no psychometrist yet I know I didn't understand one *iota* of that Economist's Greek. Theory holds in a world of just me then, but given the world we have—our world of many—it's at least a safe bet that Hannah's getting a lot of regular old capitulation in The Economist's recapitulation.

"Think about it like this," he says with warmth. "You hear about a town in complete collapse and sure enough you find they've just lost a major source of revenue *hence* a major source of employment. Yet, how many times do you hear of a town that's lost a major source of revenue going into complete collapse?" He leans forward and puts his elbows on the desk. Speaks with chopping hand gestures. "In other words, towns in complete collapse have almost certainly lost a major source of revenue, but towns that have lost a major source of revenue rarely collapse. It's something like one in ten.

"Let's talk about another fact of losses like yours Hannah. They drive the town to look for—and discover—resources sitting right under everyone's noses. Resources that stimulate the economy far better than the lost business ever could. Resources no one ever would have noticed butfor the loss of a primary money-maker. They never noticed because they never looked. They never looked because their primary money-maker kept them occupied. So it kept them distracted from more lucrative opportunities." He leans back and lets out a hopeful sigh. "Events like these often give complacency the kick in the pants it needs."

"I appreciate the optimism," Hannah says, incredulous. "However, we had that kick in the pants. We had near a half dozen kicks in the pants. We lost everything."

"No." The Economist says shaking his head, grinning. "You still have all the infrastructure in place and a people clamoring to get back to working it. This too Mayor Price is an expected phase of the processes described. No economic force ever works free of opposition. Natural or artificial. You saw what happened with your teamsters. People from all over The Belt flocked to be a part of their operation. This provoked opposition on the part of The Council. Immoral quite frankly. Certainly a hindrance. Yet you responded and reprocured your delivery contracts. From what I also hear you were instrumental in getting those tariffs repealed. These were artificial barriers. Human caused. They were met with a human response, yet so too were the natural barriers. Your solutions have seen problems but those problems have gotten smaller after each new solution attempted. It's almost like it's been trial and error every step of the way. Correct, Miss Mayor?"

"Every two steps forward and one step back of the way," she half-jests.

"Ha! And yet that makes the point! You're tinkering. You're working the kinks out. The strength of an economy doesn't lie in ingenuity and fruition alone. It lie in resilience too. Many have invented something the whole world had wanted—the best of its kind even—then thought it sufficient to simply let the world know the toy was theirs for a price. These inventors weren't prepared to break down barrier after barrier required to make even a single dollar. Their ideas get stolen and applied to stereotype. Their good names are besmirched. They're strong-armed by more coercive institutions. They lose their tools or inventory to fires caused by the tinkering itself. It happens more than you'd think... Then they're sunk.

"You've faced your share of these natural and non-natural barriers and your telegraph and teamster operations are still standing. Case in point, hail wiped out your telegraph poles so now you're burying them in the ground ensuring that won't happen a second time. You're tinkering, evolving, and making progress."

"What about morale? The townsfolk that are leaving?"

"Again, a normal response to losing a business like a mine. Folk just need to adjust and adapt. They know the new employment was gainful. They know it's still there to be had in time. People with an aptitude for the work Shale provides will move in or back. Despite some townsfolk leaving for where their aptitudes are best monetizable elsewhere, those who stay will find they have something to offer the new residents who will undoubtedly arrive. There'll be a need for serving those new folk's unique tastes in food dress entertainment and whatnot. Where of course many who can't produce such things will be paid to help those who can. You have far too little reason to think the worst Miss Mayor."

"Not to mention the fact that *we* aren't giving up on Shale, Hannah." Dotty's been in the office doorway for some time.

"Ah Miss Lamour!" greets The Economist. "I hope you don't mind Hannah, I asked Miss Lamour to join us at the end of this meeting. I think she'll be integral in Shale's renewal."

Hannah dips at her two interlocutors indicating a receptivity.

"We think so too." Dotty steps lightly into the office. "And soon! Those trenches will be done..." She appears to be figuring in her head. "...End of week! No more disruption of communications after that. No more telegraph poles lost to the elements, natural and non-natural! Pardon the saleswoman in me Hannah. I have to practice my pitching after all... With the reliability of Lamour Communication's technologies, business is expected to triple and so will your population. People will be clamoring for a piece of the Lamour Comm pie."

Hannah feels a warmth wash over her.

The economist bows in approval at the Heiress then turns back to The Mayor. He shuffles in his seat as though to mirror Hannah's lightening. "If I were you," he says, "I'd use what's working of those wires to your advantage and get some notices out to surrounding towns: *telegraph operators needed in Shale City*."

Hannah can't help let her optimism-reemerged show in her beam. She extends a hand to the economist. "Thank you. Thank you so much Mr. Summers."

He rises to take her hand. "A pleasure, Mayor Price."

He tips his hat and sets out to leave. He tips his hat again to Dotty as he passes. "Farewell ladies." He lets himself out.

"Dotty," Hannah recommences. "I hope you realize all you're doing for the people of Shale as well."

"It's my living too." Dotty chuckles, though there's a subtle pleading in it. "Hannah, there's something I want you to understand." She collects herself a little. She's blossoming into a fine businesswoman though some anxieties linger. Make themselves manifest now and again. Like now... Again... She exhales, confident she's quieted in herself whatever it is needs quieting. "I'm not an inhumane person. In fact, it's because of this that I ask the following of you: never let me get too contented with any of Lamour's more humane outcomes. I let myself get distracted by good-will, efficiency drops and people lose their jobs."

Hannah feels an urge to grin at this. However, she doesn't want to condescend Dotty's earnest if not convincing attempt at cold professionalism. She decides it best to play the folk philosof. "Bit of a mindbender isn't it? *Gotta be hard to be soft. Kinda like gotta spend money to make money*."

"That's business."

"So I've learned."

"I should be getting home,"

Dotty sparks a realization in Hannah. "I never asked you Dotty, where is home?"

She chuckles. "I have an apartment in back of the complex."

"I didn't see any apartments back there."

"There are spaces."

"Storage closets."

"Room for a bed."

"My word!" Hannah's astonished, better, disappointed in herself. "I wish I'd asked sooner. You can't stay there. Our— My place has more than enough room."

"Then we should fit you up with a terminal."

"No chance."

Dotty laughs. "Well, now I'll *have* to take you up on your offer. If for no other reason than to persuade my toughest customer. I'm going to need plenty of time to whittle you down Hannie Price."

This Hannah grins at.

THE MAYOR AND THE HEIRESS talk into the evening. Hannah sits with her sketch pad on her lap. She asked Dotty to permit her a use of her charcoals as they converse. Dotty talks about her father. His dream. His ingenuity. His business acumen. The underlying subtext of each of her anecdotes seems to be *I must though never will live up to my father's legacy.* Hannah's noticed Dotty's pessimism and is trying to diffuse it.

"One thing you have that your father didn't," Hannah begins. "And I mean this in all due respect... A—and really your father instilled this in you expressly because he lacked it... Is restraint." Dotty raises an eyebrow. It's a sign of intrigue not offense and Hannah takes it as such. She goes on. "You have a restraint your father lacked and I think that's why you've built something he never could. Shutting down those terminals was the right thing to do."

Dotty pulls at the bow on her bonnet, puffs it out obscuring even more of her. Still faces away despite increasing her obscurity. She's not sufficiently soothed. She speaks anyway. Lamentably.

"It took the loss of two souls to do it."

Hannah stands firm. "Do you have any idea the number of lives lost to iron each year? The Council's never shut down a mining operation to ensure no one die. Even after a dozen-more miners died at once it was all us mayors could do to get a shutdown and a fix. Wouldn't've done it ever if the line-up of men willing to fill a dead miner's shoes was long enough. That's the difference Dotty."

"Council members didn't have to see their faces..."

"Neither did you. You did anyway. No Council member's ever shaken the hand of a miner for the express purpose of not having to look a man in the eye gonna die in his pit. You did everything you could for the Garretts." Hannah looks down. She's conflicted about what's coming. "If it wasn't for your restraint the Garretts would have worked themselves to death long before now."

"Mayor!" Dotty says in surprise. "I—"

Hannah intercepts. "If the Mining Council'd wired the Garrett's up with that terminal how long would they have lasted?" Dotty's caught. What can she say? Just shakes her head. "The Garretts were good people and you did every-thing you could for them," Hannah assures. Heiress just keeps gesturing as though of denial. Out of an incredulity impossible to justify. Hannah sees this. "You expect restraint Dotty. You expect it of others and you demand it in yourself. Your father never did and that's why—"

"He worked himself to death."

"Now I didn't mean—"

"He did Hannah. He—" She's put her fingers to her upper lip. Eyes redden.

Hannah reaches out for Dotty's resting hand and takes hold of it. "It's ok Dotty. I didn't mean to push it. Lord knows I've never been one to talk of such things... of..." Hannah's eyes reveal a similar emotion betrayed of fluidity. *Know I'll never falt ya for this girl come what may...* "Of losing Tom."

Dotty squeezes Hannah's hand back. A bit of a reversal. "Maybe you've just never had the right ear" Dotty says. "I mean Shale isn't exactly the place for confidance."

Hannah pulls her hand free. Pats the top of Dotty's as she goes. She picks up her stick of charcoal and starts sketching a little more vigorously. Dotty's deciding whether or not Hannah ought be left to her devices when...

"You know what Tom did for a living before Mayor?" Hannah asks.

"Hmmm..." Dotty's taken a little off-guard, though her posture betrays a desire of oblige. She figures in regard to Hannah's question. Then... "Teacher, like you?"

"Nope."

"Some sort of scholar?"

"Nah."

"Don't tell me he was a lawyer?"

Hannah revels a little in the suspense she's caused. Then... "Bounty hunter," she says.

Dotty leans back stifling laughter. "No!"

"I'm serious! Good living too."

"How did he ever become a Mayor?"

"He inherited some land out here and we moved back home. Where it's all iron all the time. No crime. No bounties."

"Why not take The Sheriff's position then? From what I hear from Metro, it's the cushiest job in town. And at least Tom'd have acumen for it."

"Maybe. But before Rosa, Shale never had a sheriff. Nobody did except Carson and they only had lawmen to babysit the officials. Carson handled all lawbringing in The Belt before Rosa and judging by the outcomes of Rosa, hardly handled it at that."

"Are you saying Metro's the first Sheriff Shale's ever had?"

"I'm implying it!" Hannah smirks. "Ya know, they say Martin Shawk stopped the expansion of The West Brandon Trail but I'd like to think it The Belt that did it. If the wildlands weren't enough to stop that trail in its tracks, the sheer inertia Belters have to any activity other than mining woulda. Inertia's contagious. Enough to smother the immorality outta the devil."

"What's the West Brandon Trail?" Dotty asks.

"Where Tom died."

Dotty's stunned of this. At a loss.

"It's ok," Hannah assures. "He went out fightin'. Went out the lawbringer."

HANNAH'S TRYING TO BE STRONG about this though she knows two things: Tom's resolve and Tom's obligation.

"At least request the Marshal service escort you through the wildlands," she half-pleads.

He takes his wife's face in hands caressing that gentle

visage of hers. "Hannie how many times have I chased some scoundrel into lands like those? Worse?"

She frowns. "You're not that man anymore."

"What?" Tom chuckles. "You think mayorin's tamed me?" He moves a couple paces back from Hannah, suggestiveness in every step. He stops. Whips open his duster revealing two revolvers. One's holstered near-horizontal at his front waist sitting like an offset belt buckle. The other holster sits at the side of his waist conventional-like. Side pistol's meant for his right hand though, oddly, the buckle pistol's meant for the right hand too. He whips the duster closed. "Does that give you peace of mind?"

"No." She stares defiant at him.

"Ease?"

"A little…" She simpers.

She leaps forward latching on hugging him tight as she can. He holds the back of her head gently to his chest. It's time to go. "Time for us to get to work," he says pulling away. She won't let him. He leans back in and kisses her on the forehead as he breaks free. A second kiss is blown as he backs away.

Up on the saddle of his quarter horse he reassures. "I'll be back darlin'. With Shale's deliverance." He takes up the reins. "I love you Hannie Price."

He rides.

15

———

THE PRESCRIPTION, PART II

Tom'd left The Belt that morning in search of an enterprising endeavor to bring back to Shale. He intended to ride into Stemfield, a town north The Belt. He'd meet with the Labor Chair, some local farmers, and determine whether or not the unarable could be made arable. Whether or not with the right amount of seasoning, Shale's red mud could ever hold a crop. That was the intent. What he actually rode into that evening was a town an hour and a half away from becoming the next of The West Brandon Trail. A town in the midst of its recession.

"I AM SO SO SORRY Mayor Price! I couldn't be more embarrassed." This isn't the first time the Labor Chair—also the mayor it turns out—has said this. He met Tom carrying that contrition and he hauled it all the way back into his office. He's sat Tom down across from him at his desk and continues the lament. "Near half the town maybe more just up and left. Farmers were some, sure, though mostly the hands took off. I've never in my forty-five years—"

"How many did you say live here Mr. Moore?" Tom's cut him off, abrupt.

"W—well we're a small town in terms of population Mr. Price but... *But!* We've got the longest Main Street in Karn County! I'm proud to say."

"The population Mr. Moore." Tom presses.

"Aw it's true, sir. It is a bit misleading. We're basically a cluster of ten-acre homesteads. The sheer size of the homesteads account for the length of Main but... *But!* we had a bit of an uptick in our population since last year! Going back to October we had a population of j—just fourteen. Now it's twenty-five! Well, it was twenty-five... But you gotta believe Mayor Price, twenty-five or fourteen, we're three farming families strong, a general store, and my bank! O—our industriousness more than makes up for our—"

"Mr. Moore!" Tom shouts, setting the Labor Chair/Mayor/Banker silent, aback. He leans closer. "Have you accounted for the people having left? Think very carefully Mr. Moore."

"Well there's some inkling—"

"All new folk?"

Mr. Moore looks a little surprised. "W—Why yes. By preliminary accounts—"

"All men?"

"Yes."

Tom's eyes go wide. A pensive wide. "I don't imagine a farmer has a need for blasting like a minin' man does?"

"Maybe not a *need* to be precise. Though a good store of dynamite has helped us make short work of the stumps Out South. *Out South*'s what we call the fields we farm south of the tracks. You'd have saw 'em coming in. But yes, dynamite makes much shorter work of a stubborn tree ruining otherwise useful grassland."

Tom's eyes go back narrow.

THE PROTO RED-EYES—THE ingratiators responsible for laying the West Brandon Trail—would return after a recession like a fist opening up into a bucket of gold dust. They'd enter town at one end of Main as a mass and start spreading out like fingers splaying. Moving through every alleyway and side street all the way down the length of town. Some of the Red-Eyes remained at the top of Main, killing whoever would make a run from a house or storefront believed passed over by the runagates. Them greedy fingers would splay out and flank down the length of town only to pour out the other end and converge to march back up its center.

Like clenching fingers taking a covetous vicious handful.

People who crossed paths with any Red-Eye at any point in his pillaging were murdered of course. According to whichever way was most expedient. The tougher of the grown had to get a quick bullet. However, the weaker folk not able to put up any kind of a fight—children and elderly especially—were dispatched-with via whatever means was most cost-effective.

The Ingratiators of Stemfield return in much the same manner. Eleven original Red-Eyes plus seven. Six of them stay standing at the tip of Main. Six splay out to the east. Six splay out to the west. The splayers have finished following pattern. They converge at the other end of Main Street and ride back to the waiting six. Everything went according to plan save for one thing...

"The townsfolk?"

"There's fourteen. Three families. The Mayor. The kid who runs the general store."

"They're still here," says *Lead Red-Eye.* "Wildlands is

death and they didn't pass us to the north. Burn it all. Burn everyth—"

H'yaw!

There's a clamor at the other end of Main. All-a-sudden a covered wagon zips across that end, flying parallel the train tracks. The twelve *Pillager Red-Eyes* ride off after it in thoughtless haste. Lead Red-Eye holds an arm out to the five of his Inner-Circle readying reins. Circle holds its position.

The wagon's near disappeared over the west horizon by the time the Pillager Red-Eyes rip around the corner of Main after it. Pillagers get a bead on the wagon and spur-in to close the gap. Cart's dipped completely over the horizon as the pillagers begin the same descent. Be on it in a matter of minutes.

But it don't matter.

As them riders recede off over the horizon, Tom comes slinking out from behind a granary next the tracks. He confirms the coast's clear and gives a little wave. The towns-folk come out from behind the granary too and follow *The Bounty Hunter*. He leads them down the back road that runs behind the shops. He's careful to keep everyone clear of the end of Main and out of sight of the Inner-Circle.

MR. MOORE LETS EVERYONE INTO the back door of his bank and leads them to the vault room.

"What's this Mayor?" a resident asks.

"Tom?" Mr. Moore gestures to The Bounty Hunter for an explanation.

"We can't fight them off and we can't run," Hunter says. "They're all over these lands and they look just like your neighbors to ya. They look that way because that's exactly what they've been. That's what they do. No choice except to hide—"

CREEENK!

Mr. Moore swings the vault door further open. Vault's been picked clean by the runagates.

"In there?" says another resident, apprehensive.

"Yes," says The Hunter.

"They'll burn us out!"

"This building's pure stone," Hunter reminds. "Won't burn. Besides, they'd have to know you're in here first which they won't because..." He leans down to one of the children in that vault. A little girl about three-years-old hugging onto her mama's skirt. He grins at her and continues. "...You're. Gonna. Be. Extra. Quiet." He punctuates each word with a playful finger twitch to the tip of the little girl's nose. She smiles then buries herself back into mama's dress.

Some of the grown-ups aren't so easily pacified.

"We'll suffocate!" one says.

"No no," Mr. Moore assures shaking his head. "A vault ain't airtight for the very reason a person could get locked inside... I—I could get locked inside. P—point is, I checked!" Mayor nods at Hunter.

He starts the vault door closing. "Good luck everyone."

"You're not staying with us?"

Hunter shakes his head. "Someone's gotta get that telegraph back up and let the comin' law know you're in here."

Townsfolk sadden.

Hunter speaks as assuredly as is honest. "I'll see y'all," he says swinging the door closed.

"Tom!" says Mr. Moore through the last sliver of vault door. Hunter stops. Mr. Moore continues. "Got a rifle and some shells under the counter."

Hunter pats Mr. Moore's shoulder appreciatively. He seals the mayor and the townsfolk in.

THE BOUNTY HUNTER'S SNUCK BACK behind that granary. Only telegraph terminal in town is in the station-house about twenty yards to the west of it. Station-house is really a glorified gazebo. A roof over an otherwise open-air counter-space built up of pine logs. It's used primarily for selling train tickets and sending telegraphs of course.

Peeking around the side of the granary toward the north end of town, Hunter can see Lead Red-Eye and his men remaining pillars. *Could just make a break for the station-house Tom.* He hears a rumbling. *Starting to look like ya ain't got no choice!* Pillaging Red-Eyes are bringing back that runaway wagon. Of course they are. They'll pilfer anything a beast can budge.

Red-Eyes have forced The Hunter's play. He sprints for the station-house. Simultaneous to this, Lead Red-Eye draws his pistol. He fires it into the air just as Hunter dives over the counter. Pillager Driver whips the wagon team and Pillager Outriders dig in the spurs. They weren't doddling before yet they're really moving now.

Hunter sits with his back against the station-house counter, hunkered, out of sight. He has Mr. Moore's rifle at the ready. He's listening for the wagon clamor to get sufficiently loud to know it's sufficiently close. Got a little time. He reaches out for the telegraph key and gives it a few wraps. No spark.

Dead.

Rumble intensifies.

He shuffles to the westernmost edge of the counter closest the approaching wagon. Can use every inch. He lays the rifle across his lap. Closes his eyes. Listens. Sound of the clamor's growing... Growing... Now!

Hunter pops up and levels the rifle across the station-house counter. He starts unloading at the wagon hitch.

SHK-CHK POW! SHK-CHK POW! SHK-CHK POW! SHK-CHK POW!

Wagon's flyin' so his window for doing whatever it is he's doing is narrow.

SHK-CHK POW! SHK-CHK POW!

He drives the lead into the hitching pole splintering it just enough that the next bump shreds it. The team of horses breaks free. They run off and don't stop as the busted hitch dips plunging itself in the dirt. Wagon's wrenched upward catapulted to a sudden stop. Driver flies off and into the grit below sliding shredding. He's hamburger.

"Shit!" shouts one of the Outrider Red-Eyes. Then...

SHK-CHK POW! SHK-CHK POW! SHK-CHK POW!

Hunter takes out three Riders from their horses. Animals get spooked at the gunfire and rear on the Outriders in the saddle. Remaining abandon their mounts. One dummy jumps off on the side of his horse facing Hunter. Exposed.

SHK-CHK POW!

That's one more dead Red-Eye thanks to stolen horses ain't conditioned to handle gunfire.

SHK-CHK POW!

Hunter fires off over all's heads and the rest of the horses tear out leaving the remaining Red-Eyes to their lonesome.

SHK-CHK POW!

He takes out one more, last, as the living six scramble to unholster pistols. Hunter ducks under the counter as they return fire. It's a steady barrage of pistol lead hitting the station-house but Hunter's untouchable thanks to the pine log construction. He still shuffles away from where the Red-Eyes are firing: where they saw him last standin'. Keep 'em on their toes. He shuffles as the pops of those pistols keep on. Until...

A muffled shout's heard. "...your fire! Hold your—"

Silence.

Then...

"You still alive in there farmer?" asks one of the runagates.

"I counted twelve of you bastards," Hunter shouts from behind the barrier. "I count six after the round-and-round. Ready to pack it in?" Hunter starts sliding some shells into the rifle's loading gate.

Laughter from the Red-Eyes.

Remaining six stand in a semi-circle around the wagon. Hunter don't know that though. Doesn't need to.

Last bullet through the gate... "You inspect that wagon you stole?"

"Think it's pretty funny making us chase after a bunch of sacks of rapeseed doncha?" says the same voice. He must be the group's representative. "We're gonna eat you slow and kickin' for that!"

"Ain't rapeseed ya fools!"

"Already got everything of yours worth taking. What little there was of that! Might as well be sacks of cowshit."

"You really oughtta had a look."

One of the Red-Eyes' curiosity is piqued. He climbs into the wagon as the runagate Representative yammers on.

"Your pissant little town's bank had just a couple-hundred bucks and a coin collection in it! You people ain't got shit. I bet whatever's in those sacks ain't worth the carry or am I wrong farmer?"

Hunter doesn't answer. Pulls one of Mr. Moore's stump blowers from out his pocket.

"You hear me?" The Representative's getting impatient.

The Red-Eye Wagon Inspector is feeling over those sacks in the dark. He manages to get a grip on one and tears a sizable enough hole in its jute. He reaches for a match.

Hunter reaches for a match too.

Inspector strikes his match against his buckle. Holds the flame to the hole in the sack leaning in to get a better look.

Hunter flicks his match with his thumbnail. Put's the flame to the wick of the stump blower.

"Alright asshole, tell me what's in them sacks!" demands Representative.

Inspector's eyes bulge out at the sight. Immediately blows out the match.

"What's in the fuckin' wagon farmer? Answer me!"

"Here's a hint," says The Bounty Hunter as he lobs his dynamite up and over the station-house counter. Representative's head arcs according to the same curve of the lit explosive heading right for a hole in the wagon canvas.

Inspector's trying to get the hell out of the wagon. He's tripping over those slippery sacks in the dark just as that stick drops right through the canvas and into the tear of jute!

"*Shiiiiiit!*" shout Representative and Inspector in unison when...

KABOOM!

Wagon goes up just like you'd expect a wagon full of dynamite to. Representative and Inspector Red-Eye disintegrate instantly and two of the remaining four runagates die as the concussion and debris tear them to pieces. Last two of them pillagers survived by near-miracle. Found themselves up front of the other three running. Both managed to trip onto their faces just before the explosion. Representativedisintegrated weakened the concussion just enough that it killed, yet didn't dust the closest to him. Closer two then weakened the concussion further so as to only knock the lucky two unconscious. *Lucky* for whatever luck is worth to a Red-Eye.

OVER ON THE OTHER SIDE of town, Lead Red-Eye and his Inner-Circle watch the mushrooming fireball of the explosion eat itself up to nothing.

"We gonna do something?" asks one of the henchmen.

Leader's hand goes up once more. They wait.

LUCKY RED-EYES GET TO their feet. They're dazed though acting more vengeful than, say, happy to be alive. One of the two with the most wherewithal taps the other on the shoulder. Points to the destroyed station house. They draw their pistols and lumber toward. It's now just a rectangle of a pine log counter. Explosion blew the roof to splinters and all the way onto the railroad tracks. Pair lunge over the counter and point their pistols to the last known location of The Bounty Hunter.

BANG! BANG! BANG!...

That's two six shooters. That's twelve pops. They're empty. They're spilling spent casings onta the ground as Hunter walks up behind.

"Shoulda checked them sacks," he scoffs.

The two goons lunge at Hunter like it's all they have left because it is. Hunter side-steps them clobbering one with pistol butt as he passes. Does the same to the other as he turns. Two on the ground dazed and groaning. Hunter walks away from them whistling.

.   .   .

HE RETURNS WITH THE DAZED men's horses. He picks up the least woozy of the two and flops him over the saddle. He takes the horse's bridle and uses the reins to bind the runagate's hands to his boots under horse belly.

MEMBERS OF THE INNER-CIRCLE hear a rumbling. A few of them draw. Out of the darkness of Main comes a horse full gallop. The Red-Eyes recognize their compatriot tied over the back of the animal. The horse blows right on past the Circle and heads out of town. Ain't stopping.

"Now?" says the same impatient henchman.

Leader's hand goes up in that similar gesture.

HUNTER'S WASTING NO TIME. LASHED the last outrider-equipped horse to rebar to cool and's sifted through the rubble of the boom. He's found and's clearing off the telegraph terminal. He tries pulling it off its pedestal but it's on there fast. He wobbles the pedestal a little and although heavy, it isn't anchored to anything. He starts dragging it to the opening of the station house. He wrenches then regrips wrenches then regrips getting about six inches of distance each wrench. He peers down Main each time he gets those inches to confirm Leader and his men still statues.

Pedestal gets to the station platform under a telegraph pole. Hunter attends a last time to those statues. Deliberates hardly at all. *Think a'them folk fella. You know your oughts.* He shoots out one of the pole insulators.

.   .   .

LEADERS HAND GOES DOWN IN a chopping motion. Two of his henchmen ride out toward The Bounty Hunter.

HUNTER'S DRAGGED the braid of the pole. Laid it through the tooth of the terminal key and's giving it a few whacks with the butt of his pistol. Tooth chews at the wires severing the braid.

As he connects the frayed ends to the pedestal he hears the cantor, faint. He's just about got the terminal wired and he knows if he lets his adrenaline push him to haste he'll lose his smoothness. He continues the job at-pace. He could take them riders on of course. Probably win. Yet if they get the upper hand by some fluke, townsfolk rot in that vault. His ethic is clear. He knows what's gotta be done. Those oughts.

The Circle Red-Eyes draw their pistols.

Hunter turns his back to the riders approaching. Needs to focus on one thing at a time.

Red-Eyes aim.

BANG! BANG!

Miss.

Hunter finishes wiring. Starts hammering that key. He's got a spark.

BANG! BANG!

Red-Eyes miss again. Not by much.

DIT DIT DIT DASH DIT...

This better work!

BANG!

DIT DIT DIT DASH DIT...

BANG! BANG!

One got him! In the back. Just the fat. Pluck it out later.

DIT DIT DIT DASH DIT...

BANG!

Miss.

DIT DIT DIT DASH DIT...

BANG!

Grazed the thigh.

DIT DIT DIT DASH DIT...

The hoof beats stop. Heard them stop just at the opposite side of the station-house.

DIT DIT DIT DASH DIT...

They gotta be reloading.

DIT DIT DIT DASH DIT...

Last of their shells are through the gates.

DIT DIT DIT DASH DIT...

They re-raise those pistols...

DIT DIT DIT DASH DIT...

Aim...

DIT DIT DIT DASH DIT...

Then...

BEEP BEEP BEEP BEEP goes the sounder.

Hunter spins pulling from that buckle holster.

POP! POP!

Red-Eyes are corpses.

INNER-CIRCLE GAZE ON INTO the darkness punctuated by the burning remains of that wagon.

"They'd be back by now," says a henchman.

Leader finally readies his reins, intending to ride on.

The four of the circle ride out to the south. Ride as a row.

They cross the center length of Main and...

The Bounty Hunter appears at the south tip. He's back on his quarter horse. Got a kerosene-soaked flaming rag-wrap at the end of his rifle barrel burning like a torch. He halts his mount. Surveys the four men down the way. Issues a challenge.

"You bastard runagates wanna see this through? I'll be waiting in the Wildlands! Let's see how much of a trail you can blaze in there!" *BOOM!* Rifle fires bursting streams of flaming torch into the air!

He yanks the reins and the horse begins to pivot. Time to get the hell out. *Come along if you will ya scum. Won't find any quarry here!* But something causes an itch in his peripheral vision. He pivots the horse back to one. Narrows his eyes down the street. He slumps in the saddle, dejected.

You fool!

It's the kid who runs the general store. Really, he's twenty-two, yet for all intents and purposes... He's slinking along the boardwalk in front of his store carrying a coach gun.

Damned fool! How'd you miss him?

Hunter shakes his head in disgust. He whips the horse around again and gallops out the south of town.

The kid keeps slinking along, coach gun firm in his grip. He's fixated on Leader and his men and he's jittery. There they are though. He's getting closer. He can see them clear. Just stone statues. *CREEK!* It's a twisting rusted weathervane to his back. Kid spins to catch it. Realizes what he's done. He turns back quick to face the Red-Eyes.

Gone!

Kid steps off the boardwalk and into the street. He's trying to get a better look to where those men made themselves conspicuous for far too long to just disappear now. Where the hell'd they—

THUMP!

A henchman's boot hits the kid from behind sending

him face-first into the grit and coach gun flying away. Kid rotates on his ass trying to better see the four Red-Eyes staring down at him from horseback. His mouth goes slack-jawed just a second before...

SMASH!

The quarter horse flies out the storefront window behind The Inner-Circle. Crash sends Circle members wrenching their horses around to catch the event. They see only the horse. Just the horse because that was the ruse. They pivot back to kid only to see The Bounty Hunter in his place. Kid's safe behind for as long as he don't move.

No suspense here. The four draw on Hunter. Hunter's quicker. Calculus he's running on who's the faster Red-Eye pans out.

BOOM! BOOM! BOOM! BOOM!

One shot one dispatched runagate. Oddly, the group's now dead Leader was killed third. Pretty slow.

Last henchman's only been shot out in the arm. He's dropped his pistol but he's got a hold-away. He's reaching for it.

"Don't," begs the Bounty Hunter.

Red-Eye keeps reaching. Reaching across his belly for that hold-out. Hunter's got him in his sights. It's no contest. Doesn't want to do it but the Red-Eye keeps reaching. Doesn't want to do it but...

BOOM!

Buckshot blows out the front of The Hunter's chest and lodges in the shoulder of the reaching Red-Eye. Buckshot kills Tom instantly but only compounds the runagate's wounds. As Tom's corpse falls, the kid's revealed behind him, coach gun in his hands barrel wafting blue smoke. Kid starts screaming at the Red-Eye. Screaming something about being one of them. *Look what I did. Just for you. Take me with you! I'm one—*

SPLAT!

Kid's head's cleaved. Wounded Red-Eye's finally reached that hold-out. He holsters it anew. Nurses the buck in his shoulder a little and rides on.

HANNIE WIPES THE TEARS FROM her eyes. Dotty's silent. Rapt.

"So that was it," Hannah sums. "They found those townsfolk in that vault a couple days later dazed and a little ripe though alive. They didn't remember much. However, they kept talking about the man from The Belt who saved them."

"I... I don't know what to say Hannah."

"Neither do I other than I can't believe I kept the story bottled up like that for so long. I don't think I could tell it again if I tried."

"It's harrowing."

"No. No Dotty. Not because of the pain of it. I... I don't know how else to put it. It's like... Like I've set it free. Like it's gone."

"I'm honored to have heard. I—" She's at a loss.

Hannah reaches out and takes Dotty's hand once more.

"It's ok."

"Shale was so lucky to have Tom," Dotty blurts as though she feels she need say something. Like now's not the time for any of that awkwardness of hers.

"I know."

"Sorry!" she shouts. "That was a platitude. The town is lucky to have had him that's a fact. B—but I just said it because it seemed like the thing to say."

"It's ok Dotty, really."

"No it isn't. The truth is Hannah this town's *luckier* to have you." Hannah nods at this in choppy ups and downs. Her face loses expression. Dotty notices. "I'm sorry," the heiress says crestfallen.

Hannah realizes immediately the harm of humility. She realizes the position Dotty put herself in sayin' what she did. To say it only for Hannah's lack of faith in herself to overshadow an appreciation so difficult to express. To cut Dotty down.

"I..." Dotty tries to muster *only* to stifle herself again, ashamed. She turns downward.

Hannah pulls Dotty's hand closer. Squeezes. She immerses herself in the Heiress a second. She must. She immerses herself in this woman currently consumed by a need to allay her. Allay anyone most likely. A woman who you'd suspect would subserve herself to all before herself in a situation like this. Trying her damnedest in her awkwardness to please. To say all the right things. Who'd die if anyone ever failed to benefit beyond her and who'd die if they ever knew her intent. A woman completely out her element drownin' in everyone else's.

Hannah realizes a thing more... "There's a certain honesty in you Dotty Lamour." She takes her hand out from Dotty's grasp. Places it on the dorsum. Pats. "A trust."

The Heiress is sent deeper into her loss. "I just wish I—"

"Don't." A beat of a silence. Then... "Let it be my turn for some honesty. I'm *not* the person Shale needs. If it weren't Tom's dream I don't know if I could even go on living in this town. This town doesn't need me. This town doesn't need Tom. Job's done. That economist was right. The infrastructure's laid. This town doesn't need anyone like us just someone to set it free. The watch has been wound. Let it tick."

Dotty shakes her head. "I don't want to disparage. I don't Hannah. But the people of Shale would revolt if there wasn't someone telling them what to do. As harsh as that sounds."

"Then a leader in name only. Someone who, when the time is right, will reveal to the townsfolk they've been their own best executors all along. A leader in name only where in the time leading up to this reveal and the time subsequent to it, there's a trust." Hannah takes the sketchpad back in her grip. Sketches with a vigor unmatched this evening. "There's a trust in *you* Dotty Lamour."

"W—What are you saying?"

Hannah flips her sketch pad to reveal a near-perfect rendering of The Heiress in portrait above a 'For Mayor' chyron.

Dotty's amazed at the rendering, though taken off guard. "N—Now, I came here to sell you on a terminal not be sold myself!" She smiles as though there's no controlling it. "I'm flattered. I really am. But I have a vision to see through myself." A look of realization in her grin. "You..." Smile's even wider. Chuckles. "*You* saleswoman!"

They laugh at this.

Hannah shakes the portrait. "This will be sitting on my desk just waiting for when you throw your hat in the ring. I'll whittle you down Dotty Lamour. I have ten months."

16

THE DIAGNOSIS

A new morning. Hannah steps out onto her veranda moving toward the easterly portion. There's a contentment in those steps. She's convalescing over thoughts of Dotty and The Economist's assurances. She leans onto the rail. A closure's present as she looks out to Tom. It's as though she can finally feel the love that left with him the day he rode out. A love unadulterated by obligation. She smiles. A little September in her June.

ACROSS THE WAY FROM HANNAH'S, the Molybohas are doing a little shopping. Metro carries Vicki in his arms as he Kate and Anya inspect the floor model furniture lining the outside of Will and Rosey's shop. *Boardwalk model* might be the better expression?

Kate peruses in apprehension. She's been worried about constituting an upper crust of Shale for quite a while now. Especially considering the town's general hardship. Her farmers market's really booming and she don't know what to do about it. Metro told her she might as well be comfortable in her stewin' so here they are.

Problem is, Will and Rosey are doing damn well themselves having furnished near all of Rosa in its renewal. All while selling boutique goods to Carson. The Molybohas get along great with Will and Rosey, but in the midst of everyone else's struggles, Kate feels their cross-patronage akin to the Vanderbilts moving in with the Rockefellers. Like she's helping build a walled-off little kingdom on a hill. Then...

"Moma I want to try it," Anya says reaching out and rocking a rocking chair.

"It isn't a hobbyhorse dove."

"Moma please!" the four-year-old insists.

Will pops his head out the shop door. "Aw go ahead and give her a go Mrs. M. I'd hate to think my furniture not durable enough to withstand a curious four-year-old!"

"If it's ok..."

Will nods assuredly.

Kate lifts Anya onto a chair that seems to be rocking before the girl's even sat. Matter of instinct. Rocking a rocking chair never had or ever will require teaching anyone how to do so!

On Anya rocks.

"I've got just the piece for you two," Will boasts. "An artifact of the old country of yours made with the tools of the old country of my father's. Come on in!" He waves them on. The couple look to Anya. Will assures them, "She'll be fine out here you two. Only take a second."

The couple gesture at each other as though expressing *maybe this is reasonable?* Kate turns to Anya.

"You stay right here in this chair you understand?"

"Yes yes moma," she promises as she ups the intensity of her rocking.

Kate Metro and Vikki-in-arms enter the shop.

THEY WERE REALLY ONLY IN there a minute...

KATE'S THE FIRST TO EXIT. Vicki must have been transferred to her arms at some point cuz Kate's holding her now. She immediately looks to confirm Anya in that chair. Chair's still rocking though only slightly.

It's empty.

"Anya!" Kate cries as Metro flies out the door around her.

He tears out into the street stopping his forward movement as he gets to its center. He spins trying to cover as much ground as he can as quick as he can. It's like adrenaline comes in different flavors because when Metro's got it pumping in the presence of gunfire, for instance, he feels a fear—'course he does—but also an exhilaration as though of adventure. When he's got it pumping through his veins at the awareness of his missing little girl it's like someone's ripping his insides out top-to-bottom starting at the fist-sized lump in his throat. He keeps spinning and shouting Anya's name seeing nothing.

He stops.

He starts sidling to his right facing Will and Rosey's shop. He's moving north as it's only the end of town to the south. He sees the storefront. Sees Kate frozen and Will running out to look to the other side of town anyway. He sidles on peering into the only side alley the furniture store has. He catches the bottom hem of Anya's little dress. It's caught in the wind and fluttering in and out of his view. He sprints in the direction of it.

He gets to the *sight*. Anya's there, standing. She's silent, yet standing. Not upset in any way, just watching. As curious about whatever she's attending to as she was about that rocking chair when... Metro scoops her up into his arms turning her to face him.

"Anya! You're alright?"

"Yes," she says matter of factly.

Oh that dynamic! A father wanting to puke his guts out out of a worrying trauma as the object of which remains blissfully unaware she even induced it. Metro stifles the manifest shock. He's careful not to frighten the little girl. Looking at his sweetheart almost lost, his instinct kicks in. Instinct to preserve her innocence like it's a treasure far too easily squandered because it is. He does hug her tight though, feeling a pressure at his heart as he squeezes. He can't hold on forever. He lets go realizing the pressure felt was more tangible than first thought.

"Oh Anya!" Kate arrives. She immediately hands Vicki to Metro in that mama-papa shuffle where each have a child in arms then two seconds later they still do only it's a different child. Metro watches as a weeping Kate holds onto Anya kissing her endlessly. Anya winces and laughs at this at once. So much for downplaying the trauma... Metro also sees what caused that pressure against his chest. Anya has a small artifact in her hands.

"Baby, what is that you're holding?"

"From church."

She holds it out. It's the empty cross. Its size indicates it's meant to be displayed like by hanging on a wall. Kate looks at Metro with concern.

"Who gave that to you?" Metro asks.

"A man and a woman."

"Where?"

Anya points down the alley.

Incongruously though intentionally, Metro moves out of the alley toward the street, brushing past Will arriving. He moves down the street toward the south of town. Kate and Will follow.

As the edge of Shale comes into view, Metro sees a couple walking in a direction consistent with Anya's account. He leans in to his little girl in Kate's arms. "Anya who gave you that cross?" he asks. Kate pivots to ensure a glimpse of everything in the area. Anya points to the couple without hesitation. Metro hands Vicki off to Will.

"Kateryna, wait in store with Will and Rosey."

He jogs toward the couple.

HUSBAND GLANCES OVER HIS SHOULDER. He catches sight of Metro approaching. Mad Popa's just a few yards away. He tries hastening his wife along. The angry lawman just picks up the pace closing the gap. Metro circles around to the front of the couple noticing two more empty crosses hanging around their necks.

"Can we help ya *coss*—"

He grabs the husband by the hair on the back of his head and yanks giving the man's chin to the sky. Husband's wide-eyed, busting his eyeballs trying to see horizontal with a face held vertical. Trying to see the lawman that's got him. Man's wife's staring too, petrified. Metro puts his fingers into the man's mouth and appears to be rooting around. What he's doing is fixing his grip on that upper lip. He pulls it up. Gums are blue.

"Missionary work?" Metro asks. "Trying to get back in

good graces after your relapse?" He lets go of the man's head shoving it forward.

"Lost cause," says the man.

"Don't you talk about my daughter that way!"

Man shakes his head. Points to the west. To the church. "There's your cause *lost*," he says.

Metro's already marching in that direction.

HANNAH'S MOVED TO THE NORTH-facing side of her veranda just about to head over to the office. She's decided to linger a second like she used to in calmer times. She can see on down Main Street. She's hopeful for the first time in a long—

A scream!

WE'RE INSIDE THE CHURCH LOOKING at the door newly fashioned and installed. It's pristine with cross inlays routered into the walnut. Meticulous. It's a heavy door too. Not so heavy that...

BOOM!

Sheriff boots it open and starts pounding through the antechamber. Man intends a reckoning for the Pastor and his blue-toothed proselytes. But...

He's halted by a sight over the threshold of the nave..

He stares into the room wide-eyed. Goes pale.

A WOMAN IN HER WHITE Sunday finest—ain't Sunday by the way—has come stumbling down Main. She appears to be in a stupor. Dotty joins Hannah on the veranda having heard the first few screams. Cries of the bystanders continue as the woman lumbers. She looks like she's bleeding buckets out her mouth dripping down her already red-stained jowls and all over her top. Enough people continue reacting in a fear inducing a clamor. All others not moaning or screaming musta let their curiosity win out. Rosey Will Kate and the girls have stepped onto the front entrance of the furniture store to investigate.

The Mayor dashes out from her veranda toward town, Dotty following.

METRO SCANS THE CENTER OF worship. Supine automata permeate. They're not sleeping and they're not dead just splayed. Flesh automata that appear to have had the bottoms of their faces ripped off. Looks like a flophouse for victims of a dentistry gone medieval. Looks like it but Metro's read what this is.

One of the congregants' noses twitches, snorts. She rolls over catching sight of Metro and begins lifting herself, groping and leveraging against those nearest her. Agitation rouses groped congregants causing a chain reaction throughout the nave. All eventually get to their feet mumbling and groaning. Doesn't sound like they're in pain *more* lament. They're rotating and shuffling in place, none moving forward other than the Pastor. He comes stumbling through the crowd toward Metro dazed to hell with clear attention fixed on The Flying Cossack.

Congregants react to their Pastor like a switch is flipped. Their rotating and shuffling continues though not in place. All are shuffling toward Metro reaching out and clawing at the air as though coming to collect him piece by piece. *Just bolt for the door Met. Then they'd follow ya down the road. Who knows what trouble they'll find in town.* He grabs onto a large standing cross and rips it free of its moorings.

OUTSIDE, METRO SLIPS THE BOTTOM of the cross through the door handles barring the church exit. Who knows how long it will hold? The cross *is* solid walnut thinks Metro as he heads back to his family.

ROUNDING THE CORNER OF THE furniture shop he sees Doc Smart tending to the Red-Mawed woman. A confusing sight. He looks on to his left relieved to see his girls just observing everything from the boardwalk. He gestures for them to stay where they are as he hustles to join Hannah and Dotty standing a few feet back from Doc.

Doc's gotten the woman to lay on a blanket and is attempting treatment. He hovers a stethoscope not even in his ears all around the red stains on the woman's dress. The woman begins to writhe. She appears euphoric.

"Everything will be alright ma'am." Doc hands his stethoscope to his assistant suggesting he carry on the Doc's doing of nothing with it. He rises to consult with Hannah Metro and Dotty. "Physically she's fine," he assures. He points to the woman's chest. "That's not blood."

"I know," Hannah says glancing at Metro. This causes the Doc to tilt his head in some curiosity. The euphoric woman starts giggling.

"As odd as it sounds Miss Mayor, if I could make just a single diagnosis... Based on observation I'd say... She's drunk."

Metro interjects. "I have some worse news—"
SMASH!

Flesh Automata pour out of the church!

THE WOMAN IN HER SUNDAY finest was a longtime resident of shale. A spinster named Harriet McMurtle. Once admitted to a convalescence home in Rosa her good health returned just fine.

The church stumblers turned out to be an easy handle as well. The stupor affecting them left 'em menacing though otherwise uncoordinated. Metro Dep and a few good Samaritans were able to shepherd them back into the church nearly without incident.

Nearly.

A single stumbler managed to get a hold of Dep at one point and it was near impossible to break her free. Took four grown men to pry the single automaton off and not before her grip bruised Dep's arm to the bone. Stumblers turned out to be like porcupines. Slow and docile, but get too close…

There was a bigger problem than a need to perfect a method for corralling the stupefied church-goers however. Unlike Harriet, their good health didn't return.

Once the Pastor and his proselytes were sealed back into that church, the intention was to turn the hall of worship into a temporary hospice until everyone sobered up, exorcised their demons, or whatever else they had to do to get straight. Doc and his apprentice agreed to treat the congregants on the condition they'd be sufficiently restrained. They were.

They were penned into the nave by an elliptical wrought iron fence opening into a wooden cattle chute. The chute was used to trap a single stumbler for feeding and watering. Necessary, as they had to be force-fed until they were sufficiently sobered. The cow chute was also intended to allow for the releasing of those sufficiently sobered.

THERE WERE NO RELEASES. NO one was sobering. Jowls were dripping as much crimson as they were the day Metro busted in on them.

It wasn't until Doc went to the well out back to replenish his store of drinking water that he learned the source of the discoloration. Well water pumped out blood red. Hardly a bit more investigating revealed Harriet's well bled the same. Didn't take much epidemiology to figure out, since the only difference between stumbling townsfolk and non was the drinking of that blood, the drinking of that blood must have caused the stumblin'.

Finding the source of a problem solves the problem right? Wrong! How do you unspike a well? For that matter how do you ensure the problem not worsen? You didn't. And Shale couldn't.

See, Harriet lived about fifty yards off the south-west edge of town in a small cluster of houses closest the mine. Her well water was likely the first to turn along with the church's.

And I say *first* because the problem is indeed a progressive one. Half the town's well water's tainted now. They've already started a water ration to ensure the last of the untainted wells don't run dry. It was only a week ago that Harriet's and the church's turned. Just a matter of days before the whole of Shale's wells are blood.

Nobody knows how to stop it. They certainly don't know how to reverse it. They don't even know how to explain it.

· · ·

"IRON IN THE WATER!" SAYS *The Geologist* sloshing some of Hannah's well water around the dipper. He finishes observing whatever he's observing and sets it down on top the well. "The wellspring that feeds your town ran right around your mine. The dam's bursting flooded that wellspring. Now it runs around *and* through the mine. Groundwater's just *rinsing the vanes* as we say, taking the iron with it. Happens all the time. It'll dissipate." He tilts his head and his eyes bulge a little. I think he's trying to assure.

Not to digress but you ever meet one of those people who's always got the right answer for everything? Not because he's learned mind you, but because he stops you in the middle of your question to tell you what you're *really* asking and what you're *really* asking is always a question he has the answer to? Well...

"What are the—"

"Harms of consumption? None if you let the iron settle. I'd give the water about five minutes before drinking it."

"No. I was asking about—"

"The timespan for dissipation is anywhere from three weeks to six months."

"No." Hannah tries again. "The effects of drinking iron-rich water—"

"You want to know if drinking this water will help with iron deficiency? I wouldn't recommend it. The particulate is too heavy to serve as any kind of supplement. There wouldn't be any health benefits."

"Iron-rich water doesn't cause intoxication," Hannah says rapid-fire.

"Of course not!" The Geologist scoffs.

"This water does." She manages to get this out in one shot.

The geologist frowns. Purses his lips and sighs through

them. The pursing causes a slight flapping as the air releases. He doesn't have much to say when evidence contradictory to his hypothesis is on the table...

"Sometimes..." he tries. "When... Sometimes... Excessive iron in the blood—much the same as deficiencies of iron in the blood—can cause symptoms that mirror intoxication... *Aha heh.*"

"I thought you said the particulate's too heavy for any kind of supplement. Wouldn't that mean no accumulation of iron in the blood?"

That lip-flapping sigh again...

"It could be something in addition to the iron," he relents.

"And that's exactly what I was hoping you could help me identify."

"I'm a scientist madam. I don't divine answers from the ether. I'll need time to collect samples. Carry out the proper analysis—"

Divined that 'rinsing the vanes' explanation real quick! No wonder Burke gave you a two out of ten.

"Are you familiar with the troubles of Santa Rosa doctor?"

"Just what I've read."

"I've been reading up on it too. What little is known, one thing is certain. The townspeople were controlled through spiking the water supply with what they called *beet-boil.*"

Geologist scoffs again. "Now you know as well as I do beet juice is purple damn near black in a pooled state."

"And you know it's not really beetroot. They make it from some sort of flower. Saltwater's a more nourishing product. Too much of *The Boil* will give you visions they say. A little more, a near unbreakable thirst for it."

"Well this is not that."

"That's why I was hoping you could carry out that analysis—"

"I'm not a botanist madam."

"There are no bot—" Hannah changes tack. "By process of elimination doctor. A qualified geologist could rule out all earthen explanations leaving us with a smaller pool of explanations—"

"My my, a mayor who's also an expert in contrapositive deduction! Why even deign to request a vulgar positivist such as I contribute?"

"There's no need to be petty—"

"*Petty*? I prove what *is* discoloring your water and you want me to prove what *isn't*. All because of some hair-brained idea that no geological explanation will suffice, meaning you believe my geological explanation will not suffice! And I'm being petty!"

"I just fear your ideological immune system is at work here doctor—"

"*Ideological* what?"

"You seem to be favoring your first guess rather than exploring other possibilities. As an exercise, I used to encourage the schoolchildren to—"

"*Guess! Favoring!* Madam a geologist no more plays favorites with consistent *hypotheses* than he does grits of dirt in the road. My opinion is as expert as they come, so unless you're suggesting I don't come the same, this is my final appraisal."

"Though you admit your appraisal left room for something in addition to iron?"

"Not *that*! Height is dead and The Red-Eye gang disbanded!"

"Those looking to achieve the same ends could use their methods—"

"Copycats? Preposterous! What could they have to gain from a town on its last legs."

Hannah flushes. Grinds teeth a little. She eyes that dipper full of water no more settled than when The Geologist sat it down.

She picks it up.

"Want a sip?" She offers the dipper to The Geologist. "It's been five minutes."

"Uh... Hmmm... *Ahem*! Won't suit my hemochromatosis. Haven't yet had my phlebotomy."

Hannah isn't lowering the dipper.

Geologist relents. "I—If... And this is a general rule... I'm not endorsing your hypothesis... If you want to remove harmful impurities from water, boil it in heavy fabric before consumption."

Hannah lowers the dipper.

TOOK LESS THAN A WEEK for the rest of those wells to go. It was decided that Shale residents between the ages of 15 and 65 would drink the well water that had been boiled. Two fire wagons were purchased from Carson, care of Will Rosey and the Molybohas. Fresh water would be brought in on those wagons for children and the elderly. There was barely enough yet enough.

Local water tastes like laundry now, but there's been no more stumblin'. A little daze but no stumblin'. Only fabric to boil's in clothing and bedding so everyone's walking around Shale looking like a tangerine. Not stumblin' though. *Yet.*

17

SECOND OPINION

City's lost all its delivery contracts. Lost all its teamster contracts in general. Telegraph poles are still down and the burying of those lines has slowed to a crawl. Contaminated water's keeping everybody other than the children and the elderly in a perpetual state of mild intoxication. Mild at minimum. A few people eventually succumbed to stumblin' and had to be corralled at the church. Then a few more... Then more...

Rate was increasing and it was just a matter of time.

Drinking that laundered water's like trying to get off whiskey drinking nothing but beer. Church filled up in just a few weeks then the jail. A much larger wrought iron cage and cow chute was built by Dep Metro and Jon inside town hall. It won't fill up, if only because the hall's sized to hold all adults in the municipality!

At first the few automata present were given the kids' water in the hopes they'd sober up. There were three problems with this. First, once they sobered up and were let loose, they'd immediately go back to the unwashed well water. Second, the rate at which people were succumbing was too great for the clean water to keep up. Third, sobering up caused a withdrawal that was torturous. Anyone over 50 who attempted sobering almost certainly died. Shale lost six residents in the last two weeks to it alone. Church was filling up and all sober folk could do was keep the stumblers stumblin'.

Some of Shale remained stalwart. Mostly those who were stalwart from the very beginning of the degradation. In a selfless self-serving kinda way—as well as a selfless selfless kinda way—Metro and Jon rode off into Carson to get the kids' water along with multiple weeks' worth of undelivered mail. It was self-serving in that The Sheriff was sure the mail contained another package of clippings for him. Selfless in that he was desperate for that bundle to contain information on proving and curing beet-boil addiction. It was straightforwardly selfless selfless in that he was getting the vulnerable their water and everybody their mail.

The trip was largely uneventful. However, they travelled by day. About a dozen or so Shale folk had left for redder mud in the weeks prior on trips that would require camping in the night. They haven't been heard from since. It is hoped they arrived at their destinations safely and their not writing was due the assumption that no correspondence would arrive anyway. This is the hope, but have you ever known anyone to not put a postcard in the mail to at least try to allay a loved one's fears? Even if the allaying wouldn't come off?

THE RESEARCH CONTINUES. INDEED, ANOTHER bundle's arrived for The Sheriff in one of the lapsed mail drops. He's looking over them by lantern light again though this time in the Will and Rosey furnished comfort of his own home.

He's perpetually sipping at a cup of coffee too. A real balancing act as he needs the caffeine to keep up with the midnight oil while not overdoing it with the laundered water.

He's skimmed the bulk of the material and the only thing close to helpful in addressing Boil addiction is a botany paper. Paper's recently been republished to include an important addendum. Of course, Metro ain't a botanist. Kate kinda is, in an informal sense, but she's sleepin'. But Metro definitely ain't a botanist so he just jumps right to the article's conclusion like he's a goddamn tenured academic or something.

Conclusion

Though harmless in its natural or 'wild' state, duacubane root (DR) is highly toxic in concentration. Desiccated chemically separated DR can consist of upwards of 98% tropane alkaloids, lethal to humans at doses as low as 5 milligrams (due the presence of lopolamine). Though non-lethal in an ultra-dilute state, DR is known to cause severe hallucinations and euphoria. DR is highly addictive (IA rating of 18). The epidemiology of DR addiction suggests largely poor prognoses for sufferers. Withdrawal symptoms are offen lethal themselves and relapse occurs in near 98% of those recovered. To date, there is no intervention known to safely and effectively treat DR addiction and recovery.

Addendum: The Santa Rosa Anomaly

Though the epidemiology of DR addiction remains largely unchanged, it is worth noting the unprecedented recovery rate of the cohort known as 'The Santa Rosans'. Though only observational, subsequent physiological and toxicological assessments confirmed the average Addiction Severity Index rating for DR addicted Santa Rosans a mere 8 (comparable to severe caffeine addiction). Santa Rosans saw a whopping 99.67% success rat of treatment of their DR addiction. Although these outcomes wood not be possible without a pharmacological component to treatment protocols, to date, what pharmaceutical intervention/s contributed tooties results restrains unknown.

Metro's going to need another read-through of that addendum. He yawns. Caffeine's losing the fight. However, Shale's already lost if he can't get a lead on how to reverse the stumblin' fast. He tries again to comprehend:

Anddensum: The Satan Rose Inallamy

Dough the hippopotamology of DR aardvarktion...

His eyes blur a little. He shakes his head.
Some time...
He knows he stopped shaking his head about five minutes ago. The room doesn't seem to've figured it out. His kitchen window's jumping up and down.
"The addiction severity rating is only eight y' varmint!"
Did he read that? Or did the article read it to him?

SHOCK!

He hears a noise outside and goes to it. Instantly. He's outside now. Blink of an eye. There's a figure in the street.

It's that Shadow. The one that killed the Wilder. Just standing there hunched. Poised even? It *is* poised! In an instant it lurches upward whipping off any and all shadow. Shadow cloak is immaterial. It evaporates into the dark. To nothing. Red eyes are revealed and them eyes drip profuse. Figure's looking like he's intending something. He is. He bursts away! Makes a run for it into hell?

Metro floats after him. He floats after the disciple losing sight of him entering the woods. If only he could float higher than the few feet off the ground he is. He'd just spot 'em up on high. Bird's eye!

He's lost him. He's lost himself. He's deep in those woods. Seems that floating was a short-lived trick. His feet are on the ground again. No floating his way out of here. He can't discern a way out. He feels like he's sinking deeper with every step forward. It's all a sinking feeling in that direction so he tries backing up to avoid the swallow. Sinkiness of the earth has abated though the ground's still sponge. All-a-sudden he's stopped! Not by the marshmallow on which he treads but by something sturdy at his back. A tree? Can't be! He can't see the trees for the forest. He turns to assess the barrier only to trip falling backward into the awaiting sponge. The barrier looms. It's the Killer. The Shadow-turned-Red-Eye-Disciple. Back and snarling. Bearing ratty yellow teeth.

Then...

Plurality of disciples emerges from out original Red-Eye's back. One after another. There're three to each side of him in seconds fanning out in some weird wing-spreading recursion like the *Center* disciple's two mirrors facing each other. Recursion stops at ten offspring. Ten bearing down on The Sheriff with the same gnarled chompers as Center.

Sheriff ain't got his gun. Ain't got his wits either thanks the well water. Hell, he ain't even got his shoes. It's eleven Red-Eyes moving in on him pulling what appear to be serrated machetes from dried-up leather sheaths. Sheaths shred to nothing before machetes are half-drawn.

Bearing down and moving in, they cry those red viscous tears at him...

...They pounce!

CRACK!

Machete blades don't make crackin' sounds!

That's because no blade's been swung. A blonde bearded monolith has appeared out of nowhere toppling the disciple at the tip of Center's left wing. Did it with a smash from a moose femur! Before the other disciples can act, three more Wilders jump out the shadows. All grip those same calcified deer clubs.

Metro scoots back to clear out of the ring of the fracas. Despite his illusions, he derives Haidt's disciples not identical as they fight differently. Some can't fight the Wilders for shit. Four of them to be exact. First thing they do is break their machete blades swinging at them femurs like they're just asking for a ball-joint to the chops.

WHAP! WHAP! WHAP! WHAP! All four of the inept topple. That leaves six disciples against four Wilders. Remaining disciples know not to swipe their blades at them bones so they just poke and stab. Wilders just parry and dodge.

Two Wilders face each other at about ten paces. They're fighting a disciple each so proxemics determine those disciples' backs to each other. Disciples keep on with that poking and the Wilders keep on with that dodging until simultaneous to each other, each Wilder throws his club away. Just throws it away right on past the disciple he's facing.

Wilders didn't throw them bones to trash of course. They threw them at the backs of the heads of each other's opponent as them dummy Red-Eyes just stood there reveling in the upper hand they thought they had seconds before...

THUMP! THUMP!

Backs of both their heads get whomped by flying femurs. They're out cold.

Four on four.

Metro tries getting up to join, but the daze is still ringing his bell. Everything spins. He relents. Falls back. Just acts the spectator.

Four on three.

Four on two with all machetes busted.

Seems like no contest for the Wilders. Shouldn't be long now—

Scratch that! Three on two as Center's snagged a femur from one of the Wilders and cracked him unconscious. Center's swinging at the three Wilders as his last remaining wingman stumbles into him. Guy was just trying to help but... Center without a beat clocks his clumsy compatriot out cold. He sidesteps the wingman's crumpled body and welcomes the Wilders back to the fight. Remaining three move in.

Center sweeps the ankles of the closest, taking him down supine. Before the laid-up Wilder can even lift his head, Center puts him to sleep with a swing of the bone pendulum-like up his chin. Center hunkers to avoid the last two Wilders charging. They run past and while he's down there, Center swoops out the legs of one charging wilder then stands to face the other.

Upright Wilder turns, lifts his bone like he's gonna chop Center in two with it. Center jabs the Wilder in his nose blinding him in pain and tears then spins, femur extended, clocking him out cold. Center pulls this off just as tripped Wilder—now back on his feet and the last of his brethren in the game—shoves him from behind. Wilder picks up a discarded club and waits for Center to turn. Second the two are face to face they clash.

Clubs smash into each other like cutlasses in a dual. Wilder makes the mistake of trying for Center every few strikes while Center just focuses on smashing at the middle of his opponent's club. Wilder swings a desperate unbalancing swing horizontally as Center jumps back dodging it with ease. Center spins, bringing his club back-handed right into the middle of Wilder's. Grinds Wilder's bone to make his bread.

Weapon's dust so Wilder just dives right in! Pounces! Center knows the pattern. Third times *also* the charm with another ankle swoop. He takes the Wilder to his back.

Supine warrior stares up at Center. Stares up with an expression that says *won't be long now...* Center Red-Eye lifts his femur like an axe chopping only he ain't intending to split any log. He's looking to pulp a melon. Won't be long now...

SCWIPP! SCHLITCH!

An arrow pierces through the darkness. Arrowhead slices between the hamstring and kneecap of Center's legs pinning them together. He lets out one of the howliest most pitiable screams of pain you've ever heard, still holding that bone over his head with a grip loosening. Bone falls to the ground forcing Center to wave his arms overhead searching for a new center of balance. He's silent. The shooting pain has backed up into his lungs and crowded the air needed for screams anew. He twitches. He tries to be still as stillness is his only analgesic. Needs his balance for stillness but needs to move to keep his balance. Stillness hastens a tipping. Balance gives in to the paradox. Balance is forfeit. Gone. Center topples like a felled tree onto the Wilder below.

The archer slips out of the shadows, bow in hand, quiver at her back and some sort of sack slung across her shoulder. "Get up," the Wilder Queen orders her warrior still conscious. Conscious Wilder rolls the catatonic Center off him. He gets to his feet. He's hobbled a little. Queen approaches. Drops that pouch onto the ground letting it sit open on its flat waxen bottom.

Wilder and Queen immediately commence to pulling pig strips out of that pouch to bind the felled Red-Eyes. They bind the feet and legs of all but Center. His legs are still arrow-bound. They slap the other three Wilder warriors awake as they work past them.

Finishing the job, they move to our Sheriff still lost in his wooz. He can't move. Can't believe his eyes. The four warriors surround him. They squat down and grab hold.

THEY'RE CARRYING HIM SUPINE TWO-Wilders-by-two as the Queen of the Wildlanders walks on ahead. He hears her voice as he floats. *Understand that what we do in this Belt is no trespass. Your people use The Bark improperly. Even with our warnings. Understand that I can't say with certainty my son's actions were NOT a trespass. You didn't save his life lawman. You didn't take it either. You even sanctified him in death. Consider this a debt repaid.*

Something is slipped into Metro's moshonka. They

carry-on carrying him. They carry him to... His bed? How'd he get here? So fast? He feels as though he can't breathe a second. He swallows hard just before they toss him next to a sleeping Kate and...

BOOM!

Daylight.

He pops awake, the daze worn off completely.

METRO PEERS INTO A LITTLE circular mirror that sits atop he and Kate's chest of drawers. It hovers over a tin base bound between two forking strips of tin. Strips extend from the base allowing the mirror to swivel upward and down.

He tilts the mirror at all angles examining his face. He comes across as Morg Munson did last fall: that chafing at his chin. He succumbed to the stumblin' last night. Was one of those automata. No doubt about it. Yet here he is sober as the day he was born.

He grabs his latest bundle and stuffs it into his moshonka. He ties the pouch onto his hip and heads out the house.

HE WALKS ALONE. HE WALKS along the perimeter road to the south of Shale, dipping into the back alley before Main.

DOTTY'S LEFT HANNAH'S PLACE FOR the complex. Hannah follows the same path at present, it being about five minutes later. Less of a commute for Hannah so less of a need to head out early? Not really. Not when your clocking-in is the second you start worrying about the town you're expected to run. That is, the very moment her eyes pop open after the restless useless sleep she's been getting. She moves down Main toward her office.

Metro moves out the alley.

HE'S AT HANNAH'S DOORSTEP AGAIN dropping off more food for thought. He pulls the bundle out the moshonka. As it pulls free he feels something else leave the pouch. It was moved along by the bulk of the letters. The object flutters down Metro's thigh as it falls, before...

FLACK!

That clenches it. Something broad flat and solid hit the slats near the welcome mat. He leaves the bundle and starts looking around for what fell. Though barely noticeable against the brown of the decking, he sees a pasteboard envelope. He picks it up examining it real quick. Scrawled onto the envelope in charcoal is

T:I:I

He'll examine it further back at the office. Right now he has to finish what he's—

His finger feels a fibrous material at the flip side the envelope like a strand hanging out the flap. He turns it over. It is a strand hanging out the flap. Is that what I think it is? Quickly he lifts the envelope open looking at its contents. It's pure Bark!

A face of astonishment. "Geezus—"

A voice behind. "Not the type of economy to be entering the entrepreneurship... Especially when you've already got a cushy government job."

He stuffs the envelope into his moshonka. He spins to meet the voice.

"Mayor."

She moves past him to pick up the bundle at her doorstep. "We tried home delivery too remember? Didn't work." She opens the bundle more interested in its contents now than continuing the flippancy. Metro's just glad she ain't asking about that envelope. "Geologist laughed at me when I suggested the boil," she acknowledges.

"I thought you might laugh too. Something tells me I could have dispensed with the discretion long ago."

"So you don't believe our folk busting the church at its seams just victims of hemochromatosis?"

"I'd say not. Everything is consistent with that flower root." He points at the bundle. "You read you see."

"Not the wellspring rinsing the vanes?"

"No. Read."

"So where do we stand? Mrs. Burke's reined in The Council—at least up to Burke Sr's death. Even now Council'd never poison a town full of men marked for slave labor."

"They would not."

"Do you think they killed Burke?"

"I don't know. If so, they defied Burke Sr for the first time in the history of The Council. I can't imagine Mrs. Burke not smoking out betrayers and making them pay. However, I don't know—"

"Think Dotty did it?" Hannah don't want to ask but she said she needs to know where everything stands and she meant it.

Metro speaks cautiously. "Her only motive was Burke Jr second-guessing her. She's lionized him since. All but admitted he was gray eminence behind Lamour's latest innovations. Though I not confirm anything. And you know her better than I—"

"Not a chance she did it. Have dinner with us. You'll see."

"I don't suspect her Hannah. *Ees* just... The technical motive." He rubs his chin. Sighs. "There is another possibility."

"What is it?"

"In all honesty?"

"I can take it."

"I'm thinking more myself. That aforementioned laughter..."

"Then *you* can take it."

Metro lets her have it. "I think we have copycats. Of Haidt's Red-Eye Gang."

Hannah shudders. Words evoke in her the thing she thought lost. An image of the Proto Red-Eyes riding into Stemfield flashes before the mind's eye. Tom in his last moments. *Oh God.*

"...iss Mayor?" Metro's reaching out to Hannah with a look of concern. He makes contact with her shoulder, startling her out of her daydream.

"S—Sorry," she stutters. "I—I think it must be that boil. I guess we're all in a bit of a fog these days?" She chuckles still a little shaken.

Metro tips his brim despite not being soberer in weeks. What's he going to tell her? Some Wilders cured him in a dream? One outlandish revelation at a time.

"Copycats?" she asks.

"Red-Eyes not captured by Shawk are far too small in number. Dependent in every way on Haidt too."

"That's exactly the problem," Hannah adds. "You read what I read. No Haidt, no Red-Eyes. Copycats couldn't pull off a fraction of the mayhem."

"So, no Red-Eyes then?"

"Not necessarily."

Metro furrows his brow at the implication.

Hannah notices. "One outlandish revelation at a time Sheriff?"

He shrugs.

"Not the wellspring rinsing the vanes?" She gives the mundane one last try.

Sheriff smiles. Asks Hannah to take a walk with him.

18

HELP

P*lease respond if received STOP Anyone respond please STOP This is Shale City STOP Many residents ventured out in last weeks STOP Haven't returned STOP Rescue team sent STOP Hasn't returned STOP Desperate for help STOP Many sick STOP Many missing STOP*

THEY WALK TO THE CHURCH. Would look almost leisurely if not for the circumstances.

The pair approach Rosey. She's been standing guard at the church ever since Will went missing with the rescue party. If she couldn't leave after him she was going to direct her vigilance somewhere useful she figured.

She's wobbly like everyone these days. You can see the chafe accumulating.

"How are things Rosey?" Hannah asks.

Rosey tilts up in her wooz. She squints. There's some sort of realization. "H—Hannah... Picking the hen feathers..." Her head's bobbing up and down. "Adulterators you know..." Head bobs back down without rising. Hannah takes a hold of Rosey and pulls her close cradling her head to her shoulder. The Sheriff watches stone-faced. Stonier and stonier he's gotten the worse things get. The more things warrant breaking down and balling without hope the more he turns to that stone.

Sheriff moves to the start of the church's renovations. To the first few boards the fire failed to reach. He feels for the last few bucket-brigade-soaked white-washed slats not damaged enough to be removed in the rebuild.

Hannah notices. She sits Rosey down onto the steps, gently, and joins The Sheriff.

"Permit me ma'am?" he asks prying his fingers under one of those water-damaged slats. Hannah gestures in assent. "Your geologist claimed the well water turned red after the dam burst?"

"Yes."

THRATCH!

He tears off a good length of siding. He puts it over his knee lengthwise and...

CRACK!

Snaps it down the run of the middle over that knee. He reveals the center of the slat to The Mayor. It's dyed blood red to its core.

He points over The Mayor's shoulder.

"They put this out with that well water," he says. "The day *before* the dam burst."

. . .

METRO'S SPLIT OFF FROM HANNAH moving toward her office. He's continuing toward the jail when...

There's a rumble at their feet. Some screams in the distance. The pair stop in the midst of their respective trajectories. *What now? Dam's burst. Mine's soup. No clouds for any ungodly hail. Stumblers are locked away.* If this were cattle country it would have to be a stampede but ain't no cattle till the west end of The Belt. *What now?*

One of the children's water wagons. It's ripping around the corner at the north end of Main. It picks up speed at a tremendous rate. Unearthly! Who put the team on it? Who the hell's even driving it?

Metro gestures to Hannah's office suggesting she get inside. She moves. He braces himself as though standing semi-bowlegged and boots-planted is gonna stop a runaway wagon loaded down with three tons of water. Wagon ain't even moving straight but weaving. Metro sees everyone 'cept himself's gotten to boardwalks though it don't matter none. If that wagon weaves any wider it'll tear right through them walkways then them people.

He waves in futility. *Get inside!* All just stand staring as the wagon weaves wider and wider rocking the tank near over with each swerve. Team of horses just keep building up that centripetal sideways whipping momentum.

As the wagon gets closer Metro catches something. He pulls the brim of his hat down to cut maximal glare. Squints. Horses haven't taken flight though they have wings. Same beet-boil wings them confused cattle were brandishing back in Rosa. Horses look just as baffled. Truth be told they're near as easily confused an animal.

As the winged-beasts' swath whips back perpendicular

the street, the horses decide to keep on in that direction and barrel forward. They run as though possessed at speeds ethereal with a singular focus. The jail!

Team veers away at the last second. Hitch—already shoulda been kindling—snaps clean sending the horses running off down the boardwalk and the water wagon spinning smashing right through the front of the jail.

Hundreds of gallons of the children's water pour out onto the street turning the dry grit of Main to red slop. A couple of the stumblers in the first cage come washing out in the deluge. Cage musta smashed open the wagon and the wagon musta smashed open the cage in some sort of chicken or egg conundrum ending in a gizzard omelet.

Dep's come running from out of the saloon, meeting Metro at the jail.

"Did you see that?" he shouts in disbelief.

"Does it matter?" Sheriff grabs a lariat off a hitching. He tosses it to Dep who immediately ropes one of the stumblers.

"This way!" Sheriff waves on. Dep, his *Fettered* stumbler, and the *Unbound* stumbler move toward Sheriff. Unbound ambles up front followed by Fettered, driven by Dep's lariat.

Sheriff stops at the saloon hotel, maneuvers around Unbound. Shoves the stumbler a good ten feet away south and down into the dirt. He waits for Dep and Fettered to get closer.

"Hold him," Sheriff orders. Dep pulls Fettered still at about three feet of rope. Fettered reaches out for Sheriff. Fingertips nearly tickling his throat. "Hand me the slack." Dep throws the hoops of remaining lariat over Fettered's head and into Sheriff's hands. Sheriff sends that slack over the second-floor balcony flagstaff and grabs what dangles down at him. "Topple 'em!" Dep pulls Fettered down to back supine in the dust. "Hoist!" Dep runs to Sheriff-side of Fettered.

The two wrench on the slack. Dep leaves Sheriff to mind the rope a second so he can shove Unbound back a few feet. This buys the lawmen a few seconds. They continue the pull lifting Fettered up then off his feet and into the air dangling.

"Hold," Sheriff says. Dep grips the rope tight in both hands and The Sheriff lets go, taking the slack after Dep's grip. Deputy struggles a little trying to keep the stumbler dangling. Sheriff tempts Unbound back closer and closer. Close enough. He whips that slack around Unbound as many times as is needed then ropes him like a calf. "Now!"

Both lawmen let go of the rope. Unbound rises as Fettered lowers. Metro puts his hands under the feet of the slightly heavier Fettered to halt the displacement. The two lawmen get clear of the dingle-danglin' stumblers.

"I keep an eye on them. You check on the others. Bring back some shackles."

Dep runs off toward the jail as Metro does the tending. Really, all Metro's doing is looking down to the jail watching his babies' water turn to red mud.

WE'RE IN HANNAH'S OFFICE. IT'S just her and Metro. If Dep were here it would be all the officials left of Shale.

"It doesn't matter," Metro says. "One wagon remaining or none, who will be left to provide the children the water? This is our only hope."

Hannah relents.

METRO RETURNS HOME TO SEE Anya tending to Viktoriya, the

two girls playing on the kitchen floor. He approaches. Cautious.

"Popa!" Anya greets. Vikki smiles.

"Where is moma, Anya?"

"In the garden," the four-year-old says pointing.

"Have you been fed?"

"Before moma went into the garden."

"Do you know how long she's been outside dove?"

The child thinks a second. Resolve. "As long as Alice's Adventures."

Metro ponders this too. Realizes, "When I read you and Vikki the story the other night? That much time?"

"Yes."

He gets a slight look of melancholy. Feels a tightening grip at his throat. He scoops the girls up into his arms and carries them toward the back door. He can't help holding them tight, cherishing the few Alice's Adventures he has left with them.

He walks them out to see moma in the backyard. To say goodbye. The stone in him is crumbling. His eyes well as he approaches Kate. The girls are confused at this side of him. His vision blurs. He can barely see his beloved tending her garden. He blinks out the tears.

"My love I—"

She turns. She's automata.

The blood drains from the lower half of her face.

The girls scream. Metro falls to the ground, his sight washed out again. He lets go of everything. This is that hopeless balling... Vikki sits crying too but Anya moves toward her moma, the little girl's confusion compounded. A push of love. A pull of fright. She's within grasp of the groping growling witless Kate, arms outstretched in a grotesque empty welcoming of the girl. A clawing from moma.

"M—Moma w—what is wrong?"

Anya enters her moma's arms.

Popa wrenches her out.

"No baby."

He moves away. Both girls in his arms.

"Moma!" Anya screams.

"Moma's not well. She needs time to rest."

THE WAGON IS NEAR LOADED with the children. They only have room for the youngest and oldest of Shale. Metro will drive. The only Shale resident to return. He sits with Anya on his lap trying to calm her, hoping the trauma not so severe she won't recover. He sits next to The Smiths, a couple in their late seventies. Mrs. Smith holds Vikki. Vikki's contented and Metro's fooling himself into believing she will stay that way.

In back in the wagon proper, the elderly tend to the children. They try their damnedest though the elderly are tired and the children scared. Many of the parents aren't there to see them off. They've succumbed to the poison long ago. Some haven't yet succumbed but are too witless to understand the severity of the situation. This only confuses the traumas the children experience losing them. The lucky ones have parents to leave heartbroken wailing at the side of the wagon holding onto little hands in grips broken in precious seconds.

Maria stands next to Metro looking up at him. She promises to take special care of Kate. Metro asks if she's doing the same for Jon. She shakes her head.

"Good. We promised. Everyone must be treated the

same or else last of us will have no reason not to submit to favoritism."

He sets out.

THERE'S NO LOCATION THAT WAGON can get before nightfall. Not that it matters. Shale residents who went missing last rarely had a need to camp or travel by moonlight and they disappeared all the same. At least by daylight there's a chance of seeing it coming. Sun'll be set in an hour over that wagon. Maybe the day'll last a fraction of a tick more what with the wagon heading west chasing after the light. More light will be granted too due the fact that Metro will not stop.

Anya sleeps between Mr. and Mrs. Smith. Vikki sleeps in Mrs. Smith's arms. Mrs. Smith sleeps on her husband's shoulder. Children in back have calmed too and most are resting. Mr. Smith doesn't sleep. He sits taking things in. He takes in everything with an awareness so effortless it borders on clairvoyant. Earlier on and only naturally, Anya didn't want to let go of Metro making it difficult to steer. It was Mr. Smith's telling Anya what bird or what other beastie was coming up around the bend or over this-hill-or-that that got her calmed and eventually settled. Smith could tell the animal by the call or the chirp. Some of the time, I swear, by the rustle alone! He could call them back too. He'd call and there the bird would fly or the prairie dog would pop. He let sing with this bellow sounded half like wood creaking and half like a bull getting kicked in the testicles. Made all the kiddies roar with laughter. And yet Mr. Smith swore to 'em all, said on the way back there'll be a bull moose chasing a cow. *Mark my words* he said *it'll be there when we come home.*

He got quiet after that.

He's been quiet for a time. Though, as the sun gets lower there's less for him to see.

"They call you *Galician* Mr. Molyboha," he says, breaking the silence. "However you ain't are you? You're from a... Pardon me... Kate told me once. Sounded like *Carson* though not our Carson."

Metro feels a certain pang of somethin' at this. He'd like to think himself a humble man. Stoic too. Not a man needing attention praise or affirmation. Yet he's also aware he's barreling down the road to ruin for all he can tell having lost Kate to the boil trying to deliver these people—his girls—their salvation and he don't know what he needs right now but that pang's told him he needs something. That pang's told him he got it too. It's Mr. Smith's iron trap of a concern for the particulars of his homeland that's made him feel... Welcome.

"Pronunciation is close enough," he answers. "And that is my origin. All my life."

Mr. Smith nods. Grins. "You joke, yet you bring up an interesting point about the facts of our ways our residency and our nativity. We can stop practicing our ways. We can change the place we call home. We can't change where we're from. Not originally. I take it you meant the latter idea because you say *all your life*, though you may also have meant a conscious decision to never lose a grip on your ways."

Metro smiles. "You're right to attribute the latter to me, though if you were describing my wife you'd be right to attribute the former."

"I'm sorry about Kate," Smith laments. Metro goes stone. Smith notices this too. "I—I only ask about your heritage as I saw in an Atlas where Galicia was and I remember Carson. It wasn't in Galicia."

"No. Much further east. To the south as well."

"And yet they call you all *Galician*. Especially up north."

"That they do."

"Can I ask…" he pauses for permission.

"I imagine you can."

"Why put up with it?"

"I have nothing against Galicia."

"But the camps…"

"No camps in Shale."

"You know what I mean. It's not exactly a term of endearment and it's just plain wrong on the facts."

"Well, if Shale ever tried to put me in a camp then maybe I complain. If they ever try to put my wife, m—my daughters, in camp then I more than complain."

He pauses at a crunching sound. Scans around.

"Mule deer," Smith says.

Metro feels a relief. Sees Mr. Smith is waiting for closure on his point. There's that *welcome* again.

"I don't care about their words," Metro continues. "I care about what word is vehicle for. Disagreeable words that don't betray ill-intent or ill-will are immaterial to me. Agreeable words that manage to betray such ills… Those words make me wary. They are very common these days."

"And disagreeable words that betray ills?"

"At least I see ills coming."

"Makes sense." Smith appears to have realized something. Appears a little discouraged. "I don't know that I could stand up for myself if there was a need like you mention. You and your missus though," he livens a little, "now that there's a kettle of a different brass—"

Metro veers abruptly. He steers the wagon north into the head of a dry ravine. The jostling is only a little more intense than some of the more potholed stretches of road, so the passengers are minimally disturbed. All except Mr. Smith. In keeping with pattern, he's more than aware.

"I thought we were going to Carson, Sheriff."

"We must go where no one can know. Where they cannot follow."

"What if they need to rescue—"

"There will be no one left to rescue you."

"Then why couldn't you have told 'em?"

"Because there will be people *only* they will not find you to rescue you."

Mr. Smith's head lowers. He understands this too as he's crestfallen. "Won't they have followed us from town—"

"Yes."

THE CARRIAGE RUMBLES ON ALONG the dry riverbed, flanked by the ravine's high steep cutbanks. Sun ain't quite set though it might as well be snuffed. Ravine's put the escapees into a hole hiding all remaining sunlight behind the east cut. The carriage continues on.

"Do you hear that?" asks Mr. Smith.

"What is it?"

"You feel it?"

"No."

Metro fights the urge to slow the cart to better assess. Wouldn't make a difference to the coming force anyway.

"A rumbling from the tops of the valley walls." Mr. Smith's searching around in all directions.

"Be brave Mr. Smith."

Smith realizes Metro's implicature. He calms himself so as to not cause any further agitation but... "They're all around us Sheriff."

"Be brave. For the children."

The rumbling swells.

BOOM! BOOM!

A pair of blasts from behind the wagon. All riders startle awake. Rocks and dirt tumble down the banks completely barricading the entire of the riverbed behind. There will be no passage there. The rumble continues to swell despite the geology having settled.

Children can't help but whimper. They're trying to move to see. The elderly do the same.

"Be brave! For the children!"

The Smiths hold onto Anya and Viktoriya. They begin to pray. They put their empty crosses into the girls' tiny hands and clasp their own around the babies'. Smith reaches out to the crucifix at Metro's chest and holds onto it too. Be brave. Then...

Men on beasts of horses easily five hands higher than any Clydesdale pour out the tops of the ravine edges. They swarm toward the wagon. The old folks are petrified. The children are balling.

Metro tries for calm. "It's ok."

The massive blonde warriors atop their massive steeds flow in and ride majestically at pace the residents of Shale. The rumble of the hoofs is tremendous. This might be cause for greater fear in the passengers but the surreality of it has them stunned.

Lead outrider moves up alongside The Sheriff. Sheriff tilts upward at him. Rider tilts down to the lawbringer. His eyes narrow at the Smiths and the children.

"All are well?"

Metro flicks the brim of his hat. "I never got a chance to thank you," he says.

Wilder Warrior puts a palm the size of a Derby brim on Metro's shoulder. Shakes a *you're welcome* into him.

"Any chance you see Shale folk in the wilds?"

"You're missing people too?" the Wilder asks.

"Yes."

"We haven't seen. We suspect south of our lands between Shale and the territory lines, that's where they were taken. We are not as welcome in the tame as you however. You know better the state."

Metro has a look of accord.

Wilder lightens. "Your pursuers. The men with the eyes. They can no longer follow."

Metro lets out the deepest of sighs. *Thank God!*

THE WAGON ARRIVES AT THE intended destination. The Wilder escort breaks away and rides off back to their homeland and outta the tame.

It's a huge fort. Fifteen-foot high walls of bound poplar logs with rampart design. People mill about along the walkways above though it isn't clear if they're operating in any kind of guard capacity.

Metro moves toward the large gate glancing up at the nebulous figures atop the wall. He hammers onto the right of a pair of immense swinging doors. He uses his forearm since the rap of his knuckles would never announce him.

CREEEK! Go them gate doors.

"Metro Molyboha!" shouts Reeve Johnson. He's as boisterous as anything as his bohemians move in to welcome the children and help everyone carry their belongings. Reeve wraps an arm around Metro and leads him over the threshold.

Children of the RM await the children of Shale City as children do. Apprehensive and indifferent to the ceremony of it though curious and receptive to new friends. It's late for them if not by much. The Reeve's people guide the newly arrived children into the circle and bring the elders to some seats.

"How was the trip?" asks the Reeve.

"Largely uneventful thanks to our escorts," Metro responds.

Reeve leans in for some sort of aside. "The Queen there?" he asks in all seriousness.

"I don't believe so."

"Ahhh!" Cap leans back genuinely disappointed like he's missed out on something by proxy.

They sit themselves at a picnic table next to the palisade. Two of the Reeve's people bring the men a pair of wooden tankards and begin filling them with water. Metro observes the clear substance with interest as it pours. He looks to his girls playing. That stoicism falters a little. Eyes blur.

"I could offer you something a little fancier Sheriff. You need only—" Metro turns back to Cap, a noticeable redness in his eyes. "I—I forgot Metro." Cap's sentimentalism's shining through his aloofness a little too. "Despite our reputation around here, there's nobody more nurturing than a Rural Shaler. They'll be well taken care of."

"Thank you," Metro says. "I'm not sure how Shale City could ever repay you."

Cap don't miss a beat. "One man's poison is another man's pleasure..." Metro stares at him in puzzlement. Cap grins. "Shoulda brought me some of that boil Sheriff!"

Metro shakes his head. Teetering on aback. He considers the swath of the man across him. Is he kidding?

"That stuff will send you around the bend," he warns.

"It better!"

"It's horribly addictive."

"You don't know the RM, Metro! Boil'll grow dependent

on us before we ever grow dependent on it. Hell, they used to ween us off the tit with the beet-boil!" Metro can't help chuckle a little. Cap goes a little somber a second more. Lucky to get any seriousness out of him at all... "We're of a different constitution around here. But we have our priorities straight." He gestures over to the children.

Metro's appreciative.

Apropos of everything, Anya comes running to her father with another child in tow.

"Popa, this is my new friend Theodore." Anya shakes Theodore's hand as she says this trying to get a handle on social custom.

Theodore starts shaking back and says to Cap, "Daddy, this is my new friend Anya."

The lawman realizes. Cap winks.

Metro's attention goes back to his daughter and Theodore. "Nice to meet you Theodore. You and Anya go play a little longer. But Anya, it is already past bedtime."

"A little longer Popa?"

"A little."

The pair run off to rejoin the others.

"Don't worry," Cap guffaws. "Teddy's a real charmer like his daddy but his decorum is impeccable just like his mama."

Metro chuckles then finishes his water thirstily. Before his tankard is even lowered it's getting refilled.

"Thank you."

He surveys, sees all the health. Even in its best days he'd never seen half this vivaciousness in Shale City.

"How'd your people take the loss of the telegraph services?" he asks.

Cap shrugs. "Hell, when everything ya do is cash-in-hand and whatever else the land provides... Didn't really put a dent in us."

"Not even the people new to the RM?"

"They were so close to Shale City they were basically yours."

"*Ours*?" Metro asks.

"They weren't living in *our* neck of the woods."

"They weren't?"

"Did I imagine that?" Cap puzzles a little.

"Imagine losing a hundred residents?"

"Maybe I dreamt it?" Metro's losing Cap. Cap angles his head up and away, contemplative. "I imagine them folk disappearing?"

"Imagine an absence?"

"You got a point Metro. I usually see things that aren't really there. I don't tend to *not* see things that really are." Cap appears to be seriously trying to figure things. Resolve. "Hell, I'd talk to Li'l Dotty Lamour about that. How many'd she say she lost?"

"That's the problem. She lost everybody shortly after the lines went down and it's been too dangerous to account for them."

"Hmmm. I guess I'll say this much for the RM. We're one part communal one part private at once. If yer not built for that ya tend to just leave. No ceremony. If ya are and ya want to light out nonetheless, you just leave. No ceremony. No ceremony when anyone leaves the RM."

"I see."

Cap nods. Then scoots himself backward in his chair. Slaps both his knees. "Whelp! My brain is shutting down on me as you can probably tell. I'm going to take my leave and let you spend those last precious hours you have here with your little ones." Cap stands. Wobbles a little.

"Thank you for everything Cap."

"Already said that," he fires, trying to hide that sentimentalism again. "You stop those fugitives and we'll bring your babies home." Metro's taken aback. Cap notices—as much as Cap has ever noticed anything in his life. "Oh I know all about them runagates giving you the trouble," he says gravely. "Knew by the look in your people's eyes. Know that look well. You're standing in the asshole end of the West Brandon Trail. Where Shawk sent all them folk meant to die in the town that would be them runagates' last. He saved those people's lives sending them here."

"Sounds like you did."

"Bah!"

He wanders off.

METRO SPENT THE REST OF the evening and as much of the following day with his daughters as he could. If they had their moma with them they would have been more contented than they'd ever been in months. But they didn't have Kate and the frequency with which Anya asked for her didn't abate. The girl knew in a way more of the heart than of the mind that moma needed more than rest.

Metro hated himself for leaving his girls and he hated himself more for lying to them about coming back. *Popa's only going to work like I do every day* he lied. He left a teary-eyed Anya and a Vikki too young to understand. Vikki was at least blessed to be soothed by the mere presence of her older sister. But Anya watched him through that familiar teary-eyed blur, standing steady not moving until popa dipped off over the horizon vanishing completely.

He hated himself for lying to them like he had but they were going to survive all this. Be truly happy in time.

He won't be back to this place but they'll be happy here.

19

———

NO ONE

Metro's returned.

Riding into the north end of Main he sees a few stumblers are out and unaccounted for. They haven't escaped. They just haven't been rounded up. It's only stumblers on the street. Sufficiently docile stumbler's, though Metro's still careful not to agitate them. He notices the defacement too. The graffiti that had been emerging over the weeks is now everywhere. It started as the half-gibberish of a bunch of discontented drunks and's metastasized into the all-out-gibberish of the stumbler. How they even hold a brush or bucket of tar?

Town's crumbling. Stone façade of the bank is falling away. Siding of the General store is near completely ripped away.

Sheriff knows what he's read and he recognizes these signs. Yet the almost-certain cause of these signs ain't at the fore of his mind just yet. First third of his trip back he wasn't sure if anything other than Kate and the girls could ever take that fore.

Somewhere among the noise of the mental screams a single name.

HE WON'T GO TO HIS home. Not until it *is* home. He's checked the jail and although completely unmanned, the stumblers are still in their cages. He stands in the town-hall-turned-prison. It's unmanned too though the wrought iron and the cow chute are holding.

Among the crowd of automata she emerges. She's gaunt. Gray save for the poppy chafe. She sashays slightly while she spins. She spins almost as a means of propulsion though there's otherwise no life left in her. When he thinks she's caught sight of him he waves. It's as though he's driven to do so of some bygone impulse. She faces him for the half-second her rotation allows. He swallows hard like he's swallowing his whole throat. She spins away.

SOMEWHERE AMONG THE NOISE OF the mind screams a single name...

"HAIDT! CAN ONLY BE!" HANNAH'S shouting this through the wrought iron come to surround her Queen Anne. Dotty stands close to Hannah. Hands on her shoulders consoling her. Gesture seems rote at this point.

"Haidt is dead ma'am. However, his men—"

"You agreed we'd push this. This is where it's taken us. This is his handiwork. Like a goddamn artist about it down to the last brushstroke! You tell me. Is this a forgery?" She gestures all around.

He does look where she gestures. Then back through the

compound bars in which Hannah Dotty and Dep stand. Are they all that's left? The wrought iron is makeshift though seems durable.

"What are you drinking in here ma'am?"

"Oh what the hell ya think!" she screams. She stifles. She stares downward. "Sorry," she offers meekly.

"*Ees* okay."

"I—I'm just... I'm not crazy Metro. I—I'm just... I'm just mad to all hell is all!"

And she is! He saw it the second he got to within sight of her compound. Her standing solemn waiting for him. However, there's a last test. Is this really resolve in her or has she lost her wits? Her righteous anger notwithstanding...

"What would you have me do Hannah?"

"If he can do this to Rosa right under them folk's noses then surely he can fool the right folk into believing he's dead."

Definitely got her wits. What she says is true, yet how?

"He went from that train to a hanging rope to nothing in between," Metro offers.

"He went into that train wearing that mask of his. A lotta other men were on that train too, in the dark t'boot. He left that train wearing a face nobody'd ever seen in the dark or the light."

Definitely got her wits.

He tips his brim. "I will ride out though not before tending to you. Who else is here?"

"You're looking at us," Dep says, approaching.

"If you continue to drink that poison you'll turn and you'll only have caged yourselves in with stumblers not fenced any out."

"What do you propose?"

"I saw our last water wagon still intact. I fill it and bring food. Then you all hunker down."

Hannah realizes something. "What about the marauders? How'll— How'd you avoid them?"

"I am blessed," he jokes. A joke that swings from the gallows.

"*Blessed,*" Hannah chuckles. Focuses in the direction of his home. "I'm sorry that everything happened this way Metro."

"It's not over yet." He takes his horse by the reins and prepares to mount. A pause. "Anyone other than me is an ingratiator. Let no one in except me."

He rides.

SHERIFF DON'T KNOW WHERE TO begin. Everything he's done playing Pinkerton man up to now has been about seeking objects immediate to his hypotheses. Church water pump might have explained that red shirt, so he went to the church pump. The Council telegraph poles might have explained the absence of Council technicians at Burke's hanging, so he went to them poles. Them slats might have confirmed the well water red, which would explain the red shirt, so he went to them slats. Haidt's unobservable presence might explain the state of Shale, so he'll go... Where?

Now you see the nature of the problem.

So far any evidence of Haidt attacking Shale is evidence of a competent imitator doing the same. Sheriff needs a piece of evidence that could only exist if Haidt was truly the culprit. Yet, he knows if Haidt *was* at the center of all this, the miscreant's first move would be to deny any such evidence.

Absence of evidence is evidence of presence? Technically *it is* given the assumed modus operandi, which is a pretty dogshit clue if you ask me as you'd have it the same whether Haidt were alive or dead. Can't look for the man's *effect* Metro concludes. Can only look for the *man*. Search for Haidt alive or dead? Guess'n so.

It's a manhunt.

Lucky for The Sheriff, he read in the Pinkerton Manuals how to proceed in these cases. First, talk to the folk who're last to see the subject. Subject's supposed to have been alive at that point a' course...

Shit. What the hell am I even doing?

He feels like he'd have more luck going around flippin' the hats off every man he passes lookin' each one of 'em in the eye and confirming *not Haidt not Haidt not Haidt not Haidt...*

He rides on.

THE ROUTE TO CARSON TAKES him past the mine and those stone statues of guards minding it. Presumptuousness in a Council uniform. Only ever standing among all the chaos and insidiousness. Never moving. Wouldn't need to either they're so over-armed. Even a single of their mounted Gatling guns would shred a Belt's worth of Red-Eyes in seconds. Not that the Red-Eyes would ever just walk up directly. Not their style.

Two hours of daylight left and Sheriff needs a hint. A hint as to how the forceful arm of the bureaucrat could just stand minding the bureaucrat's presumpted property through the whole of Shale's decline.

He swerves in and rides up to the gate.

The two men working the entrance eye him warily. Surely they know him by the badge and their briefings?

They don't budge but their posture's attack-ready out of bed in the morning.

"Step aside men," says a third guard.

The first two clear the gate. One of them opens a padlock latching a chain that binds the swinging door. Lock clicks open and the two ends of the chain fall to the side. Guard pulls open the gate a crack and his *Boss* exits. Boss walks over with a noticeable limp like he's favoring his hip. He's a bit past middle-age so he couldn't have gotten as far along in this job as he has without his share of scraps. The mere fact he's survived this long makes him ideal leadership material too. That said, fact that he's leadership material makes him officious unwavering and petty? I guess we shall see.

"Can I help you Sheriff?" he says, cold.

Sheriff leans forward in his saddle. Lays his hands criss-cross over the horn. "You men realize Shale is in collapse?"

"Your trouble's are why we're here."

"Never thought of coming to our aid?"

"We're here to maintain viability."

"*Viability*? Mine is destroyed. Shale nearly the same."

Boss stands silent.

Of course they would... Sheriff shakes his head. "Brave protectors. Keeping the peasants from stealing the ashes of the altar."

"Altar?"

"The altar The Council is praying burns itself whole again."

Boss gets curt. "Sir, our jurisdiction is The Council's property only."

"My jurisdiction is the municipality in which you stand like cowards as Shale burns."

Boss stiffens. "We gonna have a problem here Sheriff?"

Sheriff relaxes more. "Eventually."

Boss backs up. He and his two lackeys put hands on holsters. Off the way those twin Gatling guns swivel inward and down, vanishing point of their twin trajectories on Sheriff.

He waves off the gunmen. "Our people who left haven't been heard from since. That means these lands are almost certainly crawling with marauders."

"We ain't seen nothin'," says a lackey.

"Quiet!" orders Boss not dumb enough to be so cocky. "Kinda marauders?" he asks in genuine interest.

"Kind like shadow. The kind you never see coming unless they want you too. Where then, it's too late."

"Scary tale," Boss scoffs. "But there ain't nobody who can hide in them shadows from us."

Guess he is *just* dumb enough to be this cocky...

I didn't say IN the shadows. "Don't look for the dark in the shadows boys. I don't imagine you'd be willing to harbor any of our survivors?"

"Not a chance sir."

Sheriff exhales. Doesn't sigh, just exhales. "Well, night is coming quick. It will be even more dangerous then. I go."

Boss just turns and walks back to the gate. One of his lackeys spits.

ROUTE TAKES THE SHERIFF PAST the collapsed dam too. Another dilapidated structure of The Council's. Useless and also minded by the same men in Council uniforms. No need to stop. It'll only be the same exchange and the less Metro has to travel by lantern before Carson the better. He just continues ferrying himself along the now tripled width of Rubrum River.

· · ·

HE'S ARRIVED IN CARSON AND'S now wondering *how the hell do you carry out a manhunt for a man who for all intents and purposes is dead and buried up on a hill?* For one, you could prove the man really up on that hill. Then you've found him and hunt's over. Of course, there's no way Pettimore Swade would ever press the coroner to exhume the corpse of a man he unlawfully hanged. And neither does The Sheriff wish to involve Swade in any of this until absolutely necessary. If at all.

Protocol Metro. Talk to the last to see the man hunted.

He takes in the expanse of Carson City.

What the hell are ya even doing? Might as well try the hat-flipping trick...

SHERIFF WALKS THROUGH THE SMALL front yard of The Carson Mortuary. He passes some rows of caskets turned on their ends. They lean up against each other piling back toward the front steps. He ups those steps and knocks on the door. A man who must be the town's *Undertaker* opens it a crack.

"Yes... *Officer*?" He's guessing at what Metro's badge must mean.

"*Sheriff*. Of Shale City."

Undertaker's eyes widen. Rightfully so. "S—Sheriff Molyboha! It's very... It's very late."

"I apologize. I'm hoping to take little of your time."

"I must admit Sheriff, considering what's been happening in your town, I take it I'd be remiss if I didn't at least let you explain your reason for calling."

Metro flicks his brim in appreciation. "I'm carrying out an investigation into the recent unfortunateness you alluded to. I'm following up on a possible connection to—" He falters a little. Gotta be careful about what of the subject matter he betrays. Can't just blurt out that he's hunting a man he thinks may have faked a hanging burial or both—all in the law hub of The Belt! "T—to the passengers who arrived in the jail car last Aug—"

"Haidt's car. You wanna know about that off-the-books hanging."

"In a sense. Really, I'm seeking information about what happened after—"

"Pardon me Sheriff," the Undertaker interrupts again, short. "Has Marshal Swade permitted this investigation of yours?"

"In all honesty, I haven't spoken to him yet—"

"Come in."

The Undertaker moves aside, holding the door for Metro to enter.

HE GLANCES AROUND THE LARGE open-concept home. The entire first floor is solely for business purposes. There are many lab tables and work benches with bottles of chemicals atop them. Some variety of instruments are present as well as filing cabinets a desk and desk organizers. There are, of course, a number of examination tables too.

Something strikes the Sheriff as anomalous. There're no discernible smells other than what you'd find in a house of this build. He doesn't realize it, but he's been sniffing since he was invited in.

"Don't worry Sheriff," the Undertaker assures. "There are no cadavers here at present. I wouldn't have permitted your entry if there were."

"Thank you."

"Shale's a small town," The Undertaker begins in slight intimation. "But after what you've experienced, I wouldn't have taken you to be wary of death."

"It's more—" Metro shakes his head. "It doesn't matter. Could I ask you a few questions about the dead prisoner?"

Undertaker gets a look of impatience. "Sheriff, pardon me for my forwardness, but with all we've been hearing about your town and with you all but confirming it, no one would think you crazy if you just came out and said you don't believe that hanged prisoner Haidt. Only one who really believes it is Swade anyhow."

Sheriff chuckles in some relief.

"One other particular to get clear on," the Undertaker adds. "It was dead *prisoners* plural. Two."

"Two from that car?" Metro asks in surprise.

"The prisoner hanged and a prisoner who died in transit of severe alcohol withdrawal."

Metro's eyes close. He's running every possible tale he can tell after adding this new fact to the old. Nothing useful comes to mind. No new theories. He's trying to subtract a death after all, not add another. Better keep probing.

"Was there anything unusual about this prisoner?"

"Busted jaw."

"You mean Haidt?"

"No. I should have clarified. The drunk."

"Both? They both had a broken jaw? You didn't find that strange?"

"I found those men the product of their handler."

"Swade?"

Undertaker is silent.

"I can assure you I don't work for Swade," Metro says.

"Every lawman in this territory does one way or another."

"Then permit me to tell a story where all you have to do is amend or not?"

"I—I think I can abide that," the Undertaker agrees.

Metro continues. "Particularly rambunctious prisoners on that car, with a particular lawman supervising it, frequently leave with broken jaws. It is as though that injury the trademark of this particular lawman. Conversely, when that lawman's not in supervision, the prisoners never have such injury. So, whenever this lawman is on board, it would not be unusual to see a broken jaw, maybe two or more." Metro looks the Undertaker in the eye. "Care to amend?"

Undertaker's silent. Metro continues his inquiry.

"May I see the personal effects of the drunk prisoner?"

"I got them. Though a darn underwhelming lot if you ask me." Undertaker moves to a stack of drawers of a desk organizer. He waves Metro over as he starts pulling out different drawers hoping to find the right one. "Bear with me. It's been quite some time since I've done an inventory." He keeps pulling yet can't seem to find the drawer at issue.

Metro watches as all the belongings of people-deceased appear and disappear. With each drawer opened and each drawer closed it's a glimpse at the last vestiges of them people-gone, plucked from them as though the spoils of persistin'. In all of them drawers, one after another, a host of items last to touch the dead just sit. Metro feels an unease.

Undertaker gives up and goes to a manifest on his desk. He starts flipping through it. Satisfied, he closes it and moves back to a drawer that must have the correct index. He doesn't just pull it open but all the way out of the slot. He carries it over to an examination table.

"Like I said, a paltry lot if ya ask me."

"I didn't," Sheriff answers with a hint of disgust. "Quite the collection you have…"

The Undertaker puts the drawer down on the slab abruptly, gestures in sharp waves that The Sheriff may now peruse at his leisure.

Sheriff finds only a cracked monocle, brass cufflinks, and a bottle of Dauphin Rye with a half-ounce remaining. Paltry maybe, though there's something about that rye that strikes him as interesting. He holds up the mickey bottle and swishes that half-ounce around.

"This exactly as you found it?" Sheriff holds the bottle out to the Undertaker.

"It is. Why do you ask?"

"You ever know a drunk to leave just a single sip at the bottom of a bottle?"

"Can't say that's ordinary, no."

"Said he had the shakes," Sheriff insinuates. "How'd you know?"

"Jailers said it."

"He have any of the usual bruising on him?"

"Nah."

"You'd notice?"

"I tend to keep account of things like that."

"Why?"

"A courtesy," the Undertaker says, hint of indignation. "I'm not the last to see them alive. However, I am the last to see them before the funeral dollin'. Kin sometimes want to know how their loved ones were at the last, before being readied for the casket. *They seem at peace?* and all." He eyes the Sheriff now. A seriousness. "Kin don't appreciate me lying or mincing words."

"They tip better for the truth, hmm?"

"Wouldn't take it if they did." Undertaker says this as though maintaining dignity.

"Yet you make a habit of pilfering the dead?" Sheriff holds up a cufflink.

"I make a habit, sir, of holding onto a man's affects for twelve months to the day. Then I do with them affects what I will. All kin and kind and townsfolk know I got them and know how long I hold them. They need only inquire. If they didn't, and I didn't dispatch with the materials, there'd be a mountain of mostly hanged-men's dinky treasures out back a mile high." Eyes narrow. "Now, you've insulted me enough *Galician*. And I don't say that with animus and I didn't say it in slur though I do say it to remind you of how the average person treats Ukrainians in these parts where I prescribed no such treatment. You however have bore an age-old prejudice against people of my profession, everywhere, *at me* from the very second I commenced to pullin' them drawers. Do you wish for me to reduce myself? Is that what you're driving at? That I respond in kind? You will not get that satisfaction from me sir." Undertaker musters his professionalism again. "I reckon I'd notice any bruising and I. Did. Not."

Sheriff feels a sudden shame. He's got no evidence of the Undertaker's greed or lack of scruples and he knows it. Man's protocols aren't just necessary they're humane. He's also enjoyed a cordialness that would have taken six months to build with most anyone else in The Belt. Indeed the man did not say *Galician* in slur. He said it as analog to any single one of the slights he's received any given week—hell, day—since he started this job and all The Sheriff's been is a real shit!

"You are right," Metro utters in contrition. "I've been

disrespectful throughout. I apologize and I'd be much obliged if you'd answer just a few more of my questions."

"All you needed to do was ask."

"Thank you. I—I know you have good reason not to trust me—"

"Go ahead and ask."

"Did those more gregarious of jailers happen to say if it was Swade who broke the drunk's jaw?"

"Naw. They'd speculated as to another cause. Said his shakes did it."

"Yet you found no bruising?"

"None."

"This is going to sound—"

"Go ahead ask."

"You were sure the drunk dead?"

"Now, I didn't exactly check for a heartbeat, but I know a lifeless man when I see him."

"Would you know a lifeless Haidt if you saw him?"

"That depends on whether or not I believe the tales."

"And if you did?"

"Then no I wouldn't, but—"

"When you finished examining the body of the prisoner-hanged, what was done with it?"

The Undertaker lowers a shaking head. Metro caught a look of some sort of disgust just before the sinking. "I should have been clearer," the Undertaker laments. "I never examined the man hanged. I only know of his state through the facts shared by the jailers."

"What happened?"

"His ultimate end? They burned his remaining pieces somewhere along the train tracks."

"They?"

"Those for whom judicial procedure was invented Sheriff. The law-abiding who turn blood simple the second justice is put in their hands. Who reduce themselves to a cruelty worse than any murderer when allowed to adjudicate. A bunch of Carson sadists. A pack of crocodiles who Swade tossed that hanged man's corpse to." Despite no discernible odor, the Undertaker opens a bottle of a liquid deodorant. He puts a little on his hankie and holds it under his nose. "I sincerely believe, Sheriff, we don't have law and order to deter the criminal but to deter the law-abiding among us just itching to mete out the most brutal of folk justice where there's no laws of laws to stifle us. We have laws to save us from ourselves not criminals. However, I ramble..."

"Normally I would want to hear more of your views on justice. In better times maybe?" Undertaker dips in assent. Metro continues. "Where did the drunk man's body end up?"

"Now that's a shorter tale. Me and the gravedigger buried him up on the burying hill without ceremony. He's under the name *Bill Carson*."

"That is quite the coincidence."

"Not if you knew what the namesake of Carson got up to."

AS SHERIFF GETS TO THE bottom of the mortuary steps he spins to face the Undertaker a last time. A little contrition lingers. "Once again, very much obliged."

The Undertaker'd make a gesture of closure but one last thing needs settling. "Understand," his end begins. "People in my line Sheriff, we don't undertake the dead because we're numb to it all. We undertake the dead because we believe life so valuable folk ought have dignity even after."

"I agree with your sentiment." There's that closure. However... One resolution frees the mind to seek another... "Sorry," he says. "Could I ask one more—"

"Ask."

"Do you know where I can find Martin Shawk?"

"Nope. Nobody does."

"Well," Sheriff says. "I thank you again." He starts walking when...

"Hold on!" The Undertaker calls after him, taking out a notepad. He's scribbling on the top ticket. He tears it away and walks it down to The Sheriff. "In a manner of speaking," He hands over the note, "there's one lady who might just know."

Sheriff reads at the note,

Martha Shawk nee Spruce b. 2032 d. 2090.
Santa Rosa Cemetery Santa Rosa.

THERE'RE GASPS AND WHISPERS.

FROM Shale.

Goes to that Greek church.

I thought all them people godforsaken.

Godforsaken and dead.

Patrons are amazed at the sight of the Sheriff walking into The Carson Hotel.

The desk agent can't help commenting along the lines of the chorus. "We thought the worst of Shale sir. No one dared enter your municipality in over a month. No communications... Workers were missing... Well, we just thought the worst is all."

"You thought right." Sheriff agrees, though his tone suggests a reluctance to entertain any more of the desk agent's sympathies. Frankly, the sympathies of others won't get it done at this point. "If you excuse me," he says, Spartan. "I just need a couple hours rest. Any room will do."

20

OUT THE WINDOW!

Time to go to work Hannie Price!

There's smoke. Heavy like a blanket. *Hannie!* It's smoke. Like a molasses turning the fluids of the throat to a treacle of shrapnel. Creosote. *Hannie! Time to get to it!* Her nose burns. It's hot in there like someone lit a five-square-foot bonfire in a four-square-foot outhouse. *Hannie! Hannie! Cool times better times Hannie!*

The window smashes! Smashes from the outside-in causing glass to scatter in and smoke to waft out. As the smoke escapes from the second floor, Hannah's breath of smog transforms to a familiar icy vapor. She gasps awake!

"Hannah!" Dep shouts from the yard. "It's goin' up! Goddamn it Hannah can you hear me?"

She jumps out of the bed, feet on the wool runner next to it. She steps for the window but the second her bare foot hits the hardwood it ain't a *SIZZLE!* though it is a scalding heat. Enough to make her leap backward. She barely catches the mattress as she flies. She drags herself back onto it by her elbows.

Haste got her nothing but a scalded foot so she slows.

Deliberates. Attempts an assessment. First things first, she needs to breathe. She pulls a pillowcase free and wraps it around her mouth and nose. A little help.

"Hannah! It's climbing!"

Coming Dep.

Feet back on the runner, she tosses the bare pillow onto the hardwood next the window. She folds up her comforter to make a path over the glass. Now that she's proper-insulated from the cooking and the cutting she moves.

"Oh thank God!" Dep shouts as Hannah emerges out the window. "The whole place has gone up at the ground floor! Is there a ladder?"

"The back shed," she shouts getting onto the overhang. "Bring it around the other side."

Dep's confused but Hannah's already running barefoot around the veranda roof in that direction. He heads for the shed and figures he'll get answers later.

HE KICKS OPEN THE SHED door and the instant he catches sight of the ladder, *WHOOF!* Thing goes up in flames. "What the shit hell's happenin'?" He lunges at the ladder like maybe he can grab it and run it out to Hannah before it's ash then comes to his senses.

He eyes a conveniently placed water bucket next to him on the workbench. Reflexively, he tosses it. *WHOOF!* Whatever's in it's an accelerant and more of the shed goes up in flames. "Gimme a shiiiit break!" He runs back to the side of the house Hannah was moving toward. Flames are rising: a flickering fixture at the edge of the overhang now.

He moves around the corner of the Queen Anne in time to see Hannah dragging Dotty out the other bedroom window laying her lifeless body onto the top of the veranda.

He scans around in an ever-growing loss. In sum to the fire roarin', that wrought fence that was their only refuge is toppled at near every section.

"Where's the ladder?" Hannah shouts.

"You wouldn't believe it. It's gone. Just wait there and—" He stops a second. He's woozy. He's been acting on adrenaline up to now but he had to come crashing down some time. Come-down's made him lightheaded. He shakes off as much of it as he can though ain't much shakes free. "Just wait and I'll figure something out!"

The fire's climbed to inside the second floor, periodically poking out the windows.

Dep's searching for something to get Hannah and Dotty off that roof but that broke down fence has him worried. He's preoccupied with it. A lost security. What if the stumblers head toward the fire? He needs to find something about twelve feet long 'n sturdy with a structure like rungs to climb on though all he can think about are those twelve-foot-long lengths of downed iron-barred— The fence!

He grabs a section of it and drags it perpendicular to the edge of the veranda. "You and Dotty keep clear!" he shouts. He lifts the end of the length furthest from the house. He walks under it raising it like he's a moving fulcrum. Elevates it more and more as he gets closer to Hannah and Dotty. At the tipping point he lets gravity take over and the top of the section crashes forward latching onto the veranda roof. He scurries up to help as the fire rages.

"Oh god!" he says as he catches sight of Dotty. "Did she hit her head?"

"It's just a sleeping turban," Hannah assures trying to angle Dotty toward Dep.

He pulls her toward him from under the arms. As he pulls, her legs slip off the roof dragging the rest of her along with them. Hannah screams! Dep can barely hold Dotty as she hangs from the edge of the ladder. It's too far a drop to just let her go. He struggles.

"H—Hannah see if you can climb down around me and I'll hand Dotty down."

Hannah tries. There's room to pass, though any jostling could cause Dep to drop Dotty. She's slow about those steps past him but she can feel the heat the fire's put to the iron. She knows the searing Dep's enduring. She jumps as soon as she's past him and rolls. She sticks the landing and moves back to the precarious pair, her arms open. She can just barely reach Dotty's ankles.

"You're going to have to let go and I'll try to catch her."

Dep jostles his head as though a nod. He can't talk cuz his gritting teeth are the only thing keeping the pain of that flaming steel from overwhelming him. Hannah moves her feet closer to Dep and leans her shoulders as far back as she can. The only way this is going to work is if Dotty lands on Hannah like she's landing on a slide.

"Ok let her go!"

Dep starts shaking his hold on Dotty loose. She goes! She slides down Hannah at first, as was the plan, but Hannah can't keep her balance and falls backward. This breaks the fall however and Dotty rides Hannah down like a falling tree. *THUMP!* to the ground they go.

Hannah immediately rolls Dotty onto her back on the lawn and tries rousing her. Dep's already down the fence and moving to Hannah's side as she tends.

"Dotty! Dotty!" Hannah lightly slaps at the heiress' cheeks.

"I heard," Dep starts. "I heard if people ain't breathing you can kickstart their lungs by breathing for them."

"How?" Hannah asks with her ear to Dotty's chest.

"I know how it's done I just can't explain it."

"Then do it!" Hannah demands.

"I—I'd gotta breathe into her mouth..."

"Goddamn it Dep! Now's not the time to be bashful!"

"Ok." He leans down to Dotty's face. He plugs her nose and props her mouth open by pulling down on her chin. He breathes deep into her.

Nothing.

"Try again!" Hannah shouts.

He does.

Nothing.

"Keep trying!"

"You're supposed to give it a second."

He waits. Tries again.

Nothing.

Waits.

Tries—

AHUHHHHHH!

Dotty bursts alive again and immediately lets loose with a choking hacking cough. Hannah and Dep sit her up. Dotty coughs out all she can before needing to catch more breath. She does so watching on at the house in disbelief. It's fully engulfed.

"WHUUUT— WHUUUT HAPPENED?" she croaks with a voice that sounds like she just had a pound of tobacco and a gallon of whiskey for breakfast.

Hannah's trying for an answer. Realizes she woke up in the middle of all this too. The two ladies turn to Dep.

"I—I don't know... I just... I was just watching the fence and I... I just... I woke up on the lawn." He notices something as the fire illuminates more and more of the surroundings. "Dotty your face. It's like you've—"

"It's not her Dep," Hannah says pointing to his chin.

He rubs at it. On his hands is the reddest of boil flickering in the firelight. It's still wet. "What the hell?" He realizes immediately the only possible source of the boil he'd drunk.

He gets up in some sort of positivist fervor and rushes over to the water wagon. He fills a dipper and starts looking, moving around the yard searching for something. He finds the last remaining white-washed surface on the house and heads for it. It's the bottom step of Hannah's back entrance. He tosses the dipper's contents at it from a good six feet away—though still too close to that roaring fire for his tastes. Liquid splashes with an unmistakable blood red.

He heads back around to the side of the house the girls are at. He's peering into the dipper as he speaks "You all aren't going to believe this—" He glances up only to see Dotty cradling Hannah down on the lawn. Hannah's weeping as the last of her world goes up to ember.

Dep drops the object of his attention. In his shame he walks right past the two women and stands with his back to them. He faces the dark outskirts of Shale between the danger and Hannah. He does the job he shouldn't have let that poison stop him from doing in the first place.

NEXT MORNING AND IT'S COME to this...

Metro was the asshole with the Undertaker but there's no way in hell, no matter what bastardization of decorum he could ever muster, he'll be the asshole next to Swade. Be that as it may, he needs information from our local touchy tyrant narcissist jawbreaker so he's gonna have to be extra ginger about things.

.   .   .

"YEAH I KNOW A' YOU," Swade says rocking himself in a lavish-as-hell swivel chair courtesy of The Federals. "Yer Hannah Price's little pet. Wants one of my deputy jobs. Kinda nervy doncha think? Showing up for what? An interview? After letting your town go t'shit like that?"

Concentrate.

"I'm not here about job."

"*Ab-yout j-yob!*" Swade caricatures this in a hush meant to entertain none but himself. He keeps on a' rockin' too. Good news about his tax-funded comfort though, by the cutting-edge nature of that chair, them tax dollars had to go straight to who pays 'em most: Will and Rosey. To Shale.

Think of Shale. Of Kate. The girls.

"I'm investigating similarities between Shale's troubles and attack on—"

"Y'all got somethin' against the word *the* in Russia or somethin'?"

"I'm investigating—"

"You had your chance *sher-yiff*. You could have asked for the US Marshal's services from the beginning and ya didn't. Thought you were better than us."

Change tack Metro. You won't get any professional courtesy.

Swade continues. "You and Madam thought if you just sucked the ass of that mama's boy's Burke's—" He stumbles over his tongue. "That mama boy's burke ma— Shit!"

"*That mama's boy Burke's mama?*"

"Think yer smart doncha?"

"Average. Man don't even have to be that to manage such a phrase."

Swade flushes. "Now you're definitely not getting any of the US Marshal's services."

"By the looks of how you run things, nobody is."

"You son-of-a—"

"I want answers you buffoon!"

Swade kicks his chair back and away from his heavy oak desk as Metro slides downward and out of sight. Petty Swade makes a grab for the Colt at his hip but Metro's already popped up at his side of the desk, spinning him in his chair. He pushes him up against the wall holding him there. Swade's got his gun out but Metro's got him pinned. It's just a man in his rocking chair thrashing about with all the range of motion of a baby in a Mei Tai.

"Son-of-a-bitchin' shit'll!"

Metro disarms Swade and lets him free. Swade swivels back around trying to get angry words out only to spin right into the handle of his own colt. *SMASH!* Metro's laid into him across the jaw. Bloody-lip-Swade prepares to lunge but Metro's got the colt on him. Petty ain't so dumb he don't know when the better man's got the drop on him. He just sits there nursing his jaw.

Pistol fixed on Swade from the hip, Metro moves back to the guest side of the desk. "That's not even half as bad as that poor drunk got it," he says, sitting.

"Whuch the fwuk aw you tahing abow?"

"What are *you* talking about? You're not hurt that bad. Speak clearly."

Swade stops nursing his jaw. Spits a gob of bloody saliva onto the floor "I don't know what yew're tawking about."

"I'm talking about the night you hanged Haidt. You broke his jaw and the jaw of the drunk next to him."

"Fuck you."

"Your jailers gave you up."

"Traitors."

"Maybe I lie?"

"Naw, those fwuckin' twaitors have lodged more complaints against me than the prisoners."

"And yet here you are…"

"Complaints are *shunted* back to my office."

"Checks and balances?"

"Lookit, I bwoke that mis-kweant's jaw and I'd do it ten times again but I didn't touch that drunk."

"Then how'd his jaw get broken?"

"Goddamn souse had the shakes stho bad he coulda rattled his own jaw off his face!"

"You know what? I believe you when you say you didn't accost the drunk. You want to know what I think happened?"

"You're not satisfied with my explanation?"

"That the drunk shook his head so hard his jaw fell off? That wasn't joke?"

"You got a better explanation?"

"I just asked if you wanted to hear it."

"Well pardon the fuck outta me Sheriff! Or did you forget I just got my bell rung?"

"Yes, a slight rap to the chin is why you can't think properly. Here's what I think happened. I think Haidt broke that drunk's jaw then painted the man's busted face. Like demon. Then he posed as the drunk and faked death. You sent Haidt to the mortuary and you hanged the wrong man. An innocent man who couldn't tell you anyway because of his injuries."

Swade chuckles. "Now you think I'm stupid but I'm smart enough to know when you're mockin' me with your tubsext— shit!"

"*Subtext.*"

"I'm smart enough to know you're mocking me *sneak-like* and I'm smart enough to know no one's mistakin' that drunk for Haidt. That drunk couldn't'a stopped shakin' for a second if he tried."

"He could if Haidt had been giving him rye whiskey in the proper measure." Metro pulls the mickey bottle out of his moshonka. "This was found among the man's personal effects."

"Haidt was bound ya fool."

"He got out of his bonds just fine to get the drop on you. In fact, it was his scaring you so bad that caused you to break his jaw. Though not before he was put back in his shackles and made defenseless..."

Swade flushes once more. "You better hope I never get the drop on you—"

"And you better hope I never prove your illegal hanging *not even* an illegal hanging of Haidt." With that Metro stands, still holding Swade's Colt on him.

Then...

He breaks aim and releases the cylinder. Shells dump onto Swade's desk. Swade looks like he's about to make a move when Metro puts his hand on his own pistol. "You forget I still have mine." He starts backing up toward the door of the Marshal's office.

As Sheriff gets close enough to the door for Swade's tastes, the tyrant barks out. "That pistol's Federal pwoperty!"

Metro stops at the door. Assesses the pistol, holds it up. "I mail it to The Federals then. Maybe they *shunt* it back to you." He walks out with the colt.

Swade sits a second half-stewing half-half-deliberating over what to do next when...

Pistol slides through the envelope slot of the office door.

So much for ginger...

21

COWBOYS FROM HELL

"If you thank me one more time Metro I swear I'm gonna succumb to the hopelessness of living in a world where fulfilling such a mere minor obligation is so rare it must be met with the most profuse and unending of gratitudes! Is this what we've sunk to?"

"Alright," Metro chuckles. "I stop, though never have any doubts."

"Done! Now shut up!"

The Undertaker has driven Metro and the Gravedigger up to the cemetery on the hill. He turns his left-hand carriage lantern sideways as they move along a row of plots of interest. Gravedigger scans those illuminated markers as the Undertaker continues inching the hearse forward.

GRAVEDIGGER TAPS ON THE UNDERTAKER'S shoulder. Hearse halts and everyone exits. Gravedigger hops out the back grabbing a couple of digging spades as he goes. Undertaker takes both carriage lanterns along with him and hangs them onto the side of the hearse. He directs them to the wooden cross that reads:

Bill Carson

The men start digging. Two on one off.

BACK IN SHALE, HANNAH AND Dep had managed to sneak Dotty past the stumblers and barricade themselves into Hannah's office. They had food and about two gallons of laundered boil but Dotty's lungs were badly damaged by the smoke and she needed medicine. Out of desperation, Hannah and Dep secured Dotty in the office and set out to find anyone who could help.

They're riding to the mine currently, hoping to implore The Council guards.

So far there've been no marauders.

UP IN THE BELL TOWER of the cemetery chapel, Swade watches three men dig. What's he intending? Run down and arrest the trio for grave robbing? The undertaker has ulti-mate authority on exhumation outside of official US Marshal's Service business *and* Swade was too dumb to make Metro's investigation official US Marshal's Service business.

He ain't *so* dumb he don't understand the consequences of anyone finding anyone other than Haidt in that grave. Given such, the Department of Justice would have no choice but to open an internal investigation into Swade's activities. And there won't be any *shunting* of investigative duties back to his office this time.

He aims a .30-06. It's state-of-the-art scoped property of The Federals, of course, and the reticles on Metro. He just kills The Sheriff see and the Undertaker and The Gravedigger get scared off. The Sheriff's out of the investigation and even if that wily Undertaker has any inkling, he'll just sit and stew in his cowardice and resentment as always. Most importantly, whoever's in that grave stays there.

Reticle's on Sheriff but even in the directed-light of those carriage lanterns it's hard to make out the dot at the center of the scope's view. Swade needs Metro to stand still a second so he can contrast the black dot of his reticle against the mustachio-induced joviality of The Sheriff's face. Metro goes on digging any longer and Swade's gonna have to refill that whole damn grave.

THE SPADE'S HANDED OFF AS Metro takes a moment's rest. He puts his hands on his knees and lowers his head a second to catch his breath.

"Damnit! Lift that head up of yours ya dirt-shit!" Swade whispers this through grit teeth. "Much obliged…"

He's got the dot on Metro's cheek as Metro stands in profile overseeing things.

"Say goodbye to that dumb smile of yours mother-fuck!" Finger goes to trigger and…

THUMP!

Swade goes down. Someone's whomped him good and's lugging him around the dark of the bell tower.

DONG!

Metro's attention goes to the tower. He squints trying to catch sight of whatever's up there. He swears he sees one of them shadows carrying—

"Alright!" shouts the Undertaker diverting Metro's attention. "Let's get those lanterns over here. Sheriff get ready."

Metro jumps into the grave, legs in the inches between the casket and the dirt wall. Gravedigger and Undertaker hold the lanterns on him from above. He puts a prybar between the lid and the casket proper and notices there's already substantial give.

He slips his fingers under the loosened lid then... A thought creeps in. What inference are you going to draw in any case here Metro? Somebody in there? Nobody? Broken jaw? Intact? What tells you Haidt's alive or dead? *Jesus Christ!* He hadn't even considered! He'd just been barreling on putting pieces together lucky enough to have emerged from protocol, cooperation of helpful folk, and manipulation of miscreant folk easily manipulated.

What the hell would he learn about Haidt from whatever's in this casket? No man or no broken jaw *then* neither the drunk nor Haidt down there. That's it. Anything else he gives up the ghost? There's no way to tell who *any* eleven-month-rotted corpse is, broke jaw or otherwise. Even if he proves the body ain't Haidt what does that tell 'em about where Haidt's at? Coulda actually been hanged along those train tracks for all he knows! Could be lounging on a beach in the tropics for all anyone knows! Could be—

You're overthinking things.

He pops the lid off. Undertaker and Gravedigger lean in with them lanterns. Dust settles.

"Oh thank God!" says Undertaker in haste. Catches himself. "I—I'm sorry Metro." It's plain as day. A corpse many months decomposed with a jaw broken in several places. "I—I know this stifles your investigation— There's the integrity of the examiner's office on the line too. Then again your problems are bigger than—"

"*Ees* ok," Metro laments. He lifts himself out of the hole as the Undertaker puts the lantern down to aid him.

"So what now?" Undertaker asks.

"Eat crow. Tell Marshal."

"Not him!"

"Would you rather this case be reopened someday and Swade comes to you looking for this information? All because I didn't give it to him tonight?"

Lantern starts shaking a little in Undertaker's hand. "Y— You got a point there."

"NOT A CHANCE MA'AM," BOSS says to The Mayor.

"You gotta be kidding me!" Dep protests. "You got the goddamn Council's treasure trove at yer disposal and ya can't help three lousy people just lost a whole town!"

Hannah grips onto Dep's arm pulling him back. He turns to her. She shakes her head.

Not a chance with these men Dep.

THE SHERIFF HOPS OFF THE Undertaker's carriage. He waves as Undertaker and Gravedigger roll on home.

Metro moves up the block a few storefronts to the one he's calling on. He was let off those lots back so Swade wouldn't see The Undertaker fraternizing with anyone hastening his downfall. Nice gesture on Metro's part. He ups the Marshal's steps and knocks. No response.

"Swade!"

Nothing.

All the lights are on but the Marshal's office windows are clerestory. Sheriff can't see a damn thing inside just standing on the boardwalk.

"I have information regarding the case we discussed. It's protocol." He tries the knob. Locked. *Oh why the hell not let him have it Metro! You knew it was gonna come to this.* "You were right."

Nothing.

People are peeking out of storefront doors and windows at the shouting Sheriff.

Well this ain't workin'. He waits for the busybodies to disperse then grabs one of two adjacent wooden crates out front. He stacks it on top the other. He climbs up to get a look through an office window. He can see Swade's swivel chair with its back to us. A right hand hangs over the armrest. Metro squints. He sees what's almost certainly blood pooled under dangling fingers.

Exigence.

He kicks through the locked door and hurries to the chair. Spins it. No suspense just grotesquery.

It's Swade alright. His jaw's snapped near off. Skull's split in two lengthwise the center. The butt of his coach gun's jammed down his throat right up to the flute! Busted jaw drips with either boil or blood but the pattern of the drip is as contrived a message as could be. Hell, the whole of the brutality is as contrived a message as could be.

HAIDT OR NOT, THE CURE will be the same.

DOTTY'S HANGING ON BUT THAT wheeze of hers is getting worse. Hannah and Dep hover over her blotting at her forehead. Laundered water's at a constant simmer in the hopes the vapor'll ease the rot in her lungs.

"What did you see out there?" Dotty rasps.

"Nothing. Bureaucracy."

"Too bitter a pill."

Hannah smiles one of those *if these were only better times* smiles. "I'd bring ya Doc Smart…"

"Why not? Stumblin' couldn't have made his bedside manner any worse." Dotty chuckles.

She goes into a coughing fit.

LANTERN ILLUMINATES THE TOMBSTONE. WE see written on it,

Martha Shawk nee Spruce b. 2032 d. 2090.

At the base of the tombstone an envelope is lain. On top of that envelope a piece of taconite is placed.

MOON AIN'T FULL THOUGH IT'S full enough. It was just a matter of time thinks Metro. Yet, it sure happened quicker than he thought it would. The mine gate's swung wide open and guards are gone. *I don't have time for this.*

Shit!

He swerves in and rides up to the entrance. Caution increases the closer he gets.

THERE'RE NO BODIES. NEITHER STUMBLIN' nor slain.

He moves for that Gatling gun to see if they even got a shot off. He sets his directional lantern onto a crate to the left of the weapon and has a look. No spent casings. No bullets in the magazine either. No bullets anywhere but it don't matter. Gun's trashed. Doesn't even have firing pins. It's a complete façade.

Council nickel and diming these men? These men really so cocky they think six shooters and pretend Gatling guns'll scare off or fight off the creatures in Shale shadows?

Ain't anything's gonna answer that question out here. Metro sees nothing out the bag so the situation inside the mine'll have to write the chapter.

GUARDS WERE CONSIDERATE ENOUGH TO keep the mine lanterns fueled. He lights each one along the first-level corridor in the order he passes them. He checks each room in the order he passes too. All there've been are storage and utility rooms and they've been empty all along the way.

The dark of the corridor would spook Metro if he took any time to think about it and... he just did. He realizes he's lighting up the back of him with those lanterns for whatever may be ahead of him in the dark. He's as good as standing upwind facing the sun. He grabs one of the lit lanterns off its mount and tosses it as far down the corridor as he can. It smashes open spilling kerosine in a six-foot by three-foot flaming swath. Nothing scurries out of the light so, so far so good. But...

CRAM! CRAM! CRAM!

Clamor of the toss has caused a thumping up the corridor. It's coming from the sleeping quarters just ahead the lantern fire. Metro moves to it passing over a door with *Repairs* written on it.

There's a four-by-four bracketed across the entrance of the quarters. The pounding continues from the other side.

"Who's in there?" Metro shouts.

Pounding stops.

Then...

"Who y' think y' dolt!"

Then...

"Now how the hell y' think he's gonna know it's you y' narcissimo! Think he can see through two inches of pine?"

"He could recognize my voice!"

"You don't even know who's on the other side to recognize it!"

"Bob? Carp?" Metro shouts.

Quiet a second.

Then...

"Told you he could recognize my voice y' fool!"

"Oh you got lucky like y' always do! Like when y' inherited that bar under my hotel!"

"Hotel's *over* my bar!"

Metro swings the door open. It *is* Carp! It *is* Bob! It's the missing Shalers!

"Sheriff! Oh thank god!" Carp latches onto Metro in a clingy hug. "We couldn't spend another minute in there with that belligerent!"

"*Why you...*"

Metro tunes the curmudgeons out.

He shines his lantern around the room. He's looking at familiar faces all with questions he hopes he'll have the wherewithal to answer. He's running an inventory in his head. He ain't sure if he's accounted for everyone missing though everyone he's accounted for is here. And they're all sober as anything. Healthy if not slightly annoyed. Oddly plump...

"How did you all—"

"Metro! What's going on?" says a familiar voice.

He moves the lantern over to that voice. It *is*! "Will!" Sheriff shakes Will's shoulder warmly and excitedly. "I'll try to explain everything when we have a minute. We're not safe just yet. I need you to answer some questions for me first.

Starting with what happened in here? What did they do to the guards?"

"Guards?" Will asks, standing himself up off the floor.

"The Council guards out front. Surely your captors would have dealt with them when they brought you in?"

"Our captors *are* our guards." Everybody nods in agreement with Will.

Surely they're in a delirium thinks Metro. Visions of those pathetic hangers-on flash in his head. Poor souls desperate for the Red-Eyes to make them kin. He examines Will's eyes. Man doesn't seem to have lost his senses. *Be mindful anyway Metro.* "Wait here," he orders. "I'm going to check to the end of the corridor."

HE MOVES PAST THE LAST of that broken lantern's kerosine burning up. There's only one more room to check before the soup. It appears to be just another supply closet. Door's not barred so he pulls down on the little iron tab that unlatches the lock at the other side. Real cautious about it. *Last place for those Red-Eyes to hide.*

BOOM!

Metro kicks the door open with a smash then twists away from the opening out of sight. He extends his directional lantern into the entrance only allowing the arm holding it to cross into the doorframe. Blinding of the light affects the appearance of a man in the doorway. Lantern at his hip.

No reaction.

Metro inches over. Peers inside. He's hit by a smell of copper and sour. Death. Blooded death. They may call it a closet but this room is massive. Three times as big as any other so far. From the door he can only make out amorphous piles of materials. Nothing can be individuated by the lantern beam just yet.

"Sheriff?"

JEEEZZZZ! Metro jumps. It's Will.

"You shouldn't be here Will!" Metro says this over his shoulder.

"That's an understatement. However, since I am..."

"Well just stay in the doorway." Metro moves in.

"What's the state of Shale?" Will asks as curious as anyone should be in his position.

"It's bad," Metro says swinging the lantern around the room.

"How's Rosey?" He asks this more subdued. He's obligated to ask yet knows his friend would have already shared any good news if there were good news to share. Still has to know.

Metro stops what he's doing a second. He doesn't face the brother. "She's in the church now." Will slumps against the door frame. Metro allays. "But she's alive. She's young and she's strong. We can get her off the boil yet."

"Y—yeah. Yeah." Will's last *yeah* was hopeful. Reinvigorating even. Is he fooling himself? It doesn't matter. He's gotta keep his thoughts about Rosey's chances out of mind if he's gonna be of any help here. "Those Rosa folk," he says. "They got off the boil."

"That's right Will."

Will is right Metro. Rosa did it. Yet nobody knows how. Not even you. But Rosa did it!

Metro continues the reconnoiter. Lumps of materials turn out to be piles of Council guard uniforms. He makes out a workbench at the opposite side of the room from where he stands. He moves toward it. He hops over a pile of uniforms and nearly stumbles face-first into a cluster of severed hands and feet at the bench. *What the hell?* There are cutting cleaving and sawing implements next to the appendages. There's some sort of sack of something twisting hanging in the corner to the left of the workbench. It brushes up against Metro's shoulder in its rotating.

He puts the lantern down on the bench—not before using it to brush someone's left foot out of the way. He holds onto the sack and feels something familiar. It's not really a sack. It's a canvas tarp. He whips it off. *Shit!*

It's a Council guard hung up on a butcher's hook. You can tell he's a Council guard because he's wearing one of those grey coverall uniforms. Strange thing is, the right leg of the uniform is torn off at the thigh. It's torn off at the thigh because that's where they applied the tourniquet. They applied the tourniquet, of course, to stop the guard from bleeding to death while they cut chunks of meat from his thigh down to the ankle. Clean to the bone. He's dead, so the tourniquet failed. The coveralls are also torn open down the center. Coveralls are torn open down the center because, despite the guard succumbing to the flaying, they tried preserving what meat was left of him. He's completely gutted. Dressed out like a deer.

"My god they've been eating him!" Will shouts from over Metro's shoulder.

JEEEEZZZZZUS! Will!

"S—sorry. What in the hell is going on Sheriff?"

"I only see guard in this room. Did they ever take any of you away?" Sheriff grabs his lantern and starts leading Will out. Been in this abattoir long enough.

"No. We're all accounted for, pretty sure." Will says this as he's hustled back out into the corridor.

"This may be difficult to answer Will... Did they ever make you eat any of this meat?"

Will shakes his head. "Just fed us water and some sort of sugary porridge."

"No meat?"

"I think it was steel-cut oats."

Metro stops the walk. "Did they have a leader?"

Will wobbles his head. It's one of those *no-wait?-yes!* gestures. "Just a guy a little older than the rest. Told the others what to do."

Metro's jogging his memory. Going through the information he'd read on the Runagates. "Gruff? Told them to *shut up* a lot?"

"Yeah, as a matter of fact. Especially if they got rough with us."

"They didn't hurt you? Almost conspicuously so?"

Will's aback. There's a puzzlement. "Yeah, *again*. Went out of their way to keep us comfortable. Didn't approve of us moving around much—" Will realizes the Sheriff's testing some sort of hypothesis. "J—Just what do you think they were up to Sheriff?"

"They were fattening you up Will. They were going to eat you after they ran out of dead guards. Or *live*, judging by that butchered man's state." Metro starts walking again and can sense that Will ain't following. He stops. He hears Will begin to retch. He backs up to the barfing rescuer. "It's ok." He pats him on the back.

"I mean my god!" *RALF!* "Yet it makes perfect sense!"

"It *is* consistent. Their leader Will, anything else about him stand out?"

"Like I said, older," Will tries. He wipes his lower lip. "Fifty, fifty-five. Looked rough. *Weathered* I guess you'd say, had a hitch in his step—"

"What?"

"Walked funny," Will adds.

An image of that hobbling Boss. *Not a chance sir.* "Guard or captor?"

"The Boss."

Metro's growing agitated. "No. Was he a guard or your captor?"

"I told you Sheriff. Those guards *were* our captors. That guy hangin' back there brought me in himself."

"When?"

Pfflffl... Will flaps his lips as he considers the timespan. "Gotta be three weeks ago at least."

Metro goes pale. A horror'd epiphany.

BOSS AS WELL AS THE guards from mine and dam ride shoulder to shoulder storming toward Shale City. Boss whips a finger in the air. He and his men slather beet-boil onto their cheekbones transforming themselves into Red-Eyes.

"WHAT IS IT SHERIFF?"

METRO'S hustled Will back to the sleeping quarters.

"You all must stay here," he says to the Shalers. "It is the safest place for now. Bar the sleeper door and I'll try to bar the outside gate with whatever I can."

"You're leaving?"

"We have people still in Shale. I'll be back."

22

WOODSTOCK

Boss and his men sit on horseback at the south end of town.

STHEWEEEET! goes Boss' piercing finger-whistle.

At the whistle, not all but *only* working men new to Shale pour out the side alleys of Main. They're swiping the blood boil under their eyes as they emerge. Boss whips his finger into the air and three Guard-Red-Eyes ride over to the church.

One of the guards dismounts and hustles up to the door. He gives the handle a test. Locked. He yanks at it a few times aggressively. Guess he's not a *Knocker*? Another of the guards takes a lariat off his saddle and cantors up to the bell tower. He's hooping the lariat over his head by the time he arrives. Knocker Red-Eye just watches *Lasso* Red-Eye intently. Lasso lassoes the massive wooden cross sitting atop the tower. He wraps the other end of the lariat around his saddle horn then inches the horse back. Cross gives way. Falls to the ground and lands in one piece.

*Wait*ing Red-Eye dismounts and joins Knocker and

Lasso at the cross. The three pick it up like a battering ram and move toward the church door. They swing it three times for practice to get the pendulum arc just right. Satisfied, they rear it back for real this time and let fly. *CRACK!*

Meanwhile the worker Red-Eyes have amassed around Boss and remaining Guards. Boss surveys the scene. There's an insistence in the assay. One of the worker Red-Eyes notices. Designates himself the speaker of the group. He points down Main.

"In The Mayor's office."

Boss rides in that direction as all the henchmen, mounted or otherwise, follow.

CRACK! CRACK! CRUNCH!

The cross has broken through the door of the church and the three Red-Eyes aren't done with it. They carry it through the antechamber toward the cow chute. The stumblers inside the pen become restless at the sight of their would-be liberators.

SMASH!

The cross breaks through the head gate of the chute. Inside the squeeze, a large bucket of boil had sat. A vestige of a time when the captives were fed a daily allotment of boil to stifle withdrawal. It ain't sitting anymore. The smashing of the gate's toppled it. The squeeze and the cross are soaking in the blood as...

SMASH!

The cross is through the entrance gate of the chute.

Knocker Lasso and Wait get clear the path as the automata stumble out by the dozens.

Outside Hannah's office, Boss stands at the steps.

"Are you seeing this Hannah?" Dep's looking through a gap in the barricade.

"Remember Rosa?" Hannah's looking through a similar gap.

"I thought Haidt's gang was dead!"

"Can't kill an affinity."

Boss tries one last time to push in the barricaded door as Hannah and Dep brace it from the other side. Boss backs up down the steps and into the street. He pulls out a match and flicks it lit with his thumbnail. He reaches into his duster with his free hand and pulls out a stick of dynamite. He lights its twelve-inch fuse.

"You got a minute to tear down that barricade or I'm tearing it down for ya."

"Holy shit!" grits Dep, panicking.

"Get to the back. Cover Dotty," Hannah pleads.

Ten-inches of fuse...

Dep and Hannah grab as much material as they can to cover Dotty and themselves.

Nine-inches...

Boss raises his arm. His men stand surrounding him encouraging him with strange lusty grimaces fixed on that fuse. This will be the commencement of something grand. Boss rears his arm back for the toss holding that cocked arm poised a second. He revels in the rumble of the stumblin' Red-Maws behind him coming up Main. *Holds...* He can hear the smashing of Knocker Lasso and Wait gotten to the town hall prison, opening its doors with that cross key. *Holds...* More rumbles to undoubtedly follow.

Holds...

Eight-inches...

Boss gets done with the reveling. Time for the toss. He rears a few more overdetermining inches then... Whips that arm forward like a slingshot! Hand opens. Lets go of the dynamite when...

WHAHCHHIH!

Dynamite don't fly! It's tied. Held fast against Boss' wrist. Caught and bound just at the point of release! Lassoed! Noosed more like!

Six-inches...

Arm's raised and going nowhere. Boss keeps trying to throw against the tension. Can't. It's instinct driving that arm. Confused stifled instinct. Then, like a fool, Boss turns to face his captor. Allows the rope to wrap further around the lit dynamite in hand binding it more. What Boss beholds in the turn is Metro. Lariat in hand taut. Lawman's standing atop the back of Shale's last water wagon.

Four-inches...

Boss lowers his arm to get some slack for escape but Sheriff's quicker to use it. He loops the slack over a crossarm of one of Lamour's telegraph poles. Starts backing up along the tank. Pulls the lariat with him. Boss' arm's right back up. Metro keeps on. Rope keeps pulling. Boss rises off his feet.

Two-inches of fuse...

Boss' men scatter.

Dangling, looking like a twisting writhing Statue of Liberty, Boss makes one last futile reach with his free hand. No good. Goes still. Physics twists the defeated Red-Eye to face Metro a last time.

"Let me go," he snarls.

Fuse is down to the primer...

"No chance."

BOOM!

Loss a' d' Boss!

AS THE CLOUD OF PINK dust settles Metro carries out a quick survey. Stumblers pour out of Town Hall and Church stumblers come up to join them. Boss' men are only dazed and'll be ambulatory soon.

Metro runs the length of the tank and jumps off the back of it to ground. Lucky for him that dynamite-man burst the office door open a crack without turning its barricade to shrapnel. He leans half through the opening, shouting.

"Gotta go!"

"Sheriff?" yells Dep.

Metro's pushing more of the debris away from the entrance as Dep and Hannah join in the teardown. They clear a large enough path to allow Hannah to move through. She stares at Metro imploringly. "Dotty's in the back."

"Tell her to hurry—" but he can see in her eyes something ain't right. "You drive the wagon." He runs into the office.

STUMBLERS ARE STUMBLING BUT THE water wagon ain't caught their attention yet. Hannah's angling it around Boss' stunned Red-Eyes as Dep and Metro exit carrying Dotty.

BANG! BANG!

Knocker Lasso and Wait have cottoned to the escape and are trying to get through the mass of automata at the town hall landing. They're firing their guns wildly into the air half to hasten the stumblers, half out of a futile attempt to hit that wagon.

"Ignore them for now," Metro assures as he sets his end of Dotty down. He climbs onto the wagon. Dep's holding Dotty up by the arms as Metro reaches down for her. "Hoist her up!"

Town Hall and Church stumblers hear The Sheriff's voice and amble toward the wagon. Former stumblers are coming up from behind and latter stumblers are moving in at the front.

"Set 'em off!" Hannah shouts.

Dep lifts Dotty up by her waist and Metro grabs her by the arms. He pulls as Dep pushes. He drags her the remainder of the distance to the top of the wagon and lays her flat. She's out but he can hear her wheezing. He turns to Dep and reaches for him. Dep grabs on when...

A pair of hands wrap around his ankle!

"Oh dammit! One of 'ems got me Sheriff!" Dep starts pulling. Moving Metro further down than himself up. Metro braces to keep from toppling off. He attends to Dep. Frowns.

"Just a Red-Eye! Shake him off!"

"Ah geez!" Dep's relieved at the sight of the half-conscious Red-Eye. Then...

"Shake him the hell off Dep!"

"Shit!" Dep starts doing a jig. The Red-Eye, though not possessed of the strength of a stumbler, has a grip tighter than expected.

Metro holds tightest. "Drive Hannah!"

She yips the horses moving. Metro's trying his damnedest to counterbalance Dep against that Red-Eye when... Finally! The rattling breaks the demon free and Metro pulls Dep aboard.

"Stumblers!" Hannah shouts as the Church Maws swarm the front of the wagon.

"Just go slow. Through."

Hannah angles the wagon carefully into the crowd. Dep and Metro are making sure none go under the wheels when...

BANG! BANG! Knocker Lasso and Wait are finally on the street running and gunning. Thankfully, they're still a couple hundred yards away. Dotty starts a coughing fit. Blood's coming up.

"Damn it!" Metro gives his six-shooter to Dep like Dep knows what to do with it. Dep does. He lays his belly onto the wagon to get prone. Starts firing. Knocker Lasso and Wait scatter to the boardwalks to take cover. This slows 'em, only now they have crates and sacks and barrels to hide 'em on their way forward.

BANG! BANG!

Metro moves toward the bench. "Hannah! Dotty!"

She looks back. *Oh no.* Hands the reins to Metro. He takes them and slides into shotgun as Hannah moves back over the tank.

BANG! BANG! BANG!!

She picks Dotty up and angles her forward, rubbing her back. Blood spatters but the coughing's easing. Hannah sits Dotty back up straight. She's wheezing though steadily and without anything more coming up.

BANG! BANG!

Knocker's lead's punctured the water tank. beet-boil spurts out the hole. Stumblers split away from the front of the wagon and start moving back toward the flowing intoxicant.

Dotty regards Hannah with as much of a lightness as she can muster. Blood at her bottom lip. She reaches out and takes her savior's arm away from her back and shoulder and takes its hand in hers. She shakes it with little strength yet joyously. Her regard carries all gratitude in the world.

"Thank you Hannah Price. I feel..." It's mostly her voice if a little raspy still. "I feel for the first time in my life... *Welcome.*" Grip goes limp. Hannah fails to notice in the grief of things. Dotty's eyes roll back as she topples, spilling over the edge of the wagon and down.

"No!" Hannah cries. Frantic. "Stop!" Metro glances back to see Dotty floating a second on that sea of automata. Faces forward again. Face is hopelessness. "Stop Metro!"

He doesn't. "We can't."

Hannah watches as the stumblers recede in the distance dragging Dotty away. They tear at her finery as they move. Her alabaster skin viciously pawed. They Rip that turban to shreds. Her near-white flowing tendrils torn by the roots.

Hannah positions herself over Metro's shoulders. Takes hold. Shakes. Strikes him even. "Stop damn it!"

BANG! BANG!

Metro takes Hannah's hand. Doesn't pry it off. Doesn't try to stop the blows. Just holds it, squeezes. Hannah sinks. Turns back atop the wagon as it picks up speed. She's looking back toward town. Knocker Lasso and Wait have given up their chase though that's not what she fixates on. She fixes further down Main, at the stumblers hauling Dotty's body into Town Hall.

THE MORNING SUN HITS MARTHA Shawk's gravestone. It hits that piece of taconite too. That's all it hits. Envelope's gone.

Man will be callin' on me soon.

I still got a bit more time to finish the tale...

THE SURVIVORS WATCH AS THE smoke of the fires of Shale rise over the horizon. Folk are low in that mining pit, so the smoke rising's all they see. That and the top of the church bell tower without cross. They'd be able to see the top of the rotunda of Hannah's Queen Anne too if not for...

"They will start with the businesses of Main," Metro assures. "They'll burn the wood and crumble the stone."

"When will they get to our homes?" Will asks.

"They don't burn the homes. They take slats from them to build their wooden Loomers."

"Loomers?" asks Will.

"What about Hannah's house?" asks another Shaler, pre-empting an answer to Will's follow-up. "They burned that didn't they?"

"That is an anomaly," Metro admits.

"So they'll be coming for our homes?"

"No."

"What's that ma'am?"

"No," Hannah repeats, sitting slouching on a wooden crate, despondent. "No it ain't any damn anomaly."

"How so?"

She straightens her posture a little. "House had Tom in it. Still does as far as them Red-Eyes are concerned."

"What's that mean Mayor?"

She's lost again. Posture weakens again.

"Mayor?"

"Hannah?"

Shit Hannah girl, what have you started? Tom's watch-words *If you can't face them people...* start echoing in that head of hers. She twists away from the crowd. Rips at those tear ducts.

"*Come what may...*" she hushes.

"What was that?"

She turns back to the crowd. "That Queen Anne and those shops down Main represent to that mobbed-up collective the only thing able to defy them in this Belt far as *I'm* concerned."

It's all ears on Hannah. Folk no longer carin' to observe them fires no more.

Well get to it girl. Her posture goes right-straight like she's schoolmarmin' herself all-a-sudden then...

"*Spirit,*" she starts. "Now understand this. I ain't about to say mining ain't hard but mining's cake compared to defying that council with work other than minin'. Defying them mayors too. Them Federals. The church. Defying the people of this world thinking everything's a wound-watch they wound ticking away in perfect time worried the slightest of iconoclasm's gonna set that watch to spittin' gears. Folk too damn benighted to realize it's the iconoclasm that did the windin' to begin with.

"There's nothing in this world top-downers fear more than *spirit* and there's nobody more spirited in this world than a man woman or child sayin' *I'm goin' it alone come what may! Come near-certain failure. Settin' The Council and The Mayors of this Belt against me in so doing. To make something for myself and kin and kind in a natural world enough against me besides those unnatural folk the same! They won't stifle my machinations!* That's spirit!" Hannah stands and ambles in the direction of that defunct Gatling gun. Talks as she walks. "That's spirit, and The Council can't tame it and them Red-Eyes can't tame it and both those mobs know it so they'd just as soon kill it than submit to it. Yet, by burnin' them shops they've played their hands. Betrayed the fact they don't know the difference between the symbol of the spirit and the matter of it. Spirit lays in the heart. In Tom's. In Will's..." Will attends. Hannah smiles at him. "In Rosey's."

"You're forgetting *someone,* fearless leader." There's insinuation in Will, acquaintin' itself to his admiration.

"I—I ain't that." Hannah fumfers. Some wind out of her sails. "I just love my husband's all."

"Ah horseshit Hannah!" Bob says, offended. Surprise surprise right? Though there's something about this offense of Bob's that's different. "That last part may be true. The first part is wet horseshit! Us of the Chamber of Commerce never saw you as any bureaucrat or stifler or some *Miss Stay-tees Quo!* You got more a Tom in y' than Dalt Pettimore. Hell more Tom in y' than ol' Morg Munson even! More Tom than Tom! You've stood up to that council more times than anyone ever has in the whole Belt and are still kickin' to talk about it. If that ain't spirit girl, then hell if I know what is!"

Hannah tilts her head back, not shaking it in disagreement yet. She's more searching for a reason not to have to, when...

"He's right," says Carp.

Say's Carp! Man who's never agreed to a damn thing Bob's ever had to say in his life! Would disagree with Bob saying *Carp I'm a disagreeable bastard all the goddamn time!* and now this? Carp's seconding has hastened the nods of all other survivors in sight.

Hannah chuckles. Tips the invisible brim of an invisible hat at the folk then puts her hand on the top barrel of that Gatling gun. "Can we get this working?"

"Could always look around for parts..."

23

———

DESDEMONA

Their search of the upper-level has brought them to the end of the corridor. Where the low of the grade meets the soup.

"What are those?" Metro asks for anyone in the know. He's fixed on what appear to be twin boilers. They're on wheels poking out of the flood waters.

"Engines for the conveyors," answers Karl, an ex-miner.

"Do they work?"

Karl shakes his head. "That was Brett Garrett's expertise."

Metro gets wistful a second then... "He would be of value here that's for sure. Is there anything you can do with these Karl?"

"Hell, put the team on 'em and pull 'em out into the light of day I guess. Take it from there."

"Sounds good."

Hannah nudges Will. "What did you guys find in there?" She's pointing across multiple doors of the corridor. One of them doors is the one to the meat.

"M—mostly nothing…" Will glances at Metro with a bit of a wide-eye. Metro gestures to drop it.

"What about in here?" Hannah's digit's fixed on the shop door Metro passed over freeing the townsfolk.

"You're right!" Metro moves to the door. Tugs the padlock. "Will, the first supply room on the way in, I was sure I saw a ball pean hammer and a flat chisel. Could you bring them?" Will hops to it. Metro turns to Hannah. "Ma'am I'm not certain what's in here. You might not want to see."

"Those Red-Eyes camping here right under my nose this whole time? There's not a shred of detail I want to be deprived of ever again, especially knowingly!"

"Then I should tell you. The Red-Eyes don't live off of any oatmeal like their captives. In the room at the end of the corridor there's—"

"Got 'em!" Shouts Will. Guy's fast.

"Tell me later but tell me," Hannah insists as she and Metro step aside. Will goes to work.

CRINK! CRINK! CRINK! CRINK-CHUNK!

Fourth time's the charm. Lock pops.

Metro hands the directional lantern to Will who holds it over everyone's heads as they enter.

"On the left Will."

Will moves the lantern beam to the area requested.

"On those."

He hovers the illumination over more wall-mounted lanterns. Metro lights them up. Not much help though there's a workbench illuminated. Some nondescript items on it. There's a supply closet and many lidless crates on the floor.

No Red-Eye-Made lunches. Thank God.

Metro grabs the lantern from Will and shines it closer to

the workbench. Gatling ammo and a broken firing pin are revealed.

"Shells are useless without this." Metro picks up the pin. The tip is sheered off.

"What's that?" asks Will.

"For the gun outside."

"Let me see?" He holds the lantern closer. Examines. Shifts. "They work with those?" He's pointing at the firing springs next the box of ammo.

"Yeah."

"I can make these."

"How?"

"I make similar at the shop all the time."

"You don't even know if your shop's still standing."

"Don't need it. Just need that." He's pointing at the metal lathe to the right of the workbench. "Just get those folk out there to file me a few four-inch pieces of rebar."

Hannah and Metro Shrug a *why not?* at each other.

"Alright I'll get them started on the cutting." Will makes for the door. Stops. "How many you need?"

"Eight is ideal though even one will fire a barrel."

"I can do eight."

He leaves.

"Well," Hannah says. "We might be able to make a last stand yet."

"First things first..."

Metro moves the lantern to the open crate. It's empty. He picks up the lid leaning to its side and puts it back on top. Lid says *Dynamite.*

"Shit!" the two say in unison.

Metro moves the lantern around. Does a quick count of crates.

"That's way more than what's needed to bust up a few storefronts," he thinks out loud.

"Enough to blow a dam?" Hannah suggests.

Metro raises an eyebrow. Nods. "It's at least consistent. Though even after that they'd have crates to spare."

Hannah shakes her head. She's resigned to something.

"What is it?"

"These men. They're not some force of nature or apparition. Some myth." Keeps shaking that head of hers. "They're just... They're just conmen. Meticulous cruel con-men."

"Good. We can stop what is mundane."

"The Council?"

"*Touché.*"

"Speaking of... The Council just let these guys sit on one of their mines for a year?"

"Council's domain is immense. Maybe right hand not know actions of left?"

"Damn it!" she huffs. "Which prospect hurts worse? Council commissioning these assholes to run us out of Shale? Or these assholes proving Council members the ignorant fools we all knew they were but who've managed to get the better of us for forty years?"

Metro grins. "Rats flipping switches."

"What?"

"Rats flipping switches. Give one hundred rats one hundred paddles to press in some number in some order for a food pellet. Ninety-nine rats starve while one figures out the combination. Do this one hundred times and you have one-hundred rats who always eat. Yet rats know nothing. They just got lucky with conditioning is all. Council's just rats flipping switches. Found the combination they needed to steal iron."

Hannah grins like Metro grins. "So how do you stop 'em from flipping those switches?"

"You don't. You stop giving them food pellets."

She tilts in some sort of satisfaction at the thought. "What about this?" She points at the supply closet.

Metro grabs the lantern off the bench and gestures for Hannah to open the doors.

Metro recognizes some blasting caps and wire. He hands Hannah the Lantern and starts pulling the materials off the shelf. He sets them onto the bench.

"More ingredients for their terrorism." He pulls some metal containers off the shelf below where the blasting materials sat. "Lock boxes." He turns back to the closet. There's no light. "Hannah?"

She's still got the beam fixed on those containers.

"What is it?"

"I've seen these before," she says.

"Lock boxes?"

"No. These are something else." She starts moving the lantern beam around. "Where's that chisel?"

"Here." Metro moves past Hannah to the end of the bench at the door. He picks up the hammer and chisel.

Hannah tilts her head toward the box. Metro gets it. Goes to work.

He sets the box on its end and readies the tools over the padlock.

CRINK-CHUNK! Lock busts open.

"First crack at it!" Metro says holding the lock in slightest of boyish glee.

Hannah's silent at this. Holding the lantern and waiting for Metro to finish the job. *Oh well...* He swings the door open to reveal some sort of cylinder. It's difficult to make out in the dark of the lockbox. Metro pushes at the tube and it jostles a little. Whatever it is it's held firm if not fast. He holds the box out to Hannah gesturing for her to take it. She puts the lantern down and takes the box in her grip. Metro puts both hands to the tube and yanks. Cylinder breaks free.

Hannah swaps out the box for the lantern again. She's about to move the beam to the object in Metro's arms when she notices a peculiarity. She brings the lantern as close to the box as she can. What she beholds is a pair of metal brackets each with a circled cursive 'L' stamped into them.

An image of a Lamour tech installing her office's telegraph terminal flashes to mind. Tech's sliding the cylindrical power cell into the lock box under the terminal. *The electricity in this power cell will stop your heart...* Horror comes across Hannah's face. She spins, shining the lantern on Metro.

"That's a Lamour power cell!" Metro's eyes go wide despite the glare in his face. "Get rid of it!"

Instinctively, he spins to throw the power cell out the door only to toss it at Will returning with a piece of rebar. Will drops the rebar to catch what's tossed at the exact moment Hannah shines the lantern on him.

Hannah and Metro scream as the power cell breaks apart in Will's hands!

AHHHHHHHHHHH! Hannah and Metro scream as Will convulses, shakes, and starts screaming himself. All in apparent anguish!

AHHHHHHHHHHHHHHHHHHHHHHHHHHHHHHHH! AHHHHHHHHHHHHHHHHHHH! AHHHHH... Will screams, just shaking and convulsing with a look of pure shock! *AHHHHHHHHHHHHHHHHHHH... AHHHH WHHAAAAT...* "...the hell you two!" He's stopped with the screeching and stares angrily at Hannah and Metro. "You scared the shit out of me with that wailing!" He holds up the power cell in multiple pieces. "What even is this?"

"Will?" Hannah and Metro ask in unison.

"Yeah?"

"You're not dead?"

"Naw but these pants have had it!"

"We thought you were electrocuted! You were convulsing."

"How would you react if two maniacs threw whatever the hell this is at ya coming around the bend only to start screamin' like banshees?"

Will dumps the power cell parts into Metro's arms and kneels down to find that piece of rebar. "Could use some of that light down here."

There's no light.

"I don't understand..." Metro admits.

He and Hannah are examining the broken cell. It's just a tin canister. Empty. Will gets fed up working in the dark and leaves to see if anyone will loan him a change of pants.

"It's a fake?" Metro continues. "Were they planning to impersonate Lamour operatives?"

"How?" Hannah ponders. "No technicians were ever added. Dotty vouched for every one that came with her."

"Sell fake equipment in other towns?"

"For what money? If people didn't notice a lack of Lamour lines around them they'd surely notice the lack of messages coming in. Can't fake that. Besides, this looks genuine." Hannah picks up the lockbox. "I have one of these in my office."

She runs her thumb over the Lamour emblem on the power cell bracket. There's a flash of Metro dropping those same brackets onto her desk. *Dotty is a suspect...* A flash of Dotty grimacing at Mrs. Garrett and Waylan Burke for asking about a lack of iron. A lack of spark.. A flash of a rendering of Haidt with those silver wispy tendrils. A flash of Dotty's silver wispy tendrils slipping free from her sleeping turban as she's dragged away. *My father's dream...*

"My father's dream." Hannah glances down to the cuff of her top. At a portion that caught the blood Dotty'd coughed up.

"What was that Hannah?" Metro asks, confused.

She shows Metro the red of her cuff. *Like poppy pedal...*

"Dotty is Haidt's daughter."

Hannah goes faint. S'collapsing. Metro catches her.

24

LIBRIUM

etro ain't sure if Hannah passed out due the shock of her realization or the fact she hasn't slept a solid sober night in days. She sleeps now though. A couple hours won't hurt.

Alright put her in gear! He hears coming from out front the mine.

HE EXITS TO SEE KARL'S gotten the steam engines for the conveyors going. The belts are submerged and unsalvage-able so he's testing a motor on a wheelbarrow using the barrow's wheel well and a length of chain around it and the engine's drive drum.

CHAIN'S ROLLING OVER JUST FINE until the Shaler holding the barrow lets it slip. The slip causes slack in the chain and the slack causes the chain to roll over itself and knot in the drum. Now the drum's *winding* instead of *conveying* and the chain loop is shrinking as more and more of it wraps around the drum. Shrinking loop drags the wheelbarrow toward the motor mechanisms.

Karl's trying to wrangle effectiveness out of all involved as he turns to the winding motor. "Put it out of goddamn gear!" He shouts at the Shaler minding it. Just then the wheelbarrow tumbles past him with the *Barrow-Minder* chasing after. Karl chases after the chaser shouting, "Leave it alone! She'll rip your arms off!" Barrow-Minder doesn't appear to have heard. Keeps on. So does Karl. Catches up to Barrow-Minder only inches before he'd'a been tangled up in that chain when...

Shit!

CRUNCH! CRASH! CRUNCH!

Wheelbarrow's dragged into the drum and spun-smashed to bits in seconds. Pulped! It's just the drive turning now, whipping that snarl of a chain around the drum. Round and round it goes as *Motor-Minder* wrenches on the immovable gear shifter. Karl pulls him out of the way, steps on the clutch bar and pulls the lever shifting the drive out of gear. Drive stops. Chain stops.

"I... I'm sorry Karl," says Motor-Minder. Contrition all over his face.

"My fault," says Karl, contrition all over his. He stares off into the mine. Shakes his head. "I ain't no Brett Garrett. I ain't no boss man." He moves to the drum. Tries to unsnarl the chain as though this impossible task's just the distraction.

"What's the assessment?" Metro asks not acknowledging anyone's errors or contrition—would be a disproportion of iniquity. A profanity among the saints.

Just as Metro's question's posed, Karl manages to yank the last of that snarled chain free. He grins at those links a second just sitting free of each others' encumbrances. Grins at the impossibility of what he's done. He bows in recognition of something only he'll ever know and rises to brief Metro.

"Well as ya saw," he begins. "The belts are soaked but we ain't got no iron to move around here anyhow. As you also saw, these things make for a pretty good winch. Power of these motors could drag that mine inside out if ya ask me. *If ya ask me.*"

"That's a use. Where could we apply it?"

"In this refugee camp? I can't imagine. However, the damn things are on wheels so if there's an object you can get to by team you can drag at it with these motors."

"Sheriff!" shouts Will from up on one of the gun turrets.

"Good work Karl!" Sheriff tips his hat. He moves on to Will.

Will's got the gun at the ready. "Eight barrels," he says. "Eight pins. Eight shells in the magazine. Want to christen it?" He moves aside allowing Metro access to the crank.

"Why not..." Metro gets a second's glee of a kid on Christmas morning. He grabs hold of that crank and...

POOM! POOM! POOM! POOM! POOM! RRRITCH! POOM! POOM!

All except one of the shells fire into the dirt outside the complex.

"Excellent," Metro says.

"That one's off by a half millimeter or so," says Will pointing at the pin that didn't fire the shell. "As good as a mile. Wouldn't have happened if I had my micrometers. I'll have it fixed in the hour." And he will.

HANNAH ROUSES TO SEE METRO in the door of the sleeping quarters. His back to her. Keeping watch.

"How long was I out?" she asks.

"About two hours," he says over his shoulder.

"If I had any more faith in me being a use I'd say that was two hours wasted."

Metro turns. Matches her flippancy. "It was and it wasn't." he says. "We've managed to secure the compound and you got some much-needed rest."

She chuckles. "We're all needing it yet I'm the only one with the nerve to take it." Then... "Dotty's going to raze the hell out of Shale. Do what her daddy never could."

Metro's still a tittle incredulous. "She went to a lot of trouble. Setting up a state-of-the-art operation like that just to ingratiate herself..."

"No real trouble when you think about it. Only thing they needed was that concrete shell. Quite the upgrade from camping in the woods. They blow that gate and hole up here while they build their complex. Store their explosives to blow the rest of the dam. Store a handful of telegraph machinery to use for appearance's sake. Everything else is just a bunch of sham copper and wood connecting nothing. Those telegraph poles were never destroyed by sabotage or the elements. Not by the Council! Those poles never *were* to begin with! You see any of 'em out in the RM?"

"Only rubble said to be what was left. After the *hail* of course. The *sabotage*." Metro snaps his fingers. "Cap mentioned never meeting any people new to the RM. Thought they all just lived at the city limits and assimilated with us."

"Just names on a ledger and bandit money for taxes."

"Probably not even that. You think Cap does any accounting?"

Hannah shrugs a *probably not.*

"People were paid commissions?" Metro adds. "There were incoming and outgoing messages?"

"One big loop heading out from that complex and coming back in. Commissions just more bandit money."

Metro's reaching. "They taught them that amalgamation method?"

"Badly. Maybe even just told us we knew it. Have to see our outgoing nonsense to know we weren't fluent and..."

"...Only Dotty and the technicians saw that," Metro fills. "Yet, what could possibly be their motive?"

"You asking because you think *no motive no Red-Eyes* and we go back to the drawing board?"

"There is not an explanation other than Red-Eyes though it can't be right. Only insane people destroy without any conceivable motive. Yet insane people could never carry off a plan so intricate."

"Santa Rosa?"

A beat.

"*Touché.*"

DOTTY'S TECHNICIANS MOVE OUT THE Lamour complex like on a mission. Kinda are. They march shoulder to shoulder into Shale from up on the hill. As they pound on, they transform themselves into The Inner-Circle. Boil's washed under and dripping from their eyes.

"WHAT NOW?" HANNAH ASKS.

"WE have no communication. You are still half-drunk. Our best plan is to gather fresh water at the river, wait here and sober up. Then I ride to Carson and—" Metro sighs in some sort of half-resignation. Hannah notices.

"What?"

"Marshal Swade is dead. Dotty had him killed."

"There must be an interim Marshal in place? Some deputy?"

"*Maybyee.* But a deputy appointed by Swade."

"Shit!"

Metro puts his hand on his moshonka kneading it again. He feels something anomalous. It's that envelope of Bark. He pulls it out and examines it once more.

T:I:I

Your people use the Bark improperly...

"Your people use the Bark improperly."

"What's that?"

Metro's turn for epiphany. He's remembering the night he went into that fugue. How quickly he came out of it too. A vision at mind's eye. It's of the Wildlanders before they tossed him onto his bed. They're pouring something down his throat. That was why the strange sensation.

"*Proper use?*" He rubs his thumb over the 'T:I:I' on the envelope. He covers the ':I:I'. He covers the 'T:'... The ':I:I'... The 'T:'... The ':I:I'. He lingers on the 'T:'...

"*Tea?* Tea!"

"What is it!"

"A hope."

25

LEGION

Kate's still the loner even on the stumble. Soon as the Red-Eyes freed her she headed right back to her garden. She's loping around it in the moonlight. She's noticeably frailer but her being freed's allowed her more of the boil. Sounds horrible, however, at this point any further withdrawal would kill her.

She reaches out for a half-black tomato rotted on the vine. Gropes at it a few times knocking it swinging as though on a pendulum. Eventually it lands in her opened palm. She pulverizes it watching it ooze out her fingers.

Huh huh... It's almost like she's amused by this.

She moves on to the potatoes. Their leaves are shredded by the bugs. Crusted-over protruding tubers long ago greened from lack of hilling catch her attention. She's stomping over to them when...

WHUSH!

She's lassoed.

She groans and changes course. She lumbers toward her lassoer which is easy as he's pulling her in this direction. The second proximity favors it, she takes the lassoer's wrist in her hand. It's the most powerful of pressures he's ever felt. She grimaces at him. He doesn't see it. He just looks into her eyes as she squeezes. Metro's dying too much to feel the unpleasantness of the pain in flesh. It's all asymbolia but the heartache.

He whips the arm she's got the death grip on up and over and around her back. He scoops her off her feet and into his arms, carrying her toward the house. She growls and chuckles a craggy scoffing chuckle at him. Hannah holds the door.

Inside, he lays her onto their bed. She's roped around the belly and forearms yet she's still got him in Beowulf's grip. He crouches beside her next the bed. He doesn't fight her hold on his wrist though he lays his free arm across her holding her still.

"Hannah, there is my canteen with clean water on the dresser," he says. "With it is a small paper envelope. Please boil a cup of that water and brew the entire of that envelope in it." Hannah obliges. No hesitation. She takes the indicated materials. "Be extra careful not to waste that."

She leaves and with barely fifteen seconds passing comes back into the bedroom. She's staring warily into a coffee cop. "This what I think it is?"

"Yes."

The graveness in his voice and the pain in his expression indicate he knows what he's doing. She returns to the kettle.

The tea brews.

HE TRIES GIVING KATE THE Bark. He can only work with his one free hand so Hannah braces Kate's head still for him. Tea's only a little more than lukewarm yet Kate writhes and growls like he's pouring limestone onto canker sores. It's heart-rending work but he's got to make sure she gets it all in.

IT'S DONE.

SHE ROLLS HER head back. She groans but the craggy bellow is pitching up to a voice more recognizable. At least it's Kate again in that pain thinks Metro but now it's Kate in that pain. A cry of a voice he loves. A voice he hasn't heard in far too long though it's still a cry. He lowers his head. She loosens her grip. He puts both his hands to her cheeks his lips to her forehead. Wash of tears aids the fever breaking.

"Dmytro?"

"K—Kateryna?"

SHE WAKES, LUCID IF GROGGY.

"The children?"

"Safe."

"Where?"

He chuckles. How can he not? "Y—You don't want to know. Just... Just understand there are people we never thought would be our allies in this who've turned out to be so much more."

She latches unto him. "I believe. Since troubles, it's all I've ever seen in this town."

FIRES BURN ALL ALONG MAIN. There's much rubble too. Rubble of what's burned and of what's crumbled. There's a rumble on the outskirts of Shale City. It's a familiar sound.

A massive *Beasts-Bigger-Than-Clydesdales-Driven* water wagon approaches. Biggest water wagon you'll ever see in the territory. Fifteen-hundred gallons! Wagon comes to a stop at the south end of Main just in front of what remains of Hannah's Queen Anne.

Red-Eyes and Red-Maws have built a Loomer over the Anne's rubble. That wooden skeleton of a man of one-by-four slats. What I told you about at the start of this tale. Shaped like a wood-frame conjuror working his hands over a cauldron. Head like the Loomis method and with boil splashed under the eyeless sockets. A real blasphemy.

Another blasphemy in all this is Tom's stone. Tom's gone.

Wagon's shotgun rider throws a saddle bag over his shoulder and grabs a pair of tin pump sprayers sitting between he and I. He hops off the wagon and gestures for me to follow my usual route: a spiral around the outskirts of town that works its way to the middle. My job is to recruit as many volunteer firefighters along the way as I can.

Rider walks on down Main. Formed.

KATE'S SITTING UP IN HER and Metro's bed. Metro kneels beside her holding her hand. Hannah's in the other room keeping watch through the front window. Kate's managed to get a couple of the last of her non-rotten tomatoes in her and's gotten some strength back.

Her returning vigor and clarity of mind only bring a grief we'd expect of a woman of her knowledge. Knowing her babies are a half-day's ride off. She's anxious. The sooner Shale's healing the sooner she'll be holding them babies again. Getting to hastening Shale's healing will take her mind off those lonely babies and allow her her part in making it whole. Yet, there's a nagging thought that keeps creeping in. She can't help entertain it.

"What is the plan?" she asks Metro.

"For you to rest."

"I get over my hangovers sweating. Besides, you and Hannah are not going to be standing still as I rest. What will you do? Tell me beat for beat? Come on."

"Well," Metro faces the north. "That Bark cures the addiction. It cured yours Kateryna and it cured mine. We will sneak out of here and head back to the mine where you and Hannah will be safe. Then I will ride out to the wild-lands and ask the Wilder Queen for all the Bark she can spare."

"And then what Dmytro? You lasso every Shaler and pour that tea down their throats? There are nearly two hundred of them out there."

"We have to try something love."

"I know you think that." She picks up his hand. "I can see the bruise I left in that state and I couldn't stop myself. I don't want to look at it anymore and I am glad it is something that will heal because I couldn't hate myself any more —" she starts to cry. He gets up on the bed next to her and holds onto her.

"It's ok Kateryna."

She reaches out. Smoothes her thumb over his mustache. Pulls its wings outward and upward. "Why does it have to be you?"

He doesn't have an answer to this. Not now. Anya and Vikki have had refuge for weeks. Kate's been the sole driver of his actions since and he's got her back too. The content-ment that comes with this awareness hits him like a ton of bricks. All he can give Kate by way of an answer is platitude and he ain't sure why he's giving it. "Who else will do it?"

But she knows. She understands the instinct in him. "I am not a lawbringer Metro so I don't have these qualms that you do, yet I still know the selfishness in me in what it is I currently desire…"

"What is it?"

"The idea that we can just load up our carriage. Get our girls and leave this place."

"Again?" There's anger in his tone now. Not at Kate and she knows it. Too well. No more platitude. "We fled our home. We fled the north. Now we flee this place? There will always be something to run from Kateryna. They will push and they will push and they will push because they know we are the type to run when they do. They will keep at it until they push us into a corner of the world where there is finally nowhere left to run."

"Until then we'll have each other. The girls."

"In our running we leave fewer to stand their ground. They will be conquered and so those conquerors will only be stronger in their chase. We leave these people Kateryna, they perish. We leave these people, we only hasten the force at our heels."

"They'll kill you Metro!" Light tears turn to sobs. "I would have killed you! You can't save them all."

"Naw," says a presence in the doorway. "But I know who can…"

METRO POPS OUT OF BED with his six-shooter on me before he's even fetched his slippers. I turn my palms out at him. As good as showing my belly. I think he understands the gesture. He eyes me up and down and if I didn't know any better I'd think there was a sense of relief in him more than anything else. Y'see—

"You're a Wilder," he says to me. "In a Deputy Marshal's badge."

"That I am," I say. "And that I wear."

I hear Hannah coming toward me so I step inside and into the bedroom to let her through.

"I'm sorry Metro," she says. "I—"

"That's ok ma'am," I intercept. "I let myself in the back door."

"How'd you know we were in here?" asks Metro.

I pull that letter he left on Martha's grave out my pocket. "Your house is the next stop on my twistin' into town. That said..." I hand him the note. "You are Sheriff Metro Molyboha and this is your address?"

He tips his hat in assent.

"I'm a representative of Martin Shawk," I tell him.

"You're a Wilder!" Hannie says to me in bewilderment.

"That I am."

Sheriff betrays an air of disappointment though it ain't for my roots. "You as good as Shawk?" he asks.

"Doesn't matter. You got him too. Down 'round Main."

He looks on in relief at where I point. "And you?" he asks me.

I continue the pointin' only I move my finger a little lower and over, gesturing out the window. "I put out the fires."

"Not enough water," Metro says, assessing the wagon out back.

"That's not for that. That's for the townsfolk."

"What is it?"

"Just the purest of what the county's wellsprings have to offer. Remineralized with my own concoction. My people's *blessing* as I like to call it." At this point I notice Mrs. Molyboha's lucidity despite her red maw. "Though I take it you already know?" I stifle myself again here as, despite the missus' lucidity, Mayor's suffering a decent amount of wooz herself. That was my negligence. Of course she'd been living off the same boil. "Here," I say as I offer Hannah the flute from my hip.

She takes it. Turns to Metro. He gestures assent like he's sipping from his thumb. She turns back at me and shrugs. She drinks. Thirstily.

"Drink half that," I say. "Up up! Get at least two pints in ya. You're next Sheriff."

He shakes his head at me. "I know of the Wilder's blessing too."

"Very good then!"

As I said, Hannah drank quickly. Like she hadn't had such a potion in years. Truth be told she hadn't had that potion ever. By the last ounce you could see the color returning to her cheeks and the good sense evident in her eyes.

"Won't fix y'all instantly but it'll right you and them townsfolk enough to get the beet buckets on them fires."

Then...

BOOM! BOOM! BANG!

"That's Marsh. This ends tonight. You politicians head toward them shots. I'll continue roundin' up a fire brigade."

"I join you," Kate says.

"What?" Metro responds. Slight protest in tone.

Kate furrows. "I'm not lawman or legislator. I don't shoot gun. I can be of help on that..." She points to the water wagon. She's silent for a good three seconds then... "I can be of help on that?" She's waving at me.

"Oh you were askin' ma'am! Of course!" I nod. "Recruitin's the reason for the role."

Kate nods back at me then turns to Metro. She embraces him. Looks deep into his eyes.

"Besides dove, I want to lord over Pastor fact that it took a Wildlander and a 'Galician' to cure him."

"That is petty woman."

"Questionable morality?"

"Yes."

"Then you are welcome husband."

"What?"

"*Questionable morality but morality nonetheless,*" she says with her simper. "*I don't want to raise my children in an amoral world...* Well, here's your reprieve."

Never loved her more. Never would've still, even if she hadn't made the gesture.

She kisses him on the tip of his nose. "We go now..." she says not moving. Then... "We go now?"

Ah! She's asking again.

We go now.

THE SHERIFF AND THE MAYOR move through the alleys making their way to Main. There are many more vacant lots. Vacant butfor the rubble and the Loomers. Bank's gone. General Store's gone. Make no mistake, them shops were an empty gift box for a long time and now there ain't even the box.

On their way the pair pass the odd pig-gut-bound Red-Eye. They count six so far. How many left then? What was it? A dozen that came with Dotty. Five at the mine and five at the dam. Then there's the operator men who moved to town leaving up to a maximum of—

Three.

Sorry. Not *three* operators, three henchmen. Knocker Lasso and Wait. Trio greets Metro and Hannah as the pair round the corner to the Loomer lot of the General Store.

The henchmen stand at the Loomer looming over the vestiges. All four in seeming anticipation.

All henchmen have some sort of weapon out. Knocker's got a Colt eight-shot revolver at the hip. Lasso's got a bull-whip. Wait's got a pair of sawed-off .410 shotguns—one in each hand. Hannah and Metro stand halted. All pointable weapons pointed at them. All bleeding eyes stare daggers at them.

BANG! BANG!

Knocker shoots to shit The Sheriff's revolver still in its holster.

BANG!

He shoots The Sheriff's gun belt off.

BANG! BANG!

Now the moshonka's gone. Sheriff winces.

BOOM! BOOM!

One of Wait's .410 blasts blows Hannah's chest open sending her flying onto her back. Other blast blew Metro's chest open too, though his extra mass kept him on his feet. Don't matter none. The second Lasso saw Metro not falling he lashed the shot-up lawman's ankles and toppled him.

Hannah and Metro lay nursing their stinging wounds.

"Am I dyin'?" Hannah groans.

"Rock salt," Metro says licking at the jam at the tip of his fingers.

"Hold 'em," Knocker says as he flips his pistol around doing that fancy shit we've all seen hundreds of times *before* before finally holstering it. He reaches for his hunting knife as Lasso crouches next to Metro, poking at his chest wounds. Wait's dumping the .410 shells.

Knocker swaggers over slowly. Cuts at the air with that hunting knife as...

A hand reaches out from behind. Pulls Knocker's eight-shot back out the holster and drives the butt of it into the back of his head. *WHOMP!* Knocker goes down to his knees as hand relieves him of his hunting knife too. *CRASH!* The upright half of the kneeling Red-Eye's booted into the dirt to join the prone.

"Son of a bitch!" say the other Red-Eyes.

Wait's hurrying to get some lethal rounds into those .410s all while Lasso rushes to unwrap his whip from Sheriff's ankles. Their eyes fix on Shawk as they complete their respective tasks.

Wait gets a round into one of his .410s just as Shawk tosses the hunting knife upward in hand. Wait chunks the action of the .410 closed. Hunting knife inverts allowing Shawk a grip of the blade. Wait aims. Shawk throws the knife sending it spinning end-over-end and the handle square into Wait's nose. *SMASH!* Wait drops the .410 to cradle his busted face. Screams through blood-oozing palms.

Lasso's gotten that whip free and's rising to meet Shawk. Lawman moves right on past like Lasso wunt nuthin'. Shawk's hustling to where the crying Wait stands. Not slowing at all as he nears. He uses this momentum to hoof the blood-nosed blood-eye in the gut sending him flying into, and kinda through, the slats of the wall behind.

WHAHCHIHH!

Lasso's cracked that whip-tip sending it flying for Shawk's neck. Shawk just reaches out and catches it like he's a goddamn myth. He wraps the slack of the whip around his left hand holding it tight. Yanks! Lasso's too dumb to let go so Shawk brings him stumbling toward. As Lasso stumbles over, Shawk pulls his already cocked left arm back further, clenching his raw-hide-wrapped fist tighter. Close enough! He launches that fist forward *SMACK!* into Lasso's approaching accommodating unsuspecting glass jaw. Lasso takes it like it's terminal and spins himself into a crumbling heap.

Red-Eye's are down but they ain't out. Shawk rushes to the now sat-up Hannah and Metro examining their wounds. He looks unimpressed. Goes back to get the saddle bags he set aside. He brings 'em to the pair. Tosses 'em onto the ground.

"No point sittin' there lettin' your adrenaline pool," Shawk says. "Only make the salt burn more fierce."

He reaches into a bag and grabs a handful of pig strips. He hands a few to Hannah then a few to Metro and turns around to the unconscious Knocker. He loops the strip around Knocker's legs first.

"Start with the legs," he says. "Get a layer wrapped about to half-shin then start workin' on the wrists. If they're conscious work on the wrists first."

The pair help get to work with the bindin'.

Hannah and Metro follow Shawk down the alley back the direction they came. Salt wounds are burning like the man said they would in calm. Shawk carries his saddlebags and a lariat he stole from Lasso.

Incidentally, his grey has turned to damn-near white since retirement. He's huffing and puffing a little harder these days from a little less these days. Last hunt took it out of him. Took a lot of it out of him and now he's right back on that demon's trail.

On their way down the alley, Hannah and Metro notice some newly bound Red-Eyes.

"You came right up behind us," Hannah observes.

"You walked right past me," Shawk says.

"Where?"

"Hope you don't mind Mayor, I set up shop in your office. I followed you out the back door."

"Don't have a back door."

"There's always a back door." Shawk says this in serendipity. He rolls some barrels sideways on their bottoms then lifts a pallet away from the wall of Hannah's office. It appears he's broken some slats out to about thigh height. A length of fine grey sewing thread spans the *ad hoc* passageway connected by thumbtacks. He pulls the right tack off and sticks it into an already-established hole above the left. Satisfied, he ducks under and waves Hannah and Metro on to follow.

Inside we see the front of the office rebarricaded. At the rear, Shawk slides a row of oak file cabinets across the passage. Metro moves to help him as Hannah pulls various items out of her desk. She finds some matches and strikes one. She's moving it toward a lantern when...

"Put that out Hannah!" Shawk grits. He moves past her toward the front of the office. "We don't need it yet."

She snuffs it with whips in the wind.

Shawk waves her and Metro over to him at the front barricade.

"Got a problem here," he says, pointing through a gap next the window.

Hannah and Metro take turns looking. They see that the remaining stumblers have amassed outside Town Hall.

"There's a lot of 'em," Hannah acknowledges. "Too much for your deputy?"

"It's not that," Shawk says. "They never cluster like this without a Red-Eye. Like sheep with a sheepdog."

"I don't see any," Metro admits.

"Exactly. Yet they're there. Have to be." Shawk's pensive a

second. "Besides the irreverence for 'em would be nothing to wipe the blood from their eyes and slather the same under their maws. Last of the Red-Eyes are gonna make us hunt. Try for an ambush I reckon. Which ones?"

"Well, we can't just walk out there and start taking a census..." Hannah jokes from the gallows.

Metro chuckles as Shawk watches unmoved. He's watching contemplative. Gears are turning though nothin's yet the product.

It's about this time I fly by on my fire wagon. I'd say Kate and I cured about two-thirds the southside of town and now them cured folk are working on them southside fires. Time to head for the east. Let Marsh deal with the center mass as well as the Inner-Circle up north.

In all my rumbling I cause a helpful mundanity. A Loomer in the lot next to Town Hall loses a single slat of its arm. A minor concern but it appears to have exercised the hell out of a few stumblers who're moving swiftly to it. With what anyone who's ever observed a stumbler would think impossible dexterity, half hold the slat to where it fell and half bind it back in place with hammers and tacks.

"That's it!" Shawk bursts. "Hannah, you can light that lantern now."

She does.

She turns the lamp up to half its illumination.

"Haidt!" Shawk says.

Metro goes alert—hand on gun—then realizes the ostensiveness of the utterance. Shawk's pointing at the *For Mayor* sketch on Hannah's desk.

Hannah realizes the point of the gesture too. "Yes, we know unfortunately."

"We know *now*." Metro adds.

"You never noticed before?" Shawk asks.

"It wasn't until we found the Red-Eyes' hideout that we learned Dotty was Haidt's daughter."

"Daughter?"

BOOM! CRASH! BOOM!

They're coming through the barricade in front.

THUMP! CRASH! THUMP!

Shawk picks up the two pump sprayers and puts them on the desk. He starts pumping one and motions for Metro to pump the other. "Hurry Metro!"

THUMP! THUMP!

"Come here Hannah!"

Hannah moves to Shawk as he takes the sprayer away from Metro. He nudges Metro toward the file cabinet blocking the backdoor. Hannah approaches and Shawk spins her around. "Let's put this on." He lifts the sprayer, modified to feature two shoulder straps evidently. Hannah extends her right arm and Shawk slips the right strap over it. He repeats the process for the left. She wears the pump like a backpack. Spray nozzle in her grip.

Metro's clearing the file cabinet away.

THUMP! A Red-Maw's arm is through a hole in the front barricade.

"Leave only enough room Metro. We must reseal it."

Metro can barely squeeze between the file cabinet and the wall yet he *can* get through. He figures he's the largest so if he fits, Shawk and Hannah will.

"Come you two. We haven't much time."

26

HOWDY

They're back moving south in that alley, past one storefront after Hannah's office toward another lost lot. Shawk inches up to the edge before that lot and takes a peek. Another Loomer in there. Emptiness otherwise. He turns to Hannah and Metro.

"Metro could you go to where we bound those three? Bring one of their horses? Be careful not to alert the stumblers in Hannah's office as you pass."

Metro flicks his hat. Heads in the direction of where the fracas took place.

"Hannah," Shawk says. "Keep watch for anything unusual in the alley. See anyone other than Metro or I, whistle." He lets out a tweet that goes *WHEE HEE HEW!*

Hannah bows in oblige.

"I'll be back." He heads into the vacant lot toward the Loomer.

He's got Lasso's lariat and he's hooping it at his side. He's analyzing that wood-man's construction. Lariat's hooping over his head now. Must be done deliberating. He gives it a toss catching Loomer around the neck.

Meanwhile Metro's found Knocker's quarter horse. Gelding's sniffing at his bound-and-gagged master. "I doubt you'll miss him," Metro says to Knocker as he takes the animal by the halter. "I *know* you won't miss *him*," he says to the horse.

Knocker watches as Metro walks away having repossessed a piece of a Red-Eye's plunder. He's got a look in that red eye like he's thinking *that ain't the way this is supposed to work.* He ups the intensity of his wriggling, that's about it. What can he do?

Metro's leading the animal out to the alley as he stops short. He crouches down reaching out. It's his moshonka. He takes it in hand and ties it back onto his belt. He dusts it off letting a finger linger over one of the bullet holes a second.

SHAWK'S BACK WITH HANNAH AS Metro and the horse approach.

"Hitch the horse a second Metro."

Metro lashes the rein around a drain pipe as Shawk picks up the second pump sprayer. He spins Metro around with his free hand then puts the tank onto his shoulders. He spins Hannah around to face the same direction as Metro and gives both their tanks a few pumps. He lets the pair free to face him.

"One last thing before we begin." He says this almost in warning. "As you know, there's always an Inner-Circle. You'll see them up at the end of the road. They'll wait, never moving until all their men have failed them. Don't concern yourself with them just yet."

Hannah has a flash of the Inner-Circle of Stemfield waiting like stone. Waiting to kill Tom. She shudders.

"Hannah?"

"It's fine," she says waving off any further attention. "Let's finish the job."

THE THREE WALK OUT OF the vacant lot and on into Main. They stand shoulder to shoulder. Shawk's at the center flanked by The Sheriff and The Mayor wearing them pack pumps. Nozzles are at the ready. They face Town Hall at a diagonal taking in the whole of this new context. Scene should be the most familiar in the world to at least two of them. However, it's uncanny. It's like a picture of a corpse dressed up to look alive.

The resurrection will come though. Honest to goodness and not by some photographic fakery. Already's come in part. Trio attends to the south. The volunteers have salvaged most of Will and Rosey's shop. See Rosey resurrected and leading the brigade.

Hannah turns to the north. She sees what Shawk warned about. *You'll keep them from getting Shale like I kept them from getting Stemfield Hannie.*

All focus back on town hall, attention converging on the Red-Maw stumblers. Stumblers don't react to their scrutiny. Only tighten their cluster. Trio tries for a second or two to pick out the Red-Eyes among the Red-Maws. They're fly shit in pepper if they're there.

Shawk moves closer to the circle of stumblers as Hannah and Metro follow suit. Apropos of nothing, Shawk draws his pistol. Points it in the air and...

BANG!

Gelding flies out of the vacant lot behind them, rope of Shawk's lariat tied around his saddle horn. Gelding gallops south not missing a beat as the slack of that rope goes taut.

Rope takes the top of Loomer with it flying south. Town hall and office stumblers tear out after the head of their idol. They move with a speed as though possessed by the wind. They tear out leaving all the unwitting Red-Eyes behind isolated and confused as hell.

"Dowse 'em!" shouts Shawk as Hannah and Metro let fly with whatever juice is in them pumps. Comes out rusty and hot-looking. Soaks the Red-Eyes all over stunning them when it hits the face. Keeps 'em stumbling though not out of any theatrics anymore.

"Cross them streams!" Shawk shouts. "Hit 'em harder!"

They do! It does!

Red-Eyes are crying more than blood tears!

They cry on a little more, yet that juice alone wasn't meant to stop them. They're already starting to find their bearings.

They're about to find them completely when...

HOOODEEEE-HOOOOOO!

Shawk lets fly with that same wounded animal wail that set those zombies upon the last runagate of the West Brandon Trail. Stumblers chasing that Loomer slide to a halt in the grit. They spin to come running back to them Red-Eyes soaked in Shawk's chili.

"Might want to back up." Shawk holds out his arms taking Hannah and Metro with him as he reverses.

Stumblers swarm the Red-Eyes still too stunned to get to pistols. Stumblers pounce and go to work.

"They're tearing them apart!" Hannah screams.

"Naw," assures Shawk. "Just motherin' 'em."

"Smothering them?" Metro asks.

"Naw. Just watch."

They do. It's weird. All them iron-clawed stumblers not

letting go of those Red-Eyes until the suckling's done. But what's t' suckle? Weird weird weird!

Shawk holds his pig strips up to the North of Main. Shakes them at the Inner-Circle. They remain unmoved. "Be prepared for anything once we bind the last of their men," he says to Hannah and Metro.

He hands the pig strips out and the three go to work binding the Red-Eyes while in the arms of those Stumblers a' motherin'.

"Be careful not to get any of that chili on ya."

JOB'S DONE IN SHORT ORDER. Hannah Metro and Shawk back away from the Maws. Our three consider the north a moment as they move. Circle remains stone.

"How long are they gonna hold them like that?" Hannah asks, attending to the mothering Red-Maws once more.

"Until their babies are done feeding."

"What now then?"

Shawk's still looking up the road. "Might as well get proactive with the last of them..." And with that he starts out north. Hannah and Metro follow. "Have them pumps at the ready," he orders.

"They have guns," Metro warns.

"So do I."

The Leader of the circle holds his hand out to his men as our trio close the gap. *Stay still.* With his other hand he removes a flat oblong twine-wrapped paddle from inside his duster. He pinches the end of the twine in his fingers and lets that paddle fall. Gravity unfurls it for him.

"What's he doin'?" Hannah asks.

"Just keep moving."

Trio's about a hundred yards out as Leader starts pulling the end of that twine inward in small hoops over his head. Centripetal force sends that flat egg of a paddle moving in circles atop him. At-speed, the paddle catches the air contriving the effect of wind. It starts to rattle. It sounds like one cat growling at a second it doesn't recognize.

ROWWWRRR ROWWWRRR ROWWWRRR...

Paddle ain't a weapon. What's its function? Shawk's unfamiliar with this tactic so he's figuring with the same background knowledge as Hannah and Metro. He figures faster and he figures true. He pivots. Walks backward.

"Shit!"

The motherin' stumblers have let go and are rising, their attention on the trio. They start moving for them at about two hundred yards out.

"Shit!"

Stumblers are wind in no time. Flying.

"Shit?" Hannah asks.

Hundred and fifty yards out...

"Can we spray them?" Metro asks.

"I've tried. Just agitates 'em more," Shawk relents.

Hundred yards out...

Shawk turns back to face the Inner-Circle as Hannah and Metro follow. Red-Eyes' guns are drawn. Trio's pinned in place between the stumblers and the Circle.

Seventy-five...

Circle pull back their hammers.

Fifty...

"We got no choice," Shawk laments. "We're gonna have to charge 'em."

Hannah and Metro shake their heads *but...* "You're right."

Twenty-five...

"At my say so," Shawk orders.

Fifteen...

"Now!"

SPROOSH!

Circle goons fly off their horses. Kate's hosed 'em as we whip past heading for our trio. We roll past and swerve to put a barrier between the heroes and the stumblers.

"Get on!" I shout as Kate turns the hose to the Maws. The three climb aboard and to safety. The last few stumblers are sobering fast but a few of the more tenacious Maws have to be sprayed off the side of the wagon. *SPROOSH!*

"Look!" Hannah shouts as the remounted Inner-Circle ride off to the north. They ride past the complex and into the RM.

"The children!" Kate falters and lets go of the hose allowing the tenacious another foothold.

SPROOOOOO-YOOOOOSH!!!

Metro's put Kate's hand back on the sprayer and is helping her hose those buggers back to neighbors.

"Keep at it Kateryna. They will not get to the children."

Why's Metro so uncharacteristically unfazed? Here's why...

The Circle have returned. They've come riding back toward us over the hill of that complex. They're not slowing as they approach either. Metro and Shawk stand unmoved. Circle blows right on by our wagon and fly for the south of town.

The Inner-Circle don't ride alone.

On their heels is a familiar monolith of a man in his foot-and-a-half high derby. He's backed up by every Wilder in the territory it seems. All ride atop those Beasts-Bigger-Than-Clydesdales. Moose femurs poised.

"*Bone 'em boys!*" Cap howls as he glances over to the rider at his side. His tone of war turns suggestive and his face of fury turns wry. "You too my Queen."

Cap, the Wilders, and their Queen rocket past us pursuing the Inner-Circle. Chasing them *Out South*. Disappearing over the horizon.

IT'S NEAR SILENCE FOR A minute. The stumblers, now hungover Shale folk, are coming to and letting out the odd groan. Silence other than that.

Metro listens and Shawk knows to follow Metro's lead. Everyone else who doesn't know to follow Metro's lead knows to follow Shawk's. Metro puts his arm around Kate and she puts a hand to her husband's chest. He winces slightly. She notices his salt wounds. *It's ok* he smiles in assurance. She kisses him on the cheek as he regains focus.

He's listening into the distance when…

POOM! POOM! …

"What's that?" Kate asks.

"Guns at the mine," Metro answers.

POOM! POOM! POOM! POOM! POOM! Then… Silence again.

"They've stopped the last of the Red-Eyes."

"IS IT OVER?" KATE ASKS.

"No," says Shawk. "There's one more."

"Which more? Who more?" she says confused.

"Hai—"

Suddenly howls and moans emit from Town Hall. Sounds are carried by that smoked-out bellow of Dotty's. Howls seem nonsensical at first then...

MAAAARRRRTIN!

27

SHUT UP!

There's me—that is yer narrator—Shawk Hannah and Metro. We stand outside the Town Hall doors. Kate and the other revived Shalers are tending to the worst-off of themselves. Fires are out. Just one more rotten tooth to be pulled and Shale'll be on her way to healing. Just gotta walk through that door.

"Hannah. Metro," Shawk initiates. The pair go attentive. "You've only had contact with this *Dotty*. A false persona meant to lull you. You've never had contact with the force behind this persona. You need to understand. This force is intent on deceiving you. This force intends to seduce you. It will weaken you with promise and that promise will consist entirely of lies used to break you. Be on your guard. There will be games to be played to defeat it so we must listen for clues of weakness. We're all necessary conditions in this. However, only listen to talk that goes no further than what is immediate. Once we go through that door I can no longer help you without helping it. You need to understand this."

They don't, at least not sufficiently, but this ends tonight. They bow.

Shawk pushes open the French doors of the hall and we enter.

THE WROUGHT IRON PRISON IS gone. The fence is scrapped and pushed off to the periphery. It's near-all empty space. There's the iron detritus and there's also whatever constitutes the rankness in the air: smell's born of the stumbler's confinement. It exercises the olfactory machinery churning disgust. God knows what the chemistry of it is...

It's near-all empty space save the scrap the rankness and a five-foot-by-five-foot barred cell at the center of the hall. At the center of the cell is the figure facing us. Figure's in one of Dotty's dresses and bonnets. Its head is lowered. Obscured.

Shawk takes a step forward and somehow the three of us know to let him walk alone. He moves to the rear of the cell and stands behind the figure. He extends his left hand and places it on the figure's right shoulder.

"At last..." the figure croaks.

Then...

It whips off that dress and bonnet revealing all of itself except the shoulder Shawk holds. Dress hangs draped over the wrist. Figure's Head is shaved save for two silver tendrils —as bangs—parted and tucked behind ears. Some of that otherwise bald scalp is missing patches of skin. *Where Dotty's hair had been ripped out?* It's a familiar face. Ashen grey foundation, bleeding eyes, plaster dentures. Everything else is nudity. A porcelain-pallored emaciated nudity. A man's nudity. It's Hate.

Now to be clear, it ain't what's danglin' down there that proves the figure Haidt. It disproves any claim of the heiress being an heiress. Figure's an *heir* if any kind of a benefi- ciary... Naw, it ain't *what's* danglin' that betrays the demon, it's *how* it's danglin'. It's the fact that the poison that turned Haidt's teeth blue all those years back has apparently done the same for his manhood. Curious.

Hannah's been staring intently at the daemonium since his reveal. She ain't bashful about the cyan piping. No, it's the face that's got her most exercised. She's examining it. Looking at it and fooling herself. Believing a trust could still break through that pallor.

Shawk removes his hand. He walks around to the front of the cage as Haidt pulls Dotty's dress over his shoulders like a shawl. He sits himself down as Shawk examines the front of the Demon's confinement.

"No lock. No door," Shawk says, waving me over.

I move to him and together we give Haidt's cell a good shove. Won't budge. I lean down to examine the foundation as Haidt watches me keenly. He's doing me the courtesy of remaining still while not doing me the courtesy of ensuring he'll stay that way.

"Built right through the floor," I say rising. "Built around him." I take Shawk aside for a whisper. "Not that I have to but if'n' I were to climb into the crawl space of this hall I'd find his cell anchored five feet into the dirt. Man knows how to make the most of iron country."

"You're too kind," Haidt drawls at me.

What's the guy a lip reader?

Shawk pats me on the shoulder. Pat is directional in addition to encouraging. I know where he's sending me. I head to my wagon.

As I go, Shawk moves back to Hannah and Metro. Hannah's eyes remain narrow and daggered while Metro just waits for assessment.

"Reinforced steel. Half of it in the earth. Otherwise I'd say hitch it to a team and drag him to Carson—"

"*Him*," Hannah scoffs, walking off toward the cage.

"Hannah!"

She moves swift. Won't be deterred.

She walks right past the cage and picks up that bonnet caressing it a little.

"Ain't nothin' bringing your friend back," Haidt mocks. "Except maybe..." He alters his voice. "*Except...*" He repeats this as delicate Dotty. The voice is uncanny though we know the throat of the trickster-miscreant its source all along. Haidt stands. Dotty continues. "*We're kindred spirits you and I Hannah.*"

Hannah tears up at this. She turns and rushes for the other side of the hall. She blows past me and nearly knocks my toolbox and sawhorses out my arms as she goes.

Haidt calls after her still as Dotty. "*Thank you Hannah Price. I feel... for the first time... welcome.*"

Tears are rolling down Hannah's cheeks as she moves. She keeps on right past Shawk and Metro and out the Hall doors.

Metro intends to follow but Shawk grabs his arm. "Shale will be her best solace Metro. Follow me." He leads him to the makeshift table I'm setting up to the left of the cage. He lays his revolver onto it and his lariat along with the saddlebags and some good old-fashioned shackles. He opens the toolbox and pulls out some metal files. He hands one to me he thinks appropriate and sends me to work. "If you have any weapons," he says to Metro. "Lay them here."

"My pistol was destroyed."

Shawk understands. They look over to the filing sound coming from the cage. Them bars holding Haidt are a custom job. At least two inches in diameter. My arm'll fall off and grow back before I'll ever saw through even a single one of them bars but the aim is to not appear defeated in the presence of this force.

Goddamn trickster's flicking at my file too. Keeps knocking me off my mark.

"Quit it!"

"Too much fun," he chuckles.

He set the bars just narrow enough that I can't get a boot through 'em either!

"Quit it!"

"*You firrrrst.*" Haidt spins. "Hannie Price!" he shouts, catching Hannah reentering the hall. He says this in his own voice. "*Welcome back!*" He says this in Dotty's.

Shawk takes out a pair of vice-grip pliers and lays them on the table.

Hannah sidles up to him, contrite. "I'm sorry. I shouldn't have—"

"Hannah!" Shawk says through grit teeth. "Not—"

"Not in front of the miscreant!" Haidt anticipates. Hannah's unmoved. "Show no weakness Hannie Price!" he grimaces. You could say he's started chipping away at his target but Dotty got that ball rolling months ago. "Hannie Price! Wife of Tom!"

She spins to face him. "Don't you talk about my husband after what you made me say—"

"I didn't make you say nothin' missy! That's what us 'gratiators do or'd you forget? We lay on our charms n' we practically gotta beat you off with a stick to stop you from trying to cater!"

"You son of a bitch!"

"Hannah!" shouts Shawk. "Don't listen."

"Don't wanna know who really killed Tom?"

"Don't you say his name—"

"Again! How easily you forget my role in all this

woman!" He lifts the shawl off his shoulders revealing a smattering of rash caused by buckshot. A healed-over .45 scar sits near the center of it. Instantly, Hannah has a flash of that buckshot leaving Tom's chest and entering the runagate *cum* Haidt's. "I carry a little bit of Tom with me too." He's massaging the buck rash.

"Hannah!" Shawk renews the warning.

She leans closer to the cage. "Talk."

"Or what?" He flicks my file again.

"Stop it!" I grit at him again.

Haidt's attention goes back to Hannah. "You know I know." He nearly sings this taunt.

"It's what he wants Hannah." You'd swear there's almost a bit of pleading in Shawk here. "It doesn't matter what he knows or doesn't. He won't tell you the truth. You have the upper hand now. He isn't willing to speak and that's for the best."

Only if it's talk of what's immediate girl! ...But he got ya killed. ...And he'll do the same for you and all The Belt if ya don't end it now!

She relents. Moves away from the cage.

"What's this?" Haidt asks. "Some sort of reverse psychology, Marshal?" Shawk's stone. Haidt moves on. Sees Metro all by his lonesome. "I'm getting a bit peckish Sheriff, watching you standin' guard like that. I could just eat you up."

"Your innuendo isn't useful." Metro grabs another file and joins me sawing at the same bar though from the opposite side, intending we meet at the middle.

"Now where's there any innuendo Sheriff?" Haidt tickles Metro's shin. Metro makes a grab for his wrist but Haidt's already back at the center of the cage. "You saw that meat locker." He leans himself up against the side of the cage furthest from Metro and I. Real loungy. This puts his back to Hannah and Shawk though the pair don't bite at the contrived vulnerability. "Well," Haidt sighs. "How's this for not mincing words Sheriff? Save for maybe a pun somewhere in it. How's this... We liked to eat 'em alive. Fresher that way. Less gamy. You know we done 'em this way. You saw. And sometimes they couldn't take it. We'd leave a knife or a cleaver too close and find 'em next mealtime havin' slit their own throats. Sometimes they'd figure out they were on the menu before we even tucked into 'em and they'd do away with themselves preemptive-like." Beat. "That's how Tom got it."

Hannah tenses. She fears the miscreant can sense the fire in her flushing despite his back to her. *It's his game Hannah. Just listen.*

"Real Shame about ol' Tom," Haidt drones. "Found out the hard way we didn't bring him back to camp for his wit and his charms! Naw. When he stumbled upon those half-men half-eaten, bound and in shock, realizing *too* his fate was the plate. Couldn't bear it. Like so many before—"

"That's not how it happened." Hannah's found herself moving closer to Haidt. *Moved* closer to him? "He died in them streets."

"Hell he did."

She steps around to the other side of the cage to look him in the eye. "He was shot in the back by a fool thought it would curry favor with you."

"No Hannah, it was the other way around."

Flash of Tom blowing away the kid who ran the general store. "No!"

"Yeah. Oh yeah! It was Tom who panicked while everyone else was mobilizin'. Ran and hid in some storefront. Bet he prayed at first. Sittin' scared. In his own piss.

Looked to above like that's where salvation lay only he didn't reach high enough. Couldn't reach salvation so he just sat there trembling, letting his imagination run wild the whole time we were sackin' the place. Came to figure his only means of survivin' was to prove himself to us and maybe we'd bring him along in all our grace. Too bad old Tommy weren't orthodox like you Sheriff. Fear of fire and brimstone from the cradle might a' moved him. Fear of the hell that awaited him should he follow through with the actions he intended. If not faith in above maybe the fires below? Maybe that was Tom's salvation?"

"No." Hannah's shaking her head. "Stemfield folk said it was a man from The Belt saved them."

"Indeed it was. Though it wasn't Tom. Couldn't of been. See, back in camp Tom kept tellin' us that Mayorin' had made him soft."

You think mayorin's tamed me?

"Said he couldn't admit it at first yet it did. That's why he carried them two pistols holstered funny. It helped maintain the delusion but those guns were never loaded. Yeah, that town's savior was from The Belt alright. Only he wasn't no bounty hunter. He was a war hero. Born and raised in Carson. Fought in the Big One. Snuck into some enemy stronghold and picked them evils off one by one. Liberated a dozen POWs in the process. Did this all at the tender age of sixteen. Lied about being of age to serve. Would have gone far in the army too if all the wars hadn't dried up. Came back to Carson. Tried working at the family dry goods store. Like the army, they didn't need him either. He found out a farming town north of The Belt was a growing concern. Happiest day of his life. Thought he'd throw in with them. Thought he'd be needed. Opened up a general store there and found out he was! Then Tom blew the shit out of his front from his back to appease! We all know what happened after that..."

She's doing her damnedest to keep her composure here especially considering the grotesquery of the account. She pushes on. "You said you carried a little of Tom with you?" she asks in cross-examination. *Ah hell Hannah why not just take solace in Shawk's promise of the man's lying disposition? Because I need ya noble Tom! Don't I?* She points to Haidt's rash. "B—Bits of Tom brought along with the buckshot. I take it that's what you meant?"

Haidt simpers. "Think you're about to catch me in something Hannie? Like a lie? Lies require intent to deceive don't they? Can you divine my intentions girl?" He scoffs. "Don't matter. You think I say I got a little of Tom in me and that means from the buckshot and that means he was the one got his chest blown out? The story goes back to your cherished hero's tale? Maybe I just meant I got a little of Tom's pants-pissin' cowardice in me?" He pauses. Looks almost bored. This kills Hannie more and he knows it. "Or maybe I *did* mean the former?"

"Where'd he die?" she demands.

"Them streets."

"Not the camp?"

"Why would he have died in the camp? They found his body in them streets blown out by buckshot."

"You son of a bitch! You *are* nothing but a liar!"

"Are you relieved at that?"

"Hannah! Leave it!"

"Nothing you said was true."

"Everything I said was true."

"You said he died in the camp now it's the streets—"

"Ha! I said he found those half-men half-eaten in camp

then subsequent to that he killed himself. I didn't say the deed was done in camp."

"Why would he kill himself if he e—escaped to Stemfield?" She's vibrating.

"To avoid the plate."

"He escaped…"

"No he didn't."

"So he died in the camp?"

"Whoever said that?"

"You son of a bitch!" She collapses. Head in her hands.

Haidt grins indulgently. Turns himself away from Hannah and her tears streaming between fingers.

Shawk don't move. Doesn't run to comfort her. Can't. When you're drowning cuz you're sunk and you're sunk cuz you're anchored by the heels, there's no point reaching for the surface. You ain't getting up without going a little further down, sister.

"Keep pushing him Hannah."

She's still in that heap ignoring the imperative.

It's now that Shawk's moved. He rushes to her. Grabs her. Shakes her. "Stop this sad sack shit and get yourself out of it!" He's put firm hands on her shoulders demanding her attention.

Metro and I've stopped what we're doing to watch on. I don't mind saying we do this at a bit of a loss. Haidt's back to sitting at the center of his cage, head down.

"Time to finish it girl!" Shawk shakes.

Hannah gasps! Shoves him back full force. Leave me be I'm better!

He backs off. She moves to just an inch of Haidt's cage. Haidt's still *still* at the center though his head's up. Face smiles plaster. He rises.

Hannah resumes. "Why would Tom kill himself if he'd escaped your camp?"

Haidt moves to within inches of Hannah. "Because he didn't escape. Oh he left our camp alright. Got all the way back to the edge of town. To the south end of Main Street. Even saw the law comin' in at the other end." He turns to Shawk. "That's you Marsh." He turns back to Hannah. "Law arriving too late to save him. Ol' Marsh leading them hunters all triumphant-like. There to itemize the corpses of the townsfolk. Real heroes. Did you see him Marsh? Ya see Tom standin' there? He certainly saw you. Marsh was late Hannie. If he woulda got there only a few minutes, hell, seconds earlier then what happened next wouldn't have and you'd have ol' Tom in the flesh to drape those arms around instead of that tombstone!"

Haidt goes silent a second. Seems to revel a little. Then...

"Now *that* is a lie! That shit about Marsh gettin' to Tom in time! That's how lying's done girl! *Ahhhhh...* Here's the truth. Here it is... There was nothing Marsh could have done. See, it was me who was trackin' Tom and ol' Tommy made it real easy to keep up with his scent. Besides his stupor—his *camp fever* as we call it—he left so fast he left barefoot! You know the gravel around here's like razors. His pitter-patter turned from indentation to soup before he got to within five miles of that town. I followed that trail he blazed all the way along. By miracle Hannie if ya saw the bleedin'! Maybe it was the fever kept him going? I don't know, but that hobbled bounty killer made it real easy for me.

"Stupidity Hannah. That's what it was. He was stupid. So I played with that. I let him get to the edge of Main Street. Watched him waving and hootin' at Marsh and Marsh's men like everything was gonna be all right. I watched as the last remaining tinge of his fever dripped away and he became a man full of hope again. A man just a hootin' hollerin' hopin'. Thinking about you Hannie? Lookin' at you Marsh. I watched as that last remaining fever dripped away and he became the man you loved again Hannie Price.

"Then I took out my lariat and roped him around his neck. Dragged him clear out of those lawmen's view like it wunt nothing. Broke his neck in all the right places doin' it. Dragged him all the way into an alley before I saw he couldn't use his legs no more. I played with that too. Told him he had a choice. Told him first of course that there was no further chance of escape as he hadn't any legs. He was mine. Said *Tom, you can come back to that camp where you know your fate or, in all my grace, I'm willing to sit you up n' prop the barrel of my twelve-gauge against your heart n' let you put your finger to trigger and see your life through.* Well, which horn of that dilemma do you think that coward chose? You think he cho—

"*BOOM!* That's the horn he chose! But the damn fool shot his heart out before I could even get clear out from behind him! Maybe he wunt so stupid? Maybe he decided to go out puttin' a little of his buck in me too? Sure had his heart in the attempt—"

"There's the lie Hannah!" Shawk shouts this startling the girl out of the fugue Haidt's put her in. "I saw Tom's corpse. You saw Tom's corpse. He was shot out the front. Buckshot exited there. Couldn't be clearer. You heard the demon. Said the shot came out the back. There's the contradiction! There's his lie!"

Hannah breathes out a cold sigh. Cold relief. A plume of that frosty air. She collapses into that head-in-hands heap again. Weeping again. With her noble Tom back.

"Aw! You ruined my fun Marshal!" Haidt laughs. "Oh well, we still have the Galician to play with."

Metro pays enough attention. Can't not after witnessing such a relentless tearing open a soul like that. Haidt capitalizes.

"Want to know what that little farmer-woman of yours got up to on the boil Sheriff Molyboha? She wasn't shuckin' corn with that iron grip of hers—"

HECHHH!

Haidt's gagging. Shawk's got him around the neck with his lariat and's pulling him toward the back of the cage. He yanks the demon's head toward his waiting hand poised between the bars. He clamps those vice grips onto Haidt's protruding gagging tongue. In denouement, he closes his shackles onto Haidt's wrists. Tight.

"Let's step outside you two. He's not going anywhere." Shawk lifts Hannah up. He comforts her as they go.

28

FROM THE HEIGHTS OF HEAVEN

Shawk Hannah and Metro sit on the town hall steps. Their backs are to the propped-open front doors. Haidt is visible through them doors as well as myself still futilely filing away at them bars. At least the trickster's bound and can't flick at my file.

Hannah sits head in hands again only not of grief. She's exhausted and in no mood to do anything other than stew in the comforting emptiness of her purgation. The irony of course is there wouldn't have been anything to purge if she'd just ignored Haidt to begin with. Oh well. Catharsis has brought her back-to-one by horseshoe.

Shawk watches over her concerned. Concern for what she's just endured, concern for the beating she's been taking longer than Shale. He waits watching. Waits. Then... She lifts her head out those hands. *Eight more months...* she says. She smiles at this. Smiles over to Shawk. She says this and he lights of a little purgation himself.

. . .

METRO ASSESSES THE STATE OF things. He watches Kate attend to the revived Shalers. He watches his beloved currently. He first looked to her upon leaving the hall. Then he looked away to other events. Now he's back on her.

What did he see in addition to Kate and the people's renewal? He saw Dep Will and the Wilders come back having brought the Inner-Circle with them. Inner-Circle and the rest of the Red-Eyes sit bound in the middle of Main ready for collection. Collection by whatever the territory has left of a Marshal service? Nah. Not likely to get any help from the USMS. Yet Shale'll get those runagates to Carson.

He saw Cap Johnson teaming up a wagon just across from the Hall. Cap finished and glanced over to Metro. Cap raised an eyebrow at him. Metro tipped the brim of his hat. Cap got up in the driver's seat and headed out north.

That's what the man saw.

SHAWK'S BREATHING A LITTLE HEAVY and Metro notices.

"Everything alright?"

Lawman lets out a gust. "Job'll put the grey in ya." He points to the ash at Metro's temple and pats him on the shoulder assuredly.

Metro glances over that shoulder at the tongue-clamped Haidt. Turns back to Shawk. "Did you ever think to just shoot him where he stands?"

"Did you?"

"I thought about it. Nothing more than thought."

"You're a lawman Metro. Tell me why you do it? Besides the fact it makes you a better protector."

"That is the only reason."

"No it ain't."

"It ain't?"

"Naw. I can see it in you. I can see it in your eyes."

"And your assessment?"

"Loss: your measure of the good."

Metro's is an expression of astonishment. "I—I lost it when I moved to The Belt. I thought it would return if only—"

"No."

"No?"

"No. You lost it the day you looked into the eyes of your little girls, your wife, and realized despite being able to protect them from the corrupt of this world you could never protect them from *corruption* itself." Metro pivots in his seat to better observe this man leveling him. Shawk grins. "Fighting that kinda menace is a game of the absolute. A matter of a will that can never be yours. And that's what came to mind that day. And at that, your sense of morality slipped away from you. Ran. A defense mechanism. No moral sense *means* no morality *means* no evil to do any corrupting. No corruption of the ones you love therefore.

"The paradox of this defense was: your apathy became a constant reminder of its own cause: your fear of that corruption. Now you bring the law for two reasons. The first as a measure of good. You see the opposite in your wife and children of what you see in the depraved you hunt and that comforts you. The second as a distraction. Lawbringing distracts you from your apathy and so from your greatest fear. You surround yourself with the depraved and you feel the furthest thing from nothing, yet what it is you feel is a constant fear and resentment. Fear of the depraved for what they're capable of and a resentment of the depraved for doing what they're capable of are no substitute for the sense you've lost."

"I can't agree with you," Metro rebuts. "I don't want

apathy. I *want* my moral sense. I want morality in the world as I want my daughters to do good in the world—"

"You want your girls to *be* good in the world! The doing follows the being. Don't worry about the doing. The real question is this: what makes you think you can move so easily from no moral sense to no morality?" Shawk chuckles. "Yours is a confusion. You confuse the needle on the barometer for the weight bearing down on you. You can no more ease the pressure by smashing the barometer than you can vanquish the evil by hardening your heart in the face of it. The good and the bad are there whether you can feel them or not. If you think your apathy vanquishes evil then you haven't just let your guard down to it and your loved ones nevermore exposed to it, you've reduced yourself to a lowdown mopin' sack of waste in the process."

Metro's chuckling at the mopin' comment when... He sees it. Holy hell he feels it! Of what Shawk speaks. The faces of his little girls are at mind's eye. Clear as day. Kateryna too. She's holding infant Vikki in her arms as Anya —just a toddler—sleeps against her mother's side. He felt the most wonderful elation and love that day and he feels it even now. Not a hint of the feeling having faded.

He remembers something else. It is true. From that day on he began to numb any emotions born of evils in his world. A world that was his daughters' now too. He decided that day he would rather feel nothing than feel the pain of *even* an awareness of what might hurt or corrupt his loves. But Shawk is right. He's right to condemn such apathy. What other than this pain, this fear, could be a better motivator for ridding the world of the cause of it? He can feel it now!

"That's... That's correct. Harsh words though correct

nonetheless. What you say is true Marshal. Your prescience as well... It's like that of—"

"A lawbringer once taken to the same depths as you is all."

It all makes sense but now the task at hand floods back in. "As appreciative as I am for your council I must ask. What does all this have to do with whether or not we just walk in there and kill that man where he stands?"

"You heard me say the doing follows the being. A grade-schooler could tell ya if doing good follows being good then doing the opposite of good means being the opposite of good. If we kill that man in that cage like a sitting duck are we not doing the opposite of a good?"

"If we kill *that* man? If it means his life for the dozens of others he could take in the remainder of his lifetime. Easily. More?"

"You sure of those numbers?"

"No."

"You sure there ain't no other way?"

"Of course there are other ways."

"If we kill him where he stands at his most vulnerable, knowing there were other ways, is that not the opposite of a good?"

"I'm not sure. It is the difference between knowing there is *some* way and knowing *what* that way is. Like knowing there is someone knocking at the door yet not knowing who it is until the door is opened. What if we cannot open that door?"

"What if we could? What if we found the other way and that's how we stopped him? Would that be the opposite of a good?"

"Of course not."

"What if we kill him where he stands doing nothing

other than standing without a single second's search for that other way?"

"I think that would be opposite of a good."

"Then walking in there and killing him where he stands means our corruption. Not killing him where he stands means the possibility of our deliverance. That deliverance is necessary for your babies' deliverance as your corruption will surely mean theirs. Or am I wrong?"

Metro don't disagree.

"That's why lawmen like us don't kill 'em where they stand."

I'VE HAD ENOUGH. I COME out the hall bearing bad news.

"If he didn't already see the futility in me sawing away at that cage he's seein' it now. Might even been banking on the frustration."

"Wait a minute," Hannah suggests. "He's not going anywhere. Why don't we just bring Carson law to him? They can do whatever they need do here to see his sentence through—"

"No," Shawk says. "That won't work Hannah. He's undoubtedly thought of that. He has a way out. It's hidden in his lies and we didn't hear it. He would expect such a response from us. Likely a part of his plan."

"So what do we do?" Metro asks.

"If we can't discern from his words his means of leaving that cage we'll have to figure out a means of our own."

"Listen," I say. "Short of the hands of God himself takin' hold of that cage and tearing it in two, we ain't taking Haidt out of anything."

"A team of horses pulling from either side?" Shawk entertains.

"Every single one of a Wilders' beasts pullin' at once couldn't put a dent in Haidt's sanctuary. We need a mechanical advantage well beyond what meat can provide."

"Well what now?"

"Could start layin' down some train tracks on either side of the hall!" I jest. "Borrow a couple engines from the iron trains. Should have Haidt out by next spring!"

"Keep dreamin' fireman!" Hannah flips.

"You scoffin' at me fancying myself a railroader?"

"No!" Hannah says sly. "I'm scoffin' at the idea of The Council lending out equipment for a cause!" We have a bit of a chuckle at this. Then she stops abrupt-like. Gears are definitely turning. "Metro!" she shouts, catching his attention. "The mining conveyors?"

"Right," Metro concurs. "What about a winch powered by steam engine?" he asks me.

I begin to ponder this.

As I do, a rumbling comes from the north that only Metro can feel. His heart grows full. He glances across the way to Kate. He's paying no more mind to any of us at present, save for the following unusual request...

"Hannah can I ask you to do this? Can you take the Deputy Marshall to Karl at the mine and get those engines?"

She looks to where Metro listens. She agrees.

We head out to the mine.

Shawk re-enters Town Hall shutting the doors behind him.

Metro walks out to the middle of Main and attends to that northern rumble.

"KATERYNA?" HE PUTS HIS HANDS on his wife's shoulders. "There's something you need to see."

She turns to face him but by hardly two-thirds the way around she's burst out running. She practically knocks him over as she goes. "Oh my word!"

"Moma!"

Anya has burst out into a sprint herself, running for Kate. Mr. and Mrs. Smith had helped her and Vikki off of Cap's wagon and are bringing the girls home. Little Anya couldn't wait for their escort.

She flies into Kate's open arms as Moma lifts her baby and spins planting those kisses on her over and over again. Anya more than entertains them this time.

"You're feeling better Moma?"

"Oh yes darling!"

"But you're crying?"

"These are the tears of joy Anya. Like you remember when Vikki was born?"

Anya nods hugging onto her mother. "And your tears Popa?"

"The same," Metro says, handing Vikki to a Kate more than willing to hold both her babies at once. Hold them for all eternity if she can.

The family embraces.

SHALE'S BABIES HAVE COME HOME. Along with its founders. All happy and healthy thanks to Cap and his folk. The boisterous Reeve couldn't bask in any of the appreciation however as he still has a few more miles to put on this night. He Dep and the Wilders loaded up that wagon with Red-Eyes and are currently running them to Carson.

The families reunited are beginning to disperse. To head home. Houses will need some scrubbing and re-siding but they're still sufficiently cozy. Wells will have to be pumped dry to allow for the wellspring to bring in clean water again. Clean water on the periphery is safely accessible though. Folk'll be well-served by that and the mineral water in the wagon till the wells fill clear.

The Molybohas still stand as one. They're paying all due gratitude to Mr. and Mrs. Smith, though it's Anya doing most of the conveying.

"And then on the way home we saw a moosk!" she boasts. "And it had *biiiggg* horns. Just like Mr. Smith said!"

"Only we call them antlers dear." The Smiths are smiling at this.

"It had *biiiggg* anklers!"

Metro laughs. Laughs joyously. In completion. He's lulled a second by the immediate. *His* world's complete but Shale's still missing a piece. Them teams dragging them engines into town remind him of that. He reaches out to shake Mr. Smith's hand and then Mrs. Smith's. She gives him a big hug instead. He tips another thank you at them. He turns to Kate.

"It won't be long now Kateryna. You take the girls home and rest. I will be back shortly."

Now come those tears ain't joy…

Metro embraces her. "He will just keep pushing if this doesn't end tonight."

She nods in understanding.

DIDN'T TAKE LONG TO GET them winches anchored. Didn't take long to get them engines stoked and ready to crank neither. What took the longest was boring out a hole at the back of the hall to run the winch cable through. They're all hooked up to that cage, though, and the engines are ready for gear.

Metro and Karl stand at either engine as Hannah Shawk and myself mind Haidt. Per Metro's plan, he and Karl will put those engines in gear simultaneous to the firing of Metro's pistol.

Inside, our miscreant has managed to get out of his shackles again and, unless he can dematerialize steel, appears to have eaten those vice-grips. He's currently flicking at one of the iron braids, of two, wrapped around the bars of his cage. Cables sit just above the center crossbar.

He's helpless to do anything to them cables as they're bolt-clasped like a permanent noose. Tight. He flicks at them nonetheless.

"Well this will be fun," he grimaces.

"You looking forward to your hanging?" Hannah asks.

"I'm looking forward to Shale's ascension. Rapture. All while Marshal beholds."

BANG!

The engines kick into gear and the lengths of cable unfurl out their respective holes of the hall.

Haidt's apathetic.

Appears to be stretching.

Raises his arms up high.

But...

He grabs onto a bar above him. He tugs it. Breaks it free. He ain't fast about it, though he is smooth. He starts unscrewing an end cap at one end of the bar.

Hannah and Shawk run to opposite sides of the cage. The sides not connected to the unfurling cables. Shawk hops over the uncoiling loop as he goes. They reach for Haidt from either side but he's standing at perfect-center. It's almost like the dimensions of his cage were designed for Hannah and Shawk's torment.

Metro sees this and starts moving toward the steps. Shawk waves him back. What could Metro do anyway? What is Shawk even doing? Hannah? Those engines are the priority. Metro recedes.

Haidt upends that bar dumping a circle of reddish-brown powder around his feet at a diameter of about his shoulder width. Hannah and Shawk lower to reach for it realizing if they can't touch Haidt's shoulders they can't touch his thermite.

The cables pull taut. Now's the real test.

The cage is creaking and croaking as pressure is put on those bars.

"Damn it!" Shawk exclaims. "Get away Hannah!"

The pair back off as Haidt begins twisting the cap off the other end of that bar. Croaks and creaks intensify. He pulls a single match out the top and dumps the remaining contents onto the thermite. Contents are gray with the granulation of gunpowder.

CROOOOAAAAAAAAKKKKKKKKK... BOOM!

Both sides of the cage fly away as Haidt strikes that match. Hannah Shawk and I run to grab him but the flame is already on the gunpowder. Powder goes up in a flash igniting the thermite along with it. The heat is immense though nowhere near as immense as the flashing white. We can't see a damn thing!

Metro's come flying into the hall shielding himself like the rest of us.

It's burning hot yet it's burning fast. Won't be much longer.

Just as the flash and the flame begin to dim there's a tremendous crash at the bottom of the cage. I open my eyes in time to see the floor swallowing up the last of that flash. Everything goes out in that swallow. It's just an empty cage with a burned-out hole at the bottom ate the fire!

"Son of a bitch! Should have known!"

We move in, about to stick our faces into that hole just as a blast of flame erupts from it only to suck back in like a vacuum!

Outside, the skirting over the hall's crawlspace explodes outward in all directions. Flames follow the bust-out. Bastard runagate's set the whole hall ablaze from the bottom up!

FIRE'S CLIMBING UP THE BACK of the hall and smoke's billowing out the hole in the wall of the winch as *CRASH!* Shawk comes smashing out! His pistol's already drawn. It's just Karl at the engine.

"What the hell happened Marshal?"

"Did you see him? Anything?"

"Just you."

OUT FRONT, METRO HANNAH AND I had conducted a similar search with the same results. Haidt's gone and the Hall's going near as fast. He had us sitting on a literal powder keg the whole time. His plan the whole time. Son-of-a-bitchin' miscreant!

Shawk moves swiftly through the lot to the south of the hall. His arm's up shielding his face from the heat of the inferno.

"Anything?" he asks, joining us at the boardwalk of Hannah's office.

We shake our heads.

"I should have heard what he was saying." Shawk says this eyeing that roaring hall completely engulfed.

"So what the hell are we supposed to do now—"

DING! DING! DING! DA-DING! DING! DING! ...

"What of the earth is that?" I ask peeking into Hannah's office in all my confusion.

"Box Boss!" Hannah and Metro shout in unison.

"The complex," Hannah says, walking back out into the street to face that concrete mass on the hill.

Metro's already setting out as Shawk holds a hand to him. "You stay here," he says. "You all stay here." He's breathing heavy again. "This task is mine alone to see through."

"I can be of help!"

"We don't know what's waiting for us up on that hill," Shawk reminds. "We do know I'm the only one he won't simply *end* the second I get too close." Hannah and Metro's collective expression goes curious. "You heard him," Shawk obliges. "He wants *me* to behold."

He pats Metro on the shoulder. Metro's solemn yet won't dispute the man's logic. He moves to Hannie. He reaches out for her shoulder as she latches onto him hugging. He hugs back in the way a lawman would.

Metro and Hannah stand vigil as he sets out for the complex. Sets out bathed in the amber strobe of the dwindling fires of that hall.

There'll be no bucket brigade to save this institution. The watch has been wound. Let it tick.

29

SHOWDOWN

Rapture... What's the demon up to? The Marshal beholds... Shale's Ascension? 'It's hidden in his lies...' *DING! DING! DING! DA-DING! DING! DING! ...*

She hasn't stopped watching that hill since Shawk set out for it.

"It's all cut and dried from here ma'am," I say from the office boardwalk trying to allay her concerns. *DING!* "Haidt's cunnin' though he falls real easy once Marshal gets him in his grip." Here I ramble. Can't help it. I'm concerned the same. *DING! DING!* "Cunnin' but he must be losing a step. Minus that cage, his trick's the exact same he pulled down the road in Santa Rosa. Minus that wired-up house on the hill too I s'pose. Now *that* is truly an elaborate way to ingratiate oneself into a community. Wire up the dam to blow. Wire up the town to grow. Surely there are more cost-effective measures—" *DA-DING!*

"Wire up the town to blow?"

DING! DING! DING! DA-DING! DING! DING! ...

"Naw ma'am, I said *wire up the town to gr—*"

"I can't hear myself think."

"Sorry ma'am. I do ramble."

"No. Oh no no. Not you. That damn dingin'!"

She bolts for the toolbox at the back of my wagon and digs. She takes out a stone chisel then runs into her office.

She moves past an uneasy Metro. He's sitting on a barrel at the boardwalk seemingly lost in reflection. Watching the bonfire across the street. He rises the second she moves past as though in concern. He doesn't follow her.

I *do* follow her. There's a curiosity sure but also… Really it's just curiosity.

She slips the chisel into the padlock shackle that secures the terminal door. Starts prying downward at it. Instinctively I latch onto the chisel for extra leverage. We wrench until…

POP!

She pulls the broke shackle through the locking rings and opens the terminal door. It's a power cell like any other. She reaches in and chunks it off its brackets. Box Boss keeps right on a dingin'.

"What the hell?"

"What is it Mayor?"

She angles the power cell nipple at me. "*This* is supposed to power *this*." Cell's nipple now indicates the terminal. "But this isn't *really* supposed to power this… Supposed to be a fake… Empty…" She shakes the cell. Definitely not empty. Has a solid mass thumpin' around in it. "But what's powering that then?" Nipple's back pointing at the terminal. "And what the hell am I holding? Hold this a second." She hands me the cell then rips the dingin' embosser arm right off the terminal.

Thank. You. Ma'am!

· · ·

SHAWK SIDLES UP TO THE door of the complex. He saw on approach it was wide open. Haidt's in there waiting. Time for the end game but what's the strategy? Won't know until he looks I reckon.

He drops his saddlebags to save himself from any extra burden. He's about to spin into that doorway when... Metro sidles up!

"Son of a—" He shakes his head. "Told you to wait," Shawk admonishes in whisper.

"I tell you what. I let you go in first," Metro gallows.

Shawk grimaces. "You *will* wait here. Wait for my sign."

Metro tips his hat.

Shawk's been pointing a finger at Metro while admonishing. Now he wags it like he's all our dads. Like he's saying *do as you're told*. Then apropos of nothing... He spins around and into the doorway of the complex.

He's hit in the face by pure adulterated surreality.

It's a demon of a fly smack in the middle of that copper cobweb. Haidt's somehow strung himself up by wires extending out from him in all directions. They splay him spread-eagle... Floatin'... Grinnin' plaster... Blue dong a danglin'.

Shawk takes a single step over the threshold when...

"Whoa whoa there Marshal," the demon admonishes. "You do anything to move me and I send a wire to Shale that'll be my final love letter."

Outside the door a listening Metro feels the weight of those words. An intuition. Better, a sentiment. He glances over his shoulder. Up to a grouping of copper wires. Grouping's coming out a weather head at the corner of the complex.

The grouping eventually spreads out across to a dozen

different telegraph poles each feeding into Shale. One of them wires must run along down to Main and right into...

...HANNAH'S OFFICE.

SHE HOLDS THAT power cell in her hands giving it a once-over. Cautious. If her hypothesizing's correct she's going to have to be extra—

SMASH!

She spikes it onto the floor. I look at her. She looks at me. "Outta time..." she says.

She picks up the cell. Its lid's busted off. Appears to be connected to the inside of the cell by some sort of thread. She pulls it upward. Gentle-like. The thread's a wire that lifts along with it a bundle of dynamite.

It's a flash of images of near every residence of Shale. House after house after house. People's homes! A Labor tech in every one wiring that residence up. Not with electricity for communication but detonation! Not to send telegraphs but to send us to bits!

"*Even after blowing the dam they'd have crates to spare...*" she mutters. "*Shale's ascension* he said. *While the Marshal beholds...*"

Our eyes go wide like we're competing to pop 'em out our skulls the faster.

Hannah tears out holding that bundle.

"YOU DO ANYTHING TO MOVE me and I send a wire to Shale that'll be my final love letter."

Shawk gestures ever so subtly to Metro. *The wires.* But Metro knows. Metro goes.

Shawk steps over the threshold.

"Now Marshal," Haidt sings out. "I warned you—"

Shawk filters out Haidt's caterwauling. It goes on unrelenting make no mistake though we won't hear it for a time. He examines the scene free of the singy-songing.

Sees a plunger detonator sitting about fifteen feet to the left of Haidt. Gotta be a decoy. Why else the dozens and dozens of wires extending from the miscreant in every direction? Then he catches it. Each of Haidt's wires is connected to a tug detonator. A detonator with a pull-away thread attached to it. *Tug* that thread free and you spin a little magnet in a copper coil just enough to cause a spark of current. Then *BOOM!* goes whatever explosive's on the receiving end of that spark.

Shawk figures most of those wires only serve to hold Haidt in the air. For the theatrics of things. No way the detonators attached to those suspensions are real. Though frail, Haidt's body weight would have already set them off. They're anchors.

Nature of the miscreant betrays a bit of his plan too. Though the claimed intention is to have Shawk believe it was his movin' of Haidt that caused detonation, Haidt'll want complete control over all of this. Haidt'll *have* complete control over all of this.

The only real detonators will be attached to the demon's clenched fists Shawk reckons. The only part of him that can vary any of the tensions needed to cause a spark. He counts five live wires in total. Three in Haidt's left hand and two in his right.

He takes a deep breath and concentrates on his mission. This allows some of Haidt to filter back in.

"...arrest Marshal. Then you'll finally see—"

Marshal draws.

BANG! BANG! BANG! BANG! BANG! BANG! BANG!

He was right. He hit all five tugs and near as he can hear no boom. No boom save for the pop of the derringer smoking in Haidt's hand. Got Shawk in the upper chest though Shawk managed to get one in Haidt only lower. Wouldn't have been a contest for him if he hadn't five of the demon's detonators to handle.

Shawk crumples, short of breath. He drags himself to the left of the facility door.

Still hanging by those wires, Haidt realizes he's short of breath too. He reaches down to where the hole in his collapsed lung is. "I'm touched," he wheezes. He notices Shawk in that heap. Haidt wheezes heavier in a scoffing almost jubilant tone. "That wunt no kill shot Marshal!" he laughs.

"Took the wind out me nonetheless," Shawk laments.

"Get up!" Haidt demands.

"Didn't have much of it left. Figure you took the last." He slumps over.

"No! No! *NO!*" Haidt screams. Bloody spittle coughing out his mouth as he does. He starts pulling at the wires suspending him. "You need to see! You need to lose!" He collapses onto the floor in front of that copper heart. He tries to get up. His wounds are too great.

He crawls.

"YOU DO ANYTHING TO MOVE me and I send a wire to Shale that'll be my final love letter."

Shawk steps inside the complex.

Metro moves under the weather-head of telegraph

wires. He tracks along the grouping, seeing that it extends out about thirty meters before splitting to feed each pole to town. *Just shoot 'em down Metro.* He grabs for the pistol he forgot was destroyed by Knocker.

Damn!

He moves back along the complex wall to Shawk's saddlebags hoping to find something useful. He dumps 'em out onto the complex' landing. One bag's just got them pig strips. In the other he finds a pocket knife, some flint, a can of beans, a small hatchet— Hatchet! It's tiny though it's the best tool he's got.

He heads out to the nearest pole.

He climbs to the top of it and hacks off a wire held against the crossarm. He follows that severed wire to the next pole and does the same. His hacking's given him a decent length.

As he jogs back to the complex he makes a snare out of one end of the wire and loops it around the head of the hatchet. He's pulling that loop tight as he arrives back.

He tosses the hatchet over the grouping at the weather head. He takes both ends of the tossed wire in hands and pulls down. Just what he was hoping for. There's slack inside the complex. He yanks harder and the rest of that slack pulls free.

He moves along following the lowered grouping to find where it splits. On his way he picks up a rock just about the size of a baseball. At the split he begins hacking at each bifurcating braid of wire until all are severed.

Now what? he thinks holding the frayed end of the grouping in his hand.

"METRO!"

HANNAH'S APPROACHING, CARRYING THAT BUNDLE of dynamite. She gets to Metro out of breath and doesn't take any time to catch it. She holds the bundle out to him. It's still connected to the power cell cap.

"Whole town's wired with these." She puts the dynamite in Metro's empty hand so he can examine it. "Dotty's power cells weren't empty after all."

Metro holds up the grouping of severed ends in his other hand. It's like a copper yucca plant. "And *this* fed *this*." He brings the yucca in one hand nearer the explosives in the other.

Hannah tears up in relief. She'd sigh but she'd have had to catch that aforementioned breath to do it. Then...

BANG! BANG! BANG! BANG! BANG! BANG! BANG!

She turns to those shots as Metro assesses his items in-hands. He appears to have figured on something.

HE WALKS UP TO THE open door, hands behind back holdin' that bundle. Not even through the doorway, he sees Haidt sitting on the complex floor staring in his direction if only obliquely.

"What's this? The consolation prize?" Haidt wheezes. Gaze still fixed.

"You are under arrest," Metro says stepping into the complex.

Second he enters, his peripherals feel a pinch. He attends to the source. Sees Shawk keeled over. Not moving. *No...* He crouches down to him as the last game begins.

"Uh-uh," Haidt warns pointing over his shoulder to the plunger detonator behind him. "Leave Marsh be or I'll blow my last kiss."

Metro stands. "No you won't."

"Confident. Where ya goin' with it?"

"I'm not playing your games."

"You're beating around the bush 'bout stoppin' me..."

Metro bites. Pulls that bundle of dynamite out from behind. "All wires are severed except this..." He angles the bundle at Haidt showing him the single thread of copper wired to the lid. Shows the demon it's live. "Try anything, we go up but Shale makes it."

Haidt smirks. "Always have a redundancy Sheriff." He wipes at the blood collecting under his lower lip. He ain't a Red-Maw yet but as his lungs fill with fluid backing up and out his mouth he's getting close. "Ain't nothin' connected to your bundle. Marshal insured of that."

Metro's not entertaining Haidt's last shit. He's listened though only for the knowledge and there ain't none. The demon is a lyin' sack.

Either Shawk defused those bombs or he didn't but it don't take Haidt to tell you that. It's one of those tautologies again. Gotta be true. Now, which horn of it makes it so? Say Shawk didn't defuse those bombs, present bundle included? Then it's as Sheriff said and the men in this complex'll go up while Shale lives. Now, what if Shawk did defuse 'em? If he did he did it from where he keels. If he did it from where he keels he did it at a distance. If he did it at a distance he did it by bullet.

Metro scans around cagey trying to catch a clue. Shawk didn't take all those six shots just to hit Haidt a single time in the lung. He was shooting at something else—

Got it! Bullet hole in the wall next to a tug detonator. Last few inches of shot-out thread still dangle from it. Goddamn Shawk's a deadeye and a half alright but his shot only took the tug out of Haidt's hand. It didn't put that detonator out of commiss—

"Clever calculus!" Haidt relents. He's pivoting at his hips as he says this. Like he's twisting to see over his shoulder. Twist ain't stopping! He's breaking his own spine in forcing his torso away from the lawmen. His legs still sit pointing south but his belly chest and visage face due north.

Didn't even hear a snap.

The grotesquery breaks Metro from any further deliberation. He just readies himself at Haidt's last words.

"That there's the real Key that's gonna get the whole world talkin'!" The demon's pointing at the plunger detonator. "Y'all assumed Burke's trenches were laid for show too? Empty conduits down there to keep up the ruse?" Metro moves a few steps forward. "Uh-uh!"

Was that *uh-uh* Haidt scoffing or Haidt warning? Metro stops his stepping nonetheless.

"Copper-pure flows in them veins!" Haidt reveals. "All the way down to every power cell in every house in that city."

Metro goes pale. Copper in the conduits in those trenches! Electric fingers splaying. Carrying detonation down to Shale after all. Dotty's promise: *get them trenches finished and them homes wired up by next week.*

Metro snaps out of the dream. Stares past Haidt and to that Shale-Razing plunger.

"That's the redundancy Sheriff! That there's the last word!"

And with that, Haidt jumps to his feet spinning and landing. Tips of his toes have joined his torso in facing that plunge. He breaks out into a wheezy dash for it.

Metro's already running too though he ain't figured on anything yet. That's ok. He don't need his wits. He's got his sense! His wired bundle of dynamite in arms too. He ain't tearing out for Haidt however. He's going for that tug detonator at the wall opposite the demon's plunger.

Amidst the action, that copper heart sits in arrest. It's equidistant to Haidt's plunger at our left and Metro's tug at our right. Equidistant, really, the life-taking and life-saving store of electrons just waiting for our *BOOM!*

Haidt's a myth as he moves. Got a shot-out lung full of blood and yet there he flies for that plunge. Vibration in his steps is blurring his visage mixing the whites of his eyes with the red of the boil beneath. Fire.

Metro ain't a myth but a man. A father. Running for the life of the women he loves back in the home he made for them. It's Anya it's Viktoriya it's Kateryna moving him forward. He sees them in every step. He's loving them more in every step. Cherish these visions boy!

FOOOSH! The two leap for their targets in simultaneity. Haidt's already dead in the air fixing to ensure his corpse hits that plunge in posthumous genocide. Metro's flying with one hand reaching out for that tug wire as the other lets fly with the dynamite. Bundle's tossed. Arcing across the complex *Hail Mary* for the Demon's quarry. Haidt's corpse is square over the plunge as Metro's hand catches that wire. Haidt's coming down. Coming down. Coming down as dynamite hits plunge solid! Drives it a billion miles away from the descending demon. Tug wire's pulled. Dynamite's stopped dead on a dime like a cue ball hitting the Eight. Corpse is coming in for a landing. Tug detonator clicks. Demon flops onto the dynamite in time for...

KABOOM!

Man's dust. Man's dead. Man's Hate.

. . .

HANNAH'S KNOCKED OFF HER FEET by the blast. Walls of the complex are still up but the blast took the roof off in a billion little pieces a lot of 'em Haidt. Ain't looking to be landing any time soon.

She props herself up onto her elbows. She stares forward. Sees the dust and rubble of the complex settling in front of her. She immediately rolls onto her belly to see Shale behind her. Her town's bruised battered and still standing. She closes her eyes. *Thank God!*

She rolls back supine and sits herself up. Watches on at the complex once more. Concrete and steel buildings don't burn when you blow them up. Materials just sort of sit there after the dust settles. Looks like a person you haven't yet confirmed passed though somehow know is gone all the same. You know it ain't sleep though the death's not given in the stillness. It's the absence. The spirit has left the soul.

WHO KNOWS HOW MUCH TIME has passed. Hannah still sits watching on like she's waiting. Half-expecting.

"I'm sorry Tom. I'm so so sorry."

A hand reaches out to Haidt's plunger. It wrenches from it the wires that up to the wrenching were still connected to Shale. Not no more. Shale's singing free. Alright boys job's not quite done. The hand reaches out to Shawk and jostles him on the shoulder. The hand reaches out to Metro and cleans off debris. Time to get to work.

"I'M SO SO SORRY."

A mass approaches Hannah from behind. She doesn't startle. She doesn't unsettle. There's an immediate comfort. She somehow knows. She turns to see Jon and Maria standing behind her—the whole of Shale behind them. Come to be with Hannah. Come to heal.

I was there too. I told her real quick so as to not monopolize her time, we got all the townsfolk out their houses. Told her we're well on our way to cleaning out them terminals. It'll be a campout tonight for Shale folk but we're well on our way.

Kateryna has come too, though not for Hannah. It's obvious who she and the girls have come out for. She ambles out in front of the crowd. She holds Vikki in her arms and leads Anya by the hand. She doesn't see Dmytro. She feels faint. Anya instinctively latches onto her Moma at the hip. Then...

Kate's braced by two hands on her shoulders steadying her. It's Hannah. She looks to a Kate imploring her to say what Hannah knows she can't.

Hannah stares into Moma's welling eyes. She's beginning to shake her head ever so slightly when...

FOOOOOOM! VZZZZZZZZT! BOOM!

The entrance to the complex is alive with activity. There's electrical arcing everywhere: a white-hot fire ensuring Hannah and Kate can't see a damn thing just yet. None can see until... Against the glow... Silhouettes of the two men appear. They're stumbling. They hold each other up supporting each other *ex nihilo* as the white flash-frame beams behind them.

Kate can't believe her eyes. "You've got some real brass in that moshonka," she grins.

Curious! A third man emerges. He's not stumbling but ushering the first two men along from behind, guiding them.

The three's silhouettes begin to melt away into feature.

Back into our heroes as they move toward the townsfolk and into the light of the moon.

"Moma who is that man helping Popa and his new friend?"

"I don't know dove."

Oh but Hannie does. Hannie smiles. Hell, Hannie beams.

He's returned. Returned with Shale's deliverance.

www.ingramcontent.com/pod-product-compliance
Lightning Source LLC
Chambersburg PA
CBHW030924120726

47906CB00002B/482